ASCEND

C.MILLER

THE
REAVE SERIES

REAVE

ELUDE

ASCEND

TO FALL

PROLOGUE

STORIES

AS THE LITTLE GIRL WAS CRAWLING into bed, she asked, "Will you tell me a story, Father?"

Once she was properly settled with the thin blanket used for warmer weather pulled up to her chest, her father sat down at the edge of the bed beside her. She stared at him in eagerness and expectance and, with her right hand, loosely gripped the fabric covering her.

He grinned a little before saying, "I'm not so sure I feel like it tonight."

"Oh, but Father, you *must*." Her green eyes widened as she tightened her grip on the blanket. "You always tell me stories every single night when you're home. I don't think I could sleep without them." She did indeed have a great deal of trouble sleeping soundly when he was not near. The lack of stories only had as much to do with that as it did.

He tilted his head ever so slightly to one side, the same way he always did when he was playing with her. "I think you may be getting a little too old for stories. Aren't you tired of hearing them by now?"

"Of course I'm not!" the little girl exclaimed. "And I'll never be too old to hear your stories, Father. *Please* tell me one."

He gave in, as she thought he would. He teased her with the stories nearly every night, and—no matter how he protested—he always gave in. Still, the prospect always frightened her. She often had difficulty discerning when he was joking with her or playing anything but a set game, as she had the tendency to take things literally and would rarely base any statement on tone of voice opposed to words said. She was old enough that she should've been able to tell the difference better than what she could. He kept waiting for the day she would realize . . .

He was only playing.

He kept waiting for her to realize she did not need to put up the same argument, that it wasn't the argument getting her what she wanted.

He worried about her with that, as he worried about her in so many regards, but . . . He often found her way of being amusing.

"Which one would you like to hear?" His grin had transformed into a huge smile because he loved his daughter so, and seeing her happy brought an indescribable amount of joy to his world. She was always happy to hear his stories and, when she was, he was *almost* able to let all his concerns melt away for a brief moment.

He didn't always let her choose, so she was very excited when she said, "The one about the two men."

She watched his smile falter the smallest amount, but she was too young to understand the reasons why it happened. She was quite accustomed to seeing the change or altering of that expression.

He asked for clarification, "About the kings or the brothers?"

She did not see the relief on his face, though she was looking directly at it when she replied with, "The kings. And not the one where you make the brothers kings and tell their story differently."

She couldn't remember the first time she'd caught him doing as much in altering the stories he told, but he could, as it had been rather purposeful. She was also too young to understand his reasons for doing most things, though he did wonder how long that would last. Time passed so quickly.

"I don't know why you enjoy hearing about the kings." He shook his head. "It's not a very nice story." So few of them were, as imaginations only stretched so far when burdened by reality.

"That's the one I want." She moved a bit and then clutched the blanket tightly in both her hands over her chest, saying nothing else and making it clear that she had no intention of answering his inquiry.

He would only tell her stories once she was properly ready for bed, but he did not mind if her legs were wiggling in excitement beneath the blanket. Appearances mattered in some ways, as did concealment. Everything mattered, though some things were more important than others. Some things were more important than others, depending on the company.

"Once upon a time . . ." He began the story then paused to smile genuinely.

She wiggled even more because she always loved it when he started them that way.

"There were two young kings and each of them ruled one half of all the land. They split the world down the middle and they each held one half of it in their hands." After holding out both his hands to signify as much to her, he brought them back to himself and continued on. "They were good men and all the people in their kingdoms loved them dearly. They worked together despite the distance separating them, as separation does not matter so much when there's no true absence. There were no wars. All people were treated equally. The kings loved every person as though they were their own children. Happiness flourished in the hearts and lives of all."

He paused again, hoping she would ask that he stop the story where it was, but he knew she would not. It would've been so happy where it sat, but a story was not a story worth telling unless it strayed. He continued on.

"One of the kings heard whispers that some men who lived outside the protected realms of their kingdoms had plans to murder him. A long plan, to not only eliminate the king but also destroy what he'd built by ripping out the heart of it. The other king came to the kingdom of his friend, and the two of them formulated a plan to prevent that from happening to either. They could not continue to do good if they were dead. It seemed the only way."

The little girl said, "The Reavers."

"Yes." Her father nodded. "They were intended to be good. Very smart, very strong. A personal Guard for each of the beloved kings. So they were trained extensively in the art of war from a very young age, and when the kings saw how exceptional their new soldiers were when trained in such a way, they began training more of them to protect their respective kingdoms rather than simply their persons." He stopped and forced a smile at her, reaching a finger out and poking her on the tip of her nose. "I don't know why you enjoy this story."

"Go *on*," she urged. "You're getting to the sad part."

It was harder then for him to keep the smile on his face, but he managed it. The strain of it made his eyes crinkle slightly at the corners. The little girl loved seeing his eyes that way because she thought it meant he was happy. His eyes always crinkled when he smiled at her.

"As the kings aged . . ." he went on, "they discovered what separation truly meant. The closeness of *understanding* and *trust* had made the physical distance between them not seem so great. They lost the very things that had held them together throughout the years, slipping so slowly through their fingers that no one could discover whose hand slackened first.

"Paranoia developed like a disease inside their minds and beings, each believing that the other was secretly trying to steal their Reavers. The damage of that began there—inside them—then spread through the long reach of their hands. They adjusted their training and began teaching their Reavers how to infiltrate the kingdom of the other king. Each began stealing the children who were in training from the other king, and then they began taking seemingly random children from their parents if they thought those children might benefit their purpose. Eventually . . . they began taking them as infants according to bloodlines. Stealing life as soon as it entered the world from the people who'd created it."

He paused and rubbed at the stubble on his chin. The little girl reached out and pushed his hand out of the way so she could do it for him. She loved the way his stubble felt beneath her fingers. He shook his head, but she did not know at what.

"Go on," she told him quietly that time.

She heard him take in a deep breath and then release it, but he did as she asked.

"One king sent some of his Reavers to murder the other king because he'd heard from his spies that he was intending to do the same. No one even knew whether it was true or simply a story. After one king was dead, his Reavers went to return the favor, but there was no need. The Reavers had already murdered their own king, his wife, and all his heirs." He pursed his lips for a moment. "No more kings."

The little girl said, "Because the Reavers were evil."

Her father smiled sadly and nodded. "The kings took away their humanity, replacing it with knowledge and training. They raised them from birth to be monsters without feeling, to live and die *only* for the purpose chosen for them. But they taught them how to think in the wrong ways because the kings never imagined they would revolt against them. When you teach someone from infancy that action should only be taken with just cause and you give such an order on mere *speculation* . . . What were they to do?" He stared off for a moment. "You cannot ignore what you are, even when the person who made you that expects as much."

He brought his attention back to his daughter. "After the kings were gone, the small bit of good the Reavers had inside them was destroyed. It was erased from their training and their hearts. When you take away a person's humanity, they're no longer a person and they no longer behave as such."

He stared at his daughter in silence for a time, looking at her face while he pondered over *humanity* for what felt like the millionth time to him. She was also silent, watching his face.

He wondered . . .

Why did it not upset her? She was old enough to understand certain things as well as could be expected, *better* in some regards. He could not understand why stories of murder and horrendous people did *nothing* to her. He'd been so concerned he'd made her the way she was, but he'd tried so hard. He'd done his best at something he'd not been taught to do.

If he hadn't caused her to be the way she was, he was still responsible. His blood ran in her veins.

Eventually he asked, "Will you allow me to tell you a happy story tomorrow night?"

The little girl shook her head. "I want to hear the one about the brothers tomorrow night."

He asked, "Why is it that you won't let me tell you happy stories any longer when you have a say in which are told?"

She hadn't asked for or agreed to one in quite some time. He'd not wanted to inquire about it before, convincing himself it was only a phase she was sure to grow out of. Wishful thinking, because she was not growing out of it.

Her response to that was, "Because the sad ones seem more real."

"Why is that?"

"You always seem sad when you tell me the sad stories," she told him, "but you never seem happy when you tell me the happy ones."

He forced another smile at her as he poked her on the nose once more. He hurriedly got into bed behind her so she would not know how her words had affected him. But the little girl knew, as he knew she would. She knew as much as she could—*what* but not *why*. She was growing old enough to begin knowing far too many things her father did not want her to.

She rolled over and wiped away a tear that was rolling down his cheek. "Would you like for me to tell you a story?"

He smiled, confused, because she'd never offered that or even given any indication that she had a story to tell. "Of course. I'd love to hear any story you would ever have to tell me."

"There was a girl . . ." she began, "and she loved her father very much. They were happy and did what they wanted all the time. But she was sad when he went away."

Her father laughed, but another tear fell from his eye. "Is that all you could think of?"

She gave a tight shrug of her shoulders. "It's all I know." She wiped another tear off his face and whispered, "I want to hear a happy story tomorrow night, Father."

"Time to go to sleep," he told her quickly because he knew she was lying to him. Already he could see truth on her face when there should've been none. The blankness of a simple truth that was really a lie. He would've believed her, had he not known with certainty that her words hadn't been true.

She rolled over, putting her back to him, and she waited.

He pulled her close to him and whispered the same words he whispered to her every night. "Go to sleep now, Flower. I've got your back. I love you. You're safe."

And then he waited for her to say, "I love *you*, Father." That much, at least, was true. She loved him so much.

The little girl closed her eyes and made a promise to herself that she would never ask her father to tell her another sad story again. She fell asleep knowing she was loved, and she was safe, while her father lay awake thinking over lies and waiting.

CHAPTER ONE

HARD

I WAS IN JARSIL.

I was in the very hell my father had told me I would never look upon again. He'd brought me just outside it all those years ago, and we'd stared off at it from a distance where trees ended and openness began before ending suddenly. Then those mountains shot out of the world, reaching for the sky. It was a hell made and surrounded by stone, sort of nestled inside a crook of it. He'd hidden me inside his jacket and whispered the lie.

How ironic was it that he was the one to bring me back and trap me here?

I would've laughed, if I had it in me to do as much.

The day after our arrival, my father had sought me out. I presume he'd had every intention of chastising me for destroying nearly everything inside the space he'd given me to live in, but when he saw me staring vacantly out the window of my new prison . . . I didn't believe he had it in him. He couldn't follow through.

"Aren't you glad to be done with the traveling?" The remarkably happy tone his voice had when asking the question hadn't matched the glimpse I'd caught of his face as he'd been walking up. His face during approach had indeed appeared as though he'd had every intention of chastising.

I'd seen the expression a very small handful of times as a child and despised it. It might've been amusing as an adult, were anything amusing.

I'd not responded to him in any way, only stood there blinking as I stared off at what laid beyond the window. I hadn't cared then if he saw the tears falling down my face as I'd cared every other time that he'd been close enough to see them since returning from the dead, apart from a very small handful. He hadn't had it in him to chastise me for the destruction I'd caused, and I hadn't had it in me to wipe those tears away.

"Aster," he said quietly. "You look as though you're locked away in a dungeon. You're home now."

His words almost stirred up the urge I'd felt the day before, to seek him out and plunge my knife into whatever part of him I could manage to reach first. Almost, but not quite. I could feel it there, agitating the painful numbness that had set in after waking in this place. It fought, but it could not break through.

"I had a home once." My voice had been quieter than his as I stared at the brightly colored flowers growing just outside, their very presence mocking me. "I had that and a father who loved me dearly. He left me starving in our home and, after a time, I came to accept that he had died. My home is some little house in the wilderness that I shared with that man. Every place I have been since has been a prison." I clenched my jaw as it quivered, until it was stable enough to say, "Stone walls, keeping me contained. Do you think me so ignorant that I can't see this?" I brought my hand up, touching the stone next to the window. It was a struggle to manage even that.

"I am not dead, Flower." He could not deny that I was what he'd claimed I wasn't when he knew I knew better.

Locked away.

He had been blurry from tears when I'd looked at him to calmly say, "You are not my father." I resumed staring out the window, not caring at all for the expression I'd seen on his face. That face—his presence, his *existence*—mocked me more than any bit of brightness out a window ever could. It was an insult to the life I'd led in his absence and all the lengths I'd gone to in order to overcome it in whatever ways I could. All the pain. "Please leave me alone."

I'd heard the door close only moments later and pretended I was not watching his retreating figure.

I'd pretended I was not imagining myself doing the exact same thing as a child—standing in the doorway and crying as I watched the image of his back walking away. But I *was* imagining it, as it would've been impossible to not. Even when he didn't stop to turn and hold a hand in the air . . . I still pictured it. That he didn't stop and turn back told me . . .

He was not my father.

It did not matter that no one was present to either see what I was pretending to not do or see through that to what I *was* doing. No one would know. No one but him had a chance to. Those memories had never been spoken of. There was no point, when memories did nothing but *hurt*.

It had not been very long after that before Chase opened the door and approached behind me, though every second felt like a lifetime.

An entire lifetime with nowhere to go, no options.

"Your father told me you could use some company," he had said to my back.

When I made no effort to move, he'd gone on uncomfortably. I knew what his voice sounded like when he was uncomfortable.

"I know you probably want Jas, but he's . . . not here."

"I know." I'd barely said the words.

I knew that Jastin had gone off somewhere as soon as I'd woken in the middle of the first night. I'd been staring out the window ever since and had not seen him once after. I knew he'd gone to that pregnant girl I'd seen when first arriving in Jarsil—whoever she was—because he'd not told me where he was going when I'd asked him. It was the only thing that made any sense. It was the only reason I could think of for him not telling me the answer to such a simple question.

I'd been waiting for him, knowing he would never leave me to deal with all this alone. He wouldn't just leave me here, trapped between these walls, not knowing what to do, where to turn, or which direction to take.

But most of the day had passed and he was nowhere to be seen. I had to accept that he was leaving me to go it alone.

I'd been wrong.

So I'd allowed Chase to hold onto me in a chair while silent tears fell down my blank face, and I'd cried until all my tears were depleted. It had left me with an empty feeling I'd not recovered from in what I thought was a month spent in this hell my father had dragged me to and contained me inside.

I TRAINED.

After that first full day of being in Jarsil and coming to terms with my situation, I'd trained relentlessly. Because my body had lost during travel so much of what I'd worked on before it, combatives were out of the question. Chandler and Stelin were attempting to build back up what I'd lost. I was attempting to surpass it.

I spoke to no one unless asked a direct question that I had some desire to answer, and I did not have a desire to answer anything unless it pertained directly to my training. I did not acknowledge remarks or questions, but I listened when I needed to and also sometimes when I didn't. I'd tuned out most things that couldn't hold even the slightest bit of relevance to anything. I was determined not to become distracted by nonsense. I had a goal, and I would achieve it. I couldn't do much of anything, but I *could* do that.

I ran and did movements until I became ill. From the time the sun rose in the morning until it went down again in the evening, I was doing that. I took breaks to eat and rehydrate when they told me it was time, and I did not stop otherwise. When I became ill, or fainted, I would recover and continue on. I ignored the protests from my body—sometimes screams and sometimes small groans—and I did what was necessary.

When the night came, I would cry, no matter how hard I tried to not. Then I would find myself walking to my designated training area with my designated Reapers trailing along after me like an extensive shadow in the darkness. I would continue training alone into the night until I stopped crying.

I'd missed the feeling of exhaustion, of working so hard on something I wanted to work on until I could no longer move or think properly at all. My head was fuzzy and I preferred it that way. I did not want to think, and the haziness helped with that. Hard work and determination occasionally had its benefits. It was odd to discover that something once found negative could turn positive with a change of situations. Circumstantial exceptions.

Every time I saw Jastin, I found that I did not want to *feel*, either. I could not find anything satisfactory enough to be done for that as I had with proper thinking.

I would not look at him intentionally, nor would I speak to him—not after asking him three separate instances where he went when he was gone.

Each of those times he'd responded with the same answer without the slightest bit of variation.

"Don't worry about it."

He never gave me anything more than that. Not a thing.

Sometimes I could nearly convince myself that what happened between the two of us had some strange, unknown thing to do with traveling together and that it was not as real as I knew it to be. Sometimes I could nearly convince myself it was all right or that I did not care either way. Most of the time I knew better. I knew bonds could not be so easily broken—not without the proper amount of force—and that it wasn't so simple.

So I would train until I no longer thought about it, or anything else, because thinking seemed to hurt so badly now. And pain was a distraction.

I would catch Stelin speaking to Chandler in a hushed way on occasion, as though he didn't want me to hear or possibly thought I wouldn't even notice if he could *just be discreet enough*. He was greatly impressed by me in some ways, I knew. I'd gathered as much from a few snippets I'd managed to catch, along with several instances where I'd found him looking at me. Watching. It had taken me some time to discern the way he felt, as it was not pertinent and I'd not cared to analyze it before it had struck me.

I likely would've enjoyed that knowledge before.

"It's like she's not human," I heard Stelin say once.

"She's human," was the way Chandler had responded to the statement.

I did not like feeling human, I realized.

"You're sad," Stelin had said to me one evening.

I did not know how long I'd been in Jarsil *exactly* because time was a blurry thing passing, with only periods of alternating light and darkness distinguishing any one point of it from another. I'd looked over and blinked in his direction just as he clarified.

"You work so hard because you're sad."

I'd simply turned my attention away and pretended as though he'd not spoken at all.

I could tell he became increasingly less impressed with me after that point. His eyes held something different than what they previously had when mine would catch them, and his strange form of praise halted. I did not mind how he felt about me, or why he thought I did what I did, so long as he did his job.

One night, when Chandler and Chase must've thought I was asleep in my bed, I heard them speaking with one another outside the door to my housing area. Standing guard. The small, stone structure—surrounded by gardens and the House—was massive in comparison to the servants' quarters I'd been stuck inside for the ten years before that point. Still, the walls seemed to suffocate me, and the silence that filled the space between was deafening. I perked up at the sound of the familiar and unexpected voice.

"You should talk to her," Chandler had said.

"She doesn't want me to," Chase said in response to his brother.

"Something is going on with her," Chandler stated. "I figured if anyone knew it would be Jas, but he said she won't talk to him either."

"That doesn't mean he doesn't know, Chan," Chase said. "I doubt she'd have to tell him for him to know."

Several extended seconds of silence passed before Chandler said, "I'm worried about her." He *did* sound quite concerned, which was new and as unexpected as catching them conversing. "It's like . . . I don't know, like her light went out or something."

"And what did Jas say when you told him that part?"

"That we'd never seen her light to know if it had gone out," Chandler replied.

I only just heard Chase chuckle under his breath. "Is that where he got the black eye yesterday?"

In reality, I had not been in my bed as they must've believed me to be. I'd been sitting on the floor of the main area of my housing place, staring through the darkness. I grabbed the nearest thing to me and threw it at the door, not knowing or caring what it was. I heard a throat clear on the other side, and then there was only silence, which proved what I already knew. They never would've had that particular conversation if they thought I'd overhear it.

Of course.

None of it had been mentioned to me the next day, but I'd not expected for it to be. I did catch Chandler glancing at me from the corners of his eyes a little more often than what I was accustomed. I believed he expected me to lash out about Jastin's blackened eye and the part he'd likely played in it.

I hadn't asked Jastin what had happened to his eye when I'd seen it, before or after overhearing the conversation, nor did I have any desire whatsoever to lash out because of it. Though it concerned me directly, it was not my business. Neither of them had wanted me to know. One or the other would've said, at least to my face. It had been personal to do with them.

It wasn't my business.

I did open my mouth once, almost asking Chandler why Jastin's statement had led him to do what he presumably had.

Nothing came out.

I did what I always did, or what I was determined to and could manage much better now. I worked, listened, and didn't let distractions stand in the way. I worked toward a goal I could actually accomplish, with no clue at all where I would or could go from there. It was all I could do.

I never went to bed until my body was to the point where I could not stay awake any longer. I despised the feeling of lying there exposed and alone in this place. It did not matter that Reapers were always just outside. It didn't even matter to me that Chandler might be right outside the main door. I couldn't stand not feeling another body near me or hearing no breathing in the same room.

Before coming here, I hadn't slept alone in so long that I'd unknowingly forgotten the feeling of it. There had always been someone close.

I was not necessarily afraid, but I didn't know what I was, only that I did not like it. Not at all.

I wondered if I'd allowed my mind to get accustomed to the illusion of safety in that way. I must've done without realizing, but I seemed unable to find a way around the delusion I'd let myself create. That was worrisome, and I often thought on that when my mind was working properly enough to manage it. I believed one forcing their delusions to alter their reality and the lasting effects it could have to be a worthwhile matter to ponder over.

So what I thought was a month had passed in that same way when Jastin came inside my housing area late one evening. He did not knock.

"You're angry with me." His voice was impassive as he sat down across from me on the floor. It hadn't been a question because I did not have to tell him things for him to know them, as Chase had said. Not always, with some things.

I looked at his face. The light from the candle I'd lit barely gave off enough light for me to see the honey-coloring of his eyes. I asked him the question again, knowing precisely where it would lead.

"Where do you go?"

He looked away at a wall and nodded his head slowly. I saw him purse his lips before he pushed himself up from the stone floor and walked away, letting himself back out. The injury he'd sustained during travel had fully healed. Moving was no longer a painful struggle for him that he attempted to hide, along with a sewn-up gash at his left side. He had his litheness back, no unhealed wounds, and I could no longer take care of him. And here, in this place . . . I could not take care of him when he didn't want me to. He had places to hide here. Get away.

I did not.

I felt ridiculous for it, of course, but concerning my head with such petty things was indefinably more desirable than dwelling on being trapped between the walls of my Reaper father's city.

When Jastin closed the door behind him, I blew out the candle, my left hand reaching under my shirt on my right side. I sat there, alone in the darkness, running my fingers over a slightly raised scar that only Stanley knew I had.

As I did that, I thought on *weakness*. Sometimes weaknesses were so obvious, visible to anyone who stopped and looked you in the eyes. Sometimes they were far more difficult, only visible if allowed, or necessary, or accidental.

It was beneficial, though such a shame, how easily one weakness could be misconstrued and mistaken for another.

15

STELIN CAME UP BESIDE ME as I was punching the dangling contraption the day after Jastin hadn't given me any verbal response to the question at all. At least it had been something different. I'd been trying all morning to not compare the interaction with Jastin to an early test and proven point with my brother, but my mind couldn't help making the connection every so often. I was having yet another internal debate about trust when Stelin spoke.

"Have you thought about asking him who she is?"

I continued punching the contraption, pretended he was not there, and disregarded the words that had come out of his mouth. They'd not been even remotely important, giving them no reason to take up space inside my head which was otherwise occupied on more than one thing.

A minute or so later, he said, "I don't want to start your combative training until you've got your head on straight. Chandler agrees with me."

I punched it one more time before taking in a deep breath and looking at him.

He smiled at me, almost sadly. "I'll make a deal with you."

I raised an eyebrow at him, and he surely knew that was the only sort of response he was going to get from me for now, at least until he said something worthy of more. I was not keen on making more deals with him, but I would do so if I found his proposal beneficial. Worthwhile.

"We can start your combative training tomorrow . . ." he said, "*if* you tell me why you're not speaking to Jas."

"I've spoken to him." I turned back to the punching contraption. What a *stupid* deal.

"What question have you asked him?" I heard behind me.

"That wasn't the deal," I stated. He'd implied I hadn't spoken to Jastin at all, which I had. I wondered if Stelin would ever learn to better word the questions he asked me.

"The deal was for you to tell me why you're not speaking to him. Not speaking to him as much or the way you did before. Are you happy?" He paused. "Tell me what question."

"So you can inform Chandler, and my father, and everyone else." I punched the large bag.

"It'll stay between us."

He had made a deal with me to keep things to himself, hadn't he?

He had. We'd shaken on it, and if I trusted that pact, I could answer his question. It was not the only thing he and I had shaken on. Though I did not want to make more deals with him or fulfill what he insisted on this particular one, getting to combatives was necessary.

"I ask him where he goes." I turned back to Stelin and clenched my jaw. I stared at him defiantly, expecting to be mocked for it.

"Will it make you feel better to find out who she is?" He didn't seem to be mocking.

I said nothing and moved my eyes away from him. He did not understand the point.

"If I help you figure it out, will you promise to get your head on straight so we can start your real training?" He must've felt it necessary to add, "You made a deal with me, after all."

I'd made a deal with him that required my improvement where training was concerned. He must've thought that he had me backed into a corner with this.

I asked, "How do you know he's going to see a woman?" Had he already said something about a woman since approaching me? If that was what he wanted to blame everything on . . . I did not mind.

"Because it's the only thing I can think of that could make you behave this way," he answered. Stelin did not know me to make such an assessment, but I also didn't mind if he thought he did. "It's the only thing that makes any sense. Even if he's not, it's what you think he's doing."

It was not the only thing, and Jastin *was* doing just that, I was sure. Rather than point out as much, I said, "So you're not following him."

"No." He shook his head. "You, your brother, and your father are the only ones who have any right to follow him. Maybe aspiring to do something about your problem will get your head out of your ass. I'll help you, but I won't do it for you. You've got to help yourself first. You can't expect people to move for you." He scrunched his face at me the slightest bit. "You're so much better than this."

"Why do you act like you care?" Though I *was* curious, I couldn't hear it in my voice.

"Apart from the deal we made . . ." He barely shook his head. "When we met, you were like . . . *fire*. It's kind of pitiful, watching it sputter out." He chuckled a little beneath his breath, brought his gaze to the punching contraption, and then spoke softly. "Maybe I do have a heart."

I analyzed his face for a moment before saying, "I'm sorry."

"Why?" His brow furrowed.

"For making you feel anything."

He shook his head again. "And I'm sorry that you sound like one of us, and I'm not talking about the *normal* ones. I'm not sure you have the vaguest clue what you just sounded like." Then he walked away.

I did not need to be shouted at to do what was required of me during my training now. I did what I needed to, and neither he nor Chandler needed to watch over my shoulder to ensure I did.

That did not mean they didn't.

Stelin's words had not fazed me at all, though I was sure he'd meant for them to. He would have to try much harder if he wanted me to bleed. Harder and better.

CHAPTER TWO

LIFE

THE DAY AFTER Stelin had spoken to me on combatives was spent refreshing my memory on maneuvers, stances, and the like. Regardless of his parting words, or any other words for that matter, I believed it safe to assume he'd gotten what he wanted from the conversation. He didn't care about my personal life, which I was aware, unless it would get in the way. He did not know me well enough to know what was where.

Either way, he'd gotten what he wanted—for us to be moving on. Moving on was what I wanted—*needed*—so it had been beneficial in all regards. For me.

I paid complete attention to everything Chandler and Stelin showed me, hoping I would see something new. No one had to tell me to keep my eyes open and my mouth closed. We switched back and forth between observation and physical training periodically throughout the day. Though they said I'd likely retain more information with breaks between bouts of observation, I believed they simply needed breaks from beating on one another. They could've simply said as much. Neither were qualified to make such an assessment of my ability to retain information despite any time spent or information given.

Retaining information was not and had never been the issue.

I didn't see much of anything I'd not seen before. I'd expected a small bit of something new from Chandler, either from being in a different environment under different circumstances or him hopefully having more faith in my capabilities than what he'd had then. I'd expected a large bit of something new from Stelin, who'd been trained in a different city under different people. Apart from a few new things here and there, which were so insignificant they could hardly count as bits of anything . . . it did not happen.

It was disappointing.

I did wonder once or twice if they truly felt I needed such refreshment in order to remember all the simplest aspects of combatives, which I did not. A very small part of me believed the motives behind the exercise were genuine, if not offensive, but the larger part of me didn't think so.

I was almost positive neither of them had any faith whatsoever in my capabilities. We all knew I was hopeless at combatives, at least where it pertained to my body executing what my mind knew, but it wasn't that.

I believed neither of them had faith that I could handle it mentally despite what all they knew, and it stung a bit, or tried to. But the care they were taking with me, speaking every word and demonstrating every action as though I were mentally inept . . . it was infuriating enough that the sting was essentially irrelevant and the rage it induced damn near broke through the numbness.

I kept my mouth shut, making no accusations to the obvious plan they'd clearly decided to carry out together. I pushed all thoughts of it down, as it was distracting, and I watched what they were willing to show me.

It was all less impressive after having murdered two people without putting any of it to use.

I wondered how much good the training actually did. It was something I'd thought over on more than one occasion after actually *realizing* I'd murdered two people without a bit of maneuvering in the ways they'd taught me.

The only conclusion I could come to was that it was all down to opponents and scenarios. That made it all undeniably necessary regardless of contradictory facts.

I EXPECTED MYSELF TO FEEL some form of excitement the day after being *refreshed*, as I prepared to fight Stelin. It was what I wanted, after all, what I needed. I expected excitement and was curious as to how it might feel after all the numbness, but it wasn't there inside me to be found no matter how hard I searched.

I stared at him as he smiled and said, "I'll be harder on you than Chandler was."

I did not know how sincere his threat was, but that was clearly what he wanted it to sound like if not what it actually was.

Chandler laughed. "Harder on her than pulling her arm out?"

Even if Stelin *would* go harder, he was a decent amount smaller than Chandler, which would be advantageous for me. It was unfortunate that I was so out of practice. It was even more unfortunate that I was not good to make being out of practice any sort of issue.

"Aster," Stelin said quietly when I did not respond to his teasing in any way. "We don't have to do this yet if you're not ready for it." Despite whatever deals we'd made, his words sounded sincere.

He did not understand.

"Yeah," Chandler agreed. "We haven't told anyone we were intending to do this today. Nobody expects anything from you."

I heard myself laugh once on a breath.

Chandler's face scrunched a bit and he help up a hand. "I didn't mean that how it sounded."

I looked up from the floor, to Stelin. "Let's go."

We did.

I could tell his heart was not in it as the two of us grappled around on the floor with one another. I could tell he had more of a heart than I'd ever realized when I discovered he was going easy on me because . . . he *felt badly* for me. He might not have cared about my personal issues, but he felt badly enough for me that he didn't want to hurt me.

It made me so angry.

I tried.

I tried to get him to treat me as though I were worthy of his taunting words.

The most I got for a long time was a hard slamming of my back onto the floor once. I had been through much worse with Chandler when I'd been much weaker.

I tried to be objective, to do what I was supposed to. I tried to keep a hold on my temper. Surges of anger and frustration rose up and pushed at me. Some would momentarily break through, as I was no longer accustomed to being pushed in such a way.

Numbness. I'd gotten so accustomed to it.

I would grab hold and rein the negativity all in again, reminding myself I would not learn if I couldn't keep control of myself.

An entire hour passed in that way, I was sure. An entire hour of embarrassment and wasted time. It took all that time for one bit of logic to overpower another.

I would not learn if they wouldn't teach me, either. No amount of self-control would change that.

When one bit of logic broke another, it shattered the hold I'd been keeping on myself.

I ignored the rule about not touching faces when I found myself on top of Stelin. I knew he'd allowed me to get there, and that made it so much worse. I managed to hit him three times before he grabbed hold of my arm.

Managed. I could've laughed.

He'd *let* me hit him three times.

"Where's your *head*?" He nearly shouted at me in disbelief.

"Stop treating me as though I'm not *worth* anything!" I *did* shout at him.

Not knowledge or any genuine attempt at anything. Not even worth *knowledge*.

"You want to play that game?" Stelin moved his head and spit some blood out onto the floor. "Let's play, sweetheart."

I got off him and stood up expectantly. When he did the same, I could tell he was angry. It made me happy because I *wanted* him to be angry. I wanted him to disregard whatever plans he and Chandler had agreed upon for my training. I wanted him to *fight* me. I *needed* those things. I would never learn anything if none of them would. A genuine, legitimate challenge. Something to jerk me away from where I was, in the direction I needed to go. Anything more.

The remainder of the day was spent with me fully realizing how utterly worthless I was.

Chandler had never tried to clearly show me as much, though he'd pretended he had, but Stelin seemed to have no qualms with overkill. Not once I made him.

He would make me come at him, and then he would grab hold of me on different places of my body, faster and better than I could do anything about. I would end up in front of him with his hands on my head, proving he could've snapped my neck in an instant. He could've broken my arms or legs innumerable times in much the same way.

It gave a new perspective on the question I'd been asked more than once since Reapers had come into my life or I'd come into theirs, depending upon how one looked at it.

Do you know how quickly I could kill you?

I didn't know that I would ever joke or laugh about it again, even in exasperation, but I supposed that would depend upon the situation and potentially the person. But it was hard not to poke when they poked first, at least when they did that and I could manage getting a finger on them as well. It all depended upon where you could manage to get. It was a matter of knowing where or not.

Stelin continued to prove his point long after he'd made it. He seemed determined to prove it beyond any shadow of a doubt, even after we moved on to other things.

Most of the time when I was sneaking up on him during stealth training, he would turn around and grab hold of me before I'd managed to get close enough to make my own move. It was my damned frustrated crying, I knew. At least partially. I could not quiet myself enough to sneak up on him properly, if I ever could have. Since it was a floor and there were no sticks, or underbrush, or *anything* like was out in the world . . . I might've been able to.

Chandler spouted off pointers nearly all day. I attempted so very hard to listen and put them to use.

"Don't let him get his hands on you."

That was usually followed shortly thereafter by frustrated noises or profanity on his part, due to me failing at just that.

"Aster, you need to be quiet."

"Aster, you need to stop crying."

"Aster, do you remember *anything* I taught you?"

"Aster, *where* is your *head*?"

Those were the nicer ones.

It was sometime in the early evening when we took a much-needed break, not because anyone was tired but because I needed a moment to properly cry my frustration away. I sat against a wall with my face in my hands. I did not even know if I was crying quietly or cursing loudly. I assumed it was a good deal of both, but I wasn't certain.

I'd always been so horrible at combative training. Even the time I'd hurt Chandler, I didn't know if it had been a *fluke*, as Chase had called it. I did not know, but I would imagine it had been.

Why did my means of ability bother me so badly now? The lack was not new.

No, it was not new, but when logical thoughts began breaking through . . . I knew why.

Along with my circumstances, my perspective had changed, revealing the truth.

I was in Jarsil, and I was utterly alone. Being useless on your own was much different from a person having your back until that changed.

That realization finally striking me, harder than any point Stelin could ever make, sent the numbness back in to take over.

I'd expected to continue on after I was done with my fit, but before I'd properly composed myself and had the faith that I could handle more of Stelin's points, he crouched down beside me. "We'll continue with that tomorrow."

I removed my face from my hands and nodded my head slowly.

"I'll stay with you if you want to run or punch something," he said. "Okay?"

"Okay," I replied, my voice quiet. I wiped the tears from my face and went to the punching contraption.

Stelin stayed with me until long after dark. He did not have to.

THE FOLLOWING DAY was almost exactly the same in the sense of points being proven, as was the next. Stelin did not relent nor deviate even slightly from the path I'd forced him to take. After a bit of time, I numbed myself to the embarrassment of it, in a sense. I tried to learn through it.

The longer Stelin spent tossing me around, the more comfortable he seemed to grow with it. Or perhaps he could tell when my embarrassment somewhat faded. I was unsure, but I began finding less hesitation from him. He kept on the path even after the initial anger or frustration on his part had faded to nothing. He kept on.

I knew it was a good thing despite the shame it brought upon me. I felt as if I were a ragdoll—my limbs incapable of moving unless they were being moved for me by someone else.

It was humiliating, because I was trying *so hard* and couldn't manage. I knew what I was supposed to do, and I just . . . couldn't do it.

After several days of the same, I'd cried out all my tears for it. What did the failings truly matter, so long as I was moving forward—albeit slowly—and not regressing? I could not become any worse, after all. I could only either stay the same or improve so long as I was trying, and I refused to stay in the same place of something I didn't have to.

I thought of what Chase had told me many months before. Honor did not matter so much in the grand scheme of things. I understood now that having honor when another did not could be the very thing that got you killed. It, along with any other quality or choice, could easily get in the way if you allowed it.

Pride was no different in that regard. I couldn't let it stand in the way of my goal, so I pushed it down.

The harder I pushed against it, the more and harder I could focus on what was important.

At some point, I remembered to listen to my breathing at all times while I was awake. Breathing mattered, as everything mattered. An unintentionally loud breath could be just as detrimental as stomping.

Everything mattered.

I'd managed to jump onto Stelin's back three times in one day during stealth training because of my focus being where it should. Each time, he would put me on the floor before I could get one of my hands around the front of his neck to mimic slitting his throat. After some time with him, I found his capability and speed of reaction to be the most impressive thing about him. I believed it could—on occasion and in reality—cause him to be a much more formidable opponent than most would likely give him credit for.

It was in the evening on that same day of small accomplishments when I jumped differently.

I did not bodily throw myself onto him as I had all the other times. I focused on what I *could* do and ensured my hand would be the very first thing to touch him. Slitting a Reaper's throat before they could get you off them was my intended goal. I was not skilled enough to play with a kill like they did or attempt to teach them lessons, nor did I have any desire to do so. Quickness and efficiency was the priority. I did not think I would ever be capable of truly fighting a Reaper head-on, no matter how much I trained for it. They had too much time on me.

I'd been expecting to be thrown to the floor as usual, for Stelin to turn and grab hold. I'd not been expecting to catch the full force of his elbow to my gut. I supposed I'd unwittingly let my guard down in the monotony of it all, or perhaps I'd been focusing on the wrong things.

Either way, I was not prepared for it, physically or mentally. I didn't know that it would've made a difference.

I felt as though I were flying backward and was only able to contemplate the strangeness of flying with no air in my lungs before sharp pains began tearing apart near my stomach. I began vomiting immediately after I hit the floor. I distantly heard Chandler shouting.

"*How hard* did you *hit her*?"

"Not very." Stelin sounded as if he were in shock.

One of my hands shot to my stomach because the pain would not stop. Surely it should not have been so bad. I'd seen many people hit in the same way without this sort of effect. Did preparation make so much of a difference? I felt my face contorting after the heaving.

It was all so strange. I'd been beaten with a whip until my back was turned into nothing more than a massive area of scar tissue, but I'd not ever felt anything like this before. There were so many sorts of pain. This was just a new sort of it.

Why hadn't anyone told me this hurt so badly?

"Oh my god." I barely heard Chandler say, "She's pregnant," before I vomited again.

And I barely heard Stelin say, "Was."

As soon as the newest wave of nausea abated enough to stop my body from expelling whatever was inside my stomach, I felt my shoulders being shaken. I'd only just opened my eyes when Chandler shouted at me.

"Why didn't you *tell* anyone?"

"She didn't know," Stelin answered for me.

I didn't know what caused them to come to the conclusion they had. It was preposterous, though. I'd only been intimate the once, and *surely* it wasn't—

It hurt so badly.

Chandler and I stared into one another's eyes, and he said the words *oh my god* several more times. His hands were still on me, quite gentle, but he looked at Stelin.

I closed my eyes again, just in time for him to say, "Her father is going to *kill you.*"

"He's not going to find out," Stelin said. "She wouldn't want him to know, and I think we can all agree it's in *everyone's* best interest to keep this between us."

It felt like forever until Chandler seemed to locate a portion of his composure. "I have to get Chase."

That seemed to be the only thing that could somewhat drag me out of the unspeakable agony I was feeling. Hadn't he heard Stelin? If they were right . . .

"*No,*" I said desperately through tears I hadn't even realized were falling.

Chandler said, "Aster, it was *his* baby."

I ignored him as I continued clutching at my stomach. It hurt so badly.

"Jastin," I said. "I need Jastin." No matter what had happened or how things had changed . . . I needed him.

No matter what had changed . . . he *owed* me.

"Go get him," Stelin said. "And I don't suggest you tell your brother what just happened. It's her right to let him know herself. I doubt she'd ever forgive you for it. I'd take that into consideration."

I heard no more speaking, but I felt a hand take the one of mine that was not at my stomach.

I knew it was Stelin.

At some point, he whispered, "I'm so sorry."

I squeezed his hand as my body shook on the floor. His words seemed to be the only thing that was real in the world until I felt a hand on my face sometime later.

I knew that hand, even though it had been a while since I'd felt it last.

I did not open my eyes when I heard Jastin say, "Sonofabitch," under his breath.

I did not open my eyes when I was covered with something and scooped up into his arms.

He whispered, "I've got you."

I latched onto him with my then-vacant hand.

I disregarded him when he said, "I'll deal with the two of you later."

I disregarded him when he spoke to two people who inquired about me on the way to wherever we were going, presumably my living quarters if he had any sense. I didn't know how much sense he actually had, but I hoped. I ignored him because the things he said in response to them were inexplicably unpleasant to hear. I suspected he would pay for those remarks later, in some way or another.

I distantly knew he was speaking to me, also presumably when no one else was near, but I didn't care what he was saying. I only cared that he was there. I knew he would get me where I needed to go, at the very least. Had hope that he would. Faith.

It was not long before we were back in my living area and he'd put me on my bed. It hadn't been misplaced.

"You're bleeding everywhere," he told me. "I don't know what to do."

I opened my eyes for the first time in what felt like an eternity and saw him standing there with his widened eyes and a hand over his mouth as he stared at me.

"Will you just stay with me?" I asked through my teeth. It would be all right if he just stayed and had my back for a little while.

It would be all right if he was just . . . *here*.

"I feel like I should get a healer." He shook his head. "This isn't like being cut. I don't know what to do. I can't sew it up or something. I wouldn't think it could be this bad, given you weren't very . . ."

"Please don't," I begged. I could not let my father find out about this, and he most certainly would if anyone else did. He might regardless, in which case . . . I had no idea what would happen.

He would probably kill Chase. Likely Stelin as well, as Chandler had said.

Possibly worse.

I couldn't think about that, so I said, "Just stay."

It was as Jastin was walking around to the other side of the bed that I realized . . .

"I got blood all over you."

He didn't so much as look down at himself to see the extent of it when he crawled into bed with me. "I don't care."

For a long time, I laid there on my back with him on his side next to me. In the beginning I'd been holding onto my stomach as he touched my face, but then he put his hand on my abdomen and rubbed it gently. In my peripherals, I could see him watching my face, likely to ensure he was not doing more harm than good with the action. It felt better than my grabbing.

I assumed my reaction was a mental thing, as his touching did not take away the physical hurting. Still . . . it was better.

"This is much worse than having your arm pulled out," I told him through my teeth when I thought I could manage it. My breathing was still ragged and sharp, and even that was somehow painful. I said what I had because I did not want to say what I wanted to say. But I couldn't help myself because my head seemed to be mostly shut off from dealing with pain. "Will you stay?"

"Aster, you could have fifty of his babies and I'd still be here with you."

"That's not what I asked." It was not even *close* to what I'd asked.

"How many different times and ways do I need to tell you that I'm not going anywhere?"

"You *do* go," I told him, looking over and finding his face through my tears. "Every day you go and leave me alone with these people." I could've said so much more, but that was enough.

He seemed to deflate when he released a breath. Very slowly, he said, "I am not going anywhere." I could see the small smile on his face. Was it sad or guilty? "Do you want me to get you some Fandir root? You won't know you're hurting, then."

I shook my head. "I'd rather deal with it."

"Then try to get some rest," he urged softly. "It may not hurt so badly when you wake up."

"But you're *going* to leave." I cried. "You're going to leave as soon as I wake up." I couldn't bear to have a repeat of what he'd done when we'd first arrived, not right after this.

I couldn't bear the thought of having him there then him leaving me to manage everything alone. Not again. Not right now.

He leaned over and kissed me on the forehead. "No, I'm not." He was still leaning close to my face when he said, "I have to take care of you, don't I?"

"Just like you have to take care of Cherise." I hadn't been able to stop the words from coming out, despite the obvious differences.

He shook his head in clear confusion. "Cherise?" It took several seconds before he closed his eyes. "Oh my god." When they opened again, he blinked at me for quite a while before very slowly saying, "You think I've been going to see Cherise this entire time?"

"That pregnant girl—"

He cut me off by saying, "Oh my god," again. "Aster . . . that's my *sister*. I've been going to see my *sister* and my *nephew*."

"Why didn't you *tell me*?" A burst of anger sent another jolt of pain through my stomach. My eyes closed tightly.

He moved when I did and all he said in response was, "We'll talk about it when you're feeling better."

I wanted to tell him I hated him, but the words that came out of my mouth were, "Will you hold me?" I hated myself a little for it.

He chuckled quietly. "I've already got you. What else do you want me to do?"

I moved my face to where it was against his chest and ignored the pain of switching my position because the end result would be worth it. I'd missed being so close. "Stop letting go."

I heard him breathe out as he wrapped his arm around me and settled his hand on my back. I contemplated the absurdity of holding onto a person as they were holding onto you, and I pretended I was not bleeding everywhere. No matter how hard or what I tried to pretend, I knew that if this hadn't happened, if I weren't injured in some way . . . he would not have been here at all.

But I reminded myself that even if he left again, he was here for me when I needed him. It did not erase all the times he hadn't been, but those times didn't change the fact that . . .

He was here.

CHAPTER THREE

TO HELP

RUE TO HIS WORD, Jastin did not leave when I woke sometime in the night after being injured in whatever way I had been during training. No matter what he'd said on where he was and taking care of, him staying still surprised me. I kept waiting for him to slip away, but he didn't. He remained and essentially crammed food down my throat, saying it would help because I was weakened from losing blood. He also prevented people from bothering me. I appreciated the latter more so than the former. Much more.

I could not have counted all the people he made leave my doorstep, mostly because I didn't care about the number so long as I didn't have to deal with them. I typically only cared to be bothered with numbers when they had some sort of importance. If I didn't have to deal with them, the number was not important. Sometimes counting was good for passing time, I would give numbers that.

There was only one person Jastin could not keep away, and it was the only number that mattered in this regard. That person was the man the entire city belonged to, including the space being intruded upon, of course.

It was the morning after the incident when my father barged in, demanding to know what had happened to me.

Nothing could've been done about it, even if he'd knocked and Jastin had tried to stop it, having the time and opportunity to attempt as much.

Anders was with him and that somehow made it better, even if only just.

Jastin gave a rather interesting and questionably accurate explanation. "Very bad case of womanly time."

My father looked from him, to me. "Is that true?"

It was all down to technicalities.

"Horrendous cramping," I said, my voice vacant. That much was true, if not for the precise reason implied. Though I supposed even that was true enough in its way. For all intents and purposes, my body *had* done precisely what came with womanly time.

"Horrendous enough cramping for him to be required to pick you up and carry you?" Though my father's face was *almost* as vacant as my voice had been, it was clear by his tone that he didn't believe a single word of this.

"Rather horrendous," I said, seeing Jastin carefully stepping away in my peripherals. "I don't believe I'll be moving for quite some time."

"You know I don't believe this, Aster."

Yes, I did.

"What other explanation is there, Father?" I didn't mind the exasperation I felt seeping into my tone. I did not have the energy to deal with him right now nor the desire to deal with him ever. If I went along with Jastin's story and no one contradicted it, what could he do? He couldn't be certain of the truth if no one confirmed it. He could only speculate.

"We were traveling for more than a month," my father said, "and I don't recall you ever having your . . . *womanly time* while we were on our journey."

It was a valid point and one that had crossed my mind on a very small handful of occasions over the last few months. I'd noticed the lack of the womanly time but had thought of a logical explanation for the absence then put it out of my mind. There were so many other things that seemed more pressing.

"Stress can prevent it from happening," I stated. "Agatha told me as much when I was younger, given my father had never informed me that one day I would begin bleeding everywhere from my most private of places. So Agatha explained to me how the world works. I would say the stress of my situation would've been sufficient enough to stop it for a short while."

That had been such a frightening day for me—the first. Agatha had assumed that, given my age before my father left, he would've at the very least *warned* me about it. Then she'd assumed I'd at some point started then been dealing with it in secret for a number of years and she'd wanted to respect my privacy. Apparently it had happened much later for me than it did most people. Agatha assured me I was normal despite that, but I failed to see the logic behind her statement.

My father stared at me for quite some time before pressing the matter further. "And what about since you've come here?"

I raised an eyebrow. "Do you believe I announce when I'm having my womanly time for everyone to hear?" I paused before saying, "I'm failing to see what you're implying."

"Are you pregnant?" His eyes had gone very wide.

I laughed uncomfortably and said, "Thankfully, I most certainly am not. I must admit I'm curious who you believe the father would be and when in the world I had the time and opportunity to become that way."

"Thankfully?" was the only word he seemed to have picked up on from my statement. I wondered if he'd heard nothing at all past that, but so long as he'd heard the first of it . . . that was the important part.

I was *not* pregnant. That was both true and the truth.

"That's what I just said, isn't it?" I asked him. "You seem shocked I would say as much. First you barge in here yelling at me as though I've done something wrong for not feeling well, and then you seem sad by what I said in response to it all."

He said nothing.

I gave him a moment before I said, "I'm very sorry to tell you that, if you're hoping to be a grandfather . . .?" I shook my head. "You'll not become one by me. But you already have a grandchild, don't you?"

I gave him another moment, this one to hopefully think about my niece in the Reaper school.

My voice was very firm when I told him, "I'll not bring a single child into this world, Father. Not if I can help it."

33

"You never want to have children?" Why did he seem so perplexed by something so simple?

"That's what I just said, isn't it?" I asked him again, my frustration rising. "I'll have to ask that you leave me be. I'm feeling quite unhappy, which happens around the time we've been speaking on as I'm sure you know, and you're making it indefinably worse."

"I was concerned about you."

"There's no need to worry, Father." I told him that rather than pointing out how *fantastic* shouting and making accusations were at showing concern. Whether those accusations were *almost* accurate was entirely beside the point. "I've gotten by without you for more than ten years. I'm quite sure I can manage without you now."

"If you need me for anything . . ." My father trailed off, speaking much softer than usual. He took in a deep breath and then let it out. "You know where I am."

He and Anders had both made it to the door before I said, "Anders."

He turned.

I asked, "Will you stay for a moment?"

My father had paused, and I watched him take and then release another breath before continuing on his way alone without another word.

Anders closed the door and came to sit down beside me.

"I'm going to ask you something I've already asked you once," I said. "Given the subject that was just spoken of, I'd appreciate it if you would answer me this time."

I paused for just an instant, wondering if he knew the question I was going to ask.

I still had to ask, "How did you never get my mother pregnant?"

"I did get her pregnant," he said quietly. "We didn't know until we went on our next mission and she had a miscarriage due to . . ." He shook his head and said nothing more on that particular matter. "After that, I found a man who claimed he knew how to stop people from having children. I went behind her back and had the procedure done. I'm sure she knew, but she never said a word of it to me."

I'd never heard of such a thing. It seemed impossible, but . . . "This . . . *procedure*," I said carefully. "Can they do the same to women?"

He blinked hard several times before he responded with, "No."

"Oh, Anders," barely came out of my mouth. "That's the first time you've directly lied to me, isn't it?"

And what a thing to lie over. There were so many other options that would've made more sense to have broken the streak for.

He simply stood and walked away at that, saying nothing more at all. While there were so many things he could've said, I supposed none of it was needed. Still . . . it was disappointing. Perhaps he felt he hadn't lied, as different parts would *surely* be dealt with in different ways, but he knew damn well I'd been asking about the procedure being possible for women as well rather than it being gone about in the same way.

I'd gotten the answer regardless, but his attempt at deception was a *massive* disappointment.

Jastin had pretended to be doing something in the small kitchen during the short exchange, at least after stretching the truth to my father for me. I suspected he didn't want to be caught doing as much and had left me alone, possibly, to have a better chance at success. I knew he'd been listening the entire time, though. He held a sandwich out to me when he came back, and I took it as he sat down beside me.

It took him a moment to speak, but when he did, I brought my attention to his face.

"I was worried you'd be sad." He smiled stiffly and said, "I guess I should've known better."

I did not want to respond to that, so I asked, "Do you believe Chandler informed Chase about it?" Along with the fact that it would possibly endanger his and their safety . . . I did not want him to know. Not yet at least, and possibly never.

"I can assure you he didn't."

I tilted my head at him in confusion, as he could not possibly be sure of such a thing when he hadn't left my side since. He could only speculate. I was simply curious what his speculation was as to Chandler's involvement.

My reaction must've made him clarify with, "He'd be breaking down the door if he knew."

Perhaps that was true, but perhaps it was not. It was probably true.

"I'm inclined to believe he would be happy we weren't having a child," I stated.

Jastin narrowed his eyes. "No, you're not."

I pursed my lips and sniffled a little. "If he had any sense, he would be."

If he had any sense, he would break down the door and proclaim his relief.

My voice sounded so distant when I added, "I don't think I would ever forgive myself for bringing a child into this world."

"Why?" he asked curiously. "And don't just tell me the world is a horrible place because I know it's more than that."

"That's enough, isn't it?" I felt my jaw beginning to quiver. I thought that was *more* than enough.

"No, I want you to tell me the full reason why."

"I can't even protect myself." I shook my head and stared down at my hands. "How could I *ever* keep a child safe?" My mother and father had both trained their entire lives and *they* couldn't manage it. How could I ever subject another person to this?

"There it is."

When I looked back over at him, he was nodding his head slowly in understanding.

He forced a smile at me and said, "Eat your sandwich."

"I don't like sandwiches," I said beneath my breath.

He put his hand on my leg and said two words I didn't want to hear, but I respected them.

"Too bad."

I took a bite.

I found myself somewhat enjoying the sandwich because he did not move his hand from off my leg as I'd expected him to. It was distracting enough for me to manage it. I kept very still, thinking he would move when I did. It was odd how something pleasant could make things you didn't like enjoyable enough.

THE NEXT SEVERAL DAYS PASSED BY in much the same way. Jastin did not once leave my side—though I kept expecting him to— as I recovered from both the physical and emotional aspects of what had happened. I cried about it more than once with varying intensity despite being happy that such a bad thing had happened.

I could not fully explain my reactions nor how I felt about the situation as a whole, as none of it made very much sense to me. The concept alone of what I'd unknowingly had and lost was baffling, but my differing feelings and thoughts about it were infinitely more so.

Logic told me that it was good, not only for myself and for . . . what I'd lost, but for others as well.

Would this have been another thing that could potentially have voided the deal my father and I had made concerning Chase and Chandler's safety? Would my father kill Chase if he knew? Would he kill Chandler the instant the deal was broken?

I was not a Reaper, but what if they would've taken what I'd lost regardless? What would've happened to it? What would it have potentially gone through due to me? What would I have done?

Though I went through so many options inside my head about the horrendous things that could've happened, each worse than the last and all of them plausible . . . I couldn't shake the overwhelming sadness I felt. No amount of logic or relief changed that I felt it.

It made no sense.

I did spend some time getting lost in thoughts simply wondering what it might've looked like, which led to thoughts about things going together to make other things, which led to a very confusing place inside my head that I had no idea what to do with. Even that Chase and Chandler came from the same place and that place had gone with my place to make something else was thought on for a moment. That was odd.

Trying to grasp that a part of me had died took some time. Parts of me had died before. My mother. My father. They'd all come from the other part of me, though. Trying to grasp something from the differing part dying was difficult. Then wondering if it was truly part of me or its own thing.

Part of me. And yet not.

It was very confusing and a great deal to take on.

Jastin sat close to me during the day as I processed and attempted to work through it all, and he slept close to me at night. I liked having him there, for a number of reasons. I did not believe I would've handled the situation well alone, if I was handling it well at all. His presence was comforting and, though it took nothing away and changed nothing at all, I felt it made the situation more bearable somehow.

It was four days after seeing my father that Chase barged in. He did not knock, so Jastin didn't have the opportunity to turn him away. Both aspects were immensely frustrating.

Upon entering, he demanded to know, "*What* is going on with the two of you?"

"What?" I asked him in confusion as I recovered from the surprise of the door opening so abruptly. Why did so many people *not knock*?

"You haven't spoken to him in over a month," Chase said. "I *know* something happened during your training the other day, but nobody will tell me what it is. Now you're not training and he won't leave your side for anything. *What* is going on?"

That wasn't what he'd initially asked, was it? They were two very different questions.

Jastin said, "Don't worry about it."

"Don't *even* get me started on you." Chase laughed. "You told me you were going to back off once we got here. Please tell me how not letting anyone near her lines up with that."

I closed my eyes and took a deep breath. "*That's* what you were doing."

That was why he'd not told me where he was going and why he'd allowed me to think he was going off to see another girl. He *had* been, only it had been his sister and not the one I'd thought. It all made sense now.

I felt my anger was somewhat misplaced when I looked at Chase and forced myself to sound as calm as I could manage to ask, "Why are you acting as though I'm a piece of property to be bargained over?" Hadn't anyone learned their lessons the last time?

"I'm not bargaining," Chase said. "He told me that of his own volition before we arrived here. Don't spin this into that."

"Then barging in here and shouting is not the way to show as much," I informed him. Why did everyone believe that was the appropriate thing to do?

It really wasn't.

"I *just* want to know what's going on," he said, speaking carefully. "My god, can't you at least give me *that* much?"

I couldn't deny that was a reasonable request.

"He's been with me because I haven't been feeling well," I stated, my voice impassive. "He's not allowed anyone near me because I haven't wished to speak with or see anyone. Is that satisfactory?"

"That might be true," Chase nodded, "but that most certainly is *not* what's going on. I am getting *so* sick of you talking in circles around me. Every single *time* he's in the picture, you start talking in circles. Every time he's not . . . you don't talk at all. What happened to fixing things and being honest with one another?"

"Chase." I closed my eyes. "I really don't feel well right now. Can we talk about this later?"

"Later *when*, Aster?" His voice rose. "Later after I've wasted my entire life waiting for it? Should I just sit here in Jarsil waiting for you while you're waiting for him?"

Idiot. He had *no idea*. . . .

I took another deep breath before Jastin said, "I'm giving you fair warning. If you don't leave like . . . *right now*, she's going to say something she'll regret. She wasn't lying when she told you she's feeling bad."

Chase asked, "Are you *speaking* for her now, too?"

I took another deep breath.

Jastin said, "Just trying to help."

I almost thought Chase was on the verge of laughing when he said, "Of course."

Relief swelled inside me when I heard the door close. I opened my eyes, finding Jastin and I alone together once more.

I looked at him to say, "Thank you."

"It's what I'm here for." Jastin shrugged, keeping his gaze at the door Chase had just left through.

"What?" I asked. "Keeping people away from me when I want them away?"

He was going to be very busy, if that were the case.

He kept his attention on the door, but he smiled a little. "Anything you want."

He should not have made yet another statement he had no intention of fulfilling. If it was different this time, he was going to be much busier than he would if he were only keeping people away.

I wouldn't hold my breath.

CHAPTER FOUR

NEVER ENOUGH

I WAS LYING IN BED with Jastin that same night as the scene with Chase, curled up with him beneath a new set of blankets. They'd just appeared in my living quarters, placed on a sofa at some point when I'd been sleeping the first night after the incident. Though Jastin insisted he'd not left at all, I initially had suspicions that he was lying. I'd slept like the dead that first night of him staying and he could've easily slipped away.

But he was insistent and accused either Chandler or Stelin of putting the blankets there. He thought if it was Chandler it would be for the caring, and that if Stelin brought them, it was an attempt at weaseling out of the threat Jastin had left them with about *dealing with later.*

If Jastin was not the culprit, which I was eventually sure he wasn't, I believed he was wrong.

Chandler had not been in Jarsil long enough to steal something even for someone else, nor would he have a valid excuse without the risk of betraying my trust to get out of it were he caught, nor would he risk doing anything to void the deal I'd made with my father. Stealing would do as much regardless of the reasoning or object, I believed, due to my father's unhappiness over his and his brother's presence. I'd seen the ways he looked at them.

Given my father had no proof when making his accusation to me, Chandler had not done it. He also simply was not the sort, and that said enough. I only had to assume he was both still here in Jarsil and alive, especially when inquiring to Jastin had caused him to laugh at me. On and off for several days. He'd laughed and not even answered the question for me.

Still, if it had been either of them, it was Stelin. He might've done it for the reason Jastin suspected. I didn't know, but if it hadn't been Jastin, it had been Stelin.

I knew that because . . . there were no flowers embroidered on the fabric. Stelin and I had made a deal.

No more flowers of any sort.

Chandler would've brought me the first or plainest blankets he could find—first out of convenience or plainest out of assumed consideration—and these were not the latter thing. The main blanket was green with white vines embroidered on it.

Vines were not flowers, so it broke no deals, but they were close enough to be irritating due to the deal. These had required some searching, as evident by the somewhat musty scent I'd had to wash out before being able to use them.

I knew I wouldn't discover who the culprit had been. If it were Jastin, he wouldn't admit to leaving. If it were Stelin, Jastin would only find out if he informed him of it. I doubted he would let me know. I was *quite* sure regardless.

I didn't bother pointing out to Jastin that people could only weasel out of things with good deeds if other people were aware of as much. I had to assume he knew regardless of not knowing why Chandler's well-being wasn't something to laugh at. If weaseling was what Stelin had done, Jastin would hear about it. He *might* tell me in which case due to me having voiced interest and him likely thinking it would tell me less than it actually would.

None of that was very important, but it was interesting to think about. And I did like my new blankets well enough despite whatever initial irritation, as they had no flowers or blood.

I still felt bad, but I was not physically hurting very much any longer, at least in comparison. I did not want to tell Jastin that, which made me feel more than slightly ridiculous and extremely pathetic.

I asked, "Why did you tell him you would back off?"

My head was on his chest and he was rubbing my arm with one of his hands. I'd been wondering about that most of the day, as it didn't line up with the events before our arrival here. And Chase had said *before*.

"Because it's what I should do," he answered easily. "Don't tell me you don't agree because I know you do."

"That may be true," I conceded. It *was* true. In one sense, I *did* agree. In another sense . . . I did not. I fought against the urge to fidget. "But what if I don't want you to?"

"Then it's all the more reason I should." He sighed. "I know where this is going. You and I came to an agreement that we wouldn't do this, that we wouldn't even talk about it."

I said, "Then let's not talk about it."

I heard him release a breath of relief that died in his throat when I put my hand on his abdomen.

"What are you doing?" he asked quickly as he grabbed hold of my hand.

It was almost amusing that he nearly sounded terrified. Almost, but not.

"Not talking," I answered.

It took him several extremely long seconds to formulate words and get them out of his mouth, and in the end, all he did was repeat himself. "What are you doing?"

"Do you remember what you said the first time you kissed me?" I asked. "You were talking about friction and said that kissing solved the problem." I believed this was similar enough.

"Aster, you and I are *so* far past that point now."

I smiled against his chest, which he must've known.

"Do you think this is funny?"

"Only slightly," I admitted, "but mostly it's just awful." I didn't understand why it was so difficult to be around him. Why couldn't I just trust him without any other feelings? Better yet . . .

Why couldn't I have just trusted someone else entirely? Someone else, without all the other nonsense.

Someone else, who I could.

"I want you to look at me," he said, "and I'm going to give you a list of reasons why not."

I moved over a bit and propped myself up with my elbow to look at him.

"You and I are lying in a bed alone together." His statement was both redundant and . . . *not*. "There's no one half-awake right next to us. Given your declaration of never wanting children, can't you see that this has *bad idea* written all over it?"

"I'm just talking about kissing." My tone sounded completely innocent.

"Aster," he said again. "Speaking of points you and I are so far past. . . . This is not the same as us kissing after I almost died and all that went along with it. This is not the same as awkward, frustration-filled first kisses. With the way we feel about each other . . . it's not a smart thing to do. Not in any way whatsoever. There's no point in you acting like you don't know as much." He pursed his lips for a moment. "The most important thing is that I'm not willing to risk losing what we have. For *what*? Something neither of us cares about at all? Something that's not even remotely important in this world? Something that doesn't compare in any way whatsoever to what we already have?"

I smiled and said, "None of that means you don't want to kiss me."

He could talk around it all he wanted, but if he didn't want to kiss me, he would just say it. At least with the way the conversation had gone.

He put his hands over his face. "What about Chase?"

"What about him?" I shrugged. "I can't make myself not feel the way I do about you and continue to love him in the same way I did, or in the way he wants me to." Especially with the way he was behaving and all that had happened. "And yes, you could break the way I feel about you intentionally, but you won't do that, will you? You can't because, if you did . . . that would destroy what we have. Trust is the only thing that cannot be destroyed by outside forces, and you would never do anything to destroy my trust for you." I was still smiling when I asked, "Would you?"

He shook his head at me in disbelief. "You're evil," he stated assuredly. "It is . . . *remarkable* how cold you are."

I laughed a little under my breath. "You love me regardless." Still, I did not quite understand what he meant, given my logical reasoning. It all made perfect sense in my head, and I didn't see how it made me evil or cold.

He frowned. "Yes, I do."

"You told me I would never hear it again," I pointed out. I would not point out that I already *had* heard it again since. Rubbing *that* in his face? I could see how that might make me a bit cold.

"Yes, well, things seemed to have spun out of my control." Unhappiness was clear in his voice. "It's not exactly something I prepared myself for." His voice was quieter when he added, "None of this was anything I prepared myself for."

"Will you kiss me?" I did not want to talk about feelings or anything else that ran to a comparative depth. I needed a break from all that, even if only a small one. I thought the kissing might help. At the very least, there could be no talking on feelings with mouths being otherwise occupied.

He sighed. "Are you insisting it of me?"

"Only if you want to." I took in a deep breath and then released it. "Don't you ever get sick of not doing things you want simply because it's the right thing not to do them? No. . . ." I pursed my lips together while I worked it out a bit more. "Why is it the wrong thing for us to kiss if we want to?"

"Do I need to repeat the list for you?" he asked, I presumed rhetorically. "It's the wrong thing because both our heads are telling us so. Do you need more reason than that?"

"Can't we stop listening to them for just a moment?" I asked. "I don't want things to change with us either. I'm simply asking for a few minutes of doing what I want." I just wanted a break from it, a small amount of good. Some sort of good.

He shook his head again. "If things get messed up between us . . . it's on you."

"You know that's not true." I smiled, excitement building up inside my chest for the first time in what felt like ages. Had he just agreed? "You don't *have* to kiss me. Just because I asked doesn't mean you have to do it. That would put it on us both. Doesn't that make you feel better?"

"And you know I would do anything you asked me to," he said in clear frustration. "I'm worried now what that's going to mean for me later."

"That's not true either." It was not even *remotely* true. "If I asked you to run away with me right now—"

"I would say, '*Yes, Star, let's go get ourselves killed.*'"

It took me a moment to make *any* sort of sense of what he'd said.

When I realized, I asked to be sure, "What did you just call me?"

He rubbed his hands over his face, clearly exasperated. "You heard me."

Had I heard him? "Will you call me that again?"

"No." He laughed as he removed his hands. And there was something about seeing his smile in the near darkness that had my face moving closer to his.

Quietly, I asked, "Maybe sometimes?"

He said, "Maybe never."

We were both still laughing when I pressed my lips against his. I realized then that I did not always need to ask. Sometimes . . . I could simply do things myself. Perhaps it was something like not knocking because you knew you were welcome inside the space you were going at whichever point. Or perhaps not, because I still thought that would be quite rude.

I could not imagine any one person being welcome inside another's space indefinitely. And if one were on the outside coming in, they couldn't possibly know if they would always be welcome or be welcome *right then.*

So no, it was not like knocking, or not, at all.

IT TOOK ME QUITE SOME TIME to fully understand what Jastin had meant when he'd spoken about us being past certain points. It took my own hands being in the process of moving down for it to dawn on me. It was a much quicker realization than the sun coming up in the sky, but almost slower in a way. It *felt* slower.

He stopped kissing me immediately when it struck me, like he knew what was going on inside my head. It seemed more like reading my mind for him than any issue with what I'd been moving to do.

Several seconds passed as I took in the sight of him shirtless on top of me. We were both breathing somewhat heavily as I stared in an almost distracted state at a knife strapped to his arm.

Perplexed, I asked him, "Where's your shirt?"

"You should know." He chuckled. "You're the one who took it off me and threw it across the room."

That was preposterous. Wasn't it?

His eyebrows rose. "Do you see now what I meant?"

"I . . . I . . ." I stopped and attempted to force my head into proper thinking. I could not remember doing what he said I'd done, but in case I *had* . . . "I don't believe we should kiss in bed again. Or in such dark." If one eliminated the factors that made a situation what it was . . .

He tilted his head and smiled at me. "Do you really think it would matter?"

Very slowly, I said, "I'm hoping it would."

It would have to, wouldn't it? The factors. . . .

I cleared my throat, wishing it would dispel the awkwardness I felt. Of course it wouldn't, only fixing this would. "Perhaps we should spend some time testing limits, to prevent ourselves from going past a certain point." In case the factors that mattered in this situation were the two of us rather than any circumstantial exceptions, but . . .

Why had it changed so much?

He grinned. "That won't work."

I blinked at him, confused again, until he clarified.

"I don't have any limits with you."

And there was something about the smile on his face paired with the words he'd said that caused me to squirm slightly where I was. I didn't understand it, but I could not stop myself from kissing him again, despite knowing I should not.

There was a very brief moment of my head yelling at me to stop and my heart cackling maliciously in response before he pulled away and rolled off me, onto his back. There was a very not-brief moment where I found myself admiring his body as he rubbed his hands over his face. Then, I realized . . .

"I thought you said you had no limits?"

"*You* have limits."

"I'm not so sure I do," I shook my head slowly, "which I'm sure you well know. It may likely make you feel better to tell yourself as much, but . . . that doesn't mean it's true."

"Then you're going to have to be the one who has the sense to keep things in line. I don't think I can do it anymore. I'm pretty sure it's your turn now anyway." He'd been trying the entire time, so I supposed that was only fair.

"If you're thinking our relationship would be destroyed by

feelings and you're depending on me to prevent that from happening . . ." I spoke very carefully, ensuring it came out the appropriate way. "I'm quite certain you and I are doomed."

"It wouldn't be worth it." He sounded so sure.

But when I whispered, "Are you sure?" and he looked over at me . . .

He did not seem so convinced.

"Are you really? Because I'm finding I'm not."

"We're stuck with half of what both of us want, Aster. We can't—" He took in a deep breath. "We can't do the things people do when they're in love and not expect the other half. We can't sleep together and not expect to have a child because of it at some point. There's only one end result to us having what we want with each other, and it's with one or both of us dead and our children taken and turned into murderers. Or worse. So yes, I can tell you right now that it would *not* be worth it."

I did not know what he meant by *worse*.

"*This* . . ." He gestured at the space between us. "This is all we can ever have." He looked up at the ceiling and kept his gaze there. "You need to decide if that's what you want, because it's all I can give you."

I pursed my lips, but I scooted up beside him and placed my head on his chest. I felt a tear fall from my eye when he wrapped his arms around me. I'd given him my answer, and he gave me his when he kissed me on the top of my head.

How could I have given him any other answer when he was the only person I could have near me? What was I supposed to do?

I knew that safety was only an illusion, but . . . I didn't want to go it alone. Not here. He was all I had, the only thing that felt . . . *solid*. Or *somewhat* solid. How could I have given him any other answer?

Why couldn't I have trusted *anyone* else? Someone. Anyone. Why did no one else trust or believe in me?

The thought of continually looking someone in the eye and seeing there was no sight . . .

What he was offering may not have been enough, but . . . it was better than nothing. It was better than worse than nothing. To convince myself I could tolerate all that came along with it, I thought on the fact that I wouldn't know what *enough* was anyway. How could it bother me if I didn't know it? *This* . . .

It was what it was.

CHAPTER FIVE

PUSH

FIRST THING THE MORNING AFTER Jastin and I had kissed in my bed, I informed him that I was prepared to resume my training. A brief conversation on the matter followed, and he didn't once ask whether or not I was *sure* I was up for it or imply that he thought I might not be. He'd simply asked me to do the physical training, opposed to combative, until he returned from visiting with his sister and nephew. It was entirely reasonable, so I agreed. Combatives required warming up to be done properly anyway. Not that I could do them properly.

The way the matter had all been handled was a strong reminder of why I'd initially wanted his presence in my life where I didn't others. He'd never once second-guessed me directly, and having someone treat me that way now made me feel better than I had in a long while.

I had, over the days, had some very confusing thoughts that resulted in a great many internal questions as to how I felt and why I felt that way. What had been dispelling those was remembering the expressions on faces. The situation in the morning with Jastin had given me a new moment of clarity and reinforcement that caused me to feel even more prepared for the day and potentially stepping into my training room.

A small bit of irritation attempted to work its way into the good. I couldn't deny how much I'd missed that aspect of his presence since arriving in Jarsil and how it would've helped before to have him near, when trying to adapt to and accept being here.

I also couldn't deny how much I'd missed him in general. He seemed to make everything more bearable, with his jokes and his smile. His presence alone was a comfort, where trust was concerned and in other ways. It was nice to have someone close who understood a little more than the rest. Or often seemed to.

So I pushed down the irritation I felt over all he'd deprived me of and his reasons for doing as much. It didn't change that he was here now, so I focused on the good of it.

Agreeing to his terms was how I ended up running around the perimeter of my training area, attempting to ignore the aching in my body while I thought over stars. I did not mind him calling me what he had in the same way I despised being called Flower. Though my name *was* technically a flower, it was so insulting, like I was nothing more than some pretty thing to look at. I was grateful to Jastin for pointing as much out to me, causing me to really *think* about it.

It was undeniable that stars were beautiful as well, but it was not anywhere near the same. Stars were untouchable where they sat far up in the sky. I didn't know if that was his reasoning in calling me what he had, but if it had been, it was understandable. I found that I . . . *liked* it, very much. It was silly of me, I knew, but knowing it was silly did not change the fact that I liked it.

Stelin and Chandler ran on either side of me as I thought over it all, breaking up the monotony of the movement, but Chandler was the one who asked me how I was feeling. I believed Stelin had the sense to not. It wasn't that Chandler was unintelligent. Quite the opposite, really. He simply could not really see into who I was despite having been around me almost constantly for months. It made me sad, and I wondered if it would ever stop doing so, but it irked me as well.

"Would I be here if I were still feeling badly in a physical sense?" I asked him through my labored breathing.

"Sorry." Chandler mumbled the word, which was very unlike him.

His behavior caught me off guard, and I heard myself say, "It's quite all right."

I glanced up at him, unwittingly. I only realized I'd done as much when he glanced down at me. I opened my mouth to apologize, but what almost came out was being glad my father hadn't killed him. I closed my mouth, my brow furrowing. In another glance, I was quite sure he almost said something.

He did not.

Stelin drew my attention by saying, "Are you speaking again? I suppose company makes a big difference in a person's desire to speak, even in different company."

I glanced over at him briefly and saw that he was grinning. I did not respond to him. I didn't believe he expected me to.

"Aster," Chandler said quietly, which drew my attention back to him, though in a different way. "When are you going to tell Chase about what happened?"

I almost stumbled over my own feet at his question, but he quickly righted me and we continued on our way. I'd thought about that very thing over the last few days. I'd torn the situation apart, put it back together, and then tore it apart again.

After a moment spent in preparation, I informed him, "I'm not."

As expected, he stopped moving, which made me stop moving, which made Stelin stop moving.

Chandler's eyes were wide. "You're not serious."

"What would be the point?" I bent over a bit and put my hands on my knees while I tried to fully catch my breath. "It would only make him sad, wouldn't it? What's the point of telling him? Nothing has changed. Telling him won't change what happened, either."

"He has the right to know," Chandler said firmly.

I stood up straight and frowned at him. "How many times were things I had the right to know kept from me for whatever reasons? He very well may have the right to know, but it *is* my right to either tell him or not." I paused for a moment, letting that sink in. "I'm already hurting him enough, aren't I? I can't see the logic in worsening that intentionally."

"So you're acknowledging you're hurting him." Chandler nodded.

"When have I ever not?"

"Have you thought about *stopping*?"

"You give me a solution that doesn't involve removing Jastin from my life or bowing to your brother's idiocy and I'll gladly take it into consideration," I said, my voice impassive. "And if you hadn't noticed, Jastin not being around didn't *fix things* between us. I cannot erase an entire part of my life, nor can I make your brother stop behaving like an imbecile every time he doesn't understand the reasons I have for doing things. Also, if you were unaware, I have absolutely no control over him only wanting to *fix things* with me when Jastin is in some way involved. So, until you come up with some other solution . . . we're done speaking of it." I raised an eyebrow at him. "May I continue with my training?"

He held his arm out in front of him for me to do so, but he no longer accompanied Stelin and me as we ran together.

It was the first time I felt he was genuinely upset with me, and it hurt. But I kept running.

After what felt like both forever and no time at all, I barely heard Stelin mutter, "Don't worry about it."

I glanced over at him.

"He'll understand eventually."

I wanted to ask how he could be sure.

I couldn't force myself to.

I just kept running.

I did not become ill once. I was glad for that much at least.

JASTIN WAS GONE FOR SEVERAL HOURS, but not for anywhere near as long as he had been all those times before. He'd rarely been in the room with me as I'd been training, only a few instances for a few minutes at a time. I had no idea what to expect or how the addition of his presence might change the experience.

He did not sit in a corner and supervise Chandler and Stelin as they went about my combative training instruction. Though I'd thought he might do as much, I knew he was worried they wouldn't take proper care of me. He was very hands-on, which was something I'd not been expecting in the slightest.

Rather than showing me things and expecting me to miraculously be able to do them, he let me put my hands on him and do things slowly until I got the proper feel for it.

I supposed they were all quite accustomed to everyone already knowing how to do everything, because the former had been the method used thus far.

We practiced the same maneuver for the majority of the day. By the end of it when we were moving at normal speed and I got him onto his back by his arm . . . I found myself smiling.

It was as though everyone had been speaking gibberish to me where it pertained to my training. Then he finally came along and seemed to be the only one who spoke the same language as I did.

It gave me some sort of hope that—one day—I would be able to protect myself and other people, so long as he was here to help me get there.

No one else seemed able to. I didn't know if that was my fault, theirs, or simply how it was.

It was as Jastin was walking me back to my living quarters that I said, "You're a very good instructor. Have you done that before?"

He grinned. "No, Reapers always know what they're doing."

That was as I'd suspected, but it had not been what I was asking about, so I clarified. "I meant . . . normal people."

"Oh no," he said quickly. "We're not allowed to teach anyone anything we know."

"Why is that?" That was strange. Surely some of them had non-Reaper friends or . . . *something*.

"They don't want the citizens knowledgeable enough to stand a chance at revolting. There are so many more of them than there are of us. It would just be really bad."

I shrugged. "Or really good."

"I don't like the system," he said, "but no system at all would be so much worse. People are like . . ." He paused, clenching his jaw. I didn't know if he was trying to think of how to put it or if he didn't want to say it. "*Sheep*. You have to keep them in order and protect them or the wolves come in and slaughter the entire flock. I don't like it, but that's how it is."

"Yes, I can see that," I agreed after a moment of thinking over it. It was quite logical, but I didn't like it either. "It's a shame the system isn't better, that we can't do anything to fix it."

"We can't fix the world, Star."

I tried to conceal my happiness over him calling me that name again, but I was not anywhere near entirely successful. I was quite certain that I wiggled a little as I walked, without my head's permission to do so. I should've been thinking about speaking of fixing the world, rather than a name. He made me ridiculous.

Unfortunately, he noticed my lack of appropriate thought because he chuckled quietly and said, "You're so funny."

"Why is that?" Was it *funny* to be ridiculous?

"You're so . . ." He paused as he attempted to think of a word.

I glanced over at him, seeing his face scrunched in deep thought, and I knew with certainty that he was thinking rather than not wanting to say. Eventually he located the word he'd been searching for.

"*Cold.*"

I laughed. "It took you *that* long to come up with a word you've called me numerous times?"

"I don't know," he said almost dismissively. "That's how you are, at least with everyone else. I can't really put it any other way. It's hard to imagine you acting so . . . *light*. My eyes see it, but my head is telling me it's not happening, that it's not right."

"I don't know what you mean." I didn't like what he'd just said or the way it made me feel. I also didn't like that I couldn't comprehend the feeling past knowing it was unpleasant.

"You were just wiggling around over me calling you a nickname." He chuckled, but it seemed only partially amused. "Did you ever act that way with Chase?"

"Not quite, no." The discomfort I felt over his question came through in my voice when I answered it, though I kept my body still apart from walking to ensure I didn't make it more obvious. "I felt very . . . *happy* with him sometimes, and I'm certain that much was apparent to him. But if you're asking me whether or not I . . ." I cleared my throat, "*wiggled* over things he said to me, the answer would be no."

"Why do you think that is?"

"I'm not sure." I looked forward as we made our way, trying to answer him objectively. "He was quite sweet to me sometimes before you came into the picture, especially before I began training. We didn't speak or see one another often after I did. Perhaps I was so unknowledgeable about those kinds of feelings that I couldn't appropriately feel them. Perhaps I was simply so stunned anyone could feel anything for me that I . . . didn't know what to do." I sighed and forced a smile in his direction. "I don't know."

He held my gaze for an instant then brought it back to what was in front of us. "So you believe you understand feelings more now."

"I don't think I do," I told him with an uncomfortable laugh. "I don't like them, I know that much. Well . . . that's not entirely correct." I paused and closed my eyes for an instant. "I'm going to be quiet before I make a complete fool of myself." If I hadn't already done so. I likely had. Unintentional movement.

He stopped moving, which caused me to do the same.

He spent a moment looking around to ensure we were alone, which we were, before bringing his attention back to me. "What were you going to say?"

I could've told him I didn't want to answer, but would it be worse that way? Wasn't that the purpose of friends—to tell them things when they asked?

I reminded myself that there were much worse questions in the world.

Then I was struck by something much more important.

If I didn't answer a simple question . . . I would be no better with him than he'd been at his worst with me. I would be no better than my brother.

Questions could be simple while the answers to them were not.

I would answer his regardless.

I pursed my lips for a moment and felt my body contracting in anxiety. "Feelings are different with everyone, as you know. . . . I had to ask Agatha how it felt when you were in love to know that I was in love with Chase. She told me it felt like your body was too light and floating away. I felt that, and I was . . . *inexplicably* afraid. That's why it took me so long to know that—" I rethought my words. "That's why it took me so long to realize the way I felt about you."

"It doesn't feel like floating?" He sounded very curious.

"It's like . . ." I started and then stopped, trying to figure out the correct way to put something I never wanted to think about. I held my hands out in front of me. "I'm here." Then I gestured at him. "You're here. And everyone else . . ." I felt my face scrunching and my eyes close as I shook my head. "They're not there. Like you and I are the only people on the ground and everyone else is floating." I heard myself laugh awkwardly before admitting, "I just wish they'd float farther."

And then I looked at his face. His mouth was parted a bit and he was staring at me as though I were completely insane. I worried I might be.

"I'm sorry," I said quickly. "You asked, so I told you."

"That doesn't scare you?" he asked, ignoring my apology. "What you just said about that?"

"Why should a person be afraid when their feet are on the ground?" I shook my head. "I've never been afraid of you or the way I feel about you. Angry, upset, quite miserable at times, really, but . . . never afraid."

He took a step closer to me and his voice was near a whisper when he asked, "Why are you like this with me?"

I did not have a satisfactory answer to that question. I'd tried many times to make sense of it all for myself. The only thing I could tell him was, "I can't help it."

He was shaking his head when he reached a hand out and touched my face. And he kissed me as sweetly as he had the night he'd almost died. I loved and hated it at once. When he pulled his face away from mine, his hand lingered there and he wiped away a stray tear I hadn't meant to let fall.

"Why does it hurt so badly?" I whispered because of the painful feeling in my chest. It felt as though it were ripping itself apart. It made no sense.

He shook his head again as he said, "I don't know." He pursed his lips for a moment. "Is it worth it?"

I did not hesitate in saying, "Yes. I believe so."

We walked in silence the rest of the way to my living quarters, and I thought about the strange and incomprehensible pain that was induced by feelings. It was horrible and foolish at the same time. It was irresponsible. It was almost humiliating. I didn't want to feel these things.

But I couldn't stop the way my stomach turned when we arrived at the door to my quarters and I asked, "Are you staying?"

"Do you want me to?"

Tell him no, some part of me said. It would've been a lie.

Was it a lie when I was so torn?

Tell him to go would not have been a lie, but it wouldn't have answered his question.

Please tell him to go.

I nodded my head because despite any and everything . . . I wanted him to stay, and that was what he'd asked me.

"Then I'll stay." The smile that appeared on his face almost seemed . . . sad.

No. That was wrong.

It wasn't sad, but it was somewhat close to that. At least close in the sense of both being negative.

Was *disappointment* negative when we both knew better?

CHAPTER SIX

SCARY

I DID NOT FEEL as though I needed to wait until I was on the verge of falling asleep where I stood in order to lie down, so long as Jastin was there with me. I had to remind myself that, all unpleasantries aside, his presence was beneficial to me in so many ways. The pros outweighing the cons and whether or not they did as much was all a matter of how you were looking at the situation.

It was a shame that my perspective seemed to be in a constant state of fluctuation.

The two of us were lying in bed together for quite some time before he asked, "Has anyone else ever seen you wiggle like that?"

"Only my father when I was a child." It was not something I liked thinking of. It was something I liked thinking of even less than my current predicament. I liked speaking of it *far* less than I liked thinking about it. "I've not allowed anyone close enough to have too much of an effect on me since I found the sense to not." I'd found that sense a very long time ago. At least . . . I thought I had.

"Apart from me," he almost whispered.

"You seem to be the exception for all my better judgment in life." Or the thing that tore it to shreds, more like.

He said, "I'm glad."

I moved so I could see his face because I did not believe him. I couldn't believe he would even *say* such a thing, especially not seriously. Perhaps he was joking in a way that couldn't be heard, but that seemed a rather horrendous matter to joke about.

When I'd propped myself up on my elbow and was properly looking at his face, I asked, "Are you?"

He nodded his head and tucked my short hair behind one of my ears. It was *just* long enough to be done now. "You have these walls. . . ." His voice was very quiet when he spoke. "And you gather all these people around the outside. They stand there and try so hard to climb up, but you won't let them do it. Not for any reason. Then they give up and realize they're perfectly content to stand where you'll let them. It's a shame they can't see what's on the other side." He shook his head and nearly whispered again. "I don't know why you let me in."

"I didn't." I wouldn't argue one part of what he'd said, and the other wasn't important enough to waste my breath on. We weren't talking about other people. We were speaking on how he differed from them with me, which meant we were speaking about him, so I kept it on that aspect of what he'd said. His point. "I suppose there was simply a door you had a key to. I don't know if any of this was intentional on your part, but it wasn't on mine. It's simply . . . the way things are. I haven't felt as though I had any control over it."

"Doesn't that scare you?"

This situation was many things. It made me feel many things, brought about many things. I felt I was being honest enough when I said, "No."

"You *are* afraid," he said assuredly, "but I don't think you know of what."

I knew fears were always adapting—growing, dissipating, disappearing, evolving, being replaced. Mine never seemed to stay in one place for long anymore. Even the constants waxed and waned, seemingly at random. There was no point prioritizing them, but I believed I knew what they all were.

Still, he believed what he'd said, so I asked, "How could you know that if *I* don't even know?"

"Because *I'm* afraid."

"Which would naturally make me afraid of something as well." I nodded my head at his ridiculous logic. I could not fear something if I didn't have the vaguest clue what it was, and he seemed to be implying that I was afraid of something sim—

"We're partners." He shrugged, and I ignored the pleasant feeling welling up in my stomach from his words. "I'm just curious if we're afraid of the same things or the complete opposite. It's one or the other."

"What are you afraid of?" I asked him.

"We'll have a conversation about it when you figure yours out." He would not bleed unless I bled with him. Of course.

I spent a short time in silence, thinking about trust and weakness. Things that either couldn't or wouldn't be talked about. One or the other. But there were other things, so I got it back to something close enough to what it previously had been, only in a different regard.

"It's funny," I said. "I never thought Reapers felt fear before I knew any." I supposed that had been ridiculous of me, but from what I'd heard of them, I couldn't see how it was possible. As though they'd had the word bled from them. Ridiculous, no matter how it sometimes seemed.

"You've known Reapers your entire life, considering your father raised you for eight years." He narrowed his eyes at me. "Didn't you ever see him afraid?"

I didn't bother telling him I'd not known Reapers my entire life, only parts of it. I also wouldn't tell him that my father had not been a Reaper. He'd been my father and nothing more no matter what he might've been before or after. I doubted even Jastin would understand as much, so I just answered the question.

"He was sad, I remember." I frowned, thinking back on his face. I despised thinking of it. "It's so hazy for me because it was such a long time ago, but I can remember him being sad." A lot of it was also hazy from so many years spent repressing the memories. I despised it. "If he was ever afraid, he never showed me as much."

"Could you really not believe what he was when Ahren told you?" He shook his head. "You never had any inclination? Not even after being around some of us? Scars, weapons. Did you block it out?"

"He was so kind." I fought against the urge to fidget. "So caring and attentive. Patient. And I only ever noticed him sad before he left me. Before that . . . I don't know." I shook my head. "I was accustomed to the way he was and the things he did. Any scars I asked about made sense, the few weapons I saw. He only had a few of each. Scars and weapons, I mean. I wouldn't have known what I was looking for to see it properly. I didn't even know Reapers existed until he left me."

I'd never seen my father behave like a Reaper. Even now that I knew, he did not conduct himself in a way which was typical of them.

He never had that I saw. Not ever.

"Aster." Jastin's voice had gone soft. "Don't you know he didn't willingly leave you?"

"I assume you're speaking of the last time he left." I couldn't help the stiffness in my voice, but I would not have tried to. I didn't want to speak of this, not even with Jastin, and I had no qualms with him knowing as much. "Don't you understand that he left me all the time? I can remember that, as I became older, he left more frequently and was gone for longer stretches. He *did* leave me willingly. I was a child, and he left me. The other details are irrelevant."

His brow furrowed. "That's not like you."

"Why are you pushing for my father?" I demanded.

"I don't give a damn about your father. Not in this regard," he said firmly. "It's eating you alive isn't it—everything that happened? You might not want to admit it, but I know it is. You wouldn't be so hostile toward him otherwise. You only act that way toward anyone when you're hurt or angry. I'm pushing because I don't want to see you hurt or angry about anything. I'm not pushing for him. I'm pushing for *you*."

I blinked and took a deep breath as I wiped away tears of frustration from my face. "I told him I would allow him an attempt to make amends with me." I forced my voice into calmness again, though I wasn't quite certain how I managed it. "That was the deal I made to accompany him to Camden. He's made no effort. Speaking to me as though I'm a child or as if nothing at all has happened won't—" I took in another deep breath. "That's not good enough." I was not a child and so much *had* happened. I shook my head and asked, "Can we not speak about this anymore?"

When my father tried to speak to me on the things that *had* happened . . .

He had never spoken to me so much as if speaking to a child even when I'd been one.

Jastin said, "Okay. We can drop it for now."

After an extended silence, which I spent thinking over the words *for now*, he changed the subject entirely.

"My sister wants to meet you."

"Does she?" I asked my question quickly, disbelieving.

He nodded.

"Why?"

"She didn't say." He shrugged. "But if she plans on acting the same way with you that she did with Cherise . . . I'm guessing her intent is to scare you or run you off. Or both, but one would come before the other."

I laughed. "*Scare* me?"

When he said nothing, clearly not finding it as amusing as I had, I sighed.

"She's a Reaper as well, I'm sure."

"Yes," he replied. "And I hate to say it, but she's a very . . . *typical* female one. In many ways. Not all, but it's rarely all."

"Meaning she's unpleasant," I stated.

That seemed to be the consensus. Female Reapers were unpleasant, but surely they had reasons if they were.

I didn't see how all men could miss all reasons, but surely they existed.

He said, "Not to me, but to nearly everyone else, yes. We all have our exceptions."

"I'm failing to see why she would want to meet me if her intent is to scare me." I frowned. "That doesn't make any sense." Along with it making no sense, it was also ridiculous, but I didn't believe I should say as much. It was also rude. Going into a first meeting with ill intent was much ruder than not knocking, I believed.

"Female Reapers believe they're at the top of the food chain." He shook his head a little and it made me wonder if he thought it all a bit ridiculous as well. "It's basic instinct to put people of the same sex on their back if you're capable of it. And sisters?" He laughed before saying, "They're exhausting."

Unhappily, I said, "So I've heard."

Ahren had said as much before, only under completely different circumstances. Perhaps Jastin found his sister exhausting for a similar reason, meaning he was exhausting himself more often than not. Or perhaps not.

Jastin said, "You don't have to meet her if you don't want to."

Was he testing me? Was he testing or simply passing along a message?

I asked, "Would it make you happy?"

"I'm not sure it's a good idea, to be honest."

"Why?" I asked. "Because you're worried your sister will scare me away from you?"

"I'm worried she'll try, yes."

"Then I'll do it." I was pleased my voice sounded nonchalant enough when I wasn't. "So I can prove to you it wouldn't work." I wasn't concerned in the slightest over her succeeding in the attempt if that should be her intent. I was simply . . . nervous and uncomfortable over potentially meeting her. It put a somewhat nasty feeling in my stomach. Hesitantly I asked, "She wouldn't try to . . . *kill* me, would she?"

"No." He laughed. "She's not that stupid. Even if you pissed her off, she's nowhere *near* that stupid."

"That's good." If he was sure of that, I had no problem with the meeting past not wanting it to occur for all the reasons I had. One of those being a lack of wanting to potentially be pushed at futilely. That was life, though. It would also interfere with my time spent training, which I was behind on due to—

"Your father wanted to have a meeting with the group of us in the morning," he said. "I could take you to her then. It would probably be better than having some of his men watching over your shoulders for who knows how long while we're all with him. I know you won't do your training with them there."

"And leave me with your sister alone?" I asked humorlessly. "That's what you're planning?" I hadn't anticipated *in the morning*. And then I remembered . . . she *wasn't* alone.

He grinned. "Are you afraid?"

"No, but . . ." was all I could say for a time. "I've never . . . been around a child, let alone an infant."

I'd seen a few child servants in New Bethel, but I'd never been near any. I'd hardly interacted with *anyone* there apart from Agatha.

Short things here and there with a few. *Very* few and on *very* rare occasion. Never children.

"You'll be fine." He rubbed my arm. "I promise the baby won't hurt you."

As I lay there awake for quite some time thinking over it, I discovered I was not so sure on the correctness of his statement. I decided I would simply stay as far away as I possibly could from the infant regardless of it being his nephew. It was the only solution I could come up with, as I could not get out of this situation after agreeing. Not without exposing more than I wanted to. Cared to. Could. Wanted.

I suspected it was nearly an hour later when I found the sense to say, "That meeting with my father. . . . What is it about?"

"He didn't say," Jastin said, sounding very tired, "but you'll know as soon as I bring you back here."

I nodded my head because that was a more than satisfactory answer. When I really attempted to fall asleep, or was closer to working my way there, I realized Jastin hadn't said he didn't know. He'd only said that my father hadn't told him. It was not important, and I was quite accustomed to that sort of treatment, even from him.

The only difference between it and the rest of what I was accustomed to in that regard was . . . Jastin might on occasion agree to tell me things where the others never would. I could not complain about that.

I could, but I wouldn't. Not when it was more.

And Chase accused *me* of talking in circles. It was almost amusing, but it wasn't really. It couldn't be amusing when it was what it was.

CHAPTER SEVEN

KNOWING

OR THE FIRST TIME while lying so close to Jastin, I did not sleep well. I was accustomed to his presence keeping so much bad at bay that the horribleness caught me off guard. All night long, my dreams were riddled through with children and blood. I did not know whether they were all part of the same dream that kept continuing when I'd fall back asleep or countless separate ones. It was a horrendous combination regardless.

He woke me several times, likely because I'd been stirring and had woken him. I would apologize, and then he would kiss me on the top of my head.

I did wonder if I would've remembered them well if at all, had he not kept waking me. It was all so horrendous, and I felt sure I would have.

He did not ask me what I was dreaming about on any of those instances, and I imagined I would've left the children out of a potential response if he had.

Though I was sure I could've played it all off as a side effect of what had recently happened to me rather than an intense lack of desire to be around his nephew, I did not want him to connect the two. I was unsure how related they were if they were at all. I was also unsure where most of that lack of desire stemmed from.

I had my theories, but I told myself I simply had no desire to be around any child in general and there was nothing else to it. It could've been true enough whether it was true or not. I had only as much of an idea as what I did, and I felt it wasn't enough to go on.

I was not happy to put on normal clothing that morning rather than my Reaper training clothes, especially because what I'd been given to wear here was much nicer than what I was accustomed to. Different fabric that was uncomfortable for me despite being softer. It didn't feel right.

After preparing myself as much as I was able, I found myself walking with Jastin and Stanley past the outer walls of the House. I hadn't done that once since my arrival. I knew two pairs of my father's Reapers were both in front of and behind us as well, though I did not mention it.

It was horrible.

There she is. I heard the words more times than I cared to count.

The happy tones of people's voices made me want to become ill all over the beautiful cobblestoned streets, and possibly on them as well. I was quite sure that would quiet them. It was almost unfortunate that none of them came close enough. I told myself I could not do such a thing on command regardless, but the thought of it alone kept me amused for a short while.

A short while was not long enough. The longer we walked, the more attention it drew.

Where is she going?

What is she doing?

It's foolish for them to allow her out of the House so unguarded.

I can't believe he's not out with her himself.

Never let her out of my sight again if it were me.

He must trust the ones near her. I'm sure that's the only way he ever would.

It's only a matter of time before other leaders—

Oh, stop it. Nothing's going to happen to her here. No one would dare.

What about . . .

One lady quietly said, "She's quite beautiful, isn't she?"

Her female companion was not at all quiet when she responded with, "Very plain-looking to my eyes. I believe you're losing your vision. Nothing for that, my friend."

A man standing near them said, "I'm inclined to agree. I've been hearing all sorts of things these weeks. Glad to see her for myself so I can tell them she just looks like a child. I swear, half the men in the city have been drooling since she arrived. At least now I know it was nonsense."

"Clearly catching a glimpse and making more in their heads than what it is."

"Possibly that or nothing more than knowing she's his daughter and trying to convince themselves she looks a certain way. All wanting what they want. If you ask me, it's some latent attraction to her father or something and wanting to take it out on her."

"There's something odd about it, to be sure. I agree. She looks like a child. Men saying what you said would verge more on latent pedophilia than latent askewedness due to her father."

"I think she's just heard every awful word you've said."

"It's not awful."

"I saw her face. She couldn't hear. On her way to wherever, and none of us are worthy enough to be heard by her ears. See? Look at her face. Stuck there, trying to make her way with men moving people out of her path. Her face says she's not hearing a word. Selective hearing because we're not worthy."

"That's an unfair statement."

"*I* think she's quite beautiful. She carries herself well. I think you're mistaking pride for arrogance."

"I agree with that. I do think she's beautiful and doesn't look at all like a child. Something about her face. . . ."

It felt as though I had all their hands clutching at my skin. I attempted to keep my head up as I made my way, but I was not accustomed to being stared at and did not like it at all.

They would not stop looking at me. There were so many of them, and it was as though . . . there was nothing and no one else in the world for them to look at. They would just . . . stop, and watch. Some would speak. Many wouldn't. But they all stopped and watched.

At first, I tried to pay attention to the buildings we passed to distract myself, but it was not satisfactory. Long stretches passed where I saw nothing at all but stone. Well-maintained structures that varied in shades from the plain, light grey I'd grown accustomed to in New Bethel. No details.

I couldn't focus on details when all I could think about was how *visible* I was. I couldn't focus. I just wanted to disappear, but I couldn't.

It was easily and by far one of the most horrendous experiences in all my life. Despite the differences—the sun shining, the open air, the lack of skin and alcohol—I couldn't help mentally comparing the walk to the party in New Bethel where I'd first met Chase. Those differences should've made this more pleasant, but it wasn't. It couldn't be. I was just so *visible*. It was as though my father had shone a light on me in a world of darkness for one and all to see.

That meant . . .

He was not my father.

Several people attempted to speak to me, I knew, but they did not get even remotely close. I could not understand why they tried or wanted to so badly, but it almost seemed as though they simply couldn't help themselves. That was what their expressions looked like when I caught them—an absolute inability or perhaps refusal to stop themselves from attempting as much—though that took me a while to discern. It was so strange.

I realized as I made my way that I was horribly mistaken initially about the number of Reapers my father had following me. People in plain-clothes—Reapers—would come from seemingly out of nowhere and prevent *anyone* from getting near me. If they so much as stepped a foot in my direction . . . they were stopped. I was torn on how I felt about it.

I spent the majority of our time walking trying very hard to pretend as if none of it were even happening. And by the time we were stopped in front of a building that looked as if it may very well be a house of some sort . . . I hadn't even realized we'd stopped. I was rather lightheaded, so it took me a moment.

When the same dark-haired girl I'd seen staring and smiling at Jastin upon our arrival to the city opened the door . . . I wished I'd stayed inside my living quarters. I'd been wishing I could since before stepping out. I truly did not want to walk back, but I also had absolutely no desire to be where I was either.

Jastin's sister did not look at me, which made me wonder why in the world she'd bothered asking to meet me, and he hardly looked at her.

"Where's the baby?" he asked in a remarkably happy tone.

Remarkably happy, as if he hadn't just had the same experience as I had. But I supposed . . .

Even walking together?

He'd not.

"Sleeping." He was already walking past her when she said, "Don't you *dare* wake him up!"

She closed her eyes and sighed because he clearly had no intention of listening to her.

"I'm Abby," she informed me when she opened her eyes again and finally settled them in on me.

She was significantly more beautiful than I'd noticed on that initial looking, though she appeared incredibly tired where she hadn't before. I did not know where she'd gotten her dark hair, as it was quite a lot darker than Jastin's, but she had the same remarkable honey-colored eyes. They were almost a bit brighter than his, but perhaps her dark hair only made them seem that way.

"Aster," I said.

"Well, come inside." She stepped out of the way for me to pass. "I know he's woken James, and that baby will *not* stop screaming after he leaves. So I'll spend quite a long time after the two of you are gone trying to get him quiet again." She closed the door behind us.

"I'm leaving Aster here with you for a little while," Jastin said from a corner of the room. He was holding the baby when I looked at him, and . . . he did not even look like the same person. I had never seen his face so unguarded before. I wasn't quite sure what to think about it.

"Are you?" She sounded unnecessarily pleased by his statement, which I found to be quite worrisome. Why had I agreed to this?

To show him I wouldn't be scared off.

"Yes, her father called for a meeting," he said nonchalantly. He had not taken his eyes off his nephew at all.

"With you?"

"With all of us watching her."

"Oh," she said in what sounded like relief. "Well, you know what's going on, then."

Of course he did.

"I can guess." He put the baby back down in its . . . *bedding area* contraption after kissing it multiple times on the face. I still had no idea what to think. "I've got to go."

"*Oh no*," she said quickly. "You get him to go back to sleep before you leave or else the two of us won't be able to get to know one another at all."

He'd had his hand stuck in the contraption as she'd spoken, and then he said, "He's already asleep again. I told you he likes it when you rub his hands."

Exasperation was clear when she said, "I've *tried* that, Jastin."

He walked over to us and, in the process, very encouragingly said, "Keep trying." When he was in front of us, he grabbed both sides of his sister's face in his hands, and when he spoke again it was clearly a warning. "Be good."

She smiled at him, but he did not release her face until she put a hand over her heart.

And when he turned to smile at me, he clearly felt absolutely none of the anxiety I was currently feeling. Then he was gone and I was alone with his Reaper sister and her . . . baby . . . infant . . . child . . . *thing*.

I kept my gaze at the door, wishing very much that he would step back inside. Possibly declare him leaving me there a joke or that he'd thought on it just a bit harder and decided it a bad idea.

It felt to be a very bad idea.

It was not ten seconds after the door had closed that she said, "You love my brother."

My gaze shot to hers, and though it had not sounded like a question, I said, "Yes. I do."

She seemed to be watching my face very carefully. After getting the read, she nodded toward my body. "Your clothes don't match."

I shook my head, having no idea . . . "Match what?"

She smiled. "Themselves."

"Oh." My brow furrowed. "I'm not very concerned with it, to be honest. I didn't know clothes had to . . . *match*. I've always just worn whatever I was given to wear." These had been left, presumably for me because they fit. Quite a lot of clothing had been left, but I'd grabbed what was there that appeared comfortable enough. I did not understand what she meant about the matching. Perhaps she was joking. . . .

"I'm sure my brother doesn't mind."

"I wouldn't care if he did," I told her honestly. Clothes only mattered as much as they did.

She snorted. "Can we sit down?" She shook her head and sort of sighed. "I'm so tired."

I wanted to ask her why she was asking me if she could sit down in her own living area, but instead I smiled tightly and nodded. As soon as she'd sat, she started in on me.

"Jastin said you weren't feeling well. It must've been bad, for him not to visit for so long."

I'd assumed he'd told her exactly—or at least roundabout—what had happened with me, so it took me several moments to formulate anything to say. "Yes, it was quite bad."

"Feeling better now?"

I smiled another tight smile and nodded in response. I did not like the way she was speaking to me, as if a normal conversation was an interrogation. I was not a Reaper, nor was I any sort of threat to her. It was absolutely ridiculous.

It wasn't the words; it was how she was saying them.

It was *much* different from Amber.

"What was wrong with you?" She paused just long enough to add, "If you don't mind me asking."

If she didn't already know . . . "I'd rather not say anything more than that I was feeling quite bad."

"I'd imagine it's not contagious, given that Jastin didn't get sick." She sighed what I believed was a fake sigh then scrunched her face up slightly. "Wouldn't want to get the baby sick."

I assured her, "It's nothing to worry about."

She tilted her head. "Are you sure?"

I took a deep breath to calm myself down, and I spoke under my breath. "I suppose I should've prepared myself for an interrogation." *Fantastic* for a first meeting, and I should've expected nothing more or less.

If I could handle my father . . . I could *certainly* deal with Jastin's sister. But what an *odd thing* to get interrogated about.

I looked at her and said, "If you have a specific question, you're more than welcome to ask it. Given the way I feel about your brother, I won't lie to you. I'd much rather you simply ask whatever it is you want to know. It would be much simpler, wouldn't you agree?" I wouldn't lie, but there were enough ways to get around things, should that be necessary. I could hope it wouldn't.

She picked one of her legs up into her chair where she sat across from me and wrapped her arm around it. She was almost smirking when she spoke. "I'm trying to see if you're worth it."

"Worth what?"

"The death of my brother," she answered bluntly.

"You think he's going to die. . . ."

"Oh, I *know* he is." She nodded, her eyebrows up. "It's just a matter of *when*. You're smart, aren't you? He's told me you are. He thinks you're *much* smarter than what he's even sure of. Why don't you think about it a little? Unless he's wrong of course, in which case you'd be no more useful than . . ." She trailed off purposely.

"I've thought about it a *lot*," I informed her. And I didn't have the slightest interest in whatever she'd wanted me to ask about, nor would I encourage her to play.

I wouldn't let her play with me.

A few long seconds of silence passed.

"*Have* you?" She'd stopped her moving about, purposeful fidgeting, and now sat utterly still. "Have you *really*? You probably think him staying up your ass is safer than going into the field, don't you?" She paused to shake her head forcefully. "It's *not*. It's nowhere *near*. If you were *half* as smart as he's convinced you are, you'd know as much. Reapers from other cities will *always* be coming for you. It's *much* easier than going straight for your father. And eventually, my brother is going to get complacent with you because you're taking his head from him. It might not be this year, or next, but eventually . . . he's *going* to get killed. Because of *you*."

"He already almost has," I said firmly. "So yes, I've thought about it more than you could possibly imagine. If you know *anything* about that, you *must* know I'd have to be a complete imbecile to not." I paused for a moment. "What solution is there?"

"Send him away from you." She shrugged. "Say a single word to your daddy on it, and I *bet* he'll be gone. Gone from you and *much* safer. If you *love him*?" She threw up a hand. "*That* is the solution."

"I can't do that." I closed my eyes for a moment, realizing that wasn't necessarily true. I then shook my head and corrected myself. "I *could*, but I won't. What is the *point* of going through life miserable? It may keep you alive longer, but what would be the purpose of it? Why should a person care to prolong that sort of existence? Why break the most important thing in the world when there's already so little of it to be found?"

"You'd be able to forget about each other." She shrugged again. "It's human nature to adapt to things, no matter how bad the circumstances."

"Believe me, I know all about adapting to bad circumstances," I told her with a humorless laugh. "You don't know me, but I'm sure you know your brother, don't you? If you truly believe he'd be able to *forget about me* . . . I'm sorry to be the one to inform you that you don't know Jastin at all."

CHAPTER EIGHT

CHILDREN

REAPER HAD STEPPED INSIDE the living area of Jastin's sister right at the last of what I'd said to her. Despite the intrusion, she and I sat there staring at one another in the short stretch of silence that occurred after I'd enlightened her about trust and her brother's inability to forget it. I believed she might've possibly misunderstood part of that enlightenment, but so long as she'd gotten the point, that was what mattered.

I had only enough time to analyze her face and begin to contemplate the very small bit of satisfaction I felt over getting her to shut her mouth—even if only temporarily and in anger—before that Reaper spoke.

"I heard raised voices," he said, drawing both our attention away from each other and to him. "Everything good here?"

Abby sighed. "Everything's fine."

He looked away from my face, to hers, and his voice was impassive when he said, "I wasn't asking you."

"Everything is fine," I told him as well. "And it's incredibly rude to eavesdrop. She and I are having a private conversation. At least go off and pretend you aren't listening to it. Have a bit of common decency."

"If she's upsetting you—"

"She would have every right to it. Please leave." I put my hands over my face as soon as he'd closed the door, and I thought about rights.

Abby might've had no place to go behind Jastin's back in an attempt to dictate his life through someone else. She mightn't have had the place to, but he *was* her brother and she had *every* right to try and keep him safe in whatever ways she could. I just hadn't liked the way she'd gone about it.

I also hadn't liked the intrusion, not even a little. I hadn't the vaguest clue who that Reaper was. All I knew was that he belonged to my father and couldn't even have the common decency to *knock*.

Why could *no one* have the decency to *knock* before intruding?

"Exhausting, isn't it?" she asked, pulling me from my thoughts.

"I've spent the majority of my life being invisible." I removed my hands. "And now I can't breathe without everyone waiting for it and listening." I sighed before asking, "Do they take you seriously?"

Her head tilted a bit to the side and her brow furrowed. "What do you mean?"

"Because you're beautiful," I clarified.

"You're not going to win points with me by saying that."

"I've no idea what you mean by that. I'm only stating a fact," I told her. "I doubt I'd need to tell you that about how you look for you to know as much. I'm asking if the training makes them take you seriously, or if looking the way you do and being a woman makes them incapable of it regardless."

An extended stretch of silence passed while she looked at my face. Then she brought her attention to the nearest wall. "They did." The two words had been quiet when she said them, but a false smile appeared and she laughed humorlessly. "Before my time was up and I was required to produce a child, at least. Now it's like . . . I'm just a helpless girl." She shook her head. "*Idiots*."

That gave me a great deal to think on.

She snorted shortly thereafter and the expression transformed into something genuinely amused. "They held doors open for me while I was pregnant. Like I was incapable of turning a knob and pushing or pulling. It's ridiculous."

"I agree." It was one of the most ridiculous things I'd ever heard. Obviously that would in no way affect one's ability to open a door.

I was stunned when she said, "I kind of liked it."

I narrowed my eyes at her, confused and disbelieving.

She shrugged. "It seems to be the only time when male Reapers act like normal men. At least in the sense of behavior with women. In my experience." She shrugged again. "It was . . . *nice.*" She closed her eyes. "Don't tell my brother I said that."

"Tell your brother you said what?"

She smiled a little at me. At least she'd understood that.

I said, "So you're all required to have children."

She gave a stiff nod. "One by twenty," she explained, "two by twenty-five, and three by thirty. Only if you live that long, of course. A while after that . . . they give us the opportunity to *retire.* I would wonder how you couldn't know that, but you're surrounded by who you are. Or what, really."

I felt quite dumb when I asked, "Retire from . . . having children?"

"From being a Reaper," she said with a tight smile.

Her response shocked me. I'd never heard of such a thing.

"I've only seen two people who were of age actually do it. We don't know anything else. They give us the chance because they know we'll be too afraid to take it. It's just like with the children. They don't take them from us forcefully. We just . . . *hand them over.* Because it's what we do."

I was a bit surprised by the drastic turn our interaction had taken, but if she was answering questions . . . I had more. "What do they do if a person has more children?"

"Oh, they take them." She nodded, her dark eyebrows up. "We can only have them and keep them after we retire. That's the deal. It's more of a fair trade than Reapers under anyone else. We can't really complain about it."

I frowned while I thought on that for a time before carefully choosing my next words. "Jastin said Cherise was . . . *assigned* to him."

"Cherise." A laugh that could only be described as *harsh* escaped from her mouth. "I *hate* that bitch." She shook her head as if recovering from a stun. "Sorry, what was the question?"

Abby must've *really* hated Cherise, for her to have not even heard what I'd said after mentioning the name. I was unsure whether that said more about Cherise or Abby, but it certainly made her initial behavior with me a bit clearer.

I cleared my throat. "I was wondering about the assignment."

"Ah, yes," she said. "People come in and they have to go through all this nonsense—physical exams, ridiculous questions, the list goes on." She waved a hand dismissively. "Anyway, they all do it for the payment they receive. There are so many rules to it. For example . . . Cherise has three sisters. None of them are allowed to procreate with a Reaper and she can only procreate with Jastin. They get enough for their entire family for it. Food, things to trade . . . all sorts of things. More importantly?" She rubbed her thumb and first two fingers together a few times.

I shook my head. "I don't know what you mean by that."

"Currency," she said. "A lot of parents whore their older children off for it, or *try* to. Jastin spent a while when we were younger trying to convince me she was all right. I'll admit that her doing as much by choice to take care of her family *almost* won me over, but then I had the misfortune of getting to know her better. She's one of the most horrendous people I've ever come across, and honestly?" She shook her head. "The sisters are no better. One's equally horrendous if not worse. Another is equally as ignorant. I can't stand the other either."

She sighed. "Anyway, yeah. They get paid. Producing all three will set an entire family up for life unless they waste it. That happens. It's a rigged system, with the currency. Your father changed it, and it's *all* rigged. I'd take bets on him being the smartest man currently alive. If you got half of that, I'd say you're as set in the head department as Jastin thinks you are."

That was a good deal of new information to process, but I would have time for processing later so I got back on the initial subject. "What about Reapers getting random people pregnant?"

"That doesn't happen." Her reply had been firm, but then she seemed to think on it. "Well, it *happens*. . . . We just get in a *lot* of trouble for it. They keep these extensive records about who's related to who, and the random births mess up their entire system. You have to be very careful when you try to control breeding."

"That's . . . *inhumane*," I said in disbelief.

Sheep. They were treated like sheep. It went far past being punished for an action. It was being treated like livestock.

She shrugged.

"So, you're telling me that within the next two years Jastin is going to be required to have another child with her?" I asked the question once I'd recovered enough from the new information to do so.

"That's the great thing about being you." She chuckled. "I'm sure all you'd have to do is run to Daddy Dearest and tell him no. Jastin said your father is *dying* to win back your affection and favor. Maybe he'll do you a little favor in exchange for some. A favor for favor."

I was not happy at the thought of asking him for that or anything else.

Would I ask him that?

Only if Jastin asked me to do as much.

And I still was not happy when she asked, "What if he *wants* to have another child with her?"

"He doesn't," I said. "I heard him say as much before." Or close enough to it.

Had it been close enough?

She smiled. "But what if he did?"

"Then there's nothing I could do about it." Or nothing I would if I could.

"He doesn't." She chuckled again, then sighed. "You know . . . I've been so angry with him for such a long time. I *tried* talking sense into him over her, but every time he came back from a mission . . . guess where he eventually went? And then he comes home this time and tells me the *exact* same thing he always tells me before it eats away at him and he goes crawling back on his belly like a dog begging for scraps from a horrible master. '*I'm done with her.*'" She adopted a deep voice to say the words, and the tone of it implied she thought her brother was a complete idiot. "Only this was the first time I've ever actually believed him."

I said nothing.

I supposed that caused her to say, "It upsets you that he always went to her."

"In a way." I admitted as much because I'd told her I wouldn't lie to her. "Not in the sense that I feel as though he had no right to have something with another person, but because of the few things I've heard about her. What you've said and how you said it on top of that. It's difficult for me to picture him being with someone like that. Doing that."

She said, "You *are* honest."

I looked down at my hands. "Not to everyone." Not about everything.

"Did he tell you he went to see her when he got back?"

My gaze shot to hers.

"Apparently not. He didn't tell me either, but she found me and demanded to know who he was in love with, so I put two and two together. Hell, maybe he didn't. Maybe she figured it out on her own, but that girl is so stupid I sincerely doubt she could have despite the obvious signs." She pursed her lips for an instant. "I'm pretty sure seeing her face and having her speak to me was what set off my contractions and sent me into labor."

I did have to wonder what Cherise had done exactly to make Abby hate her *that* badly, but I didn't believe I should ask, nor was it any of my business nor concern. I had no connection to Abby, but *Jastin*?

There was something much more pressing with me currently anyhow.

I felt my face burning when I said, "I heard Jastin say he only gave her so many tries before he was done with her." I took a deep breath. "How does that line up with still seeing her?" Not even in the way it had just been described but at all?

"Oh, he hasn't been in love with her for quite a while, I don't believe. If he ever really was. That doesn't mean seeing her wouldn't be useful." She tilted her head and scrunched her face to add, "My brother's kind of a whore, if you didn't know." It had sounded almost apologetic rather than harsh, though the words themselves were harsh enough.

I wasn't entirely sure what my face did in response to her statement.

I believed it safe to assume my face was what caused her to say, "Apparently you didn't." She stared at me. "You're telling me you haven't slept with him?"

"I haven't told you anything on the matter," I stated.

She laughed. "Your face implied it."

"I've slept *next* to him."

"God, he must really love you." She seemed *quite* disbelieving, and that was worrisome.

I was still trying to process what she'd called her brother and what *exactly* she meant by it. If that had been inappropriate, the current topic made it seem tame in comparison. "This is *inexplicably* uncomfortable."

She shrugged. "You brought it up." Then she chuckled again. "Honestly, I thought that was why he was gone for a week. I guess you really weren't feeling well."

"I wasn't," I said stiffly. I didn't have the *vaguest* clue how *that* would've equated to him not seeing his sister for a week.

"Sorry, then." She almost seemed embarrassed, even if only a little. "For earlier. I thought you were both lying to me. He doesn't lie to me often. I thought some bad habits were carrying over with you, and it pissed me off."

I had no idea what to say to that, so I sat there uncomfortably for what felt like an eternity as she stared at me.

I eventually felt I had no choice but to ask, "What?"

"I'm just trying to figure out what it is about you that flipped my brother around." Her face was scrunched in concentration, like she thought she was peering into my soul or something. "You're pretty. I get that, but *pretty* isn't enough. Have you seen Cherise?"

"I don't know what to tell you," I said apologetically. I assumed her question had been rhetorical, but the point of it was very clear. The tone of Abby's voice when asking it implied Cherise was not *pretty* but some word that went *far* beyond it.

I didn't care in the slightest what Cherise looked like.

The way Abby was staring made me quite uneasy. I didn't know if she was trying to pick me apart without touching me or if she thought I might explain the *flipping* she'd mentioned, which I could not do. It was almost like a gift from the stars above when the baby started crying.

I quickly changed my mind about that as I fought against the urge to stick my fingers into my ears. The sound was not as loud as I would've expected, but there was an inexplicable unpleasantness to it.

Abby ran over to the other side of the room the instant the noise began and scooped him up into her arms. At first she softly shushed him, but after nearly fifteen minutes of that being a failure it turned into pleas of, "*Please* be quiet."

I had no idea what to say or do.

She was crying as well when she sat back down in the chair with him in her arms. "I'm so sorry," she told me. "I don't know how Jastin is so good with him. I just don't have it in me."

There was something so . . . *pitiful* about watching her stare down, utterly helpless to it all.

The only thing I could think of to say was, "No need to apologize."

"Why don't you like me holding your hand?" she asked the baby desperately as she touched his hand with hers. When all it did was cry louder, she closed her eyes. "Five and a half more months."

"Perhaps he's hungry?" I suggested. How often were they hungry?

"I'd just fed him shortly before you got here," she said. "I don't know what's wrong."

"Have you tried just talking to him?" I asked. "Or singing maybe?"

"I don't know any songs." She almost seemed hopeful when she asked, "Do you?"

"No," I told her apologetically. "Perhaps you could just hum?"

She immediately tried what I'd suggested, and slowly but surely . . . the crying began to get quieter. It was nearly ten minutes later when she laughed and said, "Oh my god."

I said, "Perhaps he's so upset because you are."

"He's just a baby." She laughed.

I didn't know that they were capable of such a thing, but . . . "It was simply a thought." I shrugged.

She glanced from him to me. "Do you want to look at him while he's behaving?"

"I, um . . ." I wanted to say no, but she seemed so happy that she'd finally gotten him to be quiet, and I did not have the heart to ruin her moment. I stood and stiffly walked over to the side of her chair. "He's . . . he's quite beautiful."

"When he's not crying." She laughed again.

"He has your eyes," I said as I looked at wide, nearly yellow eyes blinking up at the person who had made them.

Then she looked up at me. "Do you want to hold him?"

"No," I said quickly. Her smile faltered, which made me say, "He's just so small, and I've never been around a child. I'm afraid I would drop or hurt him." That was reasonable.

"You won't." She did not give me the opportunity to object further. She stood and extended the thing toward me.

"I don't know what to do," I said in absolute terror.

"You saw how I was holding him," she said. "Just do that. It's what they showed me. Here."

And then I had a tiny little person in my arms. Again, I did not know what my face was doing, but I was almost entirely certain it had never contorted in such a way in all my life.

I did not know if it was offensive to say, "I don't like this." I could not stop the words from coming out, even if it might've been.

"Just relax," she told me with a chuckle.

I tried to do as she said, and I looked down into her child's face. All I could see were those honey-colored eyes and it quickly made tears well in mine, though I could not quite comprehend why.

"Please take him back," I begged.

"Sure." She must've seen my face because she took her son back.

I went and replaced myself in the seat I'd been sitting in and attempted to compose myself.

CHAPTER NINE

SAFETY

IT FELT LIKE AN ETERNITY that I spent waiting for Jastin to return from the meeting with my father, though it was not anywhere near as long as I'd expected it to be. It only felt that way.

I'd sat alone for quite some time while Abby at some point fed the baby in the other room. I believed she did not want to make me any more uncomfortable with the child than I so clearly was already, which I appreciated. Even if I was mistaken about her reasons for doing so away from me . . . I still appreciated it.

Her absence had given me a good deal of uninterrupted time to think on a number of things. I was a bit embarrassed over my reaction to holding her child, but I didn't want to put thought into that particular matter. I did not like how any path of thought related to it looked from where I was standing. As it held nothing of significant importance, I put it out of my head.

I spent a small bit of that time on Cherise, wondering again what had caused Abby's intense dislike for her, if it could be called so subdued a word when she'd seemed quite serious about what had sent her into labor. Clearly it was something to do with Cherise as a person, but I wondered on specifics and potential biases if there were any of the latter. Knowing how pointless and unproductive it was to speculate on such matters without more information—and whatever more there was to know being none of my business—I put it out of my mind as well and focused on something I didn't want to.

Why hadn't Jastin informed me about the rules with children? Why hadn't he informed me that he would be required to produce another child with her? Not even one. *Two.* Two more children. Required.

I told myself it didn't matter, both the lack of disclosure and his requirement. Along with all that . . . it also was not my business, nor was it my concern unless he directly made it so.

Why did it feel as though it were? It was not.

Why hadn't he told me he'd gone to see Cherise, if Abby was correct in her assumption about him having done as much?

He'd let me think he was seeing Cherise, that he'd had another child with her in allowing me to think she'd been the pregnant girl I'd seen. I knew his reaction to my thinking that had been somewhat false, likely because he didn't want me to realize the real reason why he'd been absent all that time. Given I thought he'd been doing that very thing . . . Why not tell me as much if he had? Why act as though it were such a preposterous idea?

I didn't know what to think about any of it, but it all seemed so insignificant in comparison to other things.

None of it was my business. What he had and hadn't said or implied . . . It was not.

When Abby returned from feeding the baby, she'd put him in bed and proceeded to ask me random questions—things about the journey here, what my life had been like in New Bethel. She did not ask me any more questions about her brother or my relationship with him, at least not in the way she had before, and it no longer seemed as if she were interrogating me. I could've easily been mistaken about that as well and she could've simply adapted her tactics. It was more than possible, but I liked to think she simply wanted to know.

She asked me questions like: *What did you have to do there?* Or: *How did you and Jastin meet?*

Still, I was relieved when Jastin walked through the door, because his sister *was* quite exhausting. Even if I felt she was no longer interrogating or playing with me, I wasn't quite sure how to respond to some of her queries no matter how simple some of them seemed.

Things weren't often as simple as they seemed, but it all depended upon a number of things. I was very uncomfortable all around.

I did not feel I was *exhausting* in any similar way as what she was. But perhaps there was always something exhausting about sisters.

Jastin did not knock here either. Perhaps he was always welcome, but it still seemed rude despite relation. It was not his space; it was *her* space.

He only looked at me for an instant after entering before walking across the room and scooping the baby up into his arms.

"Hello again, Nephew," he said in a voice that sounded very strange to my ears.

Did people speak differently to infants? I had never known as much. What could be the purpose of it?

Perhaps there was always the concern that the wrong thing would set off another wave of wailing, but Jastin didn't seem concerned over it.

"How were things?" Abby asked him.

"They were," was his response. He used his normal speaking voice to respond to her, so I knew the strange speaking was not permanent, for which I was glad.

"Can't talk about it?"

"Nope," he said. "How were things here?"

He only looked up from his nephew when she said, "Good."

He looked at her, then at me, and then narrowed his eyes when they rested on his sister again.

"They were!" She laughed, and his eyes were nearly slits by the point that she said, "I finally got him to stop crying."

"Oh really?" he asked. She had successfully distracted him. "By holding his hand?"

"No, Aster suggested I hum to him because neither of us knew a song to sing."

"Did she?"

I looked down at my hands when he looked at me.

"Well, if it works . . . hopefully that will make the next five and a half months of your life a more enjoyable experience."

It seemed she wanted to change the subject when she asked, "Will you stay for a while?"

"No, I should be getting her back. But I'll stop by tomorrow."

"You're not leaving?" Confusion was clear in her voice.

My eyes darted up in time to see him look at me and say, "No."

I could not explain why his one word wasn't entirely convincing, but . . . it wasn't.

"But I thought . . ." I couldn't tell if she trailed or cut herself off. She smiled and said, "I'll see you tomorrow."

"Do you want me to get him back to sleep?" he asked.

She jumped up. "No. I'll take him."

"You remember what I told you?" He handed her the baby.

I was only able to catch a portion of the sad smile on her face when she nodded and quietly said, "I remember."

"As little attachment as possible," he said firmly. "You don't want to end up like me."

She sighed heavily. "I *remember*."

He nodded, satisfied at that, and began walking toward me.

I stood and had almost made it to the door when she said, "It was really nice to meet you, Aster." There was only sincerity and sadness in her voice.

I turned and pretended not to see the tears rolling down her cheeks when I smiled and said, "You as well."

As soon as we'd gone from her living quarters, back out on the cobblestoned streets of Jarsil where people were already stopping again at the sight of me, the small smile dropped away from Jastin's face.

I asked, "What's wrong?"

He shook his head and said nothing at all, so I tried a different approach to get something out of him.

"Did you see Cherise when we arrived here?"

"I did," he answered blankly.

"Did you sleep with her?"

He stopped moving immediately, and when I looked up at him again, I found him blinking hard at me.

"No." He shook his head. "I went to tell her I wouldn't see her anymore. Is that what the two of you talked about the entire time I was gone?"

The small bit of unhappiness I picked up on from him didn't faze me in the slightest. I didn't believe it was directed at me.

I said, "It was only briefly touched upon."

"Did Abby bring her up to throw her in your face like Ahren did?" His eyes were narrowed again.

"I don't believe so, no," I told him. "Your sister and I very quickly got things sorted between us. After a rather awkward beginning, she was quite pleasant to me. I'm sure it was genuine." Or sure enough. Or genuine enough. And pleasant enough. "You . . ." I stopped to try and find a way to force the words from my mouth. "You don't have to stop seeing her on account of me . . . if she gives you things I don't."

"I stopped seeing her for *me*." He smiled a little and nudged my arm. "Let's get you back."

I nodded and did not allow myself to show him how happy I was that he was not going to see her anymore, for whatever reasons he had. It should not have mattered to me.

Knowing it shouldn't have mattered to me personally did not change the fact that some part of me was pleased about it. Pleased and . . .

Relieved. For him.

I did not like the thought of her hurting him or him continuing to let her do as much.

Pleased and relieved, for him. In great part because the thought of him crawling on his belly made me feel physically ill.

ONCE WE WERE BACK at my living quarters, Jastin ensured no one was near the outside of it before nearly dragging me inside and sitting me down on my bed. He did not join me in sitting there, and I realized by the expression on his face that I was going to learn something important and potentially unpleasant. I tried to prepare myself for whatever it was, but how could I successfully prepare myself for something I didn't know, had no clue on?

"No one else was at the meeting," was the first thing he said to me on the matter.

"But I thought you said . . ." I found I could not say anything else because I was so confused.

He'd said the meeting had been for the group of them. Why had no one else been there?

"That's what he told me," he said. "But he wanted to talk to me alone first. Stanley knew. He stopped right outside your father's office after walking back with me. There *is* a real meeting, but I told him I didn't want to leave you alone with my sister all day. As soon as I explain things to you, you have to stay here and the rest of us have to go."

I felt my stomach drop before he clarified.

"Speak to him."

"What is it all about?"

He clenched his jaw for an instant before answering. "One of your father's spies in Bethel discovered that Hasting is planning another abduction attempt for you."

That was all? "Surely they couldn't get into the city."

"Oh, they could." He nodded, sounding so certain. "It doesn't matter how high or fortified the walls are. We can always get in. If we're good enough. Spies infiltrating or attempting to is one thing, but this is another. Even sending someone to attempt what he did on our way here is one thing, but you don't send throwaways into this city for something like this if you do at all."

"So . . ." I started and then paused to formulate the appropriate words. I'd been hearing threats of potential abduction attempts since my father had arrived in New Bethel. One, to my knowledge, had already been attempted. It had come so very close. But there was one curious aspect of all this. "Why did he need to speak to you alone about it *before* speaking to everyone else?"

"He said it was because I'm technically in charge of your safety." Jastin looked away and shook his head. "He was testing me."

"To see if you could come up with a satisfactory plan?"

"No." He laughed humorlessly beneath his breath. "Reapers can always come up with satisfactory plans for things like that. As long as they're not useless. He asked me whether I thought I could keep you safer by being here, or if it would be a better idea for me to lead a team to intercept the Reapers myself."

Abby's question passed through my head.

You're not leaving?

I was struggling to push down whatever unpleasant feeling that was trying to break through when I hesitantly asked, "What did you say?"

"That I needed to think about it."

"Surely there's nothing to think about," I said in disbelief. "Not unless you intend on taking me with you."

He stood there and put his hands over his face for a moment. Once he'd removed them, he said, "I'm thinking."

"You can't *leave me* here!" I exclaimed once the realization began to settle in on me.

Panic. That was the feeling. I could not fully comprehend the level of it I felt welling inside me as I watched him close his eyes and clench his jaw. My will to push against it was lost, and something broke.

"You *can't. . . .*"

"Aster, it's part of my job description. I *have* to keep you safe. We might not always like what that entails."

"It's not *about* that!" I shouted. Didn't he know what it was about? Didn't he know? "I can't let you go, not knowing whether the people with you will have your back. And you can't leave me here with people we *both* know don't have mine." I shook my head. "We can't *do* that to each other, Jastin! Not unless *everything* is a lie."

He rubbed at his forehead with several of his fingers and did not look at me to say, "I have to go."

"*Jastin*," I said in disbelief.

What was he doing? Didn't he understand? He couldn't *do* this. He couldn't . . .

He held his hands up when I stood from the bed, and his voice was calm when he said, "I'll be back later and tell you what happens."

I looked away from him and sat back down on the bed. My hand instinctively went to my mouth as I sat there in something I realized was very similar to shock.

I didn't hear him leave, but I knew he'd gone, left me here. And one thought kept popping into my head.

He can't do this to me.

A bit of logic eventually came through. It shot down the recurring thought and all that went along with it.

Yes, he can.

I BELIEVED IT WAS NEARLY TEN MINUTES after Jastin had gone when I heard a footstep by the door. I looked over at the sound and found Anders standing there.

"I've been sent to keep you company." His tone was apologetic.

"And by *keep me company* you mean you were sent to watch me." Under my breath, I added, "Like a child."

Worse than that, even.

I'd not ever been watched as a child when my father would leave me alone, apart from that bit of time the last instance he'd gone and I'd sought out his friend. Still, I'd never been left under anyone's care due to a need to be watched.

I supposed a lot of things changed as people grew.

"I'm sure Jastin informed you of what your father spoke to him about, though he was distinctly told not to." He sighed. "You should make him aware that no matter what he told your father during travel, he's not above orders, even implied ones. This particular breaking of an order will stay between us. I'm also going to warn you now that your security will be increased."

"With my father's Reapers," I said with widened eyes. I was not truly surprised by it despite the deal my father and I had made, only angry.

"Yes," he answered blankly.

"Is it even *true*?" I demanded. "Is there actually a legitimate and direct threat or is it simply a ploy to keep me under his thumb?" Walking about the city was *far* different from being surrounded by my father's men at all times.

He shrugged, and the action was full of nonchalance. "You can speak to the Reaper who informed him of the plan and attempt to make the distinction yourself, if you'd like."

"Oh, *could* I?" Sarcasm dripped from my voice.

"Yes." He smiled a bit. "I'll let you make the decision. I'll take you to that Reaper and allow you to speak with him later, when they're done with him. *Or* I'll take you just outside the door where they're having the meeting and allow you to eavesdrop on it now."

"You wouldn't," I said, feeling one of my eyebrows rise. "I doubt my father would approve of either option."

"He wouldn't." Anders laughed. "But that doesn't mean I won't do it regardless. You make the decision, but you cannot have both things."

I did believe that eavesdropping was incredibly rude, especially when personal things were being discussed between two people. When they were to be speaking about me . . .

"I want to eavesdrop on the meeting," I said without hesitation, knowing the only reason I couldn't have both was because he said so. That I could potentially have either in the first place was only because he said so.

"You know Jastin will tell you what transpires during once he returns." He chuckled. "So you're choosing the less-important and *infinitely* less-useful of the two options, aren't you?"

In his opinion, clearly.

"I don't care," I said firmly. "I *have* to know if he's leaving. That's more important to me."

"You know he'll look like a coward if he stays, don't you?" He smiled again. "Weak from love. *He* knows it. That's why your father spoke to him about it first—testing him to see which was more important to him."

"That wouldn't be why he stayed if he did," I said, my voice harsh.

"Perhaps not," Anders said thoughtfully. "But that's precisely what everyone would believe. If he stays, Aster . . . it would destroy every bit of the reputation he's built for himself over the past nine years. His entire life, even." He paused for a moment. "Do you believe you're worth that? Would you hope to do that to him?"

I stood, and through my teeth said, "Let's go."

"Not so fast." Anders grabbed hold of my arm as I was walking past.

He released me once I'd properly stopped.

"You make a deal with me right now."

I clenched my jaw in frustration over all the deals that I kept making with people, but I waited in silence for whatever it was he had to say.

"I take you there and you will be quiet," he said. "You will not make a single sound. You will not say a word. You will not interfere in any way, even if you become so tempted you can't help yourself. You *will* help yourself. You will stay where I tell you to stay and leave when I tell you to leave, no matter what you hear."

He paused again, giving me time to think it all over.

"Do you agree to my terms?"

Curious, I asked, "What would've been the terms for simply speaking to the Reaper?"

"Nothing." His eyebrows barely rose. "Apart from not telling your father I allowed it, of course. Beyond that . . . not a single thing."

"And my father doesn't know you're taking me to eavesdrop?"

He shook his head believably, but I couldn't quite figure out why any part of me believed him.

"What of the Reapers who will surely see us on the way there?" I asked. "Won't they tell my father?"

"Your father and I made a deal with one another when we took over this city together," Anders said. "We make decisions together, or some of them, though everyone believes he does it all on his own. He's the figurehead of our operation, which is precisely the way we both wanted it. He's more straightforward and infinitely more likable, though you may disagree with both those things. And, well, he is what he is.

"Part of our arrangement entailed that we were both free to do as we wished without the other having knowledge of our whereabouts and intents." A few seconds passed before he said, "You see, Aster . . . you can only be truly invisible now while in my company, or your father's. Invisible in the *only* way you can manage here. The only time your father will not be informed of what you're doing is while you're with me."

"So who's watching me and reporting back to my father while I'm training?" I demanded. "*Stelin?*" That would certainly void any deals that Stelin and I had made with one another.

"Just because you don't always have eyes on you doesn't mean you're not always seen," he said. "There are Reapers everywhere here and they know what you're doing at all times. They don't have to be inside a room to know what takes place in it."

"That's how he knew . . ." I said on a breath.

"That you were pregnant with Chase's child and had a miscarriage due to your training?" Anders asked, his voice impassive.

I said nothing.

"Your father is a *very* smart man, but the Reaper who was standing just outside your training area and overheard the gist of it is thankfully more loyal to me, even if only slightly. He came to me and I told him to tell your father as much as he could without revealing the full truth. As I said, your father is intelligent and came to the conclusion himself. Details are the difference between speculation and truth, occasionally more so than facts." He paused, raising an eyebrow. "You're welcome."

"Would he kill Chase if he knew?" I barely asked. "Or if that hadn't happened and I'd had . . . a . . . *child*?"

"No." He sounded certain. "He wouldn't risk doing anything to make you hate him. Having you followed doesn't count. Given that your safety is always in jeopardy . . . it's quite necessary. He'll take the risk of falling even farther out of your favor for that."

Though Anders seemed sure . . . I was not. Even if my father might not kill Chase for that, I didn't believe he would've done nothing. There were *many* possibilities, and none of them I would risk.

People always told their good deeds, when it would in some way benefit them to. Or nearly always, depending on. It was . . .

Sad.

"Thank you," I said quietly. "But you're making me miss the meeting."

"Only giving everyone the time to get where they're going before we make our way there." He shrugged then narrowed his eyes at me and significantly said, "You should tell Chase what happened."

"Just as you told my mother about your procedure?"

He smiled slowly and said, "Fair."

I had only taken two steps when I closed my eyes and turned back to Anders, needing to rid myself of something nagging at me. "Who did he believe caused me to be that way?"

"Jastin, of course." He nearly seemed to be on the verge of laughing at me, like he couldn't believe I'd needed to ask the question.

"That's ridiculous." When would we have even had the time or opportunity to do such things? No matter how many times Jastin and I had been alone during travel . . . it was ridiculous.

"Aster." Anders shook his head at me, and he *did* chuckle quietly then. "That is the *furthest* thing from ridiculous. You know damn well it is. Lying to yourself doesn't make something true, no matter how badly you may wish it does. You'll be *much* better off when and if you let that get through your head. Then again, if you're set on the easy path, keep headed that direction. You're certainly on course for it. Up to you."

I said nothing.

A few seconds passed before he seemed unable to stop a laugh. "Were you asking thinking it would *obviously* be Chase, or is it the other thing?"

I raised an eyebrow.

"The other thing being any of the other males surrounding you. He *did* have a moment of wondering if you might've sullied your bloodline in a way you can't even *begin* to grasp. But he didn't even consider the brother. *Too old* for you and all." He smiled quite widely at that, barely holding onto another laugh.

I just stared at him.

"That pit of discomfort in your gut, Aster?" He nodded. "That exists for a reason. You should learn to listen to it."

"I truly have no idea what you're implying or why you find it so amusing."

He reached a hand out and patted my face. "You should learn to listen to it."

I watched his hand move back to himself, and then I asked "May we go? Surely whatever this is isn't more important."

He chuckled. "We surely may."

Chapter Ten

Invisible

THE REAPERS WATCHED ANDERS AND ME intently as we passed them on our way through the House, at least until they must've figured out inside their heads what Anders was taking me to do. Perhaps it was nothing more than what Anders had told me about invisibility and the only way it could be managed here, but there seemed to be something else to it. There was the possibility that they were not accustomed to seeing me with someone who prevented them from informing my father about where I was and what I was doing, making them either confused or torn on what to do.

It could've been nothing more than that, but I was almost positive they all knew precisely what I was doing, or close enough to it. That couldn't have helped in potentially being torn on what to do, as I suspected they were not accustomed to allowing my father to be eavesdropped on.

I watched so many of them blink in what appeared to be understanding then turn their backs to us as we passed. It was oddly and immensely satisfying in some inexplicable way, like I could still disappear for a moment no matter how visible I was. They were being forced to *let* me disappear.

I nearly smiled over it several times. Nearly, until I realized it felt as though I'd gone home, in a way. And that meant I associated some part of New Bethel—even if only a feeling or way of being—with . . . *home.*

Even sneaking around inside my father's city in plain view behind his back could not amuse me enough to make up for the disgust I felt at the prospect. It could not come close.

Anders held up a hand before we rounded a corner, and I stopped in my tracks. He put a finger to his lips, pointed to his eyes with two of his fingers on his right hand, and then pointed farther down the hallway. When my gaze followed the direction he'd indicated, I found that the hallway ended with a very large and ornate wooden door.

I nodded my head and watched him sneak down there, absolutely silent as he moved. He stopped at the end, tilted his head to listen, and then gestured me forward with his hand.

I felt as though my heart were beating out of my chest—or my throat, I was unsure which—as I slowly walked down the hallway. Surely the sound would give me away. Surely everyone else could hear it as well. Surely something would happen to foil this plan and it would be my fault due to failing in some way or another.

This would be just like me following after Jastin through the trees during travel. I would do something wrong and get caught, subjecting not only myself to the punishment that followed but someone I cared for as well.

You're walking on an even surface, I reminded myself. *There are no branches, or rocks, or undergrowth to maneuver over and through. It's not dark out. You can see where you're going. You know how to walk on this surface. You've been trained to walk properly on this. If you can't walk on a floor . . .*

That set about the next wave of panic, thinking on my back being shoved against a wall, hands on my body. I'd been told what to do in frontward attacks, but I'd been too weak to make much of a difference at all, only enough to keep me safe enough before help had arrived.

I was always so useless when it mattered, and this would not be any different.

Still, I had to believe that moving was better than standing in place, no matter the consequences. I just had to *pay attention* and *be careful.* Do a proper job.

I paid mind to my breathing along with every step I took, and then . . .

I was there.

I waited for an instant to be discovered, but there was only silence.

Anders pointed to one of his ears and then to the door.

As I was moving my head closer, he put his finger over his lips again.

I could hardly make it out, but there it was.

Speaking.

I'd done it.

I'd *done* it.

"Even with increasing her security, we can't ensure they won't infiltrate the city and find a way to get to her regardless," someone said. "Even locking her inside a windowless room for the rest of her life can't ensure that."

I couldn't make out who it had been, so I put my ear all the way against the door, being *very* careful not to push on it.

"Have you thought about luring them out with her?" someone else asked. I knew it was Chandler easily. I'd never noticed his voiced carried in much the same way as that of my father's. "She'd be all for it. It would be better than running the risk that the interception team will miss them entirely."

"If she were more thoroughly trained, I would actually consider the option."

I blinked hard in confusion at my father's words, more than what I'd already been doing over Chandler's suggestion.

"*Would* you?" Chandler asked with a clearly disbelieving laugh. I was surprised to hear Chandler speaking up at all here, let alone challenging my father. Very surprised.

"Certainly," my father said. "She seems to have inherited her mother's skill at believably pretending to be so much less than what she is. I cannot tell you how many times I watched Elena successfully draw Reapers out in that way and then take them down. Her mother was exceptional."

I pursed my lips, trying to discover how I felt about my father speaking so freely of my mother to . . . *them.* A room full of people. Before I could do more than realize it had happened and discover I was unhappy about it, someone else spoke.

"She may have the natural skill for it, but as you said, she's not trained," Ahren said. "Perhaps she could do something like that in a few years, but more than likely not even then. She'd just get herself killed now, and then half of them as well."

"That's what I just said, Ahren," my father stated in exasperation.

"Only reinforcing." I wouldn't have been surprised at all if my brother had shrugged his shoulders at that.

"I overheard the entire conversation where they were planning it," someone said. I assumed it to be my father's informant due to his words and the fact that I couldn't recall ever having heard his voice before. "You won't miss them if you follow the route I indicated. They're going out of their way to avoid Maldir."

Chase asked, "And how do we know they weren't just saying it because you were there to confuse us toward their real plan?"

"Because I've been pretending to be loyal to Hasting for the last *three years*," the man said. "I've played my part well. Now let me ask you this . . ." He paused. "How did the girl come to kill one of his men?"

"She said it was because he paid no attention to her," someone stated. Had it been Stanley? I was unsure, but he *did* typically have a quiet demeanor. Stewart had laughed once when I'd mentioned that while walking, so I was inclined to believe he didn't always. He did as far as I knew.

"No," the Reaper said. "I'm asking why it came to that. How is it no one else was there and she ended up *having* to kill him?"

Chandler asked, "How do they know she did it?"

"You must not have seen the body. I wouldn't need to answer that if you had." The Reaper almost sounded as if he were on the verge of laughing. And did I detect traces of that strange accent of Bethel through the door, or was I mistaken? "She must either be a vicious little girl or simply have no head above her shoulders. She stabbed him in the back of the neck to the point his head was almost entirely detached. A little girl."

I closed my eyes tightly and bit down on my bottom lip until I tasted metal.

"That's why Hasting is sending an entire team to attempt to abduct her this time," the Reaper went on. "He's figuring that, even with the knowledge of what she did, his Reapers would still be too stupid to pay the proper attention to her. *Barbaric little girl*, he called her. It only piqued his interest, as I'm sure you can understand." He did laugh a little then. "He was at a loss as to how she could even be your child, Sir."

Jastin said, "It was my fault."

"Stop being a martyr for her, Jastin." Exasperation was again clear in my father's tone.

"It was my fault for wandering off with her," Jastin said firmly.

"Yes, that's possible," my father said. "But it was also her own fault for insisting you keep my men away from her. Perhaps your fault for listening. Perhaps her fault for simply being a stubborn ass who's unwilling to take help from anyone. There are so many circles around it that don't truly matter." His tone changed when he spoke next. "She isn't vicious, and she has more of a head than most my men. She was doing it to protect him. And she is *most assuredly* my daughter."

"She does have viciousness in her," Chandler said, his voice sounding thoughtful. "I don't believe it stems from coldness, though I won't deny that she *is* remarkably cold. I just believe she feels this desperate need to prove herself to everyone. Isn't that right, Jas?"

When Jastin didn't respond, at least verbally, Chandler went on.

"I believe it would be wise to show her you have faith in her if you truly do. I'm worried that coldness is turning into something more substantial. There's no way to come back from that. Not really. I hope very much that you and I stand on the common ground of not wanting that to happen."

"She won't give me the chance to." My father's voice was quieter than usual when he spoke.

Jastin said, "You're going about it in all the wrong ways, Sir."

"I'm finished speaking of personal aspects of my relationship with my daughter," my father said firmly. "This meeting is about her physical safety. That's currently more important by far. There's no telling what Hasting would do if he got his hands on her, but I refuse to allow it to happen, of which I'm sure he's aware. He knows I would give up my entire city to keep her safe from him. We *cannot* allow him to take her, because *everything* would fall. If he gets another city under him . . . the entire land would be at risk. Especially with the new Reapers we have and how we've been training them.

No one else would stand a chance. I don't want that on my conscience.

"Now," he went on. "He knows we're somewhat weakened from our endeavors in New Bethel, albeit far less than one would expect, and that will soon be straightened. Still, our men are spread thin right now. I have far too many of them sent out, listening for word of anyone else who might know about her. It's the perfect time for him to strike, strategically speaking. He won't get another chance like this, and I'm sure he knows it. This is his one chance to make a move." He paused for a moment. "Were he as intelligent as he should be, he would know better than this."

"You should've had Anders running the cities, Sir," the Reaper said. There was no accent. I must've been mistaken before.

"We would still be precisely where we are in this moment." My father sighed loudly. "Have you figured out who his spy is here?"

"No," the Reaper said. "I've never heard him even act as if he had one, but that's the only way he could know about her. Have you thought of his son?"

My father said, "I have."

I blinked hard at the realization that Stelin was not included in their meeting despite being so close to me daily.

"But I don't believe it is him. I fear it's someone close." My father grumbled something, though I could not make out what it was.

"Then why did you come back?" Chandler asked, I assumed in reaction to the unknown statement.

My father did not respond to his question. "Jastin," he said instead. "Have you come to a decision?"

My stomach nearly flopped out of my mouth as I waited for it.

"I have." It took what felt like forever for him to say, "I won't go." I just barely heard him release a breath. "I won't leave her."

"That kind of love is a dangerous thing to feel," the Reaper said with a small chuckle. "It's what gets people killed. Isn't that right, Sir?"

"Perhaps," my father said quietly, "but it seems to be the only thing in the world worth being killed for."

I pursed my lips and then flinched because I'd forgotten that I'd bitten the bottom one hard when I heard Chase ask, "Why didn't you just let us go?"

"Because you and your brother would both be dead and Hasting would have my daughter." My father's voice was firm again. "Whoever told him about her had already done so. I left for New Bethel as soon as I received word he knew of her whereabouts. I rode as fast as I possibly could on the chance he might make a move for her himself. He could've walked right in there. I didn't even know Agatha had found one of my men until after I'd met her. I only discovered the correspondence he'd brought to me on her behalf once we'd returned. *That's* why."

Chase said, "Nobody would've known who she was."

"She looks almost *exactly* like her mother," my father said. "Anyone who was looking for her could've easily found her that way alone. Trust me when I say he would've been looking and that he would've found her almost immediately after she stepped foot outside those walls. You *cannot imagine* what that would've meant for you, and especially not for *her*. The repercussions would've been catastrophic, but you cannot fathom what would've happened to her."

He paused, and I felt my brow furrowing.

"I understand that life seems to have dealt you a bad hand at the current point in time, but that's no excuse to be ignorant. You clearly don't know what you got involved in as well as you believe."

"*Ignorant*," Chase said quietly. "None of us know what would've happened if we'd left. Even you can only speculate. No one knows what would've happened to her or anyone else."

"No?" My father was clearly taunting him with the word, but there was also a challenge in it.

"No," Chase replied.

And Chandler was clearly giving a warning when he said, "Drop it, Chase."

"*Drop* it?" Chase asked. "Why are you acting like you know what this is about? Or is it something else?"

It took quite a while for Chandler to say, "I *do* know what this is about." He paused. "That message Agatha had sent to you . . . she said Aster asked her a question, didn't she?"

"Indeed," my father replied.

"What question?" Chase asked.

"She asked her if knowing she was going to die would be easier because she was not her real daughter," Chandler said slowly. "Was that it, Sir?"

"Indeed," my father repeated. "My daughter knew what would happen to her, had she left with you. She unfortunately could not have known that if she *had* . . . things would have ended *much* worse than with death. If she'd taken a single step outside that House, onto the streets of *any* city with anyone but *me*?" He paused. "You cannot *imagine*."

"She never . . ." Chase said and then stopped.

"Told you that she knew what would happen to her?" my father asked curiously. "I assume she kept it from you because she didn't want you to know she was afraid."

"Are you acting like you know her now, *Sir*?"

"Perhaps there *was* a different reason, but I'm going to assume you were afraid and she knew as much," my father stated blankly. "I may not know her now, but she did the very same thing to me when she was an older child. She was always so perceptive in some ways, and she lies through her teeth when the truth would be hard on a person she cares for. Is that inaccurate, Jastin?"

Was that what he thought?

Was that what he'd always . . .

Jastin said, "Don't throw me in his face, Sir."

Chase's voice was quiet—*tired*—when he spoke. "I can't deal with this anymore."

A hand was immediately in front of my face. I barely had time to look at Anders before he pointed back down the hallway.

I wanted to protest, as the meeting was not over and there was still more to be heard, but I could not. I had made a deal, after all.

CHAPTER ELEVEN

BIG AND LITTLE

THOUGH THE MEETING HADN'T BEEN OVER and there was so much more I could've potentially learned, I was unsure how I felt about what I had. There would be time to sort it all later, but when I did, I would be sorting something incomplete. Despite knowing an incomplete picture was better than none at all, I had to wonder about it.

Was it better? Was it truly better, or was it no different than being certain I would die when I left New Bethel?

I'd been so sure of it, so certain I had enough of the picture to know what laid beyond for me. I'd known I hadn't had all the facts, that important things were being withheld from me, but I'd somehow let myself think it was good enough.

It was *not* good enough.

Still, despite the potential confusion caused by an incomplete picture . . . it *was* better than nothing. Was anything ever really complete before being finished?

Only by the person creating it, if even then. I just had to remember that I was not the one creating, only observing.

I was frustrated regardless.

I did not wait until Anders and I had gotten all the way back to my living quarters to ask, "Why did you make me leave?"

"Because Chase was on the verge of storming from the room," he replied. "Can you imagine the faces of everyone in there if Chase had opened the door and caught you with your ear stuck to it?" He glanced up at the ceiling for a moment. "On second thought . . . that would surely be a sight to behold. It might've even been worth what came with it. Hindsight, and all."

I pursed my lips to refrain from smiling because a small part of me agreed. And then I flinched because I'd forgotten again that I'd bitten my bottom lip so hard. The spectacle that would surely have followed me being caught with my ear to the door and Anders just beside me might've been amusing, but I would've argued on it being worth what he'd claimed.

"So, you heard what you wanted to hear," he stated. "Did you hear anything else you found interesting?"

"We'll talk about it when we return to my quarters." A heavy frown pulled down at my mouth.

"You know it doesn't make a difference." I was unsure whether there was a bit of an apology in his words or they had been nothing more than a statement. I was also unsure if he was saying it made no difference in the sense that we were currently together, making whatever interaction we had as close to private as I could ever get here. He might've also been saying that my quarters were not as private as I liked to think. I supposed any of those were applicable.

Regardless of whichever it might've been, I felt the need to inform him, "It makes a difference to *me*."

I WAS SITTING DOWN on the large red rug that covered part of the floor of my main living area, my legs crossed in front of me. Anders was seated in a chair across from me, staring like he was trying to make sense of something.

"Why do you do that?"

I raised an eyebrow at him.

He clarified with, "Sit on the floor."

"I don't know." My response was true enough, but I quickly changed the subject. "My father . . ." I stopped and cleared my throat. Very quietly, I continued forward. "He doesn't trust Stelin."

"Not entirely, no. Enough to allow him near you, but not enough to have any sort of say in what happens pertaining to you. He *is* Hasting's son, after all. Even if he's loyal to your father and this city, or even you in a way, you still have to worry about the blood." He paused for an instant. "Are you surprised by that?"

Because I had no intention of answering his question, I spared only the briefest moment to think about blood. "Have you met him?" Interacting with Anders was not the same as interacting with most others. He paid more attention, though many might not notice the attention he paid in all the behavior that was on occasion somewhat ridiculous. "Hasting."

"He and your father have come across one another on more than one occasion. So I've seen him and I've been in his presence, but I've never been formally introduced. Your father never wanted to show his hand with me. You've no idea how bad the blood runs between them."

I *did* have an idea, but I didn't want Anders to know as much, so I said, "You'll be the one taking over officially if something happens to my father."

He nodded.

"When he first arrived while we were traveling . . ." I paused, still trying to make sense of what I was about to say, especially when paired with one particular bit of what I'd just overheard in the meeting. "Stelin made a comment for me to hear it. He said his father would love me."

"I'm sure he would find you quite amusing if he didn't kill you straightaway, which I can assure you he wouldn't do. Too many repercussions and not enough benefits. I'm unsure what you've heard of him, but he is a heartless man. You will never hear a word contrary to that. It would be like a cat, laughing at a mouse while it played with and killed it slowly."

I hadn't heard much, but I'd heard enough. It was all a matter of whether it was all true. Rather than say as much, I pointed out, "Cats can't laugh."

He shook his head and sighed. "It was just an example." He continued shaking his head for a moment. "What I'm saying is that if you were to ever find yourself face to face with him, you would likely believe you had some sort of upper hand. Mice are unbelievably fast, yes, but cats are much quicker and much smarter. If a cat were to really know what it was doing, you can't imagine all it could do. There's such a difference between the mind of a predator and that of its prey. You've not yet discovered where you fall with us."

I sat there in silence, thinking over his words. I felt he was giving me that time, but eventually he broke it.

"Hasting didn't get where he is today by brute force. He is incredibly intelligent and methodical. And heartless, as I said. Wicked combination, that is. No matter how intelligent you are, Aster . . ." He paused, shaking his head again. "Men like that will always be ahead of you. There's such a difference in the minds. You can't keep up without rising to their level. And you can't rise without becoming just like them. You cannot even hope to do such a thing when you can't discern where you stack against them."

I looked down at my legs, thinking about how difficult it was to try to figure out where people stood, if they told the truth or even just said things that were true. Why did it have to *be* this way?

"Don't you ever get sick of these spy games?" I asked, bringing my gaze back to his face. "Not knowing whom you can trust and whose word is truthful? And all the *evil. . . .*"

"Your father and I have both been sick of it for a very long time." I could hear the truth in that.

"Then why did he come back? Why did either of you?" I shook my head. "He didn't answer Chandler when he asked. Why *did* he? Why did be abandon me for *this*?"

"You're going to have to ask your father that question," he said. "It's not my right to tell you such things, no matter my involvement."

"Then let me ask you this," I said quickly, knowing I could get him to say nothing more on the question I'd asked. "Why did he act as though he has faith in me to the people in that room when he doesn't act that way toward me? *Why*? That doesn't make any sense." I shook my head again. "I'm actually inclined to believe he knew I was listening outside the door and said those things with the sole intent of me hearing them, that he sent you to me with the purpose of taking me there to listen."

"I understand it is very easy to get carried away with conspiracies in this world. . . ." Anders seemed to be putting careful deliberation into his words. "But sometimes things are pure, even if they don't seem that way. Not everything positive is done with ulterior motives, nor can one do more than speculate when other people are involved. It's all a matter of learning how to tell the difference in motivation."

I breathed out heavily. It was not so much a sigh as my frustrations making their way out of my body. There was no way for me to know what I'd asked or accused.

"Did he truly have no idea I'd planned on running away?" I asked. "Did he only come because of Hasting?"

"Oh, he knew you were intending to run away." Anders nodded. "Your brother sent correspondence and told him as much. Ahren was supposed to be slowly telling you the truth about things so you could adapt to them and come to your own logical decision on the matter."

"He didn't." Ahren had told me the truth about some things, I couldn't deny that, but not the important truths. Not any truths that might've made a difference. Not unless his hand was forced.

"No, that much was apparent to your father the instant he arrived in New Bethel," he said. "He believes Ahren is very torn between wanting what's best for you and an overwhelming jealousy. The latter of which clouds his judgment."

"Jealousy?" I shook my head, baffled by the word and the prospect of what Anders had suggested.

That was . . .

"You were allowed to live your non-Reaper life with your father for quite some time," Anders said apologetically. "I know it wasn't as long as either of you wanted, but you still had that. Having it at all is surprising enough, but for the length and still being alive?" He stared off for a moment, shaking his head and seeming to be thinking on it.

I did not interrupt his moment. I watched him in it.

That moment passed and he brought his full attention back to me, continuing. "Despite meeting your brother rather soon after you were taken . . . Ahren is not stupid. He knows your father wanted you. He had too much time with you to not, raised you. Add onto it the fact it's not public knowledge that Ahren is his son, and *then* add your relationship with Jastin on top of *that*. Well." He paused, holding his hands up for an instant. "*Jealousy.*"

"He hates me, doesn't he?" It almost came out as a whisper but not quite. I'd been wondering as much for quite some time. At first I'd thought I was mistaken, explained his behavior away with other things, but the more time passed, the more I thought it. He hadn't once even attempted speaking to me since we'd arrived in Jarsil. Not once.

"I would say a part of him does, yes." Anders nodded. "But the other part loves you. Such is the infuriating relationship between siblings."

"Do you have any?"

"Most of us do," he said with a small grin.

"Do you love them?"

"I do," he replied. "When you get older, you learn to appreciate things you take for granted while you're young. Have faith things will work out. It's better than wasting your time waiting for something you have no control over."

"I told Ahren he had to take me to see my niece." A bit of guilt came through clearly in my admission.

"Oh yes, he told your father and your father told me." Anders laughed. "Are you wondering why he hasn't done so?"

I nodded.

"It's not that he won't do it, I don't believe," he said, "but our Reapers are only allowed to see their offspring once a year. I'm sure Jastin told you as much. What you may not yet know is it's only on a specific day—the anniversary of when they're put into the system."

"Jastin said only five Reapers here see their children."

"We don't give out the numbers." Anders shook his head. "It's not very high, I can assure you. Most don't, or can't, or won't. Jastin must've asked the Reaper who brings the children to the parents. It may have been five that month or five in however long a time the Reaper saw fit to answer. Or perhaps they simply lied. But . . . it *is* more than five."

"It's sad." My voice was quiet.

"Yes, but we give them the opportunity to have children and keep them later on in life. No other Reapers are allowed that. Not anywhere." He raised an eyebrow. "You can see the purpose of it, can't you? For peace and hope, but also . . . we *have* to keep our numbers up. This was the most humane way we could come up with to accomplish that."

I felt as though I could not say anything to that. I could see the logic in it, but it was still so horrible.

Sheep.

I changed the subject by asking, "How is Bethel?"

"In appearance?"

Before I could inform him that I was not inquiring about appearances, he went on.

"Very much like Jarsil, to be honest. Only the people are not happy. They're all afraid. It's not quite like where you were before, though it is almost a mixture of Jarsil and New Bethel in a sense. It has the appearances of our city, but the bad things from your former one, only more of them. Much more."

"I spoke to one of your Reapers before I left New Bethel," I said carefully. "He mentioned that Reapers from other cities aren't like the ones to be found here."

"Oh no." Anders shook his head. "They are so far from it."

"But they're still people." Even Hasting was a person, no matter what people thought of him. Even if they were different, in some way . . . they were still people.

"No, Aster," he said. "When you take a person's humanity away from them . . . they're no longer a person."

I blinked hard and shook my head at a memory that had been buried in the recesses of my mind.

"What is it?"

I frowned. "My father told me that when I was a child."

"Did he?"

I nodded, remembering my father's voice saying the words.

"It was something your mother used to say," Anders informed me.

"Why?" Asking why she'd said it was far easier to think about than the knowledge that my father had given me a piece of my mother as a child.

Had he given me more and I just didn't know?

He looked away and forced a smile onto his face. "She always made herself cry after she killed a person. That was why she said it."

"But if she had to force herself to do it . . ." I did not want to continue.

"It made her feel better," he said, still with that tight smile. "Sometimes the little things are all we're allowed in life. And sometimes we come to realize that things are rarely as small as they appear." He paused for a moment. "It can all seem so insignificant when you're staring it directly in the face. It gets distorted when you're standing too closely. Then you walk away, find yourself at the appropriate distance, and turn around. . . . *That's* when you *truly* see it."

I waited for him to say more, but there was only silence so I asked, "See what?"

"The difference between significant and insignificant is all a matter of where you're standing." The sad smile was still on his face. "Don't think badly of her for what I told you. It's one of things that made her beautiful, no matter where you were looking from, as long as you could understand what you were seeing. But I can also tell you . . . it's something that made her the *furthest* thing from insignificant." The smile stretched a bit farther. "It made her *remarkable*."

I was going to drop it all at that, but . . . "How so?"

And Anders said, "Because she refused to let go of something they refused to let her have. Understand?"

"Herself?"

"No." He laughed stiffly under his breath. "Aster, I've told you some stories about your mother, but they're a very small piece of a life that held *far* less laughter and smiles than what it should have." He nodded. "A *great* deal of it was not so pleasant." He paused then asked me the question again. "Understand?"

Slowly, that time . . . I nodded.

CHAPTER TWELVE

PROPER

IT WAS NOT VERY LONG after Anders had talked about my mother that there was a knock at the door. Anders opened it, and I peeked over from where I was still sitting on the floor to find Chase standing there in the doorway.

"Can I talk to her?"

Anders looked over his shoulder at me and his eyes were on mine when he responded with, "Surely." He left without another word.

I remained where I sat as Chase stepped inside and closed the door behind him. He walked over and stared intently at my face, but he did not sit down with me.

In the silence, I wondered what had spurred on his wanting to speak to me. He hadn't tried to speak to me like a person in such a long time.

Had he located some shred of understanding during the last of the meeting?

Would it ever go back to a boy and a girl, standing in a garden together?

No. We could never go back to that, not when we were in such different places.

Was he even capable of understanding?

Was *I* capable of understanding?

The expression on his face told me *something* had changed, but I had no idea what it was. Not until he finally spoke.

"I'm leaving."

"*What?*" I asked in confusion and disbelief. Surely I'd heard him wrong. When I realized I hadn't, I continued sitting on the floor for a moment, dazed as I attempted to process it. Out of all the things . . . I never would've expected this. Then I remembered why I never would've expected it, so I stood and stared at his face. "I told my father he couldn't send you on any missions. It was part of the deal he and I made."

Had something happened to void it after I'd left the door where I'd been eavesdropping? I'd worried about that since the deal had been made. So many things could happen to potentially void it, all of them subject to my father's word and will. It could be made worthless the instant he decided he wanted it that way. Everyone kept speaking of favor where he and I were concerned, but I was under no delusion about where I stacked with him. He could void anything he liked, with any reasoning he liked, at any time he liked.

Chase looked away and shook his head. "Do the two of you tell each other everything?" When I said nothing, he stated, "You weren't supposed to know about this until after we'd come to a decision on it, but you clearly do."

I brought my gaze to the floor.

He sighed when I didn't respond verbally, and he said, "Your father isn't sending me. I volunteered."

My gaze shot back to his face at that, and two words fell from my mouth. "But why?"

"Because Jas wouldn't go and we all agreed one of us should be in charge of the team."

"But why *you?*" I didn't know *who* else should or could go, but . . . *someone.*

"I just—" He stopped speaking to close his eyes and take a deep breath. "I just have to."

"Of course you don't."

He didn't *have* to do it. Why would he even *say* that? How *could* he say it when he knew what *having* to do something actually meant?

"No, I really do." He paused before adding, "I might not come back."

"You're not going to *die*!" I exclaimed.

He shook his head a bit, and his voice was calm when he said, "That's not what I meant."

I blinked hard and attempted to work it all out inside my head. He meant . . .

He meant he had to go for himself.

I did not know what to say to him. I could not try to talk him out of it if he believed it would be best for him. I *could*, but I *wouldn't*. "What would you do?"

He seemed quite uncomfortable when he responded with, "I'm still thinking about it."

"I . . ." I closed my eyes. If this could possibly be the last time I ever saw him . . . "I need to tell you something."

"What is it?"

"What was wrong with me before . . ." I started slowly. My body felt as though its temperature had instantaneously risen to an unsafe level, just at the thought of telling him. But I knew I had to say it. "You got me pregnant."

"*What*?"

When I opened my eyes again, he had a hand over his mouth and his blue eyes were so wide.

"You're not serious."

I nodded stiffly. "I didn't know. Not until . . ."

"You *lost* it?"

I nodded again.

When his gaze fell on the nearest wall, there were tears welling in his eyes. "Why didn't you *tell* me?"

"I didn't want to make you sad." I didn't want to make him sad, or angry, regretful. There were so many options, none of them good and all of them close enough to the one word used as explanation. Close enough. I wiped at my own eyes. "I've already hurt you enough."

"You should've—" He cut himself off then held up a hand. "I'm not going to say something I'll regret. I've done enough of that over the past few months. So . . . I'm going to tell you I'm sorry. I'm sorry for everything I ever said to you, anything I ever did to push you away and make you feel like you couldn't come to me. Even with that. *Especially* with that."

"I don't want you to apologize," I told him quietly.

"Maybe neither of us should apologize." He wiped at his eyes with his forearm. "Maybe we were both too ignorant in the ways that mattered for this to have ever worked."

Was it like the training—not clicking as well as it could have, just because people were people? Were we all so different, even when similar, that there was no hope to find some sort of aligned understanding? Was it impossible?

He was right. We were both too ignorant with this. But . . . it still hurt.

All I felt I could do was whisper, "Are you going to come back?"

"Aster, I don't know. I'll have quite a while to think about everything when I'm gone."

I really . . . might never see him again. The knowledge tried to break through, but I pushed it down and asked, "When are you leaving?"

"Tonight."

"Do you want to stay with me for a while before?"

"No."

I looked away and nodded, hearing the one word repeatedly inside my head.

No.

He was leaving. He was leaving, and he didn't even want to stay with me before he did, not even for a little while. Did he care nothing at all for the past? Did it mean nothing to him?

Had I hurt him *that* badly, where he would just . . . *leave?*

The reality of it all finally broke through and, with it, I felt something also broke inside me. I was unsure what it was exactly, or how integral it was, but I began crying quite hysterically. I could not help myself.

He came over and pulled me up into a hug. "I wasn't expecting you to be so upset."

"*What?*" I demanded. "Did you think I would be *happy?* Do you think I don't care about you at all?"

He didn't respond, and I wondered if he *had* thought as much.

I could not explain why I did it, nor could I figure out why he allowed me to, but I kissed him.

He did not return it for very long at all, only a few seconds before taking a step back.

"I love you," he said believably.

"I love you too," I told him quietly. And I did. In a sense.

He forced a smile at me, but he could not keep it on his face. He turned his back to me and started walking.

I watched him in that moment, his back blurry through my tears, and I begged myself to say something. A part of me screamed. It screamed so loudly for him to come back, to come right back here and stay in Jarsil.

How could I lose him? How could I just let him walk away? He'd done so much for me, before I'd even realized he was doing it. He'd shown me so many things. How could I lose him?

I remained silent, apart from my crying.

He closed the door behind him without once looking back at me. And then . . . he was gone.

I WAS STILL CRYING where I'd sat back down on the floor when Jastin came later, though I was no longer hysterical. He walked inside without knocking and sat down across from me. He did not appear happy when I looked over at him and he asked, "I take it you spoke to Chase?"

I nodded in response and then gave a guilty admission. "I eavesdropped on part of the meeting." I did not want to talk about what he'd just asked me, and I believed it was obvious. I didn't care in the slightest if he was aware. Better that way, with this.

"How did you manage that?" He asked the question then answered it for himself. "Anders."

I nodded again. "He told me I could choose between that and speaking to the Reaper who had the information about the abduction."

He narrowed his eyes, which made my crying return to the point where it verged on hysterics. It almost seemed he was disappointed in my bad judgment, but it *hadn't* been. Why didn't anyone ever understand well enough? Why did they always jump to the exact same conclusion?

"I had to know if you were leaving me here alone with all these people."

"I'm not leaving."

"I know." The guilt seemed to be clawing at my stomach and chest, thinking of what Anders had said about my worth and the responses in the room to Jastin's declaration. "I heard that."

He didn't seem as unhappy as I'd anticipated when he asked, "How much did you hear?"

"Only to the point where Chase said he couldn't deal with this anymore," I answered, trying not to think of Chase at all, even when speaking of him. "Anders made me leave because he worried Chase was going to storm through the door and catch me."

"He almost did," he said. "Your father and his brother talked reason into him. Then he volunteered to go. Your father didn't want him to because he'd agreed he wouldn't send Chase or Chandler on missions, but . . . Chase volunteered." He shrugged awkwardly. "He said he would come and make sure you knew he was doing it willingly. That was the only way your father would agree to it."

"And Chandler?"

Jastin shook his head. "What about him?"

"Does this in any way void the deal I made with my father about his safety?"

"What?" Jastin's face scrunched, and he shook his head quickly. "*No.* Why would you think that?"

I didn't say anything on that matter. I asked, "Why did you come so much later? Did Chase leave before everyone else?" Had the meeting gone on that much longer or had he been giving me time?

"No," Jastin said, "but everyone left before I did."

"Why?"

He looked away and closed his eyes. I watched him take and then release a deep breath before speaking. "You remember that conversation we had while we were traveling? The one about how you thought your father was going to offer me my son? I told you I would tell you when and if that happened."

"He didn't," I said on a breath.

"No, he didn't." He closed his eyes again and clenched his jaw for a moment. "He wanted to have a conversation alone with me. He said . . ." He paused to laugh humorlessly. "He said *all* he wanted was to ensure you stayed here and that you were safe, nothing more."

"What did he offer you?" I whispered. He'd offered him *something.* That much was clear. But my father had to know that nothing apart from Jastin's son would sway him.

"In exchange for ensuring both those things . . ." he began, then took another deep breath. "I would be able to officially retire. I would no longer be a Reaper, if I wanted. On paper."

"Why would he offer you that?" I asked in confusion. "That's not proper incentive for you." That wasn't even *close*.

"That wasn't it." Though he didn't move, I could tell he was extremely uncomfortable in the stiff way he was holding his body. "He said . . ." He wouldn't meet my eyes. "He said he would never take a child away from his daughter. And that, if I were officially retired . . ."

"He offered you a child with me." I couldn't believe the words, even after they'd come out of my own mouth.

"If I accurately heard what he was saying, then yes." He nodded. "That's exactly what he did without actually saying the words."

"All the *stars*," I said beneath my breath. I shook my head, trying to process this. "You can't replace one child with another!"

"I knew he wouldn't offer me my son, Aster." Jastin's voice was quiet. "He's already been in training for too long. Taking him out when he's so young . . . it would mess up his head. It would be worse for him than staying where he is, at least until he's older and can understand. When he can make sense of what's getting put in his head."

I could not fathom the level of shock and rage that I felt inside my body and inside my head.

"I can't understand," I said through my tears. "Is it all to keep me here? Like . . . having a child would be the way to accomplish that? Or was it simply because I told him I would never have a child willingly?"

I *never* would've thought my father capable of this. This was . . .

It made me think about what Abby had said on parents whoring their children off for the payment, what they would receive in exchange.

Sheep.

I shook my head again and attempted to compose myself when Jastin said nothing in response.

I could not stop myself from saying, "What a cruel and heartless thing. . . ."

When I looked at Jastin again, I saw that he had tears in his eyes. I was so frustrated by all the crying today.

I said, "I'm sorry he hurt you."

"I'm fine." If he'd ever lied to me directly . . . it was then.

I stood up quickly. "Let's go to bed."

He shook his head. "I can't sleep right now, Aster."

"Let's just lie there," I suggested. "It may make both of us feel better."

I grabbed his hand and pulled him up from the floor, and I held his hand in both of mine as we walked together.

We were not holding one another for very long when we got in bed before I whispered, "I cannot understand why he would do that." Not to either of us.

"He said he wasn't using it as leverage when I accused him of it," Jastin said quietly. "Only that I had his permission should it happen."

After everything with my father and his refusal of that very thing, his daughter with a Reaper . . . "*Why*?"

"Because I chose not to leave you," he answered.

"He's a proper asshole."

Jastin laughed once and said, "On this occasion . . . I don't believe there's anything more appropriate to say."

CHAPTER THIRTEEN

WALK

THE NEXT SEVERAL WEEKS passed by in a miraculously uneventful manner, at least in comparison to losing part of Chase then Chase himself. They were more eventful than my first approximate month in Jarsil, but they were nowhere near as unpleasant. Not being so alone made a world of difference, if only in how I felt and not so much my circumstances. It was something.

I did do a great deal of thinking on how alone I hadn't been without realizing and how utterly I'd unknowingly failed who'd been there. It was a great deal *to* think on, certainly more than could be done in a few days.

I trained, I spent time with Jastin, and I even went and visited with Abby on three separate occasions. Those visits were more choice than necessity or obligation, and I found myself beginning to look forward to them. I couldn't quite understand why, as they interfered with time spent on other things, but anticipation for the next grew after each.

My father's Reapers were no longer comparable to an invisible shadow following behind me. They no longer attempted to conceal themselves from me or anyone else, no matter where I was or where I was going. Despite my protests, they were posted outside my living quarters while I was inside—pacing or standing around in the garden and occasionally meeting gazes with me as I sometimes watched them from windows. They watched during my training, they watched as I ate, and they followed around me in a circle every step I took.

Not *a few*. A *great many* of them.

I did not mind them being there when I would walk from where I stayed to where Abby stayed, as they prevented anyone from getting close to me. I was surprised to find that I almost felt . . . *safer*, because of it. Isolated, as I preferred. They couldn't stop the staring of course, but when it came to keeping people away from me, my father's insistence matched my desire. I would *never* admit as much. If I did, I certainly wouldn't say it that way.

There were other things during those weeks. . . .

I could not fully explain why I missed Chase, given he and I had rarely spent time with one another, or even spoke, for that matter. But I felt his absence in my gut, like some unknown part of me was missing. I suspected it was tied to whatever part of me I'd felt breaking just before he left, though I was still no closer to discovering what it had been, not for lack of trying. I only hoped it would either repair itself or stop sending pangs of some unknown and utterly unpleasant feeling throughout my body.

I wondered sometimes if I simply missed him and it was nothing more or less than that. But it wasn't as though I'd been accustomed to being near him.

Perhaps I'd grown accustomed to *knowing* he was near. I was unsure why I felt the way I did at him being gone, if it were nothing more than that.

I often felt guilty, not for how I'd felt or necessarily anything I'd directly done, but for it all as a whole. All he'd risked for me and the reasons he'd done so, the lengths to which he'd gone, and all the *time* he'd invested in one way or another.

Had he wasted it? Did he feel as though he had? Did he regret it?

They were all things I wondered, but I wouldn't have asked even if given the opportunity to do so. I *couldn't* ask, when realizing how consistently people jumped to the conclusions they did regardless of one's intention. I couldn't ask regardless due to his absence, so I told myself many a time that I was *wasting* time in thinking about it.

I couldn't always help myself despite knowing how pointless it was.

I sometimes wondered how this all appeared from Chase's perspective, if he thought me ungrateful for all he'd done. I was the furthest thing from it, but how could you repay someone for something invaluable? He'd done so much for me, but I couldn't give him what he'd wanted. He'd wanted something from a person he thought existed, not the one who'd stood in front of him. Perhaps that happened when spending a great deal of time spent looking at the same thing, but one would think that would offer clarity rather than the opposite.

I supposed it was yet another thing that depended upon perspective. Nearly everything seemed to.

I occasionally found myself wondering about him during my downtime—where he was and what he was doing. If he was all right. If he was *alive*. If he felt the same or a similar loss in his gut. If he'd thought about the joined part of us that we'd both lost. If he had the same confusion over it.

If he just missed me, perhaps. Or missed knowing I was near.

I'd not heard any word on the interception team, and if anyone else had they'd not informed me of it. That wasn't unusual and was in fact only to be expected, but I liked to think that was something Jastin *would* tell me if he knew. I couldn't be sure.

When I found the courage to ask Chandler what he intended to do if Chase did not return, he answered with, "I'm staying here either way."

I did not know whether it was loyalty or obligation to me or simply that this city was far better than his own had ever been. That level of loyalty from him would've been absurd without his brother thrown in, so I had to assume it was the latter. Or perhaps it was nothing more than a lack of anywhere to go.

It would be so easy for Chandler to slip away from all this. He would not be hunted for it, given that the majority of the Reapers from New Bethel were dead. At least I believed it safe to assume they were. And though I did not want to ask my father for favors . . . I would've found a way to ensure Chandler's safety where my father and his two cities were concerned if he left. It would be worth it.

I could not fathom his wanting to stay, even without somewhere to go. But we were different people.

I could not fathom it, but it was a relief the likes of which I was quite certain I'd never before experienced.

He'd accompanied Jastin and me to Abby's quarters the last time we'd gone. Him asking to had surprised me immensely, as he had never asked to spend time with me apart from what he did with my training or given any indication that he might want to. It had . . . *flustered* me somewhat, which he initially mistook for *being put on the spot* and *not wishing for him to accompany*. After a few awkward moments of clarification, we'd gone on our way. In silence, as was typical for Chandler in general and quite typical for moving from one place to another. But Abby was anything but.

Arriving there had been something of an uproar, as was typical, only Chandler's presence altered things and her. He altered things and her, but even the uproar of her did not alter him. But I did discover that, despite feeling I knew Chandler's way of being well, I did not know him as well as I thought. As a person. Him interacting with Abby brought a great deal of internal questioning and insight.

She even got him to hold her baby. It was a pleasant memory and one I would likely treasure for the remainder of my life—seeing Chandler terrified because of some tiny little thing in his massive arms. I would never forget the expression on his face.

Abby smiled at Chandler enough during our visit to make Jastin uncomfortable.

He'd kept his mouth shut at the time, but when we were alone later that evening, he'd said, "He's too old for her."

"About the same age difference between the two of us." I was unable to stop myself from saying, "I truly don't understand this lack of logic in belief that people are too old for people."

It wasn't like talking to Amber about Chase being too old for her. She was a child.

His brow furrowed. "What's that about?"

I shook my head. "Just something Anders said once. I understand it the other way around—people being too young for others to find interest."

"But not the other way."

Though I was unsure if he meant it as a question, I shook my head. "Besides, they've only just met. It's not as if there's anything going on between the two of them."

He said nothing more on the matter, and I fully intended on taking Chandler with us again the next time we went should he wish to go. There or anywhere else he might like to go.

Jastin would allow him to go if I wanted it, I knew, even if he did not want it.

I thought he should keep out of it, as it was not his prerogative to dictate his sister's life, just as it wasn't hers to do the same with his. If she was welcoming of who we brought with us and who we brought with us wished to accompany, I saw no reason thus far as to why that shouldn't happen. What he was concerned about was of no concern, especially not of his.

I believed my words on it helped him with it, at least to some extent. I was not concerned.

IT WAS ALMOST PRECISELY THREE WEEKS after Chase's departure when Jastin said, "I get to see my son in a week."

I looked over at him on my left where we sat on the sofa in my living quarters. "Do you still wish for me to accompany you?"

He nodded stiffly and forced a tight smile at me.

We'd not once spoken of his son nor my father's offer after that initial night of the offer being relayed, and I'd not once spoken a word to my father since then. He'd sought me out on two separate occasions, and I'd not acknowledged him past staring at him until he left.

I was . . . *inexplicably* angry with him. I'd been so sure my feelings for him couldn't become more negative than they had been, that a certain limit had been reached, but I'd been wrong. I supposed when people kept pushing past limits, going farther was inevitable. I just wondered if there was an ultimate limit, where you were pushed so far that you eventually fell out of someone's reach.

I couldn't get out of my father's reach even when believing him dea—

I did not want to think about it. I had no idea what to make of me thinking about it rather than the subject at hand. I got back to the latter.

Very quietly I told Jastin, "I'm looking forward to it."

He laughed shortly. "No, you're not."

"It's what you want," I said. "Yes, I am."

It was not a lie. You could both worry about and look forward to something, when you had multiple reasons to feel certain ways about it.

He became more anxious as the week progressed, but he was not happy. He wore his anxiety like a second skin, and I'd never seen him behave in such a way. He was distracted, sometimes not catching things people would say directly to him.

I wanted to help, but I had no idea what to do. I tried to give him his space but to also treat him no differently than what I normally would. It took some time—to figure out a satisfactory way to handle him when under different circumstances.

Many times I thought about how he'd treated me when traveling, while I'd been going through the worst parts of attempting to realize I'd turned myself into a murderer. He'd distracted me at times, and I could see now how much it had helped me. I over the week contemplated doing the same for him, or at least attempting it despite the obvious differences in the situations.

Then I realized . . . the largest difference was not the situations themselves. Looking to the past could not compare in any way to looking to the future, preparing for something in it.

So I stayed close to him when it seemed he wanted or needed me close, and I talked when and about what it seemed he wanted or needed me to. I . . . . paid attention.

It was not so different from waking a person from a bad dream, in some regards. It was closer to that than what he'd done in helping me with my situation while traveling.

The night before he would see his son, we were lying in bed together. I could feel the tension in his body and, because it was so imminent, I brought it up.

"You're not excited."

"Dreading it," he said. "I never know what to say to him."

"You'll be fine," I told him encouragingly as I rubbed the arm that he had draped over me.

That night, I kissed him on the forehead rather than the other way around, and I held him more tightly than he held me. He needed it far more than I did for a change. It was odd, but it was also understandable.

I NEARLY HAD TO FORCE JASTIN out the door on the day he'd been dreading, but once I got him going, it almost seemed as though his body just carried him the rest of the way. I walked with him through the city with my father's Reapers trailing along on all sides of us. Jastin pretended as if he didn't notice them, but I almost thought he was not pretending. He was so focused yet distracted at once.

For the first time, I found myself genuinely *glad* about the Reapers' presence, more than thinking it beneficial, or helpful, or relieving. Not only did they keep people away, but when stealing glances at Jastin's face . . . I had to wonder if he would do any good at all were we attacked or if an abduction attempt was made. I took turns stealing those glances at his face and scanning everywhere else.

Most people wouldn't dare attempting to speak to me now, not with those Reapers openly surrounding me, but a few still tried it for some reason. Some spoke with others who were nearby. Most simply stopped whatever they were doing and watched as we all passed. They watched the few that tried to approach me be intercepted. They watched the Reapers, gazes falling on hands and knives in straps.

I caught some of those gazes.

When they smiled, I would look away. Not all of them did. Some held my gaze, just standing there watching.

I searched for scars on exposed skin. Each time I found one, I would look to whichever Reaper stood between. They never looked back at me, apart from one I looked at over my shoulder.

The Reaper held my gaze with theirs and only when they grinned at me did I realize . . . it was a woman. She looked away from my face before I did hers, but I spared a short moment noticing her dark hair almost shaved off close to her head before bringing my attention forward again.

Two separate compulsions pulled at me. One, to resume my staring at the people. The other, to not look at anything. That Reaper . . . I was quite certain she'd known precisely what I was doing. So the question was whether to *play* ignorant or *be* ignorant.

The only sensible conclusion I could find was to only watch with my eyes. I didn't move my head to keep worrisome sights in view. I didn't know if it would make a difference when I'd already been caught so directly.

The walk was torturous in that way, and I found myself quite torn where my level of comfort was concerned and how it fluctuated with Jastin's level of attention. I thought many times on what Abby had said of complacency. Thinking on that was important, of course, but it did do a rather satisfactory job at keeping me from focusing on where I was actually going. I could not complain about such a thing on this occasion. So I looked, watched, thought, walked, and waited. And eventually . . . we reached our destination.

Jastin stopped once we found ourselves standing in front of a gate. The Reapers who'd accompanied us all spread out near it. He took a deep breath, opened the gate, and then stepped through.

There was fencing on the other side that you could not see through and fencing you *could* see through from the way we'd come. All along the woven-metal fencing were sharp points of varying lengths, appearing randomly and frequently. At the top, there was a tangling of that sharpness, held together with more metal. It all appeared to be pulled taut, and I had to wonder . . . If the fence was cut, would the entirety of that sharpness strike out or fall?

The people walking near gave it a *very* wide berth, but Reapers stood at intervals on the outside and between it and the high stone fencing on its other side.

There was a Reaper standing outside a door that we stopped in front of. He sighed when we came close, but it did not come across as frustrated.

"Good to finally see one." He sounded quite sincere. "Aston, right?"

Jastin nodded stiffly and the Reaper offered him a sad smile while opening the door. I was unsure how he could know which child, but . . . he had.

He almost stopped me when I moved after Jastin. I saw the intent on his face. But the Reaper took a hard look at *my* face, blinked, and said nothing at all.

He led us down a hallway, and I found myself staring in shock as we passed by rooms full of children. There were windows cut into the walls so they could be observed from the long hallway. A few Reapers also stood at intervals there, watching children who all sat in seats, stick-straight and entirely focused. None of them were speaking or laughing, not amongst themselves or to the grown Reapers who were inside the rooms with them.

I could remember speaking and laughing as a child. I'd done that often. No matter how quiet a person was, they laughed and spoke as children.

Didn't they?

In some rooms they were reading or writing. I did not want to know about what.

It was the larger room we passed that had two grown Reapers demonstrating maneuvers similar to what I was learning in front of the tiny children that I found myself grabbing for Jastin's hand. I needed to do as much, to ensure it didn't shoot to my mouth like I thought it might. My other hand I kept clenched into a fist at my side.

Jastin had his head up and stared directly in front of us, pretending he did not know what was happening all around us. But he knew.

Tears fell from my eyes when I realized . . . This was his childhood. Chase's. Chandler's. My brother's. My mother's. My father's. All of them.

What a *miserable* existence. It was *so* different seeing it, rather than imagining.

I was torn again, with one part of me thinking it was good. It gave me a better understanding on many things, and that was good. The other part was crying, saying . . . *I shouldn't have seen this. I don't want to be here.*

But I *was* where I was.

We were taken into rather large, empty room, and the Reaper shut the door behind us, leaving Jastin and me alone. There were no windows in the room, though it was well-lit with lanterns.

I rubbed Jastin's arm where he stood with one hand over the top half of his face.

"Ten minutes," he said under his breath with his eyes concealed. He breathed out loudly and repeated himself. "Ten minutes."

He straightened up when the door opened again only a few short minutes later. They were short minutes in reality, but they felt like entire lifetimes, even for me. I couldn't imagine what it had felt like to him. I attempted to maintain my composure when the same Reaper stepped inside with a child next to him.

"Ten minutes," the Reaper said before he shut us inside.

The little boy with the black hair slowly walked over to us, and the closer he came, the urge to cover my mouth with my hand became stronger.

All the stars. He looked so much like him.

I clenched both my hands into fists at my sides, only tightly enough to keep them from moving.

When the little boy was standing just in front of us, he narrowed his big, honey-colored eyes. His gaze was entirely focused on Jastin. "I remember you."

It sounded like all the air whooshed out of Jastin's lungs before he asked, "Do you?"

I could tell he was trying very hard to maintain his own composure, certainly much harder than what I was having to do to keep hold of mine. I wanted so badly to run from the room and from this place.

"Yes," the boy said. "They told me I can't tell anyone else about seeing you."

When Jastin said nothing, I unclenched one of my hands and rubbed his arm again, which brought the child's attention to me.

"Who is she?"

Jastin said, "This is Aster."

"Is she your partner?" It was incredibly unnerving how much he sounded like an adult. He nearly held himself like one as well, which should not have even been possible at that age. Unnerving and just . . . *awful.*

What did they *do* to them?

"You could say so," Jastin replied.

Aston said, "She looks too nice."

"He's much nicer than I am." I forced a smile down at the child. He looked *so much* like him.

"I don't remember you being nice." Aston looked far up at Jastin.

Jastin had just knelt down in front of his son and said, "About that . . ." when the door opened again. I knew with certainty it had not been anywhere near ten minutes yet. Jastin immediately stood again as he stared, openmouthed, at the woman who entered.

She was most definitely *not* a Reaper, as she did not carry herself correctly. She . . . *strutted.* It reminded me of a chicken in a strange way, only *very* different.

"What are you *doing* here?" Jastin demanded in something similar to shock. Was there some anger to it?

"What is *she* doing here?" the woman demanded right back at him.

And then I realized . . . *Cherise*. She must've been allowed to see her son today as well. That made sense, I supposed.

"Cherise, you've *never* come to see him," Jastin said in disbelief. "Not *ever*."

She smiled, and as she was walking toward us, she said, "I thought it was time for a change."

She didn't care about seeing her son, not at all. I knew *exactly* what this was, and all the apprehension I'd felt was replaced by anger. I struggled to keep hold on it, but keeping that hold was necessary.

I knelt down in front of the child and smiled at him. "Would you like to see how not-nice I am?"

He smiled hugely in return—with nearly the same smile Jastin had, only smaller—and nodded his head.

I might not have been able to help Jastin with his words, but I would *not* let Cherise ruin this moment for him. Once a year. He only had these moments *once a year* and so much could change in that time. So much *would* change.

As his partner . . . it was my responsibility to take care of him, and I *would*.

I stood back up and was able to intercept Cherise before she got too close to them. I did not pay attention to how beautiful she was nor to her ridiculously impeccable black hair past noticing both. She stopped moving, and she smiled at me.

I informed her, "I'm giving you five seconds after I stop speaking to turn around and leave before I force you to."

She was only able to say, "Honey, I have the right to be here. I don't care *who* your father is—" before I grabbed hold of her arm, twisting it behind her back, and turned her around. It had been five seconds and I'd given her my word.

I held onto it tightly and said, "Walk."

She didn't, so I gave her just the *tiniest* of nudges forward, which started her moving with a bit of pressure from me.

I kept her moving forward until we were at the door. "Open it."

She did not.

Very calmly, I warned, "Open it, or I break your arm."

She did.

I would've done it. With all the rage I felt toward her in that moment, I did not doubt I could have. I had the knowledge of it now; I simply had not put it to use yet. She would've been a perfect test subject, I thought. A broken arm for attempting to hurt Jastin and break this time he'd been given seemed quite justifiable in my mind.

A broken arm for disregarding what damage she could do to her own child.

As soon as I had her into the hallway, she began shouting at the Reaper standing in front of the door. "Aren't you going to *do* something?"

I waited.

The Reaper stared straight into her eyes, like I wasn't even there. "Do something about what?" He turned his back to us.

Some feeling welled up inside me at the sight of it, some strange and unknown thing. Perhaps it was many things—*too many* at once.

I started her moving, and I expected to be stopped. But each Reaper standing at those intervals observing the children moved, keeping their backs to us to the point where they couldn't have even seen us in their peripherals. It was . . . startling.

Baffling.

We were halfway down the long hallway before she tauntingly asked, "Aren't you going to go back in there? The ten minutes are nearly half up by now."

I did not respond to her. I kept walking her forward, expecting every Reaper we approached to be the one that would put a stop to this.

None of them stopped it.

"Open the door," I said once we'd reached it, my voice blank though I felt anything but.

She apparently did not need to be threatened again to do it, because she did as I asked. I shoved her not-a-tiny-bit after I'd ushered her through, releasing her with the action.

Once she'd righted herself, she turned to me with quite a large smirk on her face.

Stupid. Abby had been correct in saying as much. I could see that now, but I never could've imagined . . .

I said, "How *dare* you."

"How dare I see my son?" she asked innocently. "I gave birth to him, didn't I? As I said, I have the right to be here. You don't."

"Don't play it off like that," I warned her. "You and I both know you don't give a *damn* about your son. You didn't come here to see him. You came here to hurt Jastin, to ruin *his* moment. It's the most disgusting thing I've ever seen in all my life. And you are *so* much worse than what I heard. It's quite shocking." It was the most disgusting thing, and I'd seen so much. . . .

"Listen here." That infuriating smirk was still on her face, and it made a plethora of unpleasant feelings push a bit harder at me. "You might think you have him, sweetheart, but within the next two years?" She laughed, shaking her head. "You won't have a choice, and neither will he. And if you think I've wasted the last *six years* of my life to have some little girl—"

"I'm going to tell you what happens next, so I *suggest* you listen very carefully to ensure you miss nothing and comprehend every *word* of it." I took several steps closer. "You're going to turn around and walk away. You will never come close to him again. If you see him, you will walk the other way, even if it's the opposite of wherever you need to go."

She laughed again. "Oh, is that what's *going* to happen?"

I held the backside of my left wrist in front of her face and smiled. I pointed to the cross shape cut into it. "Do you know what this means?" I asked, keeping my voice blank. "I'm sure you do. I'm sure you've seen it enough."

"Reaper," she said through her teeth. The realization seemed to set in, and she shook her head in something I thought might've been disbelief. "You're threatening to kill me. The mother of his child? Isn't that precious?"

"No." A larger smile took over my face. "Those sisters you slept with him to provide for and take care of?" The smile fell away, and I nodded my head. "I'll kill *them*. Your parents. And *then* I will kill you. How hard could it be in comparison to a Reaper? I wouldn't care to do it." I laughed a little beneath my breath before asking, "Do you think *anyone* else would care if I did?" I shook my head. "They wouldn't."

She spent what felt like forever shaking her head at me. "What if he comes to see me?"

"He won't," I said, my voice blank again. "But I won't do anything to you or your family if he does." I took a very deep breath. "You listen to me. I've already killed for him once, and I'd gladly do it again. So unless or until he comes to you and tells you he wants you near him . . . you *will* stay away from him. And you will stay *much* farther than that from the son you disowned." Perhaps distance wasn't always a bad thing, though I never could've imagined, especially not after having stepped inside the building. But perhaps sometimes the building was better. If his own mother . . . "Do you hear me?"

"I hear you," she said snottily.

If she could be so uncaring of what she'd brought into the world . . .

Perhaps the building was sometimes better.

"*Walk*," I told her.

And she did.

CHAPTER FOURTEEN

FAMILY

I WATCHED CHERISE'S BACK as she'd been following my instruction and walking away. The few Reapers within sight watched as well. The situation was over and they could stop pretending they'd not seen anything, that they didn't know what I was doing or even where I was. One of them watched Cherise, but I could feel the gazes of all the others on me.

I remained standing there near the door, even when Cherise disappeared around a corner of stone, shooting me a glare over her shoulder just before she did. It didn't faze me in the slightest.

I wondered if she thought it did or had, whether it had been done purposely or she'd simply been unable to help or stop herself.

She passed by the one Reaper who'd been watching her, standing at that corner, and she paid them no mind.

That Reaper kept their eyes on her for nearly another minute after she disappeared from my sight before they fell on me.

I was quite certain it was the very same female who'd been walking behind me on the way here, only she did not grin at me now. She just stared at me.

I couldn't be certain it was the same one with the distance between us, but I thought it was.

Assuming Cherise was then out of that Reaper's view as well, I turned, opened the door I'd pushed Cherise through, and stepped back inside. I liked to think she kept walking to wherever she should've been, that she'd grasped what I'd told her and wasn't waiting just around the corner to return and have a worse repeat of the situation, but I did not believe much stock could be put into intelligence levels. Still, I believed she'd grasped it well enough.

I knew the ten minutes were up as I was walking down the hallway once more. I looked straight forward, ignoring the windows cut into the walls and what lay just on the other side. If not looking at something meant ignoring it. For some reason, the Reaper who'd brought Jastin's son to him was still standing outside the same door. Alone.

"I figured you would want to see him for a moment," he told me. "I also figured I could get away with it on this one occasion, given who you are." Get away with an extension of time for a father to see his son.

They were all people, in their ways. Some more than others.

"Thank you," I said quietly. "If anyone says anything to you about it, send them to me and I'll take care of it. And if his mother returns . . . don't let her anywhere near him, even if it's on the appropriate day. Please." I didn't think it was right for her to use her son like a weapon, potentially hurting him along with others. It might not have hurt him now while he was so young and couldn't understand, but someday . . .

It could.

The Reaper smiled a little in a closed way and nodded. I assumed he was the one who always showed parents to their children, or that in reverse depending upon how one wanted to look at it. It must've been a miserable job. A miserable job in a miserable place. I did not want him to get into trouble for being considerate to me or anyone else. I was quite sure I could find a way to stop anything bad from happening to him, at least on this one occasion. Some things seemed worth it.

It shouldn't have been this way in the first place, more than what other cities were permitted or not. It was still awful.

I would do what I had to if something happened and I was required to with this, and I supposed . . .

My father was who he was whether anyone cared or not. Whether anyone wanted to admit it was relevant or not.

I opened the door and stepped back inside.

Both occupants of the room looked at me in nearly the exact same way, though Aston had to turn around to give me *the face*. It was so unsettling.

I took a deep breath and calmly walked over to them. Or calmly enough to come off that way whether I was or not.

They both seemed very . . . *sad*. I found I was unhappy I'd missed all that had transpired, which was a rather strange thing to be feeling after and considering everything.

"Why are you crying?" Aston asked me when I knelt down next to Jastin in front of him.

I hadn't realized I was. "There are very bad people in the world. It makes me sad to see it."

"We're not supposed to cry." His gaze moved slowly from my eyes down to my cheek then back. "They said it makes us weak."

"Well." I knew what I was going to say, but I thought back to what Anders had recently told me about my mother. I changed my response. "They're wrong."

I expected Aston to tell me they were always right, for some reason, but he just stared at me.

"That lady . . ." he said a few seconds later. "She's . . . a bad lady?"

"Yes," I answered. I felt her doing what she had with using her son as a weapon had killed any lingering doubt inside my head on that.

People were always so biased in some way or another when personally involved. I had no more lingering doubts pertaining to Cherise's character.

"They tell us we're supposed to be good," Aston said, "but they teach us bad things. I know it's bad."

So much passed through my head at once, about good and bad. The differences between the two was one thing—that sometimes-hazy line. But there were different sorts of bad, the same as there were different sorts of pain.

I'd had my childhood stolen from me, but this little boy . . .

This little boy who looked so much like his father that I trusted so much, that I *loved* . . .

He'd never been allowed one.

It was all so . . . *bad*. And it only got worse.

I forced a smile at him as my jaw quivered. "Sometimes it's better to know bad things," I said, speaking as slowly as he'd done. "Knowledge teaches you the difference between right and wrong. When you get older, you'll have to do bad things, but it's all right. So long as you do them for the right reason . . . it's all right." I sniffled a little.

"What's the right reason?"

"To keep other people safe," I told him. "People you care for."

"Is that what you were doing?" He asked the question, and I could tell he was trying so hard to understand. "With the lady? Keeping your partner safe?"

"Keeping him and you both safe."

"Why?" His voice went so quiet.

"She came here to hurt him with you," I said, which made him frown. Then I whispered a question. "Can you keep a secret?"

Aston nodded his head.

"Aster." Jastin's voice was a warning that I promptly ignored.

"You cannot tell anyone," I told Aston. "Not your friends, not your instructors. Not *anyone*. It can be a special secret between the three of us. Would you like that?"

He smiled hugely and nodded again.

I asked, "Do you know who my father is?"

"Jastin said it's Garin," Aston said. "Our leader. Is that true?"

"It is." I nodded. "Do you know who *your* father is?"

"*Aster*," Jastin said again.

Aston frowned and shook his head slowly. Did he even know that he had one? I was surprised he knew what a father *was*, even in the simplest of definitions. He surely had no idea on the complex one. He'd not been allowed to.

"This man." I grabbed Jastin's arm and ignored my quivering jaw. "This is your father. It's why he comes to see you when he's allowed to."

Aston's eyes went wide as he took Jastin in, almost like he was seeing him for the first time.

"My . . . father," he said quietly. He seemed to be processing the information, and as soon as he had, four words fell out of his mouth. "Will you take me?"

Had he seen other children with their parents? *How?*

"He can't," I said, which brought Aston's attention back to me.

His little lip began trembling, and it broke my heart into what felt like a million tiny pieces, which all then broke a second time.

"But I'm going to make you a promise right now, all right? We're going to come see you when they allow us to. And then . . . when you get older, I'm going to give you an assignment."

"A mission?" His face sort of brightened. "You can do that?"

I forced a smile and nodded again. "One day when you're bigger and we come to see you, we're going to take you and you're going to work with us. So you have to promise me two things. The first is that you won't tell *anyone*, and the second is that you'll work *extremely* hard until that time."

He smiled hugely for a moment, but then it faltered and sputtered out. "What if you're not alive then?"

"Can you keep another secret?"

I waited until he nodded.

"Your father and I love each other very much. If you don't know the word, it means we'll keep each other alive. We have to, don't we? So we can come back for you?"

I could not tell if he was smiling or crying, but he lurched forward and latched onto me. I expected to feel awkward when I rubbed his tiny little back, but I did not. I felt only sadness. Perhaps it overshadowed the awkwardness.

He pulled away a little and asked, "Will you be my mother?"

I could feel my breathing sputtering in my nose when I said, "One day, perhaps." I took a deep breath in an attempt to compose myself. "Have a moment with your father."

He let go of me entirely and turned his attention back to Jastin.

I'd just seen Aston reach out for Jastin's teary face before I'd turned all the way around.

Aston said, "You do look like me."

The laugh Jastin made in response sounded incredibly painful. "Yeah, I do."

I walked to the halfway point from where the two of them were and the door, keeping my back to them. I could maintain my composure until I was back inside my quarters. If not until then, I could at least manage it until Aston was gone from the room. I listened to my own breathing to calm myself, focusing on slowing it.

It was only about two minutes later when the Reaper walked back inside. "I'm sorry." His voice was quiet as he passed me and went to retrieve Aston. I wasn't sure what he was apologizing for.

When the two of them were passing together and the Reaper distinctly had his head turned away, I smiled and placed my finger over my lips. Aston smiled hugely once more and nodded. He waved at me and I returned it. Then the two of them were gone.

"Did you mean that?" Jastin said when he came up behind me.

I sniffled again. "You can inform my father I'll not be going anywhere."

He did not say anything else. He turned me around and kissed me. I didn't know what sort of kiss it was, as I'd not ever been kissed that way to know. It was sad, and happy, and miserable all at once. It was so many things. It felt like everything, in a way.

Jastin still had his eyes closed long after he pulled himself away, and he wiped at them when they opened. "Let's go." He took my hand in his.

We walked.

Once we were out of the building, he looked down at our joined hands and said, "We shouldn't touch where people can see. I shouldn't have taken it in the first place."

I nodded stiffly and dropped his hand. As we walked, I did not mind that I was crying for nearly everyone in the city to see. They would not know why, and they could not get close enough to say anything to me about it.

Better for them to see the tears than know why they fell.

THE WALK BACK TO MY QUARTERS seemed both long and short at once as I attempted to process everything—what I had said, done, promised, and felt. I'd not been expecting any of it. I could never have prepared myself for it.

Would I still have gone if I'd known?

I could not discover an answer to that question no matter how hard I searched for one. I was so torn.

When we reached our destination, Jastin and I crawled into bed, but we did not lie down. We just sat there staring at one another. It felt as though the two of us were venturing off into some strange new land together. I didn't know what to think about it.

"I should tell you . . ." I began carefully, not knowing how he would handle what I was about to say. "I threatened to kill Cherise's entire family."

And he laughed. The smile on his face was the first genuine one not tinged with sadness that I'd seen in quite some time. "Did you?"

"Yes," I said guiltily. "I was very angry." I was *still* angry, but there was so much more.

"But you meant it."

"Well, yes," I admitted even more guiltily. I'd meant every single word of it.

"I would've done the same for you." His voice implied he didn't care at all, but I supposed it was understanding rather than a lack of care. Then he shook his head. "I guess you've finally realized you can do whatever you want here."

Anything apart from one thing, possibly.

Two things.

I nodded uncomfortably, thinking of all the backs I'd seen today without Anders or my father present. "I spent so much of my life thinking I could never have anything to contemplate wanting it. It's strange." The smile I gave him felt very tight on my face.

"Still," he said. "You shouldn't have told him those things, especially with how young he is. Even if you can get away with it, you shouldn't have."

"He needed a little bit of hope." I couldn't stop the sadness in my tone. "Age is no excuse not to give a person some if you can." I shook my head and felt the tears starting again in my eyes. "I couldn't help myself. He's like a tiny version of you, and it just . . ." I trailed off and struggled to find the appropriate words. "I don't know. It broke my heart." It broke my heart the likes of which I'd never experienced before, in some strange and incomprehensible way that seemed impossible.

He shook his head vacantly as he stared down at the blanket. "Do you know why I call you Star?"

"Because we can't have anything more with one another," I said as I pretended to be tracing invisible lines on the blanket. "Untouchable." Safe and untouchable despite existing and being so visible at certain times.

"That's not why." His laugh sounded uncomfortable. "It's like . . . everything is darkness. Or it was. Then you come along and light everything up, and there's no more darkness." I was *certain* his next laugh was uncomfortable. "I can't see anything else, even when I tried to."

It was almost funny, given I'd always thought Jastin was such an asshole initially, to realize . . . he was so very far from it. It was just easier to be that way. *Safer.*

I sniffled a little and wiped at my eyes. "You remember the conversation we had when traveling about the day we would go to see your son together?"

He nodded. "Have you thought of the one thing you haven't shown another person?"

"That wasn't the point of it," I said, staring down at the blanket. "The point of it was to show what we would do for one another, wasn't it?"

His brow was furrowed when I glanced at him. He said, "You've already shown me enough of that today."

"No." I continued speaking to the blanket. "It was limits. *How* far. Promising what I promised your son, staying in Jarsil . . . that's not all I'd be willing to do for you. So it's not how far, which means it's not what was spoken on."

"I can't think of anything more you could possibly do for me," he said in clear confusion.

I took an extremely deep breath and stopped staring at the blankets. Easier rarely equated to better.

"A child," I said when my eyes met his. "I can give you a child you could keep."

Chapter Fifteen

BETTER

T WAS APPARENT THAT JASTIN WAS NOT happy after what I'd said, but I hadn't really expected him to be. I continued staring into his eyes rather than down at the blanket as I tried to prepare myself for whatever would happen next. We both remained silent for a time, waiting.

I sat there, straight yet oddly relaxed, waiting for him to process my words and work through them however he found most suitable. Then again, being stiff would be relaxing after the events of the day, once getting past them.

He sat there, rigid and again openmouthed, as he'd been at the sight of Cherise. I tried not to let that bother me in any way, but despite knowing his physical response was completely logical given what I'd offered him . . . it still irked me a bit.

I would never say as much, as I was sure it was unintentional. He couldn't help himself.

I believed he spent that short time waiting for me to declare I'd been joking, or something similar, which I would not do. Perhaps he even thought I was being callous or cruel with what I'd said. *Cold*, to use the word he continued to. I liked to think he would know better. Eventually, he spoke.

"Aster." His voice was full of disbelief. "You don't even *want* children. You don't want to *be* here. You don't want *any* of that."

Very deliberately, I said, "Which is precisely why you should understand what it means for me to offer it." All those were the very last things I wanted in this world, but coupled together . . .

"What is it, *exactly*, that you're offering?" he demanded. "Just having a child and handing it over to me? Or are you saying you're wanting to spend the rest of your life having a family with me?" He shook his head. "You *don't* want that. Don't *even* try to convince me you do. No matter how you feel about me, we *both* know you as a person have *no interest* in that." He stood up quickly and began pacing around the room while rubbing at his face with his hands.

I sat there in silence, watching and giving him time. I had nothing to say on what he'd said because he wouldn't have heard anything that might've come out regardless.

"I don't even think you realize what you're saying." He still paced. "I think you're so caught up in what happened earlier that—"

"Lying to yourself doesn't make something true," I said, unyielding. "I haven't just been thinking about it today. I've been thinking about it for quite a while."

He stopped moving at that, shook his head, and finally looked at me. "I should never have told you what your father said."

"I would've thought of it on my own eventually," I stated. "Because of what you said to Chase while we were traveling. '*What would it be like not to have little Reaper children? To have a family?* It's what you want, isn't it?" I paused. "I can give you that."

"Do you *think* I would want it with you when you *don't*?" He almost shouted the words, and I realized I'd never seen him so angry before. Not even close. His face was quite red and a few veins in his neck were bulging out in a very unpleasant and alarming manner.

I didn't look away from his face, but he was far enough away that I could see his hands clenched in tight fists at his sides.

It didn't faze me in the slightest.

Calmly, I said, "I told you about all the questions Stelin asked me while we were traveling. I lied to him when I said I didn't allow myself to think on what-ifs. I don't do it often, rarely enough that I didn't even consider me telling him as much a lie." I paused again. "The world is bad. It would be incredibly dangerous to have a child, but . . . if we stay here, we may be relatively safe for our entire lives. And if we *don't* allow ourselves to have what we possibly could, then the entirety of our lives would be one giant question of *what if*. Don't you see that?"

When he said nothing, I breathed in deeply and shook my head.

"The only thing I've wanted in my adult life was *freedom*," I told him. "I've not allowed myself to think of anything else because it seemed to be the only thing that mattered." You couldn't have anything if you weren't free to. "I've realized . . . there are other things that matter equally. More so, even, perhaps. It all depends upon how you're looking at it. I can give up some of that prospect of freedom, if it means having the other things."

He still said nothing.

Very slowly, I asked, "What would being free even matter if I were free alone?"

I would never be free for the question to matter. I'd held onto the word since discovering my first glorious bit of freedom in New Bethel, clinging to it as though my very life depended on it.

I'd overheard my father say in the meeting that a certain sort of love seemed to be the only thing worth dying for.

If I knew anything at all in this world, it was that . . . my father was *wrong*. I would give up my life to live it in the way I wanted, and I would do so gladly without the slightest bit of hesitation. *That* was worth dying for.

But a realization had been slowly setting in on me for a rather long while now. I'd been pushing it down with *every ounce* of strength I had to spare, *hoping* I'd be proven wrong. Only I knew from experience that life only let you be proven wrong in the worst of ways.

My heart shattering into countless pieces while staring into the face of Jastin's child had broken whatever it was holding that realization at bay. It had finally hit me, peering into that child's nearly yellow eyes.

I would *never* have the life I wished. It was time for me to accept that I had nothing in the world to die for.

That did not mean I had nothing in the world to *live* for.

Jastin stared at me, unblinking, for such a long time. And I sat there, feeling so many incomprehensible things, unable to find any more tears willing to be shed.

"You're serious," he said in disbelief, his anger abated. "You're *actually* serious."

"I am."

Very slowly, he walked toward the bed and then sat back down on it. He took a deep breath, and when he released it said, "Let's get married."

"*What?*" Surely I'd misheard. . . .

"Let's get married." I had *not* misheard. "If you're serious."

"Are *you* serious?" I asked in disbelief. Why did my head not seem to be working any longer?

"Entirely," he said, his voice blank. I was almost worried he was in shock.

Was *I* in shock?

I cleared my throat quietly, pleading with my head to form some clear thought that at least *verged* on appropriate. "I've spent some time thinking on what I've proposed. . . ." I tried hard to find the appropriate words somewhere in this madness. "You've not spent any time at all—"

"I've thought about it." I was certain he hadn't blinked once yet. "I just never thought—" He released another deep breath. "I just never thought we could. If we're being stupid, let's be extremely stupid."

"Together," I added with a smile that I tried to hide. I was not anywhere near successful in my attempt. I should not have *been* smiling, given what had happened the last time we'd been extremely stupid together.

He'd almost died and I'd murdered the second man in my life.

I shook my head and whispered. "Are you really serious?"

He nodded and *finally* blinked. "I should've done this better." He stood immediately.

"Where are you going?" I asked as he was making his way to the door.

"To talk to your father."

"What?" I asked in confusion. "*Why?* How is talking to my father 'doing things better'?" What was he even going on about? Doing *what* better?

"I just . . . I've got to go," he said spastically. He'd made it all the way to the door, had his hand on the knob, and then paused. I watched his shoulders rise and fall before he turned to me.

When our gazes met, it was almost like it was the first time he'd actually seen me all day, or perhaps ever. He smiled and, before I knew it, he jumped back on the bed and was kissing me while I laughed at him.

"You're being ridiculous!" I told him.

"Am I?" He laughed as he kissed my cheek, and my ear, and my neck.

"*Yes*!" I pushed his face away. "It's quite disturbing."

When I got a good look at him, I realized he had the same unguarded expression he'd had while looking at his nephew, like he was not worried that showing me his true self would harm him in some way.

I smiled bashfully before saying, "I don't believe you can get any better than that."

His smile widened and he kissed me very briefly on the lips before jumping back off the bed. "I'll be back."

And then he was gone, leaving me lying alone on the bed feeling very slow and confused.

What had just happened?

What had I agreed to?

Had I agreed?

JASTIN WAS GONE for an extremely long time. While he was away, I figured out what it was *exactly* that I *had* agreed to, though I wasn't entirely certain in which way I *had*, only that I somehow had. I did not move away from the bed at all as I sat there and thought over it. I knew that my face switched back and forth between thoughtless smiles and extremely confused frowns.

I'd thought about the child. For weeks I'd been thinking about it, watching Jastin, watching all the Reapers. I'd done *so much* thinking—about him, myself, certain realities. Trust. Friendship. Love. Debt. Circumstances. The list went on and on.

But in all my thinking, I'd not ever contemplated getting married to him or anyone else, not even when it came up in conversation that I would overhear. Random people speaking of random love. I'd agreed to *marry* him and I'd never even *contemplated* it.

It was not so bad, I told myself. It did not mean that anything had to change between us. The dynamic would still be the same. There was the trust, and friendship, and love. That couldn't possibly change, not with the trust. So . . . what difference would it make if we did? It would not hurt anything, would it?

Could it?

Was it *so* wrong to allow yourself happiness in life?

I did not believe it was.

Jastin still had not returned by the point where I'd decided that being happy was perfectly acceptable. It was perfectly acceptable to allow good into your life when bad had no hopes of taking it away. Trust could not be broken by outside forces, so this was good and it couldn't be taken away.

After reaching that conclusion, I was no longer happy, because I worried that he would not come back at all. Perhaps he'd found some sense along the way and decided to leave. Perhaps I would never see him again. Perhaps I would be sitting on this bed waiting until I was old and grey, like stone. Perhaps that would be best. Perhaps it would not.

I believed I'd gone through nearly two hundred different *perhaps* scenarios inside my head before Jastin stepped back through the door.

A difference in how I'd seen him last was that he'd put on his jacket while away.

He sat down on the bed beside me and we stared at one another. I thought each of us was trying to discern whether the other had discovered sense in the other's absence.

He smiled first, or perhaps I did. I wasn't entirely sure. But we were both smiling and I supposed it was all that truly mattered.

I still did not feel like I was floating, though my head felt as if it were spinning. I was not fond of that either despite certain things seeming to stand out a bit sharper than usual in comparison to the fuzziness of everything else. It reminded me of the night he'd almost died, of when I'd murdered the unnamed Reaper from Bethel. I did not like that.

He said, "I talked to your father."

"I still don't know what you needed to speak to him about so badly." I'd tried to figure it out while he'd been gone and had come up with nothing.

He took a deep breath and then reached for my hands. "Are you *sure* about this?" he asked, apparently having no interest in informing me of what I didn't know. "About everything? About us? Are you *sure* it's worth it?"

"I am," I said quietly. If this had all taken place the day before, I was unsure how I would've responded to those questions.

His smile was not huge then, but it was no less meaningful than if it had been. I'd never seen such a smile before, but for once . . . I did not need something explained to me to understand it.

He tugged gently on my hands and his voice was quiet when he said, "Come with me."

I almost asked him where we would be going, but I pursed my lips and nodded. I did not care where we were going, so long as we were going there together. He kept my hand in his as he led me from the bedroom and then out the door.

Being extremely stupid in good company was not the worst thing in the world. Despite its catastrophic potential, it was better than being stupid alone.

More than anything, it had . . . *potential*. One person alone could not accomplish much. Two could accomplish much more.

If we'd not been so close that night during travel, he would be dead and I would've been taken to Hasting. But we'd been close enough to make it work somehow, to fight through it and come out stronger together on the other side.

Being stupid did not matter so much if you weren't when it counted. It was a way to learn—making mistakes. And doing something strange did not mean you were doing something ignorant. Potential grew, and it did not have to be bad.

Safe was an illusion. *Safer* was not. All I knew was that he and I were safer together and there was *nothing* stupid about that.

We were better together. It was only logical, in that sense.

CHAPTER SIXTEEN

TRUTH

JASTIN KEPT MY HAND IN HIS as we walked through the old stone hallways of the House together. He didn't seem to care when Reapers looked at us and watched as we passed in such a way. He didn't seem to care about their narrowed eyes or confused expressions. Despite his earlier declaration that we shouldn't be touching where people could see . . . I found I did not care in the slightest either.

I'd spent so long hiding things, so many truths and the ways I truly felt. I'd done it for as long as I could or would let myself remember. I'd done it before my life had changed and been filled with Reapers, but especially so since, after learning how necessary it was to pretend.

All my life, I'd been pretending in some way or another. And it *was* necessary. It was as necessary as breathing. Did it always *have* to be?

Couldn't there be something genuine enough in the midst of it all?

I was as torn as ever. But I felt a sense of freedom walking with him in such a way. Not in the truest sense of the word, but there were levels to freedom. And for just a *moment* . . . I was doing what I wanted. I wasn't hiding or pretending. I was touching him where people could see and damn the consequences. And damn us all for making the world the way it was.

We lived in a world where people took advantage of *everything*. Every strength could be turned into a weakness if you let it. Every person you let close could reinforce you one instant, then you turn around and enter the next only to have them used against you, or them use that closeness to their own advantages. The very thing that built you up could be what tore you down again. And how much harder would you fall when built higher? How much more would you crumble when there were more pieces to break?

How could you *ever* repair yourself from that? How many people would we hurt and be hurt by before we learned to *stop*? Was there any way to stop? Was it even possible?

Since the moment I'd realized I loved Jastin, my head and heart had been waging war with one another. Both of them knew it was dangerous, as that Reaper had said in the meeting I'd eavesdropped on. This sort of love—with friendship, and understanding, and *trust*—was such a dangerous thing to feel. It made you think with your heart and not your head because, no matter the potential repercussions, there was *just enough* logic to it.

So when my head told my heart this was unsafe for us both, my heart countered with . . . *You're never safe, but you know you're safer together.*

Then there were the more illogical points, which made no sense but still so much at the same time somehow.

If I cared for him at all, how could I put him in any sort of danger?

You'll keep him safe.

This was so dangerous for me, especially in my current circumstances. I had no idea what to do.

He'll keep you safe.

Where was the sense in a love that caused you to do things you knew you should not?

I had no satisfactory answer, but my heart was beating inside my chest, demanding to be listened to. So I felt free of my own head, as much as I was able, when I let myself *listen*. And I did not care about the Reapers staring at Jastin and me as we walked together. I did not care at all.

We went up stone stairs and down more stone hallways. So many stairs, taking us higher. But eventually he opened a door, and the cool night air rushed in on us. He led me out into it and closed that door behind us.

"Where are we?" I asked quietly.

He grinned a bit. "We're on top of the wall that surrounds the House and runs through the city."

Our location was closed off on both sides by smaller walls that reached near the top of my head. Large notches were built into its length, dipping down at intervals that would reach upper torso on me. I'd read about this sort of structure in a book once, and I knew its purpose was defense. For and from archers mostly, if I remembered correctly.

A word played somewhere at the edges of my memory. What was it?

Parapet. Was that it?

I wasn't entirely sure. It was all walls on walls.

Though they were high, when looking out through one of the gaps . . . I could almost see the entire city. The view was astonishing, and it was also extremely odd to see it from such a perspective.

Jastin walked me down a little way to some spot and rested his arms over the top of one such gap, facing the city. "They say the king used to come and stand up here sometimes, to watch over his people."

It felt like the air got knocked out of me, but I managed to find enough breath to ask, "What did you just say?"

"You probably don't know what a king is, do you?" He brought his attention to me. "They make sure no one apart from the Reapers is taught about them, but some of the people passed their own stories down. You can't forget history entirely. It was impossible to make them forget here, so best to let the Reapers know as much as we do."

"My father used to tell me stories of kings," I barely said. "When I was a child. Bedtime stories."

He blinked at me for a moment before a sad smile appeared on his face. "Then your father must've told you our history without saying what it really was."

I opened my mouth and then closed it again, briefly pursing my lips. "*Reavers.*" The word slipped out under my breath. I felt so *unbelievably* foolish.

"There's no such thing," he said apologetically. "He must've been telling you about us. His name is much more fitting, don't you think? Of course it is, if he thought of it."

I blinked back tears as it felt like the entire world was crashing down on me. In all my refusal to think about my father over the years, I'd pushed his bedtime stories from my head along with all the other memories. They'd been irrelevant, unhelpful, *painful*. The only part of those stories I'd carried with me through the years was one aspect he'd claimed as fact.

Reavers were real and they would take me from him if they could. It was what they did.

Jastin gave me a moment—not as long as what I needed, but time was time—before speaking again.

"You see those Reapers standing up here in the distance, all around the wall?" He pointed off at some of them.

I nodded, watching them. Some stood entirely still, either looking down at the city or facing the opposite direction and staring off in the darkness at what lay beyond Jarsil. Some of them walked at a slow pace but were still so focused in their watching.

"We've been doing that since the beginning of our training—watching over the city. It used to make the people feel safe because they knew that even if the king wasn't watching . . . his Reapers were. They knew we wouldn't let anything bad happen to them. That's what we were supposed to be."

Words Anders had told me several weeks before came to mind.

Very much like Jarsil, to be honest.

Quiet, I said, "Bethel and Jarsil."

"The cities of the kings, sitting at opposite ends of the world." Jastin smiled a little then shook his head. "That's why I was so happy when your father came. He had the sense to know that it wasn't the kings who destroyed everything. It was their *ideals*, their *Reapers*. A man can kill without a weapon, but if you put one in his hands . . . it's so much easier. Weapons shouldn't be capable of thought. You cannot wield a weapon that thinks for itself, no matter how hard you try."

"That's why you all kill other Reapers." That was what the Reaper had been talking about the day I'd left New Bethel.

Your father has given us a purpose.

"Breaking the system." Jastin's voice was quiet, and it almost seemed as though he were speaking to the city rather than to me. "Or that's what it was supposed to be. We're just expanding. You can't break anything unless you have the power to break it." He glanced over at me to say, "It's never going to end. Not while any Reapers are alive to keep it going. And we *will* keep it going because it's what we were made to do. It's unbreakable."

He laughed a little beneath his breath. "They think of him like a king." He nodded his head toward the lights from candles and lanterns, glowing down in the city. "It was all part of their plan when they took over, but they didn't think it would actually work. But you put a person in front of desperate, unhappy people, have them make promises and then follow through with the things they promise . . . those people become happy and they idolize the person who made them be that way. It's genius in its simplicity."

It was . . .

He smiled sadly at me again to add, "That's why they all want to speak to you."

I was quiet when I spoke. "I don't know what to say." I shook my head a bit. "That's quite a lot to take in."

"I can imagine."

I tried.

I couldn't.

When I gave up, I carefully said, "Jastin? Why did you bring me up here?"

"Several reasons." He pulled himself away from the gap in the wall and came to stand in front of me. "One of them is to tell you that your father is preparing the proper documents to make my retiring official. I'll no longer be a Reaper." That meant he'd told my father I was not going anywhere.

I stood there blinking hard at him, waiting for him to say whatever else.

"Another is to give you something."

I did not ask him what he was going to give me, as I was simply too dumbfounded to get the proper words out of my mouth.

"My mother was never married," he said, "but your father gave me something to give to you, something I couldn't have gotten from my own, were she still alive." He reached into his pocket and pulled something out of it. In the darkness I strained to see what it was. A thin chain with a circle at the end, it appeared.

"It was your mother's," he said with a different sort of sad smile that I could just barely see.

There was a moment of silence that I spent staring at what dangled from his hand, contemplating the absurdity of it. What he had in his hand had belonged to my mother. It was something physical that she'd touched. It was proof she'd existed, more proof than a drawing. It was a physical connection, and it was directly in front of me.

Jastin again gave me some time, but I was unsure that any amount of time in the world would be enough to fathom the intense feelings which had built up inside my chest. They didn't threaten to tear me apart, only wishing to exist.

Eventually, he spoke again.

"He said she wore the ring when they were alone and then put it on the necklace to hide it when they weren't. He said that . . ." He paused, almost as though he seemed wary to continue. "When she snuck away in the night to draw them away from the two of you . . . she left this on top of some letters. His letter told him to give this to someone he knew would protect you like he did her."

I wiped at my eyes with one of my hands and then reached out for the ring and necklace. He grabbed my outstretched hand with his.

My voice sounded very small when I asked, "Are we getting married?"

"I'm going to make you a promise," he said quietly without answering my question. "And then I want you to make the same one to me."

I nodded because I felt as though I might promise him anything in that moment.

"I promise that I will *always* protect you first and love you second. Nothing else matters. Can you say the same thing?"

"I promise." I sniffled, then breathed out a nearly frustrated noise and asked, "Am I finally allowed to say it directly?"

He smiled and nodded his head, so I finally said it.

"I love you."

It felt as though all the horribleness of everything washed away in that moment. Like saying those three short words had erased it all. Like I was finally giving myself permission—to live, to love, and to have something worth having in life, no matter what it could do. Not because it was logical, but because . . . it was all right.

He cupped my face in his hand and leaned down close. "We're getting married," he whispered against my lips.

We were both smiling when he kissed me.

I was quite certain we'd not even been kissing for a full minute when a Reaper came up behind me and asked, "What are the two of you *doing*? This isn't—"

I could see the shock on his face when I turned around to look at him and he realized who I was. Him cutting himself off would've been proof enough of realization, or something close in nature.

He took one glance at the ring dangling from the necklace, now in my hand, before clearing his throat and saying, "Carry on."

"It's quite all right," I told him with a smile. "We were just leaving."

I slipped the necklace over my neck with the hand that was not holding Jastin's, and I ignored the extra throat-clearing from the Reaper as we passed by him. I was quite certain I'd never smiled in such a way in all my life.

CHAPTER SEVENTEEN

THE STORY

I ATTEMPTED TO MAKE SOME SENSE of all the intense feelings I felt as Jastin and I walked through the House once more after leaving the wall. We were silent and held hands again, taking the same path we'd taken before, only in reverse. I ignored the staring Reapers as much as I ever did, but their watching fazed me even less than it had the last time I'd seen those specific faces. I had to fight the urge to touch the ring now resting beneath my shirt. I had to fight it so hard.

At some point I realized I had no hope in the world to make sense of all this, let alone any individual aspect. I still tried despite the hopelessness of it. My head wasn't working properly, but I kept trying.

Jastin and I had just stepped back into the bedroom of my living quarters when he said, "I have something else for you."

"What is it?" What more could he possibly have?

He seemed wary as he pulled something out from the inside of his jacket. An envelope, discolored from age. I was not almost wary when I took a step forward and reached out for it; I was *entirely* so.

"Your father told me this is the first time it's been in another person's possession since he found it."

I analyzed the envelope in my hands, realizing what it must be.

My father had found my mother's ring on top of letters she'd written. This was . . .

This was mine.

It was sealed with wax somewhat messily on the back. Bits of it had chipped off at the edges, but it was still there as a whole, doing what it was intended to. On the front of it was . . . nothing. How could he have known . . .?

If there had been more than one, how had he possibly known?

I removed my knife from my arm and wedged it beneath the wax, pulling it apart. Then I sat down on the bed and removed the paper from it with shaky hands. The first thing I noticed upon unfolding the letter were the tear stains on the ink. The second thing I noticed was . . .

I closed my eyes and shook my head. Tears welled and spilled from my eyes, like they'd done from my mother's when she'd held this in her own hands.

"I can't read this."

"You can wait until you're ready," he said quietly.

"*No.*" Frustration and embarrassment came upon me so suddenly, so *intensely* that I worried it would rip me apart. "I *can't*. It all looks like loops and swirls. I've never been able to read this sort of writing." I would never be able to read this myself, and . . . I was so ashamed of it. If my mind could only see full words in those loops and swirls . . .

She'd left this for me and I couldn't even—

Jastin interrupted my thoughts by asking, "Do you want your father to read it to you?"

"Will you?" I couldn't bear the thought of my father seeing me in such a state, for so many reasons. I barely said the word, "Please."

Jastin's mouth parted, and it took him a while to speak. "I don't know that I should." He watched my face and then looked away and took in a deep breath. "If that's what you want."

I nodded and held it out to him. I felt such sadness and shame when he took it away from me, more intense than it had been only moments before. But this was necessary.

I watched his eyes scan the first few lines before he closed them tightly. He said, "Sonofabitch," under his breath. When his eyes opened again, they met mine for the briefest instant before returning to the paper in his hands.

And then . . . he began speaking.

"If you're reading this . . . I'm sorry, for a great many things. I'm leaving instruction with your father not to give you this letter unless you can understand, so if you're reading it . . ." He paused to close his eyes and muttered quite a few more profanities under his breath. He clenched his jaw, unclenched it, and then proceeded forward. "If you're reading it, that means your life has been so far from what I wish for you. It means I never return from this. It means things are still horrible enough for you to understand why I had to leave you. I would *never* wish for you to understand this."

Jastin looked up from the paper at me again, clearly hoping I would not make him continue forward.

I said nothing to him as the tears fell freely down my face. I did not feel the need to wipe them away as I typically did. I didn't know that I could.

"I'm so torn," he went on. "I want you to know that I'm torn even as I'm writing this. I don't want to go, but I have to—for you, for your father. If you're reading this then you must understand why I have to do it. I cannot let them have you and I cannot let them kill your father. I have to go. It's the very last thing in this world that I want to do, but I must. And I fear it will be the very last thing I do.

"I have no qualms with telling you that I am afraid. I've been afraid all my life. I've been afraid and running for so long from one of my greatest fears. I've seen so much death in my life, and I fear that when my time comes . . . I will be repaid in full for all I've done. I know what this will be for me. I need you to know . . . I don't want to die. I have so many reasons to live.

"I'm torn," he continued, "not due to that fear, but because I don't know what you will hear about me after I'm gone. I don't know if you'll receive this letter one day and hate me for the decisions I've made and am still making as I write this, while I have the time to make them. I don't know if you'll hate me for what I've done and for what I'm doing now. I can picture you grown, sitting there with your father's eyes and ripping this into pieces because you're so angry with me. It's what I would likely do in your position. God, I hope you're more like your father.

"I shouldn't be writing things like this. I shouldn't be writing about fear or anything bad. I don't want to leave you with that, no matter how truthful it is. Not if you're holding this letter and under-stand one truth in life rather than the other. I would not wish to worsen that. I should be writing hopeful things, so that's what I will do.

"I hope so much that I'm wrong. I hope so much that you never read a single word of this. I hope so much that things will be differ-ent, that you'll be able to live and love freely in your life. I hope you're lucky enough to find people as wonderful as I've found, but I hope that absolutely nothing in your life is the same as it was in mine. Save the one thing and what amazing, beautiful things came with it. I want you to be able to have the freedom to make your own choices and not be punished when they're right. I want you to have your freedom, my beautiful daughter, as I've always wished for ours. Every day, I've wished for ours. Every day of my life that I can re-member, no matter what else was there.

"Perhaps your father will follow through with our plan, though neither of us ever truly believed in it—secret wishes whispered in the dark. It was all a story we created together, but I must admit your father has always seen more hope in the world than I could ever find. I only wish I had his eyes. His have always worked better, and I've always told myself he must be seeing things I can't, that they're there. I just have to find them. Look a bit higher.

"Perhaps when you're older, he'll actually fight for the changes so you can have a better life. Someone needs to. My god, I wish some-one would. If anyone can . . . it's him. He just doesn't know it as I write this, no matter what people say. I've always seen it. I might not have much faith in the world, but I've always had enough faith in him to make up for it. Eyes are quite irrelevant when you focus so hard on one thing.

"If you ever get separated from your father and you're in trouble, find his brother. He'll help you if he knows who you are. I hope you've heard nothing of him by the time you're reading this, but you likely will. He and your father hate one another, which is partially my fault and partially isn't, but he would still do anything for you no matter what you've heard. If your father is gone . . . find him, and I promise he will take care of you. Trust no one else in this world until you find someone worthy of it. Be very careful, even then. Trust is a slippery thing apart from when it isn't.

"I wouldn't have done things any differently if I had the chance. You need to know that. I still would have had you, and your brother. I still would've run away with your father. I would always run with and for him, as would he. Always. I feel keeping him alive has been my purpose in life, some indescribable requirement inside me. Then I saw you. That's likely no consolation, but I hope the knowledge helps you somehow in my absence. I hope you know what I mean by that. It might be consolation if you understand, but if you're reading this . . .

"This is running far too long, but it could never be long enough. Time is pushing, though, and I must push back while I can. One must do what one must. So . . . I'm going to put this down and sneak over to where you're sleeping. I'm going to give you a kiss, and then I'll be gone.

"If I could only ask you one thing . . . Give your father a kiss for me because I can't do it myself before I leave. I already regret it more than anything, but he'd wake and he would *never* let me go. I must go. I hope such wonderful things for you, so wonderful I can't even fathom. I'll give you as much of a chance for that as I can. I love you, My Flower. Your mother."

I had not been looking at Jastin for the majority of the letter. I'd sat there staring at a wall that was made blurry by my tears. Jastin came over and sat down beside me. He'd folded the letter back up and placed it inside the envelope. He handed it to me, and I clutched it tightly in my hand in a way that ensured I did no damage to it.

I struggled to control my uneven breathing, at least long enough to say what I needed to. "I need to speak to my father."

"Yeah," Jastin said softly. "Yeah, I think you do."

He was gentle when he grabbed hold of my free hand and pulled me to my feet. He wrapped his arm around me and led me from my living quarters back into the House—down hallways and up stairs. I heard him ask people where my father was. Nearly each of them gave a different answer.

In the end, we found him in the exact same room they'd held the meeting inside of. His office. Jastin knocked on the door until he answered and, when he did, I could tell he'd been crying.

"May I speak with you?" My voice was still quiet, along with shaking from the crying I was barely keeping a hold on. All I wanted to do was let it out, but I couldn't yet.

"Yes, of course." My father's voice was not carrying as it usually did.

I looked at Jastin.

He offered me a sad smile before saying, "I'll be at the end of the hall."

I nodded stiffly then followed my father inside the room, noticing something. "What's that in your hand?"

He looked down at it in a way that was almost distracted, as though he'd forgotten it was there. He uncomfortably handed it over to me.

It was the same loopy handwriting on the letter I'd been given, only the paper was not nearly pristine. It appeared as though he'd held this in his hands nearly every day over the years.

The only words I could make out were *I'm sorry* and *I love you* near the bottom.

She signed her name beautifully, though I couldn't have read that if I hadn't known what her name was.

I couldn't really *read* it. I just knew what it was. It seemed much longer than it should be.

I handed the letter back to my father and sat down on the floor near where he was standing.

He did not sit in a chair, instead sitting across from me on a rug.

"Will you tell me a story, Father?" I asked through my tears.

He looked away and nearly sobbed. "What story would you like to hear?"

"A true one," I told him.

He nodded and wiped at his eyes.

"Once upon a time . . ." he began, "there were two brothers. They were very close and loved one another dearly, though they were not supposed to. The younger brother had a secret best friend, and she was so beautiful it took his breath away when he looked at her. She had wide blue eyes that each seemed like they held an entire sky inside them and hair that was like the sunlight.

"But the two friends were very competitive with one another in their work. And one day she failed badly, badly enough that she was too ashamed to go to him with her sadness and embarrassment. So she went to the only person she could trust. She went to his older brother, because *he* trusted him. She knew that meant she could trust him as well.

"The older brother and the girl began working together," he said, "because they formed a trust without the competitiveness. The girl was magnetic; he couldn't help falling in love with her. The younger brother had never told the girl that he was in love with her too and had been most his life. He'd never acted as though he were, and she'd never had any idea that he was. He was very good at hiding things when he felt things needed to be hidden, and he'd always and only been trying to keep her safe. He'd always been watched so closely, and the higher one is, the farther they fall. She was what he loved most in the world, which was why he had to keep her safe. From himself. He never told her, so she fell in love with his older brother because *he* showed her faith and affection. But the older brother was afraid, afraid of the world and afraid of her. So he never told her that he was in love with her either.

"Something happened, something tragic. The two of them did not agree on the level of tragedy which had occurred, and she found herself once again alone at a time when one should never be alone. In her sadness, she turned to her best friend, and he took care of her as he always had anytime she would let him before. Her pride so often got in her way. One day . . . she stopped letting it. She ran off and followed the younger brother halfway across the world just to say . . . *I love you*.

"The younger brother was foolish enough to not be afraid," he said as he wiped the tears from his face, and my right hand twitched. "He told himself that determination mattered most, that he could and would do what he always had—take care of the girl who had at some point turned into the woman he loved. He was foolish and determined, so he told his best friend that he loved her, and it was all she'd wanted to hear. They realized what love *could be* together. As fantastic as they both dreamt it could be and more. Much more."

My father looked away and said, "You know the rest. I doubt you still want to hear the sad parts, now that you know they're true. Do you understand now?"

I didn't answer his question, instead reaching out and wiping a new tear from his face as it was falling down his cheek. He grabbed hold of my hand, and I did not pull it away from him.

"You left me for her," I said quietly. "Because of what she wanted."

He'd left me for my mother and her wishes.

"When you were very young and I left, I went where I said I went," he told me. "And when you were older, I still went for food, but I attempted to gather information when I went close to cities. I went closer every time." He took a deep breath. "That last one . . . I didn't stay away by choice. I was captured and held in Bethel for quite a long time. So long that Anders caught word of it and came to help me escape."

I shook my head, hardly believing . . . "He's my uncle."

"He is," my father confirmed. "Aster, the *first* thing I did was come back for you. When you weren't there, I went to Ben's house and found it empty. So I looked in the woods for you, thinking you'd run off trying to find me, or find food. I searched for *months*, trying to find *any* sign of you. I thought you were dead, and those months I spent attempting to find your body was the absolute darkest time I have ever spent in this world."

"Who even *was* he? *Ben*. He and his wife. Who *were* they?"

He sighed heavily, rubbing at his face. "A friend. Perhaps not a friend in the way many people think of the word. Perhaps something better, though. But I *very much* want to hear how you came to be separated from them."

I pursed my lips.

"It doesn't have to be now." He held up a hand. "But sometime. *Please.*"

I stared at his face, hoping so much, but . . .

"How do I know that's true?" I whispered. "*Any* of it."

"Don't you *remember*?" He sobbed. "Don't you remember how much I loved you? Did you truly think I'd willingly leave you there to die?"

"After I knew you were still alive, yes." I wiped at my face and sniffled.

He stood and walked away. I heard a drawer open and then close, and when he came back he extended something toward me—a ragdoll he'd made for me when I was a child. I took it from him gingerly, analyzing it. It too appeared as if it had been held daily for years. I hadn't left it in that state.

I felt ridiculous when I brought it to my chest and held onto it tightly, though it did not look precisely as what I'd remembered.

"If I had known you were still alive," he started, "there is *nothing* in this world that could've stopped me from getting to you. You *must* know that."

My father did not show things the way other people did. Even Reapers had quirks which occasionally gave them away, if you paid the proper attention. He had none now, if he ever had at all. No quirks, only normal sorts of reactions in comparison, but they were often difficult to detect or nonexistent where they should've been.

I'd never seen my father as *open* as he was in that moment. His face, his voice, his words all put *him* on display. And I had to wonder . . .

Had he not even left me for my mother? Had my father left me for . . . *me*?

CHAPTER EIGHTEEN

LOVE AND SAFETY

I STARED AT MY FATHER as we sat on the floor of his office together, and I thought over all the things I'd learned in such a short time. It all seemed too perfect, to the point it was unbelievable. Even the age of the objects was clear, but it was *too perfect*.

I thought of what Anders had said about things sometimes being pure, even when they didn't seem that way. What about things that seemed *too pure*? How were you supposed to tell the difference?

I hadn't the vaguest idea, and it frustrated me to no end. What was I supposed to do?

"Tell me why you've treated me the way you have," I demanded through my tears. "If all this is true . . . *why*?"

"Aster, you are almost *exactly* like your mother," my father said slowly. "In some ways. I feel as though I have to tread *so* carefully when speaking to you, and every time I do, I still place my feet wrong. So I've stayed away from you, hoping you would come to me when you were prepared to hear the truth. You've not been."

"I don't know how to tell the truth in *anything*!" I exclaimed in frustration. "Everything in this world seems like games and lies. Where were the letters?"

He just stared at me, and I couldn't help asking again.

"*Where* were the letters? How did I not find them as a child?" I *would've* remembered seeing them, whether I could read them or not.

He pointed toward his desk. "Do you see that metal box?" He waited until my gaze found it before speaking again. "They were in there, buried near a tree far enough from the house that no one but me would ever find it. I did as much when you were three. And once a year for the next five, I would dig it up, read my letter, and then find a new location to bury it all. Always near a tree far enough from the house. Just different trees." He paused for an instant. "Are you satisfied with that?"

I said nothing because . . . it was believable.

He sighed and shook his head. "Is Stelin the spy?" he asked from out of nowhere.

"*What*?"

"As far as I know, Hasting is the *only* leader who knew of your existence. There were only a small handful of people who knew you were still alive to be able to inform him. That it's him who knows is rather telling."

"You . . ." I started and then stopped. "That *is* why you put Stelin with me?"

"Mostly." He sighed again. "Even if he's not the spy, I wanted him close just in case. If he's watching you, I can't send him on missions. I've been hoping it's him. It would be a much simpler explanation." That meant he could watch Stelin, and it also meant he'd found nothing. And he was telling me as much.

"Clear this up for me, Father, if we're finally getting things straight," I said. "You told Chase he couldn't *have* me. Why should I believe that was not your reasoning for coming to New Bethel?" I was trying to find a hole *somewhere* in this.

"Aster." He stopped for a moment to shake his head again. "The last time I saw you, you were just a tiny thing. Even if logic told me you were grown now, I still thought of you that way. I still thought of you that way until I arrived in New Bethel and saw you stab a man in the heart. Perhaps you will understand one day."

"One day when I have a child, you mean."

He nodded.

"Why are you allowing me to be with Jastin when you didn't want me to be with Chase? *Why*?" I thought of what Jastin had said the day my father had arrived in New Bethel, thwarting my plans to escape.

Do you think it's Chase your father doesn't want you involved with? It's what we are in general.

My father sat there in what I thought was discomfort for quite some time before speaking. "I want you to be happy," was what he said. "And I suppose he makes you happy. I'll say nothing on reasons I believe he shouldn't, as I know very well no one will listen to reasons why not when they're in love. I suppose it's undeniable that being near him does make you the happiest I've seen you as an adult."

I . . . *believed* him. All these months of being determined of so many things, and I *believed* him.

"So you'll allow us to get married?" I asked, forcing everything I felt far enough away that it wouldn't come through in my voice. "Have children who aren't Reapers? So that I'll stay in your city?"

"I *want* you to stay," he said firmly. "I want you to stay *right here* where I can watch over you and ensure you're alive and safe. I don't care if you get married or if you don't. I don't care if you have ten children or none at all. I don't care if you promised Jastin's son that you would get him out of there once you were able. You can do anything you want and I won't stop you . . . as long as you're safe. You've *no idea* what would happen to you if I let you out of my sight again, and I *will not* allow that to happen. It's the *only* way to ensure you're alive and safe."

Almost anything was not anything, but . . . "How did you—"

"Jastin told me," he interrupted. "He didn't want his son or Francis to get in trouble with me for what happened." He paused. "Francis is the name of the Reaper who takes the children to see their parents."

"I don't like being followed by your Reapers," I told him after a short amount of time spent thinking on the countless issues. There were so many, and I had no idea how to cover them all. "Especially near my quarters."

"Aster." He sighed again. "It's for your own protection. They're all given instruction not to tell me anything about you unless it pertains to your physical safety. Not conversations, not what you're doing. That's how I knew you were hurt before. I was told that Jastin carried you from your training area wrapped in a blanket and that you looked as though you were in extreme pain. I apologize for jumping to conclusions, but . . . it was the only explanation that made sense to me. Anything else, a cut or a break . . . you would've seen a healer. I won't insist you tell me what truly happened that day."

For some reason, I contemplated telling him, but I just nodded.

I still would not inform him of that.

"Father," I began carefully. "If all this is true . . . I want you to prove it to me."

He stared at me in silence for the shortest of instants before asking, "How can I?"

"I want you to let me in on the way things work around here," I told him. "I want to know about threats, especially to my own safety, from *you*. I want . . ." I took a deep breath and then released it. "I want to help and be useful. Will you please allow that of me?"

He sat there blinking at me for what felt like forever before very slowly nodding. "I'll gladly agree to that, but you understand that means you and I will be spending time with one another?" I saw and heard the hopefulness he was trying to conceal, clear as day.

I nodded, taking a step in what I thought might be the right direction. "Father," I started quietly. "Speaking of spies . . . have you thought about my brother?"

"Ahren?" Shock appeared on his face for the briefest moment, but it was gone after only a few blinks.

"A large part of him hates me, I know," I said. "I don't wish to believe it's true, but . . . it would almost make sense." I shook my head. "I don't like to say that. Perhaps if I had a list of all the people who knew about me. . . ."

"I *have* thought about it." I could tell he was unhappy with his admission, either at the prospect or simply saying as much aloud. "I don't wish to believe it's true either."

I wondered to what degree I should worry about my brother. But I had another query, and I knew speaking of it would need to be handled with the utmost care. "He told me before, when I learned you were still alive . . . He told me you'd left our mother to fight for us."

"I've never told anyone the truth in what happened until tonight. Not Ahren, not even Anders. She wouldn't have wanted me to, and I didn't want to. I've let everyone believe what they wanted about it because it still boils down to the same thing. She died, alone, fighting for us. That alone is all that ever mattered to me."

I nodded because I could see how it would possibly be true, given what I'd heard about my mother.

Very slowly, I brought up another point. "He also told me before that you'd expected him to destroy my heart."

My father narrowed his eyes in what seemed to be confusion. "After speaking to Chase, I sent urgent correspondence to your brother, telling him to ensure you didn't do anything to get yourself killed or abducted. I suppose to him that meant the same thing."

"Would you have killed anyone else if they'd assisted in our escape?" I tried to hide the curiosity I felt.

"I likely would have, yes." There was no unhappiness or shame in his admission. Simple fact.

The curiosity I'd felt only moments before had disappeared, replaced with wariness. "Did Ahren know that?"

"I'm sure everyone who knows about you would have the sense to know it." A few seconds passed. "Why do you ask?"

"Curiosity." I answered his question with an uncomfortable smile, trying to put thoughts of rope out of my head. But the forced smile faded. "Would you have killed Chase or Chandler?"

He sighed. "I'm not going to lie to you. I wanted to kill them when I arrived there and saw that Chase was still alive. He'd gone to great lengths to make everyone believe he was dead after speaking to me about you. I knew that him still being alive meant he had intent to take you out into the world, and I can't have children getting involved in things they've no idea on. This is not a small matter. You cannot imagine the feeling of arriving there and seeing your child's life being played with. But seeing how you defended them . . . I couldn't have done it." He chuckled uncomfortably under his breath before reiterating. "I wanted to."

I did not want to think about my father killing people, but the question had been necessary.

I didn't say anything.

Softer, he said, "I know you care a great deal about Chandler."

After a few seconds, I shortly nodded.

He shook his head. "I'm not going to hurt him. I know he was going to leave with you. I know he was helping you. I am not going to hurt him."

I took in a deep breath of relief and looked away at a wall as more tears welled, but . . .

There were other necessary questions.

I had to look at him and ask, "Are you only keeping me here because you don't want me to be used against you?"

He sighed again. "Only an imbecile would *want* for a person to be used against them. But if you were to willingly do that without having all the facts . . ." He paused to shake his head. "You wouldn't know what you were getting yourself into. So, say you were angry with me and decided to make the *extremely* long trek to Bethel . . . Hasting would eat you alive. I know that better than you could ever fathom."

You've no idea how bad the blood runs between them.

"You know him," I said. "From before. From before I was even born."

"Yes, I do," he confirmed. "He was already making a play at Bethel before your mother became pregnant with you. It would've been bad enough, having two children taken away. But we knew that if he was in control of the city . . ." He took a deep breath. "We couldn't have you there. It was already worse than it was here." He stared off for a moment, his brow furrowed.

I was silent until he brought his attention back to me.

"Is it true?" I asked. "About him murdering Stelin's best friend, June? Is that true?"

"To my knowledge, yes." He did not seem so stunned that I was aware of it, but for the split second the shock was on his face, it was legitimate. "But if there's anything I've learned over the years, it's not to believe a person is dead without seeing the body, under most circumstances. Given that I didn't see her myself, all I have is the word of a few people. It sounds very much like the man."

"And do you trust who told you?"

He sighed again. "I hardly trust anyone in this world, but in this sense?" He nodded. "I do believe it occurred, mostly due to who's involved. The first source was as close to confirmation as one can get without direct involvement. The second got it even closer."

That was sufficient.

Quietly, I asked, "Are you *truly* trying to fix things?"

"It began with us wanting to destroy things," he said. "But yes, that turned into a desire to fix them. It's hopeless, isn't it?" He shook his head for a moment as if lost in the hopelessness. "Still, that doesn't mean no one should try."

"The people here . . . they seem very happy," I stated.

He smiled tightly. "I'm trying. With all I've had taken from me . . . I don't wish to see that happen to anyone." Then he breathed out almost happily and asked, "So when is the wedding?"

"*What*?" I shook my head. "Oh. Um . . . it hasn't been discussed."

"I take it you don't want anyone to know?"

I shook my head almost frantically.

"Probably a good idea, given that it would put a rather large target on Jastin's back. The two of you standing together . . . extremely so. The larger the target, the more visible it is. It's good that you're so strange. If you were anything like most women, you would want some extravagant affair."

I quickly said, "That would be *horrible*."

Something about that made him chuckle. I could not understand why a person would want their personal life on display for everyone to see. It made absolutely no sense to me whatsoever.

"May I go to sleep now? I've had quite an exhausting day." That was putting it lightly.

He laughed. "Yes, threatening to kill an entire family can do that to a person."

I almost got angry, but he went on before the feeling reached its full potential.

"Jastin didn't tell me that part. I received a formal complaint on you because of it. I must admit I was amused, until the day took such a drastic turn."

Confused, I shook my head. "A what?"

"People come to see me or some of my men when they're unhappy," he explained. "We do what we can to try to fix their problems."

I stared at him for quite some time. "Any person in your city?"

He nodded.

"What sorts of things?"

He shrugged. "Building repairs, issues with schooling, personal problems. Any and everything, I can assure you we hear it all. Stolen chickens and . . ." He paused to laugh. "As I said, any and everything."

What a strange concept. And yet it gave me a great deal to think on and perhaps made sense of a few things I'd been wondering about, pertaining to the people here.

I asked, "What did you do about the complaint on me?"

"Inquired about it," he stated. "I brought in Francis, and he explained what happened from his point of view. Then I spoke with Jastin on the matter when he arrived to speak on another subject. They both said you'd only done it to protect he and his child. So I sent a man to her house and had him inform her that there was nothing anyone could do when people bring unpleasantries upon themselves. To pacify her, I went ahead and ensured her family was given their payment for the two more Reapers Jastin would've been required to produce with her." He smiled. "I'm sure none of you will have any more issues from her. Not unless she's hopelessly ignorant. I also reinforced the order to Francis not to allow her near the child."

I felt very awkward when I said, "Thank you."

He shrugged once more. "I'm your father. I have to take care of you when I'm able, even if you don't want or care for me to." His smile turned almost sad. "Jastin will take good care of you."

"How could you know that?"

"I watched him rather closely, given that he was partnered with Ahren. He had such potential but absolutely no motivation to go along with it. And then when I saw the two of you together, it was like a light had been lit inside his head. Once you see that and have it happen to you, you never want to go back to the way things were before. I know that from experience. So I have to believe it's best for me to stay out of it."

I smiled a little. "I really should go to sleep. I believe I've cried enough today that I may sleep for two days straight." I was quite exhausted.

He stood, and I followed his lead. There was an incredibly awkward moment where the two of us simply stood there staring at one another. Then I took a deep breath and stepped forward to hug him.

He was almost wary at first, I could tell, but then he wrapped his arms around me. I felt like a child when I remembered there was something inexplicably special about hugging your father.

He had tears on his face again when I took a step back.

I smiled, reached up to wipe them away, and said, "My mother told me in the letter that I had to do something for her."

His brow furrowed hard. "What was it?"

I stood up on my tiptoes, but I still couldn't reach. It took him a moment to realize and lean down, allowing me to kiss him at the bottom of his cheek.

I wiped at my eyes as I stepped away. "Goodnight, Father."

"Goodnight, Flower," he said. "Go to sleep. Jastin will have your back. You're safe."

I nodded stiffly and walked away. When I made it down the hallway and took Jastin's hand in mine, he smiled at me. I contemplated the prospect of being loved and safe at the same time.

CHAPTER NINETEEN

ACCUSTOMED

'D NOT BEEN LYING when telling my father that I was exhausted. With all the new information and the confusion that came with realizing how much everything was changing and what those changes might mean, my head could not process it all. I felt sluggish as Jastin and I walked through the House together, making our way back to my quarters.

I knew I should be thinking about it all, attempting to adapt or preparing myself for just that. At the very least, I should've been trying to pick apart the emotions that kept coming to the surface only to be pushed down by my intense mental fatigue. Try as I might, I could do none of that.

At some point, merely walking became quite the challenge, so I focused on that and told myself there would be time for things of importance later. After all, it would do me no good to expend what little remained of my mental energy by thinking on anything when I could hardly form a complete thought, let alone a coherent one.

I was quite concerned that if I depleted the stores, I would find myself fallen over on the floor due to my inability to walk. The mental image of myself falling down a flight of stone stairs was enough to keep one foot moving in front of the other in a way I found acceptable, if not as effective as I would've liked. I had faith

Jastin would catch me before I would fall down any stone stairs, but no sort of faith should be used as an excuse not to walk for yourself.

So I shuffled my feet more than I would've liked, but we eventually reached our destination without me having fallen over.

Upon arrival at my quarters, Jastin and I headed straight to bed.

Upon arrival at the bed, he smiled at me and said, "We're getting married."

I assumed the words alone had been enough to send a new surge of energy throughout my body, but I was unsure if there were other contributing factors. Still, the surge was sent and, a few seconds later, we somehow started kissing. I was unsure who instigated, though I believed it could be argued that his statement alone had done just that. The more kissing we did, the more I seemed to wake up.

Things became incredibly awkward, though I was unsure when or for what reason exactly. I thought kissing on the bed in the dark was reasonable to do now. We were planning on getting married, after all, and I saw no issue with it when thinking rationally. It made perfect sense for us to be doing what we were.

Jastin sucked in a breath and pulled himself away though, which left me lying there frowning at him in confusion. I'd been enjoying myself.

"We should wait."

"For what?" I asked. Wait for kissing? Why and until when? That made no sense.

"For *that* . . . until we get married."

Oh.

"That's preposterous," I told him. "It's not as though neither of us have never done it before." I paused for an instant, thinking about it. "Not with one another, obviously, but that's irrelevant. Also, we were discussing having a family. And even more importantly, it would make sense to ensure we were compatible in that way beforehand."

He put his hand over his face and laughed quietly. "I'm sure we'll be fine."

"*Are* you? If I recall correctly, which I'm *quite* certain I do, you made a statement before about how I wouldn't be able to *keep up with you.* You said it was extremely off-putting, if memory serves, which it *does.* That makes me inclined to believe we would be quite a long way from *fine.*"

It had also been what made me realize people might *not* be capable of compatibility despite—

"Aster." He sighed. "You've done that *once*. Please think about this. I'm five years older than you, and I spent *six years* with Cherise. Clearly, it would only make sense for me to be more . . . *knowledgeable* than you when it comes to things of that nature. So yes, I'm sure there will be an adjustment period, but that's all right and I promise I'm not put off by it. I just said that before to mess with your head."

"Well done at being successful in your attempt," I grumbled to the ceiling. I'd tried very hard not to think about how long he'd been with her, my age at the time that would've started, and all the time they'd had together past knowing and understanding it. His words sent a more unpleasant feeling throughout me than what those thoughts usually did, which I blamed on the day and my exhaustion from it.

"Hey."

When I looked at him, he smiled almost mischievously at me.

"Do you think I wouldn't enjoy teaching you things?"

I frowned at him and then resumed staring at the ceiling. "I don't want you to teach me anything you learned with her." It came out much too harsh, and I reminded myself that I was *very* tired. But then I realized being tired and my behavior were not as related as I'd initially believed when I thought *directly* of the two of them doing things to potentially be learned and became somewhat nauseated. It hadn't been quite so bad when there was no face and body to put to the name inside my head. I didn't care what she looked like, but now the name had a face to put horrendous images together.

I felt ridiculous for my reactions and behavior, because knowledge was knowledge, wasn't it? Was this what females always felt when they loved a person who had previously been in love with someone else? I did not like this part of it at all, if it was normal. Jastin didn't act so ridiculous with me about Chase, but perhaps it was different in some way I couldn't quite grasp. I did not see how it could be, but . . . perhaps.

Jastin tried to hide the fact that he was chuckling quietly again, attempting to disguise it as a series of coughs. He was not even remotely successful in his attempt, and it sent a new wave of unpleasantness through me. I already felt ridiculous enough without his assistance.

"Feel free to experiment on me until you figure it all out your-self." He paused before adding, "If you would prefer to do it that way."

My face instantaneously felt as though it were melting away, though I didn't quite know why. We were still on the same subject. I'd been speaking of it rationally only moments before, but perhaps my discomfort stemmed from the turn it had taken. Perhaps that had nothing to do with it at all. I was unsure.

"I am . . . incredibly uncomfortable right now." I couldn't help glancing over at him, and seeing that exact same mischievous grin on his face made me say, "Stop smiling at me that way."

He bit a corner of his bottom lip for an instant before asking, "How would you like for me to smile at you?" He tried not to smile at all for a moment, and he bit it again.

And there was something about it, after examining it more thor-oughly, which caused me to say, "That's perfectly acceptable."

His eyes narrowed, but the corners of his mouth were still trying to tug themselves up. "I thought it wasn't?"

"I've changed my mind."

He chuckled a little again, but then he sighed. "I don't want you to be uncomfortable with me. Not with anything."

"It's just embarrassing," I admitted. "I don't have a clue what to do. I'm still not sure I completely understand the feeling aspect of it. And even the things I *do* understand about the feelings . . . my head tells me it's wrong." At least when it was working somewhat prop-erly.

"Why would it be wrong?" He was not laughing at all now, which made speaking about it much easier.

"I'm not sure. I suppose I just associated it with bad things for such a long time that . . . I don't know." I shook my head, frustrated. "It's as though it's taking too long for it all to be readjusted inside my head." One instant it all seemed fine, normal and natural, then the complete opposite in the next. I didn't know which it was or what to really think of it.

"There won't be anything bad about it," he said softly. "We'll take it slow so it can get properly adjusted for you. All right?"

I smiled tightly and nodded, still finding myself embarrassed despite how understanding he was being about it. Was there any possible way to *not* feel the way I did about it?

Something popped into my head just then, though I didn't want for it to. It was a question I'd asked Chase in New Bethel.

Do you wish I was more like the server girls?

Was something wrong with me?

Jastin sat up a bit, removed his shirt and tossed it somewhere across the room. When he laid back down, he held his arm up for me to scoot closer to him.

I did.

And when I draped my arm over him, my hand immediately fell over the scar on his left side. That distracted me from the current situation in a sense, taking me back to that night several months ago.

For a time, I laid there crying in silence with my head on his chest as I traced that scar over and over with my fingers. I pictured him falling to the ground and me struggling so immensely to pick him up and carry him, his limp body lying on the grass as my father checked inside the wound. I pictured him kissing me inside the carriage when we were lying there with one another after, and how *right* it was.

None of the feelings I'd felt had been wrong then, so why would they ever be?

It was so scary . . . realizing all I would've missed out on, and would miss out on in the future, if I'd not managed to get him back to the camp that night. Was that entirely selfish or was it natural to think? I realized then what it was that I was afraid of. Not necessarily of losing him. I *was*, but it was not the most important thing. I was afraid of losing all the experiences I would share with him in the future.

I resolved myself to stop thinking of it at the current point in time. Fears always changed, didn't they? Who knew what I would fear most tomorrow with the sun shining new light on the world?

Eventually I stopped crying because I didn't want to do it anymore. I'd done too much of it today. More people had seen my tears on this day than in all my life combined. I resolved myself not to think on that either, as there was nothing to be done for it now.

I knew why Jastin had taken his shirt off—to get me accustomed to feeling his skin so close. So that was what I did. I gingerly ran my hand over his abdomen and chest, finding it strange the way the muscles fit there. Strange and . . . quite wonderful. Better touching than looking, I realized. Who would've thought, when it was so enjoyable to look?

I was doing that for a decent stretch of time before he grabbed my hand and held it in his.

I knew then that the time for getting accustomed was over, at least for the night.

I took a deep breath and attempted to get my thoughts straight. When I could not manage it, I decided to get myself thinking of something else.

"Are you sad?"

"Hmm?" He finally sounded tired.

"That you'll not be a Reaper," I clarified.

"I'll always be a Reaper, Star," he said. "All that piece of paper does is say I don't have to follow by the same rules anymore. It's just like with us getting married. It won't change what we are together. Nothing can change what a person is."

"So you're not sad," I said, pushing down a sentence that still haunted my dreams.

I believe I should remind you of what you are.

"I am the *furthest* thing from sad in every fathomable way in this moment," he said believably.

I yawned. "Can we get married tomorrow?"

He laughed a little. "I don't care. As long as we tell my sister first. She'd never forgive me if I did that without telling her."

I was not fond of the thought of everyone knowing nor dealing with the repercussions of that, but I whispered, "All right." I'd almost fallen asleep within the seconds after, but I needed to say it again, simply because I could. "I love you."

He kissed my forehead and whispered, "I love you, too." There was absolutely nothing uncomfortable about it.

I fell asleep with a smile on my face because it was nice to tell and hear the truth. It had to be good.

I WAS NOT ENTIRELY COHERENT when I woke the next morning to Jastin rubbing my arm. I'd had a strange dream, of water stretching as far as the eye could see. It had been pleasant and by far one of the most beautiful dreams I'd ever had in my life. Strange, when my dreams were often so similar and horrendous.

The water had been the most brilliant blue, brighter than the sky. The sun seemed to bring out occasional muted greens, and at some points it almost appeared clear, as though it could be both something and nothing at once.

All along the water, stars moved at intervals, tiny bits of brightness bringing beauty and a further sense of intrigue to something that was already so spectacular. It reminded me of a book I'd read a few lines of in New Bethel before putting it away due to its uselessness.

And it danced across the expanses, the trees and the water and the stars in the heavens. That which was but a hope for something greater, something impossible. All beauty in the world paled in comparison to my love for her and the

It was all I'd read before moving on to a personal journal of a previous leader, which I'd found hidden behind a stack, where he recounted his time spent coming into power. His motivations, aspirations, the things he'd done, the people he'd hurt. The handwriting had made it difficult, but it had been worth the time and effort.

I only had to wonder now if the other book could've been more useful than I'd realized. Perhaps it could've explained all the water turning red in my dream. Or perhaps not.

I was imagining what it might truly look like and, wanting the redness to disappear from my mind, asked, "Will you take me to the sea one day?"

"What?" Jastin laughed. "Where did that come from?"

"Chase told me that was where he was taking me," I said. "Somewhere by the sea. I should very much like to see it so I can stop trying to imagine it."

Jastin's entire body had stiffened, and his tone had changed when he asked, "What did you just say?"

I opened my eyes and blinked at him. "What is it?" I propped myself up onto my elbow.

"Aster," he said. "Bethel sits right on the sea."

"But the sea is so large, isn't it?" I felt quite ignorant when the question groggily came out of my mouth.

"Oh yes, it is," he said assuredly. "Did he tell you where *exactly* he was planning on taking you?"

"No." I shook my head. "But Ahren and Chandler both over-heard him saying it and neither of them were suspicious over it." They would've been suspicious were there anything to be suspicious of.

Jastin muttered off an impressive stream of profanities as he jumped up and threw his shirt on. "We need to go have a conversa-tion with Chandler." His voice was firm when he added, "Right now."

I nodded my head very slowly and got out of bed because I'd never before seen the expression on Jastin's face.

CHAPTER TWENTY

THE DIFFERENCE

CHANDLER AND STELIN were both inside my training area, possibly waiting to see if I would choose to do it today, when Jastin and I arrived there. I'd had every intention of doing as much despite being a bit late, until all the strangeness. I only hoped this was cleared up quickly so Jastin's mind would be at ease and I could return to one aspect of my life that wasn't changing with the others. Return to and grasp firm hold of it. Carry on with life while keeping my feet firmly on the ground.

The two of them were both doing their own respective training. I supposed all Reapers found the time for it at some point during the day, though one had to wonder how they found it. They stopped moving when we entered and they noticed our expressions.

Jastin looked at Stelin as we walked, and he pointed behind us toward the door. "Leave."

"What's going on?" Stelin's gaze fell on my face, then Jastin's, and back again only once.

"I said *leave*."

I did not know whether it was because Stelin technically had to follow orders from him or simply due to the tone of Jastin's voice, but he did as he was instructed without any form of objection.

"What *is* going on?" Chandler asked right before Stelin had opened the door to exit.

I'd watched him go, and he'd not looked back once.

Jastin watched Stelin as well, and as soon as he'd gone, he went for Chandler. He stepped right up, past a clear invasion of personal space, and he asked, "Was Chase taking Aster to Bethel?"

Chandler did nothing more than stare at him, and I felt my brow furrow.

"Was he *taking her* to *Bethel*?" Jastin nearly shouted at him.

I expected shouting from Chandler, I truly did. But his voice was entirely calm when he responded with, "I don't know."

"Sonofa*bitch*." Jastin shook his head as though he were attempting to work everything out inside of it, like shaking it would somehow allow everything to fall into its proper place. "The interception team should've been back by now."

Chandler said, "Yes."

"Chandler." Disbelief welled up inside me, spilling out in my tone. "*Surely* you don't think it's Chase." When he did nothing more than blink at me, I said, "*Surely* you *don't*."

Chandler spoke slowly when he said, "Aster, you don't know my brother like I do."

I laughed. "*What*?"

He turned away from me and back to Jastin. "I spoke with Anders about it as soon as I woke up this morning." Chandler shook his head. "I told myself I would give him a week longer than when they were supposed to return. He said Ahren had voiced a similar concern to his father but had nothing more than a suspicion and a late team to go on."

Jastin said, "You had suspicions and you never *told* anyone?"

"He's my brother," Chandler said. "I thought she'd changed him. I *hoped* she had. I suppose it was foolish of me. I'm sure you can imagine."

"*Changed* him?" I asked. "What are you *talking* about?" This was the most ridiculous thing I'd ever heard in all my life. Was he *trying* to set Chase up?

Surely he wouldn't, but this was just so absurd.

Chandler stared at me for a moment before calmly asking, "Did he ever tell you he was the favorite in our city?"

"No." My head felt like it couldn't work correctly. What did that have to do with anything? "Stewart said something once, but . . ." Chase had never spoken on it. He'd . . .

He'd diverted the subject when I'd inquired in the way I had. In a sense.

"Aster." Chandler's voice was quiet as he shook his head. "My brother is the most intelligent and composed Reaper of his age that I have *ever* seen. You remember, don't you? You remember what happened with Camden."

I believe I should remind you of what you are.

"I don't see how that's relevant," I said quickly, not wanting the memory of hands to come back to me again. I couldn't have that right now, not with this.

Chandler looked at Jastin and asked, "What would you have done?"

"Killed him," he responded without hesitation. I watched Jastin blink several times as he tilted his head, his mouth parted. It seemed as though he were thinking very hard about a great number of things.

Chandler brought his attention back to me. "He was composed, wasn't he? Entirely? Beat him until he was almost dead and then stood up like it was nothing and walked away. You were almost *raped*, Aster. . . . *How* could he have been composed? How could he have left the bastard alive if he loved you?" He paused for the briefest instant. "You would kill someone for trying to hurt Jas, wouldn't you? Just *trying*?" Very slowly he asked, "Why didn't he kill him? Why didn't he lay another finger on him?"

"I told him I didn't want him to kill him."

"I don't care." Chandler's eyebrows rose. "He shouldn't have. Why did he?"

I blinked hard and said nothing, justifying it inside my head. Trying to.

Every answer was met with a question, leaving me with nothing substantial apart from some strange sort of pressure that seemed to be building inside my torso. I'd known when looking at Camden's face the day I killed him that he hadn't been touched since that horrendous night. I'd justified that as well, but . . .

"Do you remember the look on his face when you got me down in New Bethel? He wasn't impressed. He wasn't pleased. He was *shocked.*" One of Chandler's eyebrows rose a bit. "Do you remember?"

"Why didn't you *say* anything?" Jastin demanded.

"Because I wasn't entirely sure," Chandler said thoughtfully. "I had my suspicions, of course. I've *always* kept a watchful eye on my brother. But you see . . . ever since he was younger, he would come to me and tell me about this girl. Even when he was little, he said . . . '*She's the most beautiful thing in the world.*'" He shook his head. "So I thought *maybe* it was real. Why would he bother lying to me for nearly ten years? Why would he lie to me when he was a child? How could he even *think* to lie about that as a child?

"Still," Chandler said to Jastin. "I wanted to go with them and make sure he didn't do something with her. He wouldn't physically hurt her, I didn't believe, but after I found out who she was . . ." He paused and took a deep breath. It felt like it took forever for him to fully release it. "It was the sea comment that struck me the day we left. He'd never told me we were going to the sea. Every time I'd asked, he told me not to worry about it, that he'd had everything planned for a very long time and he would take care of her.

"Even that's not enough," Chandler went on. "So while we were traveling and the two of you got closer with one another . . . I watched his reactions. They were so misplaced. If he cared, he would try, wouldn't he? He would try to keep her affection." Chandler shook his head again. "That's what any man would do, Reaper or not."

The shortest moment passed where Chandler was silent and the weight of what he was suggesting truly began pushing on me. It felt like a slow push. Like my brother had said what felt like such a long time ago about surviving multiple stabs with time to heal between. A slow push because my mind couldn't handle it all at once. Chandler spoke before I could.

"I tried to get him to speak with her. I told him he was going to lose her, and he always said he wasn't. So was it foolishness or a lack of caring? I didn't know. I knew my brother had never been foolish, but women can do that to men, can't they? *Especially* a woman like her. She's so odd, isn't she? That'll mess with heads. But those little fits he threw?" He shook his head. "Not like him. Not at *all*. Can *any* woman do that?"

I took my chance to speak the instant he'd finished.

"You're saying he's the spy." I *couldn't* believe . . .

"I'm saying I don't know." Chandler's response was firm. "But I'm telling you right now he doesn't love you. So wouldn't it stand to reason it's him?"

"He doesn't love me. . . ." I said slowly as I nodded my head, trying to . . .

"If he loved you, Aster, he wouldn't have left," Chandler said. "He would've fought for you. He wouldn't have allowed Jastin to slip between the cracks, and we all know he could've stopped it from turning into what it did. He would've allowed me to *really* teach you how to defend yourself, without finding one new argument against after another every time I questioned it. He would've killed that piece of trash. He would've never risked getting you pregnant, knowing you were getting ready to run. And he *never* would've attacked you."

"It was pretend." The words barely fell from my mouth.

"*Was* it?" Chandler challenged. "I didn't see it. Did it *feel* pretend when it was happening?"

I looked away, my blinking becoming somewhat erratic in an attempt to prevent any tears from falling. "I was uncomfortable with being touched at all then."

"Which he *knew*," Chandler stated. "How many other ways could that have been done? How many other scenarios could've been set up?"

"It was the only thing that made sense for me to not want him." It was the only thing . . .

"Only because he made you *think* it was. Is any of that what you think love is?"

I looked into his eyes, tears blurring the sight of him then spilling from mine.

He looked at Jastin when I didn't respond. "You would've never done that, would you? You would've thought of something, *anything* else."

Quietly, Jastin said, "I would never."

Chandler brought his attention back to me. "Think about it. How many tests could that one thing have been?"

He paused as though he were giving me time to do as he'd instructed, but my mind was blank.

"How far would you go? Could he push you to do the last thing you would want? How much manipulation would it take? Can you do what he says? How desperate are you?" I did not know if it was part of his list or if he was asking me the question when he said, "Are you *that* gullible?" He shook his head. "The list can go so much farther than that."

I said nothing, staring up at Chandler's face with my jaw clenched.

"I talked to people about *after*," he said. "Did you ever wonder if he was genuinely amused by it? Do you know how much easier it is to do something when it's what you do? To put on a show and play yourself? I've followed my brother on some of his missions. I'm not going to *tell* you the things I've seen him do that would make me wonder. Much, *much* more than seducing a girl. I did see him do as much, *several* times, if you'd like to know."

I felt my mouth fall open, which made Chandler raise an eyebrow.

"Are you surprised? You shouldn't be."

"He said . . ." I started and then could not say anything else.

"I'm sorry to tell you he lied if he told you anything contradictory to that," Chandler said. "We all do it, to varying degrees of intricacy and effectiveness. Chase is the best liar I've ever seen, but I *am* curious whether he lied to you at all." He smiled the tiniest bit. "Don't you know how to lie, my friend? Haven't you figured it out?"

My mind went back to the garden in New Bethel, replaying the moment after Chase and I had shared our first kiss.

I . . . I'm sorry if I was bad at that. I've never done it before.
Neither have I.

One could pretend easily enough from drawing whatever was appropriate from something else. But the best way to lie was to tell the truth.

Tell the truth and be *very* careful.

He'd never kissed me in a garden.

He'd never kissed *me*.

I pulled myself from my thoughts and brought my attention back to Chandler. "Perhaps you're the one who's lying." Not that I couldn't believe the things he'd said after thinking about them, but because . . . Chase was not present to potentially defend himself, should there be something to defend.

"What reason would I have to lie to you? I'd get nothing from it. And believe me, if I were a spy for Hasting . . . I'd be trying to figure out ways to get you out of here, not reasons to stay."

"Perhaps you're simply biding your time," I stated.

"Maybe that's true." Chandler nodded. "But even your father knows that if Hasting is *ever* going to have the perfect time to make a strike at him . . . it's *right now*. How is waiting, waiting until you have a child your father would allow you to keep, which is *going* to happen at some point . . . How would that work, exactly?" He shrugged. "You wouldn't leave willingly. Anders told me you worked things out with your father last night, *started to* at least. How is waiting for that relationship to fully develop again beneficial to convincing you to leave?" Both his eyebrows rose. "I would've gotten you away from your father the *first* instant I could, if it were me. And I'm telling you right now—I want you *right* here."

I stared at him with my jaw again clenched, finding no way around his reasoning. "You said you all lie." I tried to be calm. "When have you lied to me?"

"And I also said to varying degrees of intricacy and effectiveness," he pointed out. "I consider me not telling you everything I know about my brother a lie, to some degree. It was intentionally misleading, wasn't it? Or allowed you to be misled. Me being blinded by my hopes allowed him to pull you into a place of deception. That is, ultimately, my fault."

I took a deep breath. "Give me some sort of proof . . . *anything* that you're not lying to me about your brother," I pleaded. I did not want to believe this of Chase. I really, truly didn't.

He stared down at me for a moment before asking, "Do you truly believe I would?"

I said nothing, but more tears welled.

He shrugged. "We've known one another for months, Aster. Spent nearly every moment of every day together. Do you truly believe I would?"

"*No*. But *please*."

He nodded his head and I was not expecting for him to take off his shirt, holding the fabric in his right hand.

"Look at me," he said evenly as he held his arms out and turned around. "Really look, Aster. How many scars do you see on me?"

It took me a moment to recover in any sense.

"Hardly any," I said upon inspection. I could not see where this could possibly be going, but wondering kept me from getting distracted.

"*Yeah.*" He took a deep breath and then released it as he spoke the word. It almost sounded . . . *dramatic*, which was not at all like him. As far as I knew. He pointed at a strange-looking scar on his arm. "This one here I got falling off a wall when I was young. I've always been terrified of heights." He sighed and pointed at one near his hip. "I got this one when I accidentally came across a Reaper from a different city while in the process of one of my missions." He raised an eyebrow. "How many others do you see?"

"A couple," I said quietly.

"How many scars does Jastin have that he didn't put there himself?"

"A few," I whispered.

Chandler spoke so slowly when he asked, "*How many scars does my brother have?*"

"Quite a lot." I hardly got the answer out of my mouth. I still did not fully know where he was going with this, but . . . I did not like it at all.

Chandler stepped back over to me and nearly got down in my face to say, "We're taught to kill quickly, Aster. Quickly and efficiently. Would you like to know why my brother has so many scars?"

I said nothing, but of course he went on.

"It's not because he's not good at what he does. It's because he *plays* with them. You saw that in him before, didn't you—with the piece of trash? I know you did. He can't *help* it." He paused. "You should know there's a difference between teaching a lesson and playing."

"Don't you all do that?" I barely said.

"We do our *job*," he said firmly. "*That* is what we do."

"Then *why* was my father going to retrieve Camden to bring back here?" I demanded.

"He wasn't going to *bring him here.*" Chandler laughed as he was speaking. "He was going to kill him. He just didn't want to say, *oh, dear daughter, I have to go kill someone really quickly and then we'll be on our way.*"

"You were there, Chandler," I stated. "You know he said he was going to retrieve something."

"Yes." Chandler nodded. "He said that to explain why he needed to leave, but then you cut in, didn't you? So . . . what was he supposed to do?" He shrugged. "I suspect he was going to allow you in there and then make you leave. Do you honestly think he would've traveled for a month with his daughter and a piece of trash who'd attempted to rape her, even with all the men he had with him? Do you *really*?" He shook his head. "It was written all over his face what he was going to do or was at least in the eyes. And if you hadn't done it yourself and asked him later why the trash wasn't there . . . Well, I'm sure he would've come up with something."

That . . .

Made sense.

"We're not *taught* to play," Chandler said firmly after a pause. "The ones who do it learn it themselves and do it for whatever reasons they do. Isn't that right, Jas?"

"Yes," Justin said. "It is." He cleared his throat. "I believe we need to have a very serious discussion with Garin."

I quickly asked, "What if we're wrong?"

It was Chandler who answered my question. "If we're right, he'll have the sense not to come back. I would think. And even if we're wrong, you should still hope he doesn't." He almost looked ashamed when he admitted, "I'm glad to be free of him." But the relief on his face could not be faked, and I thought I might've understood at least part of his desire to remain here.

He'd said . . . about not coming back. But . . .

They had both walked only a few steps away when I quietly said, "He cried."

They both turned back to me.

"When I told him about the baby . . . he cried."

Chandler asked, "Did he seem shocked?"

I nodded slowly.

"Then there's your definitive proof, Aster." He shrugged. "I'd already told him about the baby, right before he went to see you the day he left. Guess he fooled both of us, didn't he?"

"What do you mean?"

"It's easy to react the way you should when there's so little chance for it ever coming up again. You wouldn't ever talk about it willingly, and how could I say I'd told him without violating your trust? He knew you didn't want him to know. That was obvious."

My confusion over the point of what he was saying must've been apparent.

Chandler shook his head, and his voice sounded sad when he clarified with, "He cried when I told him, too." He continued staring at me, his brow furrowed. "If you still need a bit more proof, I'll tell you something else, but I promise you won't like to hear it. Do you want me to tell you?"

I stared into Chandler's eyes, nodding my head again. If he was speaking about anything . . .

"That night with the piece of trash, I'll tell you what I would've done if I'd gotten there before my brother. I'll let you know *exactly* how it would've played out." He paused before laying out the scenario. "He was distracted. Entirely focused on you. I wouldn't have even had to sneak down the hall. It would've taken a few seconds to get him off you. A few seconds to break both his hands. A few seconds to remove something from his person that he wanted out anyway. And a few seconds to grab his head and snap his neck. I might not have even tried very hard to do better than a subpar job with it so he'd be stuck like that until nature took its proper course, should that be the way life wanted things to go. That's just me." He shrugged, then brought his attention to Jastin. "What about you? Same thing?"

"Give or take," Jastin replied.

Chandler looked back to me. "Do you remember what our relationship with one another was like at that point in time?"

I didn't answer him because I believed it had been rhetorical.

"It's the *principle*. No man can stand by and let that happen to a woman." Chandler smiled a bit, stiffly, after a few seconds, but it seemed forced. "The scenario is the difference between teaching a lesson and playing. The principle separates one sort of person from another. It was right there. Everyone missed it, for whatever reason they did." His brow furrowed once more before he turned, unable to keep the smile on his face.

I looked at his back as he began stepping away, much larger than Jastin's due to larger muscles and a bit of height, not a scar to be found with easy looking.

I was watching fabric go back over, and . . .

"Because I'm his daughter."

Chandler halted, looking back at me in confusion.

"Were you only coming," I clarified as well as I could. "With us. Because he's my father."

His brow furrowed hard, and he shook his head.

"You said. Once you found out who my father was."

He took the few steps back over.

I struggled to keep my head up and tears out of my eyes as well as I could.

He said, composed, "Once I found out who you were, it concerned me that there might be differing motivation than what had been presented. Differing motivation would *not* be a good thing for you no matter what it was." His eyebrows rose. "I wasn't going to let him hurt you."

My bottom lip quivered, and I had to look away.

He began walking away.

It took me a moment to compose myself enough inside to get out, "I'm sorry."

Chandler stopped again, but Jastin hadn't started moving to be required to do so. I focused on the former, watching him raise an eyebrow at me.

"That night," I said. "In New Bethel. With the wall. I'm sorry. I never would've guessed. I'm sorry."

Chandler's mouth parted as if to speak. He glanced at Jastin. Looked back to me. "Please don't be." Glanced back at Jastin. The floor. "I need to tell you. . . ." Back to me.

I shook my head, lost.

"*I* am sorry."

My brow furrowed hard.

"For that night." Chandler glanced at a wall for a moment, his jaw clenching before he brought his gaze back to me. "I should've taken you back to your room."

The night I'd been intimate with Chase.

My jaw again quivered. I got out, "Did you sleep well?"

He chuckled beneath his breath, narrowed his eyes, and shook his head.

I'd hoped he had.

Knowing why he was sorry, I had to tell him, "I don't blame you."

He forced a stiff and tiny smile at me that said, clearly . . .

You don't have to. No matter what you say . . . I'm going to keep blaming me.

I opened my mouth to say something, but nothing came out.

Chandler continued on his way toward the door.

I looked up at Jastin.

He asked, "Do you really think now is the best time for whatever that was?"

The only acceptable and logical response to that was, "No. I just . . ." Hadn't known Chandler had been afraid when helping me to scale the wall. But acceptable and logical. "No."

He nodded and said, "No."

It hadn't been *the best time* for it, but it had been important to me.

It had been very important to me.

CHAPTER TWENTY-ONE

PAST

THEY ALLOWED ME TO BE inside the room while they were having their discussion about Chase and whether he was or was not the spy. My father, Jastin, Chandler, and Anders spoke about it in a way that seemed remarkably *free*, given I was in the room. I had to wonder whether the freedom was acceptable after what had happened with my father and me or if the subject was so personal with me that they simply thought I had the right to be present.

It took me a bit of time to make the connection and have it start really setting in on me. Despite how personal it felt—*was*—it was . . . a threat to my safety.

It was technically a threat to my safety and my father had agreed to make me aware of those. I supposed allowing me in the actual meeting where it was initially being discussed was taking his agreement one step further. Showing me that he was going to do as he said. Perhaps I was reading too much into it and potentially turning it into something it wasn't.

Either way, I did not have to ask to stay and they made no objections whatsoever toward my presence. They looked at me occasionally as though they expected my input, but I just sat there staring at nothing in their general direction.

I likely would've been pleased by it all, under any other circumstances in the world. There was *nothing* to be pleased about here.

I clearly did not want to be with Chase in the way I'd thought he wanted, but if all those things Chandler had said and implied were true . . . *how* could I have missed it? Did being so foolish about life and love truly come with such horrible consequences? Had I been *that* wrong about him? Was he really *that* good?

I supposed . . .

I supposed he was. Might've been. Was. If I had to wonder . . .

I supposed he was.

That conversation such a long time ago, talking about those *worse* Reapers who would not kill their marks quickly . . . and he'd been one of them all along. He had been talking to me about himself. *Had* he been talking about himself? Was any of this the truth or were we wrong? Who was playing this game? Was it Chase or were things simply lining up to make it appear as such?

I heard Chase's voice inside my head, asking me a question.

What would you do later, if I kept part of myself from you and you discovered it on your own?

Had he done that very thing? Had he hidden something in plain sight? Had he hidden anything at all?

If all this was true . . . he was so much worse than he had ever shown me. If all of it was all true . . . he was so much worse than I ever could've imagined.

Was I that gullible? Had I been? Was I still? I kept falling back on one thing, one question in an attempt to make *some* sort of sense of it.

Why would he do this to me?

It would've had to have been his intention from the start, wouldn't it have? And . . .

Why?

I did not like the possible answers to that question. Every time I thought of a new one, I would think of his face and his words. And every time, those thoughts seemed to substantiate something I did not want to believe.

Was I that gullible? Was I?

The decision was reached that should Chase return, he was to be taken into custody immediately for questioning and that no Reaper should attempt to apprehend him alone.

I heard Camden's voice inside my head saying . . . *And I've heard stories about that Reaper.*

Chase would not return, I was sure, nor would any of the interception team. If he was truly the spy, he would leave none of them alive. If he was not, then they had all been killed by the Reapers from Bethel by this point. Now it was only a matter of when and how they would come for me.

And they *would* come. The bad blood between my father and Hasting seemed to make it inevitable.

Stelin speculated that his father had killed my mother and, if that were true, I could understand if this were the other way around. I could understand my father being determined to in some way damage him. I simply could not understand Hasting's motivation. Was it nothing more than hatred? For what? Why now?

But I knew why now.

Me.

I was the weakness. I was the way to get to my father, and they *would* come for me.

I did not want to be taken from here. I *couldn't* be taken from here. Not with the promises I'd made and the truths I'd learned. I couldn't let that happen.

How quickly things could change. I supposed that was what happened when things being kept from you were brought to light.

WHEN THE MEETING WAS NOT ENTIRELY OVER, though things had been decided upon, Anders came over to me. I finally looked away from the wall I'd been staring at, up to his face. My voice was quiet when I said, "You're my uncle."

Perhaps discovering you'd missed and allowed a spy into the heart of all things was not the point in time to discuss less-important personal matters, but personal matters on occasion seemed quite large and pressing.

They sometimes seemed far more important.

"I am." The smile on his face seemed rather sad, but I could've been mistaken about that.

I could clearly be mistaken on a great many things.

I'd been trying to come to terms with the relation, to deal with the way it made me feel. Angry, happy, deceived, understanding, embarrassed for some reason. Betrayed, in a sense, though there was a pettiness to it in comparison to recent events. I nodded and stood up from my chair. Then, I hugged him for the first time.

"I wish you would've told me," I whispered against his chest.

"You know now." He patted me on the back. "All things happen naturally in their own time. That's all that matters."

I did not know whether it was a stroke of horrible brilliance or simply something that Anders had said, but . . . "Father." I stepped away with urgency. "The Reaper who brought you the information about my abduction. Where is he?"

"He's still here," my father replied. "I couldn't risk sending him back."

"Sonofa*bitch*," spilled out under my breath.

"Jastin," my father said. "I *know* she got that one from you."

"Be quiet, Father," I demanded, not pointing out that I'd heard him say the very same thing once before. It was entirely irrelevant. "You need to find that Reaper right now. It wasn't an abduction attempt. It was a rendezvous."

"What?" His brow furrowed.

"A rendezvous," I said. "What is the likelihood that Hasting— who, from *all* accounts is an *incredibly* intelligent man—would send a team of his Reapers into your city to abduct me when he *knows* you'll have my security so high they would never *possibly* get close?" I paused for just an instant, to let that sink in. "It was a rendezvous. Your man? He belongs to Hasting. He wasn't pretending anything with him, at least not for all of those three years. He came here to tell Chase when and where to meet up. Hasting sent one man to get another out, the more *useful* man."

My father only blinked at me for an instant before almost shouting. "Bring him in here *now!*"

"They'll know now," I said under my breath, feeling like the weight of the entire world was crashing down on me. "They'll know all about Jastin. They won't come for me." I might have been my father's weakness, but with the way it was set up . . . I was not the weakest link. "They're going to find something to use against me with—" My breath caught in my throat. "We *must* go get Abby and James. And Aston. Agatha. We have to get them and bring them here now."

"Calm down, Aster." My father held up a hand. "Nothing is going to happen in the next five minutes."

"What if it *does*?" I demanded. Things could happen and change *so* fast.

He sighed loudly. "We cannot show our hand to anyone. Aston is safe in the school. Our children are guarded like you wouldn't believe. I'll send some men to watch Jastin's sister and nephew."

"Do you promise?" I barely asked.

"I promise you that I will try my damndest to ensure nothing happens to any of them."

I nodded almost spastically, thinking about chains and just how dangerous it was to be attached to anything. I was unsure whom my father was speaking to when he went on.

"I'll send some men there now and some extra to the school as well. If Anders arrives with Bryan before I've returned, do *not* let him know we suspect anything. And if he catches on, keep him the hell away from my daughter."

I looked up in time to catch Jastin nodding, and as soon as my father had gone, he stepped over to me.

"What made you think of that?" he asked after a moment spent staring at my face.

"Anders said that everything happened naturally in its own time." I realized now that it was not any sort of brilliance, only words put in a certain order for my ears to hear. "It was too perfect, too detailed. It wasn't something happening in its time. It was set up."

It was set up perfectly enough that it would draw no suspicion. The precise route to avoid Maldir and the man running it. That made sense from what I'd heard on the journey here. It made enough sense that no one would suspect a thing with how detailed the path had been laid out. *Very* smart. Using known facts and concerns to advantage when they were truly unrelated. They needed a detailed path. Maldir and its leader gave them the excuse.

Very smart.

Almost distractedly I found myself walking toward a table that had a very large piece of canvas laid out on it. "What is this?"

"A map of the world," Jastin said from behind me.

"I didn't realize. It looks different from the only one I've seen."

"It is what it is."

"We're here." I pointed to a strange set of scribble-like markings with *Jarsil* clearly written underneath. It was surrounded by pointed shapes that I took to be mountains on two sides. I looked at the opposite side of the map and saw similar markings, sans the mountains, with *Bethel* written beneath. There was an uneven line drawn at some point between them. "Where are all the other cities?"

"This was the king's map," Jastin said. "No other cities mattered, at least on this particular map. He ruled the entirety of this side."

Though that made no sense, I moved on. "Where is New Bethel?"

He pointed to an area that was on Bethel's side of the map, though it was almost precisely between the two main cities. Still, it was distinctly closer to Bethel. "Roundabout."

"How many cities does Hasting have control over?" I asked. "How many Reapers?"

"Too many."

"My father *must* pull his Reapers out of New Bethel," I whispered quickly as a panic rose in my gut. "He *must*. How many men would we lose if he attacked the city? There's no telling how many were lost when taking over it. There's no way we could defend it when spread out so far." I shook my head, not understanding why they would do such a thing for a city so far away from their own. "All the stars."

"They weren't there to take over New Bethel, Aster," Jastin said. "They were sent to kill the Reapers. Once that was done, they were to come back."

"Then where *are* they?" I demanded. "It's been *months!*"

"Some of them *are* back." He was nearly laughing at me, I knew. Now was not any sort of time for laughing. "Some of them went to our other city and took people from New Bethel who wanted to leave with them. It's a long process, trying to ensure none of them are Reaper spies in disguise. It takes some time."

"What if we don't *have* time?"

Jastin smiled and reached out, rubbing both my arms with his hands. "It's going to be okay."

How could he even *say* that?

"Now you have a taste of what it feels like," my father said from behind us.

When I looked at him, he smiled sadly.

"Feeling you're responsible for so many people. It changes things, makes you think differently. When do you take the offensive and when the defensive? How do you take the risk when there's so much to lose? We cannot allow Hasting to have too much control, and if we sit here constantly on the defense, that's precisely what will happen. It's always only been a matter of time."

"What do we do?" I whispered.

"If I had the answer to that question, it would already be done." He did not turn around to look behind him, though I could see Anders and his companion coming down the hallway. "Time to be quiet now," my father whispered to me.

I nodded.

He looked at Jastin and Chandler—who had come up at some point—and whispered, "Prepare yourselves."

"What for?" I barely asked the question.

"A Reaper with its back pinned to a wall," Chandler replied. "Let's hope it's not as messy as it usually is."

I expected a physical pinning of a back to a wall after Chandler's words.

It did not happen.

I stayed far on the other side of the room near the map as they were questioning him, but close enough to hear.

How did you say you overheard the intel?

Can you repeat it for me one more time?

Why haven't they yet returned, do you think?

There were quite a few more of them, but it was on, "Are you *certain* you don't know who the spy is?" when the tone changed.

Bryan tilted his head a bit and knowingly said, "Interrogation."

"Simply asking the appropriate questions," my father responded. "They should've returned by now, as you well know. If there were as many men as you said . . . they shouldn't have been an issue. You know we're better-trained here than they are in Bethel."

"Trained better enough to fool you, you mean?" Bryan asked. "That's what you're accusing me of, isn't it, Sir?"

I was beginning to have doubts about my reasoning when looking at his face. He seemed so taken aback at the prospect of my father doubting him.

"Perhaps," my father said. "Though perhaps not well enough to fool my daughter."

Bryan looked at me and he smiled. My reasoning came rushing back.

"She looks pretty well-fooled to me, Sir. She's never met me. How would she come to the conclusion she's led you to? And are you willing to listen to your daughter's misplaced hunch? Females always believe they know everything, don't they? Sometimes they're correct with their gut feelings; sometimes they're not. Are you willing to bet one of your Reaper's lives on the gut instinct of a woman-child?"

"My daughter does not listen to her gut, does she, Jastin?" my father asked. "Always her head. Logic and reasoning. She's very strange." I thought I heard a smile in his voice at the end.

"Am I permitted to know what exactly it is I'm being accused of?" Bryan asked when he realized that particular tactic was not going to work.

"Treason," my father answered evenly. "Specifically: supplying me with false information knowingly, betraying your city to its enemies, conspiring against it by willingly handing over information to a spy. Not to mention that, if all this is true . . . you have the deaths of nine of my men on your hands."

"My sister was in the interception team, Sir."

"And that would make it so much more atrocious than it already is," my father said slowly as he shook his head. "Who is the spy?"

"Are you going to torture me with your daughter in the room, Sir?" he asked. "Or maybe ask her to do it for you? She probably would, wouldn't she?"

"Who is the spy?" my father repeated, sounding unfazed by the taunting.

I could see Bryan analyzing my father's face for quite some time before he smiled. "You won't do anything with your daughter in the room." Then he sighed and nodded his head toward Jastin, who appeared entirely calm. "But he will. She's already seen you paralyze someone to interrogate them, hasn't she?"

He sighed again when Jastin did not respond in any way.

"I'd rather not be paralyzed. Let's discuss a deal."

"The penalty for treason is death," my father said impassively. "There are no deals for that charge, which you know."

"No deal, no information." Bryan shrugged. "You may believe you know everything, but . . . you don't. And even if you *do*, it's nothing without confirmation. You want the information, make me an offer."

My father asked, "What do you want?"

He exhaled dramatically and answered with, "I want you to let me go. I won't go back to Hasting, because he would kill me. We all know that. So, I'll go and promise to leave and never return to either of your cities."

"Who is the spy?" my father repeated.

"Oh no." Bryan shook his head. "I want your word that you'll follow through. Let me go."

"You have my word," my father said, which caused some horrible feeling to swell up in my stomach, "and all of them have borne witness to it."

He paused and I contemplated saying something, but he'd told me to be quiet. I needed to say out of it and at least wait to see what happened.

My father said, "The spy."

"You mean the Reaper who volunteered to lead the interception team?" Bryan asked with another smile. "I suppose that's who it is." The smile fell away and his voice was no longer taunting when he continued. "My orders were to return here, give you the information I gave, and ensure someone close to the girl overheard it. There was the risk you wouldn't allow the designated person into the room to be part of the plan, so . . . if that were to happen, I was to seek out the girl myself, knowing she would tell the appropriate person who would then move on to the next part of the plan. It's someone she supposedly would've trusted with the information."

"This was a contingency," my father said. "What was the initial plan?"

"Oh, she was to be brought straight to Hasting's doorstep." Bryan chuckled. "Would've gone willingly, wouldn't she have? At least that was what he was told. So yes, this was the contingency."

"He still wants her." My father was so . . . *composed*. "What is his plan to get her?"

"*That* I'm not privy to," Bryan said with a sigh. "Couldn't risk me coming back and telling you everything, could he? Said even *you* could get the information out of me. If it's any consolation, I didn't take it as the insult he meant, Sir." Bryan smiled at my father for a moment before continuing on. "I'd imagine that Reaper will know exactly what to do to draw her out. Wouldn't you? He was very convincing, and it's clear she fell for every bit of it. Young girls get caught up in pretty things. I wouldn't blame your daughter for her gender's ignorance."

He paused and was met with only silence where he clearly expected none.

"Whatever means he'll likely use would be much cleaner than making a play for her inside your walls," he said. "That's all speculation on my part. As I said, I don't know. I just can't figure out a reason to pull the spy if not to use it to his advantage."

I found myself walking forward without my own full volition, almost as though I were being drawn in by something. My father put an arm out and stopped me before I got close.

"He won't do anything to me," I said. "He's aware it would void your deal." I spent a moment pleading with him with my eyes, begging him to trust me.

And . . . he let me pass.

I stepped close to Bryan. Not too close but close enough to see his face clearly. "May I ask you a question?"

He smiled quite widely. "Of *course*, little princess."

I disregarded his taunting, just as I'd disregarded his previous remarks.

"*Why?*" I asked. "Why betray everyone here, your sister? Why would you choose to do the wrong thing? Why would you choose to hurt people who've done *nothing* to you?" I shook my head. "*Why?*"

"That's more than one question," he said, "but they all have the same answer, and I suppose they're all close enough." He gestured toward the one window in the room. "Have you seen those people outside? Did you know they expect us to do *everything* for them?" He laughed. "Your father puts collars on wolves and tells them to be dogs. Roll over on our backs for all of them out there. At least in Bethel we get to be what we are. *That's* why." He looked over me to my father. "Am I free to go?"

My father must've nodded because Bryan turned to leave. He began walking away.

Surely they were not just going to let him go. Surely they were not. His hand was turning the doorknob when I felt my own hand reaching for my knife.

I'd not properly removed it and Bryan had not properly made it four steps down the hall before I heard a loud *thunk*.

He fell to the floor face-forward and did not move again. There was a rather large knife stuck in the base of his neck.

Reapers did not play. Reapers did their jobs.

I looked over and found Anders staring at me. He nodded toward my hand on the hilt of my knife and then winked.

And when my father said, "I gave him my word," Anders responded to it with the exact same thing I'd been thinking inside my own head.

"Yes, but I did not give him mine." Then he added something that my own head had not thought of. "At least there's no blood in your office. You can't be angry. I waited until he was *well* past the door."

I pursed my lips because it should not have been even a little amusing. I told myself it had been the delivery.

CHAPTER TWENTY-TWO

CONFUSING

CHASE WAS THE SPY. That much was undeniable now. I'd stood there inside my father's office, watching Anders retrieve his knife from where he'd thrown it. Bryan's body was then carried away to be disposed of in some unknown place by some unknown means. My father helped clean up the blood on the floor despite having taken no part in the death. I had to wonder . . .

Had Anders truly killed Bryan or had his actions and decisions killed him? I supposed means and cause were only as related as they were. Did it even matter?

Every second I spent watching the scene brought the truth down harder on me. I reached the point where I couldn't stand looking at it any longer—seeing my father scrubbing blood off the floor when he was not even responsible for its presence.

Was he responsible for it? Was the responsibility of death its own sort of chain that stretched back as far as whatever it did?

Who was responsible or at fault all depended upon how one was looking at it.

Perspective. It was all a matter of perspective.

I'd been looking at everything wrong. I could see that now, and I did not want to see anything else so I went and found a spot for myself on the floor of my father's office. I sat in front of a sofa that had its back to the scene, and I felt safe enough to think with another back behind mine between the small space that separated me from reality. So I thought about the undeniable reality of the situation rather than the reality of the scene.

Chase *was* the spy. That was confirmed. He had fooled me. Everything had been a lie. Absolutely *everything* had been a lie and I'd been too blinded to see it. How could I not have known? How could I not have seen at least *some part* of it? I'd wondered how he could do this to me, but now there was a new question I couldn't get rid of.

How could I have let this happen?

And I was *so* angry because there was this *tiny* voice inside the back of my head, wondering if we were wrong despite everything. I *had* been that gullible, and that tiny voice kept me that way. So I shut it off.

I shut it off, knowing it was the source of a greater weakness than I'd ever realized I had. Chase had known. He'd seen it there.

You think that one tiny little piece of good mixed into a giant load of bad means a person is good at their core. It doesn't. They're not a good person who does bad things. They're a bad person who does good things. You don't know how to tell the difference between the two.

I knew I should not have been so ashamed of myself. He'd managed to fool countless older Reapers who had been trained to detect deception, after all. I should not have been ashamed, but . . . I was. Immensely. I'd been the closest to it. I'd missed it.

I had been so determined not to allow myself to become blinded from things by feelings, and I'd done just that despite all the determination. But if I'd always looked at him with the same eyes, the eyes he'd opened to so many things . . . how could I have seen him any differently? I was so disappointed—with myself—because I *should have* seen it.

Jastin and I had decided to postpone informing his sister of our plans for *however long I needed*. I believed he wanted to allow me some time to grieve, as though I'd lost someone that I loved. I supposed I had, in a way, although Chase still lived. Did it count when you didn't truly know the person?

I supposed it did. The Chase I'd known and loved wasn't real, but that did not mean he had never existed.

So I grieved the loss of that fake person, the person I *had* known. It was a person I thought worthy of the pain I felt at their absence in the world, so I grieved it.

At least for a time.

Had I seen enough death yet to look into a person's eyes and see who they truly were, as Stewart had said in New Bethel? Perhaps quantity was not so important as quality, and *this* one . . .

This one was different.

Chase had stared straight into my eyes and I'd not realized the person standing in front of me wasn't even living.

I knew what it looked like now, and I would *not* make the same mistake twice. I would have to be so much smarter than I'd even realized, and they could *never* know.

This would not happen again.

"I'M SORRY," JASTIN SAID BELIEVABLY where he'd come up and sat beside me on the floor of my father's office where I still sat near the same sofa.

"Why?" I asked, curious. "You didn't do anything, so . . . why apologize?"

"Because you're sad."

"I'm not, really." I told him that rather than telling him he still had nothing to be sorry about, unless it had been said strictly for my benefit. "I'm embarrassed more than anything, I think. Ashamed of myself for not seeing it and ashamed of myself for allowing my first love to be . . ." I looked down at my hands. "Whatever he is."

"People don't have any control over love." His voice was full of apology. "I should know. And . . ." He paused for a moment. "I know that Chase would've had to have been an amazing liar for you not to have seen through him. He fooled me, too. I thought he was in love with you."

I said nothing to that.

He said nothing more.

After an extended silence, I said, "I'd like to go see Abby."

He narrowed his eyes at me, I thought to silently say it not appropriate and he didn't want to be the one to inform me of as much. Or perhaps that he expected me to already be aware of as much and was unsure how he felt about thinking I wasn't. It didn't matter.

I forced a smile. "Bad things happening aren't an excuse not to live your life. If anything, they should be motivation for you to press forward and fight for the good things. Let's go tell your sister we're getting married."

He smiled genuinely at me, but it was also tinged with sadness. I supposed inappropriateness was yet another thing that was down to perspective.

His voice sounded wary when he asked, "Are we taking Chandler?"

"I suspect we should. Perhaps it might help him feel better, though I believe he finds her exhausting. That might be precisely what he needs at the moment. Should we—"

"Should we what?" he asked when I stopped speaking and did not continue forward.

"Should we tell Ahren?" I whispered.

"Yeah, I think we should," he said softly. "We'll go see him first, okay?"

I nodded stiffly and stood.

I FELT A FEELING that was somewhat similar to panic as Jastin and I walked through the halls of the House together. Of course he would know where my brother stayed, so I was not surprised that he didn't have to search. We stopped outside a door, and Jastin knocked on it.

Ahren opened it, looked at us, and stepped aside for us to come in. He went and sat down at the edge of his bed, but we remained standing. He put his face in his hands and the first thing he said to me in *months* was, "Father told me about Chase. I was hoping I was wrong." When he looked back up at me, he had tears welling in his eyes. "I'm so sorry."

I had not believed him the last time that he'd told me he was sorry, but I believed him this time.

Circumstances made a world of difference in apologies.

"I thought . . ." He started and then stopped to look away. "I thought that letting you go with him would be the right thing for you. I had *no* idea how wrong I was. This . . . this puts me being an ass to you to shame. I almost ruined your entire life, could've destroyed our entire city. I can't ever fix that." Then he sobbed once quietly and put his face back in his hands. Sobbed, or something similar.

Very slowly, I walked over and sat down beside him on his bed. I reached my hand out for the one that was covering his face.

"I thought you were the spy," I admitted.

He did not seem angry, only blinked more tears from his eyes. He nodded in what appeared to be understanding.

"Because you hate me," I explained.

"I don't *hate* you." He sobbed, then put the hand I was not holding over his mouth and looked away again. He took a deep breath, let it out, and then brought his attention back to me. "I was angry. Jealous. But I've never hated you. You're my baby sister, Aster."

"Let's just . . . start over, all right?" I asked. "Can we do that?"

He nodded, and I wondered if it could ever be so simple.

"We, um . . . we came here to tell you something."

Quickly, he said, "You're not running away are you?"

"*What?*" I asked just as quickly. "No."

His eyes widened. "Are you *pregnant?*"

"*No,*" I said in exasperation.

He took a breath of what seemed to be relief.

"We, um . . ." I looked over at Jastin and gave him a pleading face.

He smiled and gestured with his hand for me to continue forward.

I took an extremely deep breath and looked at Ahren to get the words out as fast as I could. "Jastin and I are getting married."

Ahren blinked at me, turned his head and blinked at Jastin, and then he looked back at me. He smiled. "Are you *really?*"

"Yes," I said, but I realized it sounded more like a question than a statement when it came out of my mouth.

He laughed and grabbed hold of me. Before my head registered the fact that he'd picked me up and was very nearly bouncing me around in the air, he had already replaced my feet on the floor and moved over to Jastin.

Ahren latched onto him. "Now you'll really be my brother."

I was almost entirely certain Ahren was squeezing the life out of him, but I could see Jastin smiling. At least if my brother was killing him now, he appeared to be quite happy about it.

When he finally released him, Ahren almost seemed to be breathing in clean air for the first time in a very long time. "My god, this just made my day so much better."

"Why?" I asked. That made no sense at all.

"I was worried you'd be a complete mess right now, to be honest," Ahren said. "But to see my baby sister and my best friend so happy?"

I would've assumed that my face currently looked baffled, not happy.

Ahren breathed out deeply. "Great day. And now I can't even be angry with you for stealing him."

He laughed, and I heard myself snort.

I'd never seen my brother behave in such a way. It was quite . . . *enjoyable*. Perhaps I *did* look happy. . . .

Ahren asked, "Have you told Abby yet?"

"Doing that as soon as we leave here," Jastin told him.

Ahren laughed. "Good luck."

Jastin smiled in an odd sort of way.

I stood and walked over to the door, feeling quite awkward and more than slightly confused. Before I opened it, Ahren grabbed hold of my arm.

"Um . . ." he said stiffly. "I . . . I can see Arlene, my daughter, in a month or so."

"Do you *want* to see her?" I asked him quietly.

"Yes and no." Tears begin welling in his eyes again. "But I'm going to, even if you don't go with me."

I grabbed his hand and squeezed it in reassurance, and I smiled to say, "I'll go with you."

He nodded tightly and forced a smile, then he nudged us out the door. "Go on. I bet Abby's going to throw a fit. You'll have to tell me all about it."

ABBY DID NOT THROW A FIT, at least not one that was the likes of what I'd expected. She *squealed*, sort of like a pig, which was something I'd never heard before from anyone. Then she threw *herself* at me.

It took me several extremely long seconds to realize she was hugging and not attacking me. I could see Chandler smiling at her reaction past her shoulder. Or smiling about something. Jastin was smiling as well until he saw Chandler smiling, presumably over his sister.

Why or how that could make a person smile . . . I was at a loss.

It had almost hurt my ears. . . .

Abby said a lot of words, none of which I could make out properly because it sounded like high-pitched squeaking inside my ear. I was quite thankful when she released me and hugged her brother.

And then I was quite confused when Chandler came and hugged me. "I'm very happy for you," he said believably.

I asked, "Are you?"

He pulled away and nodded, but . . .

"You don't look happy. You never do, though."

He almost smiled, but . . . He didn't. "Are *you* happy?"

"I . . ." I thought about it. "I'm unsure how to answer that."

His brow furrowed, and I thought he was going to say something, but Abby's nondescript squealing and squeaking turned into actual speaking and drew my attention.

"When is the wedding?" I heard her ask Jastin.

"We don't know." He chuckled. "Aster wanted to do it today, but then all this stuff happened. . . ."

"*Today*?" Abby exclaimed. "That's not enough time to prepare for a *wedding*."

I informed her, "It's just going to be us."

"Us like . . . us in this room?" She gestured around. "Like all of us inside this room right now?"

I was almost entirely positive she would kill me if I did not answer her in the way she wanted. I found myself saying, "That is exactly what I mean." It had not been, but I supposed it was now.

She did not kill me.

"Do you have a dress yet?" she asked. "I bet they're making you one."

"A . . . *what*?"

"A dress," she said in confusion. When she looked harder at my face, she frowned deeply at me. "Aster, you *have* to get married in a dress."

"Says who?" That was ridiculous.

"The laws of the entire *world*," she answered in exasperation.

"There are . . . *laws* about that sort of thing?" I had never heard that there were.

She looked up at her brother. "Are you *sure* you want to marry her?"

He snorted then nodded his head.

I just couldn't understand . . . "Why are you acting so happy?"

"Because my brother is getting married to a girl that up until two seconds ago I didn't think was a complete *idiot*," she said. "And . . . Well, you two love each other, don't you? It just makes me happy."

It took me a moment to work through then get past what she'd said.

Careful, I asked, "So you would actually . . . *want* to be there?"

"Are you *serious*?" Her eyes went so wide. "My god, the entire *city* would be there if you'd let them."

My brow furrowed. "Why?"

"Because you're like . . . their *princess*," she said. "Their little psychotic princess who makes death threats and kills Reapers."

I felt quite lost when I asked, "You think I'm psychotic?"

"No." She laughed. "Just strange. Maybe a *little* psychotic, but in an incredibly good way."

I could not see any sort of sense in her logic, if it could even be called such a thing. I wondered if she somehow believed *idiot* to be some sort of compliment as well.

Her laughter soon turned into a thoughtful frown, and her tone was serious when she spoke again. "Why don't you let the city go? Make it an open-invitation sort of thing?"

"Because I don't want to put your brother in danger." My voice was firm saying that, but when really thinking about what she was asking, my skin began feeling as though it were crawling. I believed that was at least somewhat apparent when I added, "And also because I wouldn't want for them to."

"Listen, Aster." Abby held up a hand. "If those Reapers standing outside my door are any indication, Jastin's already in danger. Why not celebrate? Show everyone that, no matter what comes at you . . . you'll still be happy. Show them you won't back down to threats. That's what leaders are supposed to do—give hope to their people."

"They're not my people," I said in confusion.

"They're your *father's* people," she said, unyielding. "That makes them yours, too."

"It's not as though I would . . . *inherit them* if he died," I stated. Anders would.

"Maybe not." She smiled, and her voice was the most sincere I had ever heard it when she added, "But if it means anything to you . . . I think you would make a great leader. Just like your father."

I waited. For her to inform me that she was joking . . . I waited.

She did not.

I thought she was entirely insane, but . . . I could not deny that she believed what she'd said. Still, I thought she was entirely insane, possibly more so for that very reason.

CHAPTER TWENTY-THREE

ALMOST

I FOUND MYSELF WALKING AWAY from Abby's place in something of a daze, trying to figure out what sort of delusion she was under. Perhaps how she'd come to it in order to have gotten under it.

Chandler had remained behind with her. She'd asked if he wanted to.

I'd at first almost laughed when she asked, but then he'd said he would like to.

I'd then waited for him to declare himself going against his character and joking in such a way.

He had not done so.

It had taken me a moment to shake myself from all that and get moving from her place, to understand that I'd again *horrendously* mistook things. I'd been thinking Chandler was accompanying due to wanting to spend time outside training with me.

Jastin had been right.

I'd thought Jastin was going to protest about Chandler remaining behind, but I'd forced myself to give him a look that he must've understood enough because he said nothing at all on the matter. I had my own reservations about the two of them after realizing that might actually be a thing, but I was sure they varied from his.

He was concerned about the two of them together, which I found preposterous. I still had no idea what age had to do with anything in the sense of her potentially having interest in Chandler, and Jastin had never given me a satisfactory explanation the few instances we'd spoken on it. He continually gave reasons for his issues on it that I found either unfounded or verging on ridiculous.

I'd eventually come to the conclusion that Jastin's issues with Abby and Chandler potentially having something had absolutely nothing whatsoever to do with Chandler. Though he remained insistent that the age gap bothered him, I had to believe it was attempting to cover up a lack of something substantial. Given he could come up with nothing to justify an issue with a six-year gap, covering up seemed to be what it was.

I did wonder if it was nothing more than a brother being concerned for his sister. It was a very nice thought, but I felt he was wasting his time.

I was not concerned with Chandler's presence with Abby in that regard, nor should anyone have been if they'd heard and believed what he'd said this morning about the situation with Camden. Nor should they if they knew him at all. I did believe what he'd said, but I did also worry about her in some ways. Still, Jastin had no right to dictate his sister's life, and she'd seemed quite glad that Chandler was going to stay a while longer.

Jastin had been offended once before when I'd told him it would've been an absurd pairing the other way around, though I'd meant no offense at all to his sister. She was a lovely female in some ways, but she was not at all a person I'd thought Chandler would be interested in.

But I supposed Abby had been right without saying it directly.

I supposed that females being beautiful had more to do with things than I believed it should.

It was not my business to be bothered by, so I forced myself to think on the important matters. Because Jastin had also been right no matter what thoughts I'd had earlier on personal matters seeming pressing.

They did not matter.

There were far more important things.

I knew there were. But I did, very much, feel like the idiot she'd called me.

So I walked in that somewhat dazed state, thinking over so many things that truly mattered. I focused on the steps to take rather than the steps I was taking.

I continually pushed away the intense urge to vomit I felt every time I wondered what might be happening at my back. Urges to vomit or perhaps run back with some sort of excuse of him needing to leave.

Even through the intense focus on things to come opposed to things happening now, I noticed a Reaper intercepting a man who was attempting to make his way over to me.

He was very . . .

Old.

I couldn't explain why I was doing it, but I found myself walking over to him despite both reasoning and desire telling me I should not. There was *something* that pushed me there despite my lack of understanding. I did not know what it was, only that I felt it. Perhaps something to move my focus. Perhaps not.

The Reaper released him when I got close, but he didn't move far at all as he watched the man, intensity visible even through the blank expression. He was prepared to kill him, should doing as much be necessary. Kill him, or . . . something.

I looked away from the Reaper, to the old man. "You wanted to speak to me, Sir?"

I was quite baffled over the huge smile that overtook his face, but then it fell away. "Yes, Milady," he said. "My wife . . . she saw you walking yesterday, and she told me you were crying. We spent all night worrying about the cause of your sadness. Are you not pleased with the city, Milady?"

My mouth had dropped open, and I felt tears welling in my eyes. "You were concerned over my sadness?" How strange.

"Yes, Milady." *So sincere*. He sounded so sincere.

"May I ask you why?" My voice was quiet. I could not even see why people who knew and cared in some way for me would concern themselves over my feelings, let alone complete strangers. Why would anyone be concerned over something they were not involved in? Why would they waste the time? It was not logical.

"We've been in this city a very long time, as you can see with my age." The small laugh that came out of his mouth seemed full of humor. "And your father has made things so wonderful for us in his time here, like the stories I heard as a child of our former king. We're safe and we're well taken care of, which we've not truly been in all my many years. We should all want the daughter of this man who takes care of us to be happy." He frowned as a tear rolled down my cheek.

I quickly wiped at it.

His wrinkly brow furrowed. "Have I upset you, Milady?"

"No, Sir," I told him. "I've had a set of days that have been quite ... *trying*." I took a deep breath, released it, and then I forced a smile at him. "Please tell your wife not to be concerned over my happiness. I've very recently become engaged. Last night, in fact. My happiness is so great that I cannot even begin to fathom it. That must be why I'm currently so confused. So there is no cause for concern in that regard."

"Oh, congratulations!" he exclaimed. "I wish you all the happiness in the world, Milady." So sincere.

"And I would wish the same for you."

"My wife and I spent a very long time afraid but happy together," he said. "I've been given all I could ever ask for, to spend the remainder of my days both happy and safe with my wife. I shall die a very content man."

Was it so simple?

Could it be?

Couldn't it?

For some people.

I told him, "Then I hope you have many more years this way, to make up for all the others."

He smiled one of the most genuine smiles at me that I had ever seen in all my life. I sniffled and wiped at my eyes again because of it.

"I should've known that such a kind and wonderful man would have such a kind and wonderful daughter."

"I'm not so sure about that." I could not stop the discomfort I felt due to his words from shining through in the small laugh that escaped my mouth. "You might not say as much if you'd heard me threaten an entire family yesterday."

"Was that when you were so upset, Milady?" he asked seriously.

I nodded because it was close enough. It was *when* I'd been upset if not the entirety of why. He'd asked for *when*.

He grinned and winked at me before saying, "Well ... I'm sure it was deserved. I don't believe you would've done it otherwise."

I stood there very nearly gaping at him for quite some time before I managed to compose myself. I forced another smile at him. I did not inform him that *deserved* was all a matter of perspective. "Please have an enjoyable remainder of the evening, Sir."

"You as well, Milady." His voice was full of warmth. He'd just begun to walk away when I heard the screeching sound of a child.

"*Miss*! *Miss*!" it said repeatedly.

I only knew I was the intended recipient of its screeching when the child was intercepted by another Reaper. He grabbed her by the shoulders, keeping her in place. She didn't even seem to notice as she continued wailing, presumably for me, as she was focused my direction.

I wanted to walk away—to leave and return to my living quarters—so I could not explain why I walked over to the child instead. I again just felt as though I needed to. She seemed quite desperate.

My eyes were on the Reaper's as I approached, and his were on mine. He looked down at the child when I was almost directly in front of them. He released her but took only one step back, staying closer to her than the other had with the man.

I knelt down in front of the little girl who had tears streaming down her face.

"My *cat*," she cried.

"Your . . . *cat*?" I asked, perplexed.

"*Yes*!" She sobbed. "I left a window open and he climbed out it! I'm never going to see him again!"

I was knelt there frowning for quite a long while before I could discover anything appropriate to say to the child. I was unsure what she expected of me.

"Would you like to hear a story?" I asked her.

She blinked at me and nodded.

"Where I stayed before, there was this little white cat that came into the garden every morning at precisely the same time. And every morning, the same man in the Guard would go outside to feed and pat it. I would see him out the window as I was cleaning, and I would always wish I could pat the cat as well." I'd always wanted to know why he'd bothered and thought perhaps doing as much might grant some clarity.

"Why didn't you?" Her bottom lip quivered.

"I was not allowed to step outside," I told her with a forced smile.

I ignored her reaction to my statement, continuing on.

"For a good portion of the morning after the Guard returned indoors, I would watch the cat pounce at bugs in the grass and eat them despite having already been fed."

"I don't understand." She shook her head, and I watched a tear roll down her cheek.

"It is in a cat's nature to hunt," I said. "So, you could say that leaving the window open was really you giving your cat the freedom and permission to be what it naturally is."

She stood there frowning as she thought over my words, and she whispered a question I'd not been expecting. "You were locked away?"

I kept the forced smile on my face to nod at her.

"And I'm locking him away."

I shook my head. "The point of the story is that the cat returned every day," I told her. "But one day it stopped coming and I never saw it again. I have faith that your cat will return home to you, but . . . if you don't want him to leave again, you can keep the window closed from now on. When you go home, ensure you leave the very same window open for him to come back through."

"But what if he *doesn't*?" she cried.

"I will make a deal with you," I told her quietly. "I will return to this very spot first thing in the morning, and if your pet has not yet returned, then I shall help you scour the entire city in search of him."

"Would you really?"

I nodded.

"What am I supposed to do until then?"

"Live your life," I told her with a genuine smile, "and be happy with the knowledge that your cat is likely having so much fun on his little journey."

I watched that idea sink into her head slowly, like a light being lit in the darkness.

She smiled back at me. It was the oddest thing.

"What does he look like, in case I see him on my way?"

"He's yellow, Miss," she answered. "Yellow with orange stripeys."

I fought a laugh. "Then I shall keep a watchful eye for him. And I will hope he returns to you on his own, but will you please remember something for me?"

She nodded.

"One living thing cannot own another, only coexist. The choices we make impact those we care for, and we should all pay mind to what we choose to do." I paused for a moment. "Do you understand?"

I was unsure if she did, but she hugged me. I did not miss the way the Reaper standing by flinched, as though he were legitimately worried this child would harm me.

I only fully noticed the crowd that had gathered when the child ran away. She seemed in much brighter spirits, though that would not have been difficult. I was quite certain the Reaper was on the verge of panicking at the prospect of them all converging on me, so I quickly forced a smile at the closest onlookers and began walking away. I tried my best to not get too near anyone standing, but it was quite unavoidable. At least until a large grouping of Reapers circled around Jastin and me, cutting everyone else off. I almost felt safe in it.

Almost.

WHILE I WAS LYING IN BED with Jastin that night, I found myself running my fingers distractedly over his abdomen. He had removed his shirt again, and there was something pleasant about touching his skin while thinking of other things.

"You were great with them," he said quietly, drawing me from my thoughts. "Those people."

"Not hardly," I said. "I feel as though I should've helped the girl find her cat right then and there." I also felt as though I shouldn't have told her the last bit when she couldn't possibly understand, but it was possible she may one day. It was better to have the knowledge.

Jastin chuckled. "You know it will go back home on its own."

"If it's not killed along the way," I grumbled.

"Are you *seriously* worried about a cat right now?"

"Seems better than the alternative worries," I said quietly. *Easier.* Easier and *much* nicer.

He breathed out deeply and his voice took on a thoughtful tone when he spoke. "Maybe my sister's right."

"What about?" I asked. I'd seen Abby be correct about a number of things, but I'd also seen the opposite. Him saying what he had seemed to have come from nowhere, and I had no idea wh—

"Did you see how happy you made them?" he asked. "Just by speaking to them, acknowledging them? It's insane. Maybe she's right."

Oh. That.

Rather than saying that they were all—his sister included—actual idiots, I remained silent on that matter and all others. I kissed him on the chest and attempted to go to sleep, but all I could think over was a yellow cat with orange stripes and how torn I was on almost everything.

Almost.

"Are you all right?"

"Hmm?" I looked at Jastin's face.

"About Chandler staying behind."

My brow furrowed. "Well, I'm not thrilled about it."

He sat up. "I thought it was no one's business? Or does that only count the other way around?"

I sat up as well. "It is."

He shrugged. "Then why are you not thrilled?"

"I'd rather we not have another thing where you believe I'm insulting your sister."

"I have no idea how you believe saying he's too good for her is anything but that."

I said, plainly, "Because it's the truth and I mean no offense by it. She's lovely, in her ways. She's simply . . ."

"Oh, are you thinking of a nicer way to call her stupid?"

I said nothing to that.

"Is that what you're doing?"

"I never called her stupid. What I said is that she has odd focuses."

"But you said it to not say that you believe she's stupid."

"I believe her strengths of intelligence are interesting and differ immensely from mine. In a sense, I mean that as a compliment."

He just stared at me.

I shrugged.

He nodded. "But he's too good for her."

I nodded in response. "I understand that she's your sister. You're taking it far too personally and out of context, but you *are* biased."

"And you're not?"

My brow furrowed again. "No. I'm being objective."

"And this has nothing to do with some thing of not wanting to admit that you can't grasp him liking someone other than you?"

I laughed at that, quite loudly.

He did not.

I wasn't sure . . . "You're joking. Aren't you?"

He still did not laugh.

My brow again furrowed. "You *must* be joking."

He *still* did not laugh.

"In no world nor situation could I grasp him *liking me* in the way you're implying I believe he does."

He raised an eyebrow.

"You *do* know that's absurd, don't you?"

"Do you really believe that?"

"*Yes.*" My mouth hung open for a moment, disbelieving. "You *are* joking about all this, aren't you?"

"Let's say I might've been, but now I'm curious. . . ." He shrugged. "Why would it be *so absurd* for him to have feelings for you?"

"I can think of absolutely no reason for it to be anything but."

He put an exaggerated frown onto his face, nodding. "So the age thing is really you saying you think *you're* too young for him."

My brow furrowed again. "Well, I *would* be."

"But he's not *too old* for you."

"No."

"But you're too young for him."

"I just said that."

"Do you not understand this?" He again raised an eyebrow.

"Do *you* not?"

He held up a hand. "Do you not understand that you coming to that conclusion, thinking hard enough about it or coming to the one you did, means you've considered him an option for yourself? Do you *not* understand that, or are you being deceptive because you don't want to admit it to me?"

I said, "I haven't."

"Aster, you obviously have."

"I *haven't*."

"Aster, in *what world* does a girl come to the conclusions you have without sitting around and daydreaming about a man?"

Both my eyebrows rose as I gaped at him. "Are you being serious with me right now?"

He nodded. "Entirely."

I tried to remain calm as I said, "I understand if all you know of females is people having far too much time and option on and in their hands and using it all to sit around and *daydream* about things. In case you're unaware . . .?" I shook my head. "I am not that. Are you confused?"

He said nothing.

I explained to him, "In my internal list of personal values I've assessed of people, your sister and Chandler being on different levels is neither me daydreaming about him nor insulting your sister. I quite like your sister in some ways, and her interest in him only reinforced what I believed was a rather good internal judge of people that she—by her own admission to me—doesn't listen to as often as she should." I paused for a moment. "In case you missed things, I don't deal with unfounded accusations well. Do not take out on me your own ideas simply because you're failing to understand mine. No, Jastin. I'm not sitting around *daydreaming about Chandler*. I'd not waste my time. I live in the *real world*. In the real world, that would *never* happen." I paused again. "He's a good man. Your sister could only hope to be so lucky to find one of those and have them love her. Any woman would be lucky to. Should she be so lucky and should you be so ignorant as to try to put a stop to it, you would be attempting to deprive her of something I hope she would spend every moment grasping that she doesn't deserve, to ensure she never takes it for granted."

He stared at me for what felt like an eternity before asking, "But what if he did? Have feelings for you."

"I'll admit that his tastes aren't what I thought they were or would be, but there's no way they could be so horrendous."

His eyebrows rose. "And what of my tastes?"

"Jastin, I've met Cherise and you know her. I'm sure we both know what your tastes are."

They went higher. "Do you believe yourself similar?"

"No, of course not. But I'm well aware that you have horrendous taste in females. Thus far, I've attracted you, a rapist, and a spy I heard said earlier when Chandler thought I wasn't listening is . . ." I almost could've laughed. "*Quite possibly deranged*. On a good day." I shrugged. "I believe what I've attracted says what it does about me. So no, Jastin. I've not wasted any of my time daydreaming about Chandler. I'm well aware that he's far too good for me. If your sister *isn't* aware and fails to see it?" I nodded. "I will call her far more than *stupid* directly to her face, I can assure you of that."

A few long seconds passed. "And what of me? Do you believe I'm a good man?"

My brow furrowed, and I said, "No."

He looked away, I believed at nothing on a wall, his mouth hanging somewhat open.

I believed he was going to get out of bed, so I reached out and took his hand.

He looked down at it, and I then believed he was going to jerk it away.

I clarified. "I believe you *can* be."

He brought his gaze to my face then.

I asked, "Do you understand?"

He nodded stiffly.

"Can we drop this, please?"

He nodded again in the same way.

CHAPTER TWENTY-FOUR

ASTER

SLEEP HAD BEEN IMPOSSIBLE, or something so close to it that I had no idea on what word it would be. I'd tried, to no or little avail. I did believe I'd drifted off for a short moment or two here or there. I kept trying, until I no longer could. I then attempted to slip out of bed.

Jastin woke almost immediately. "What're you doing?"

"I have so much on my mind. I can't get it to shut itself off."

"Like what?"

"I need to speak to my father. I need to go wait for that little girl. So on and so forth."

He took in a deep breath. "Your father is probably awake. Do you want me to walk you there?"

"No. I might wait a little while. I think punching the bag might do me some good."

"Why?"

"Because I'm frustrated and can't sleep, as I said. It's rather close to morning anyway, I think."

"Do you want me to go with you?"

"No. You get more sleep. I'm sure someone's standing right outside and can escort me there." Perhaps Stanley.

"Are you sure?"

"Indeed." I leaned over and kissed him on the cheek then got out of bed. I put my training clothes on and stepped to the door, stopping to find him already back asleep. I smiled a little at the sight of it, and that felt nice.

Stanley was indeed posted outside the main door to my living quarters, and that was also nice. I was wondering about the state of the day and why two nice things had happened in a row when something unexpected happened.

Stanley initiated speaking.

"Rough night."

I stopped walking and looked up at him in the darkness.

He stopped as well. "I'm saying you had one, not saying I did."

"Oh. I'm glad." My brow furrowed. "Could you hear everything?"

"Some. Didn't need to." He stared down at me and—from what I could tell by the moonlight—seemed hesitant to ask, "Are you all right?"

My brow furrowed worse. "Yes, of course. Why?"

From what I could tell of his tone, he didn't believe me when he asked, "Are you sure?"

"Yes, of course. I'm tired and concerned, but otherwise and even still . . ." I nodded. "Why?" I wondered . . . "Were you hoping to do something about it? Perhaps hug me?"

He chuckled. "Do you need a hug?"

"No, of course not."

"Of course not." He sighed. "If it counts for anything, I think you should talk to him."

I nodded again. "Yes, I have every intention of speaking to him soon. I've been concerned since last night that I did something horrendously wrong when speaking to the ch—"

"Not your father, Aster. I meant Chandler."

"Oh." My brow furrowed again. "Well . . . I'm sure I'll see him shortly. Possibly. Unless he . . ." I cleared my throat. "I possibly will shortly. We do say hello sometimes. Aloud, I mean."

Stanley sighed. "I meant actually speak to him."

"That *is* speaking."

Another sigh. "No, dear. I mean *actually speak* to him."

My face scrunched. "Why did you call me that?"

"Call you what?"

"*Dear.*"

"I'm tired. My apologies."

"No, it was . . . It was fine. I heard . . ." I cleared my throat. "I heard a lady call her son that on the street one day." I cleared it again, my face burning. "I don't understand what you mean, though."

Stanley sighed again, rubbing at his face. He said, slowly, "Aster, for what it's worth, I believe you should explain to Chandler why you're so upset."

"I don't believe I should."

"Why not?"

"Because it's none of my business."

"You might be surprised."

"I don't know what you mean, but regardless . . . I wouldn't wish to bother him. He's not much on speaking."

"Just because he's not exceptional at it doesn't mean he dislikes to. All the time. With all people."

"True. That's possible," I conceded. I thought on it. "I suppose I could. I did believe he was wanting to be closer friends with me, in accompanying outside training, but I suppose it was liking Abby. But perhaps he might be open to the idea of . . ." I really thought on it, and I shook my head. "No, I don't believe I will."

"And what turned it from yes to no?"

"Things are fine as they are," I said. "I see him, and we have our way of being, and it's fine. Every time I get closer to anyone, they move away. Apart from Jastin, I mean. But even him for a while. My brother will hardly look at me. Stewart won't really speak to me anymore. Chase barely had anything to do with me once I started training. That might've been best, but that's sort of irrelevant in this sense. And I just . . ." I shook my head, laughing and wiping at my eyes. "I apologize. It's so frustrating that I can't shut these stupid tears off. They just happen when they happen."

"Because you're upset and don't want to lose anyone else."

"I suppose."

"Do you have such little faith in everyone?"

"It's not that. The common factor is me, Stanley."

His mouth was held parted for a moment before he said, "Aster, that's *not* your fault."

I nodded, insisting, "It *is*. And I understand. Especially after being near more people. Especially another female near in age to me. Listening to people in the city." I kept nodding. "I understand."

There was another sigh, that one lighter, and his tone changed to a lighter thing for him to say, "Have a little faith, dear. In other people *and* yourself. There are always going to be idiots, especially when dealing with people near your age of my gender. That just happens."

I laughed beneath my breath, wiping at more tears. "Yes, I've noticed."

"But sometimes everyone has moments of idiocy whether they're an idiot or not. Have some patience." He tapped me on the bottom of my chin—not to close my mouth because it already was closed but to push my head up the slightest bit higher—and said again, "And have a little faith."

It was only because of what he'd said to me on fear what seemed forever ago that I said then, "Yes, Sir."

"Come on." He nodded off. "Let's get you to your place so you can punch some things."

"Yes, that sounds ideal."

He chuckled a little.

I wanted to tell Stanley that I was glad he'd been there. I wanted to ask him why he had been, as it was not his usual time. No matter what he'd said on fear . . .

I just walked with him in silence the remainder of the way.

I WASN'T LONG INSIDE MY TRAINING ROOM with Stanley guarding the door before the door opened. I halted.

Chandler stepped inside, shared some sort of glance with Stanley while passing and the latter stepped out. When the door closed, Chandler looked at me from across the room, smiled in the small way that was typical of him when it occurred, and did his small wave that seemed mocking but I didn't believe was—more a crooking of his pointer finger than anything.

So nothing had changed.

I opened my mouth.

Closed it.

Waited for him to say something about yesterday.

That didn't happen.

I then waited for the transition from the tiny moment of niceties to *getting on with the day*.

That didn't happen either.

And that meant something had changed.

I waited. I watched him, and I waited, and it didn't happen, and I almost panicked.

I had to tell myself to walk to the other side of the room, not run. It sort of worked. And I told myself to sound calm when I asked, "What happened?"

His brow was furrowed when he glanced at me, and he didn't have to say anything verbally. I saw it on his face. *What do you mean?*

"You're over here pretending to mess about with these cloths." I gestured to the stand with them. "You would've already said . . . '*Morning nice is over.*' '*Get back to work.*' '*What're you doing?*' Something like that. Why are you not saying any of that?"

"I didn't know it was so large a thing."

I tried not to panic. "Our morning nice is the best part of my days."

He looked to me.

"I don't want to lose that just because you're seeing someone and doing . . . *things* with them. Because you did, didn't you? And that's why you're being awkward. Because you did. I don't know why that would make you feel awkward with me, but it clearly is. But it's all right, Chandler." I nodded. "I understand if you like her. I understand that she's beautiful, and I don't blame you or think less of you for it."

He still seemed confused and sounded that way as well when he said, "I'm so confused."

I admitted, "I am a bit as well, if I'm being honest."

A few seconds passed. His mouth tugged up at the corners a very small bit. They went back down after a few shorter seconds. He then shook his head. "I like to think I've been near you long enough to have a pretty good idea of things, but I honestly have no idea what you mean."

I wasn't as frustrated as I normally got at having to explain what I'd just explained. "You're for some reason acting awkward with me because of you and Abby and things, and I don't want that to change things. With us, I mean."

I was quite sure he almost laughed, but he didn't. He nodded and asked, "Is that so?"

I nodded in a different way. "Yes. I've just said several times."

He sort of narrowed his eyes. "Did you ever think that *maybe* this might be the other way around?"

I thought hard, trying to figure out what the other way around would be.

"Possibly something a bit larger than someone potentially *doing things* with someone?"

I kept thinking.

"Possibly someone *marrying* someone?"

"Oh." A few seconds passed of things falling together. "*Oh.*"

He nodded and went back to refolding the stack of cloths, and he said, sort of under his breath, "*Oh.*"

"So . . . you're worried about our morning nice as well."

"I'm worried I'm having a bad dream I can't wake up from."

I shook my head, not understanding. "What do you mean?"

He sighed, stopped what he was doing, and looked at me to say, "I think marrying that asshole would be *the* largest mistake of your life."

My face scrunched. "Chandler, as far as I was made aware yesterday, I completely fell for a spy game."

"Largest for you as a person."

I looked up at him, and I had no idea . . . "You said you were happy for me."

"Yes, well . . ." His lips pursed for a moment, and he went back to the cloths. "I've been in Jarsil for months, having your father in my ear." He mimicked my father quite well, though exaggerated, to say, "If you're to be near to her, you *must* at least *somewhat* alter your behavior. I'm *sure* she finds your manner of being somewhat endearing, but flies with honey and vinegar and all." He shrugged, stiffly. "It was the *polite* thing to say. It just came out. I guess my face couldn't manage it."

I put my hand on his arm, trying to stop him from what seemed to be a great deal of frustration being taken out in folding cloths that didn't matter at all. They didn't matter because I would do it later.

He looked to me, sort of sighing, his lips pursed into a hard line.

I said, "Don't you dare listen to *anyone* who tells you that." I shook my head. "Don't you dare. I say better no flies at all. They do nothing but spread filth anyhow."

The corners of his mouth again tugged up.

Mine followed. But then the small smile fell. "So . . . You're concerned about our morning nice."

He sighed. "On top of what I said, there was also finding out in the way I did. At the time I did."

"So not the morning nice."

Another sigh. But he nodded and said, "Yes, Aster. I'm concerned about our morning nice. It's the best part of my days, too."

"*Is* it?"

He nodded.

"Oh." I shook my head. "I had no idea."

"I had no idea it was yours."

"Oh." Though I'd already said, to ensure he truly knew . . . "It is."

"Since you're speaking straight . . ." He shook his head, his face scrunched. "What in the world about thinking less of me for *liking a woman*? Was that your way of trying to convince yourself that you wouldn't when you actually would? Because that's all very odd. Odd and more than a bit hypocritical."

"Oh. Well . . ." I thought on it. "Yes, I could see how you might think that with wording and all. I meant that . . ." My face scrunched. "Well, honestly, I thought you found her annoying. And if you found her annoying, that would mean you're interested strictly because you find her beautiful enough to find involvement worth it. Which would mean you're shallow or superficial, in most cases. But I don't believe you are. I saw you smiling last night, before all that, so perhaps you're acclimating and changing your opinion on her . . ." I tried to think of a way to put it. "Her *easily excited and occupied nature*."

He laughed, shaking his head. Not in response to anything. Just shaking. Then he asked, "What does it matter?" He shrugged. "If I were to like a woman for any reason . . .?" Another shrug. "What does it matter?"

I thought on it, my mouth open as I did until he tapped on my chin only hard enough to close it. But then . . .

"Why are you crying?"

"I just . . ." I didn't know what to say.

"We can stop with the speaking if you're that uncomfortable. It's fine."

"No, it's just . . ." I rubbed at my face, frustrated. "I don't know how to say it the right way. Because you're going to take it wrong. Everyone always takes things wrong."

"Well . . . Just try. If I take something wrong, we can get it sorted. All right?"

I dropped the hand, looking up at him.

"All right?"

I nodded. "It's just . . . I like Abby, but she's not good enough for you. I'm not insulting her. And Jastin thinks this is me *daydreaming about you* or some madness, but it's not that. She's not good enough for you, and that bothers me, but I also want you to be happy, and I want you to smile. And if she makes you smile, then I'm happy for you."

He said, "You don't look happy."

"But I *am*," I insisted. "That must be what I'm feeling. Because you're my friend, and I care for you a great deal, and I want you to be happy. And I think I'm so happy for you that I'm confused and overwhelmed by it. Because this is also what you said. You said about finding reasons to stay here. And you finding someone in that sense gives you reason to stay here, and I'm . . ." I nodded. "I'm happy. Because I want you right here."

"I *am* right here."

I nodded, trying to keep myself somewhat together.

He seemed so confused. "What about *too good for*?" He shook his head, appearing lost.

"What about it?"

"Where is that coming from?"

"Facts and the truth."

"Meaning?"

"Meaning you're a good man, Chandler. And I need to apologize to you for yesterday if you thought I at any point doubted that. I didn't. I just . . ." I tried not to sob. "I just so badly didn't want any of that to be true."

He asked, "At what point did you stop thinking I'm an asshole?"

I smiled a little through my tears to say, "I know very well that you are one."

"But a good man."

I nodded. "A good man."

"At what point?"

"Never," I replied. "There was only a point of realization."

"And at what point was that?"

I stared up at his face, and it was so clear inside my head. *The night I was very confused and found myself convinced that hands and arms could only be used for pain, and you knew I needed to be shown otherwise. When you held me and said without saying that what I'd been sure of was wrong.*

I opened my mouth.

I closed it.

I stepped past him and started making my way toward the door.

He grabbed hold of my forearm, stopping me. "What did I do?"

"What do you mean?"

He seemed somewhat on the verge of panicking. "You were just *speaking*. Crying, and speaking about feelings. And I'm watching you shutting it all back off. Why do you *do this* to yourself?"

I opened my mouth to say something, but the door opened. We both looked to it.

Stelin stood halted in the doorway. "Am I interrupting, or . . .?" He glanced over his shoulder.

"It's fine," I said. "I must tell you both that I'll surely be very late on this today, if I manage it at all. I gave someone my word on something, and I also must speak with my father."

Chandler still hadn't released my arm, so I looked back up at him.

He stared down at me for several seconds before glancing at Stelin.

I reiterated, "I *must* speak with my father. I should've done last night."

He released my arm.

I was going to go, but . . . "Please don't ever use that accent again unless your life depends on it. At least not near me."

It took him a moment to realize what I was speaking about. I watched it strike him before he smiled a little and asked, "Was it that bad?"

I nodded.

"I thought I did rather well."

"Oh. I didn't realize you meant bad in that sense. You of course did exceptionally with it."

I watched him think hard until another thing struck. His eyes widened. "I wasn't mocking you and the way you speak."

"I know."

His brow furrowed. "Then what's the problem?"

"You didn't sound like you." I shook my head shortly and barely said, "I didn't like it."

I watched his brow furrow worse.

I had to tell him, "I discovered an answer. To the question you asked me yesterday evening." I glanced at a wall only for long enough to get enough of what I needed inside to look up to him and say, "I'm trying." To be happy. I was trying as hard as I could. I cleared my throat. "I have to go."

I left the space.

AFTER TAKING CARE of the few things I needed to, I found myself walking back to the same spot where I'd promised to meet up with the girl about her cat. I could not remember how to get there exactly, as I still had no idea how to get to where Abby stayed. I would certainly get lost if required to go on my own, so I followed Jastin after he'd woken and caught up with me as I'd been doing other things. I wasn't accustomed to walking city streets, let alone attempting to navigate them. There were so many that led to the same places or seemingly nowhere at all. It was quite the disorientating experience.

I truly didn't want to see the girl again, because her presence would mean I had told her wrong. It also meant I would be required to spend who knew how long today in search of a cat that was likely dead. I hadn't the vaguest clue as to how that particular scenario should be dealt with—stumbling across her dead cat. I'd done a great deal of contemplating over it, and any means only seemed satisfactory when looking at the situation from different perspectives. I had no idea which would be best.

I hadn't the vaguest clue what to do with children in a potentially detrimental situation. I hadn't the vaguest clue how to deal with them at all. I also worried that her parents may not agree with what I considered to be a satisfactory way to handle this, should it go badly. What if they made a formal complaint on me? What if I got one of those every instance I stepped out of the House? Worse . . .

What if I potentially altered or damaged the girl in some way by trying to help? What if the parents had set things that they were attempting to teach their child and I got in the way of that?

I thought about it as I walked, still torn on the matter. I did not want the cat to be dead, but I couldn't stop from thinking it at least would've died happy, *free*. Or it would've been those things *before* it died if not when found. I liked to believe that mattered or at least counted for something.

Perhaps it was glad to be free of the girl regardless of any love or care on her part. Perhaps it just wanted to be free. What if it lived, I found it, and couldn't bring myself to give it back to her? What if it seemed so happy that I couldn't?

It wasn't as though I could gauge a cat's happiness level. That was ridiculous.

Perhaps it wanted to return and couldn't find its way? Perhaps the love and care made a difference?

I had no idea, but I believed I was putting too much into the situation. If it hadn't returned, I would help her search and there was absolutely nothing else to it until there either was or wasn't. I just wanted to be done with this so it would stop taking up space inside my head that would be better occupied by other matters.

I truly wasn't expecting for her to be there, given the sun had just barely come up in the sky. I was expecting to wait. I was *hoping* to wait despite it cutting into my time for other things and all the staring that would come with it. Staring and stress. I was hoping to wait and not see her at all, to have been right. But she was most certainly there, and she was not alone. I presumed it was her parents standing on either side of her, and in her arms was her yellow cat with orange stripes.

The smile I had on my face then was not forced in the slightest.

"He came back on his own," she told me happily when I got close, "just like you said he would."

"So he did." I stepped in front of her and her family.

There were Reapers standing by paying close attention, but they did not move to interfere in any way.

"I'm surprised you would bring him out again." I was *very* surprised.

"I thought you might like to pat him," she said. "Because you couldn't pat the cat where you were before."

I had never touched a live animal before—apart from my horse, which was more beast than animal to me—only seen the man in the Guard doing it. Very hesitantly, I bent over a bit, reached out, and patted its head.

It was *remarkably* soft.

No wonder the man in the Guard had enjoyed patting that stray cat.

Was that all it was? It was just soft?

I had to stop patting it before I found myself having some ridiculous idea that I wanted one of my own. What use was a cat past mousing? There was no use and I did not want to claim something living just to *pat it*.

I thought of my hand on Jastin the night before and felt the corners of my mouth trying to tug up harder.

I focused and brought my attention to the girl's face. "That was very kind of you."

"Very kind of you to be willing to give away your time to find a cat, Milady," her mother said when I stood back up straight. "I'm sure you don't have much of it."

"The world would be so much better of a place if we could all spare some of our kindness for others," I said with a tight smile. "I must admit I've not seen it enough in my life."

"Nor we before your father came, Milady," her father said. "I'm glad she was too young to remember the way things were here before. I wish that no one had to remember those things."

"I wish the harsh realities of our world were nothing more than unpleasant memories we could never forget," I told him thoughtfully. "It's so much better than knowing they're still out there and we're all too powerless to put a stop to it." A lack of peace might be worth it then.

He blinked at me in something I thought was confusion before the little girl pulled my attention back down to her by saying, "I've got something for you, Miss."

"What else could you *possibly* have for me this morning?" I laughed as I knelt in front of her. "You've already allowed me to pat your wandering cat."

She handed the cat up to her father and then turned around for something her body had been concealing. When she faced me again, she had a pot in her hands with dirt and a flower inside.

"It's an aster, Miss," she said. "Just like you."

My smile was tight when she handed it over to me.

"I've never seen one," I said quietly as I analyzed it.

So this was the thing my mother had named me after—a small, brightly colored purple thing with abrupt edges.

I took a deep breath and smiled again at the girl. "Would you like to know what I intend to do with this?" I did not have to look at Jastin to know he was concerned that I intended to smash the pot at the girl's feet.

She nodded.

"I'm going to take this back with me and plant it *right* outside my door. That way I can see it every day when I step outside or return, and I'll always be able to remember there's good in the world."

She beamed, even though she didn't understand. Couldn't possibly. "Thank you for everything, Miss."

I didn't think I'd done a single thing for her, so I felt very confused.

"No," I said warmly. "Thank *you*."

She smiled and hugged me again. As soon as she finished doing that, she greedily grabbed her cat from her father. It seemed more than happy to oblige and in fact seemed to try to get back to her. I watched her sort of nuzzle into it and it to do the same. I could just barely hear it making a sound over the sounds of people getting started on their days. It was a nice sound. Despite having been out, he seemed in no way wanting to escape again and be away from her.

Interesting.

I smiled at both her parents—who nodded their heads toward me—and then walked away.

I clutched the plant tightly to my chest as I made my way. When I glanced over at Jastin, I saw that he had an extremely satisfied grin on his face. It was almost infuriating.

"Oh, be quiet."

He laughed. "I didn't say anything."

"You didn't have to," I grumbled. He nudged me gently with his arm as we walked, which made me exclaim, "You're going to break my plant!" He was going to break what my mother had named me after.

I ignored the snort he made in response.

I heard footsteps on the other side of me, so I looked over and found a relatively familiar face. It was the Reaper who had been standing next to the little girl the previous night, restrained her.

"I thought you might like to know . . ." he began slowly. "As soon as you'd gone, so many who overheard your conversation began searching for that cat."

"You're joking," I said in disbelief.

He glanced at me and shook his head. "Remarkable, the things people will do." He chuckled a bit. "Your father has the same effect."

I decided to ignore that, because it made me feel quite strange for some inexplicable reason. "May I ask you . . ." I started, but he interjected.

"Why we keep even the children away from you?"

I nodded.

"Perfect strategy, isn't it? Put a child in front of a kind girl. Reaper children know how to kill and follow orders, even when they're as young as she is. There's a rather large handful of leaders who would do as much. Take the risk of irreparably damaging one of their own to eliminate such a large target. As I said, it's the perfect strategy for the perfect cover. You should be careful. Your father existing in the way he does is more infuriating than you can grasp to a great many of the others out there. Your arrival will draw the ones too afraid to come at him directly out of the woodwork. If word breaks that you're *anything* like him in *any* way?"

He didn't finish the thought. He did not need to.

He said it again. "You should be careful."

"Did *you* look for the cat as well?" I asked that because I did not like the subject of children being used. It made me think of a twelve-year-old boy cutting off a man's hands. I also did not like where he'd gone with it.

The Reaper smiled at me uncomfortably and then continued on about his business.

"You knew that would get him to leave," Jastin accused with a quiet chuckle.

"Only if he'd done so," I stated.

"But you knew he had." Jastin grinned. "He wouldn't have told you as much if he hadn't, would he have?"

Not in the way he did.

I smiled a little to myself and kept walking forward.

IT WAS AS I WAS DIGGING around in the dirt near the door to my living quarters that I had an epiphany. I looked down and blinked at the dirt, and then at the flower.

I could finish planting it. I'd told the little girl to have patience with her cat, after all. I could do the same with something that would take so much less time than what I'd asked of her, but it was difficult. It was so difficult not to abandon the small task for something infinitely more important, but it was also important in its ways. Different ways.

I resolved myself to do as exceptional of a job as I could in putting the plant into the ground. I was careful with it, but I had never planted anything before in my life to know the proper way to do it. I would do the best I could, plan where I was going before I set off, and take one careful step at a time.

I would do the absolute best I could.

When I was finished with the task, I stared down at it in a somewhat satisfied sort of way. I had put something back into the world where it rightfully belonged—reattached it, so it could have the life it deserved. Now it was time to take a step.

"I need to speak with my father," I told Jastin, who was standing behind me.

"What about?"

I was smiling down at my very own aster when I said, "I believe I know what could make us untouchable to Hasting. I should very much like to inform my father."

CHAPTER TWENTY-FIVE

KEYS

"IT'S THE PEOPLE," I TOLD MY FATHER once Jastin and I were properly inside his office with the door closed. Anders was there as well, but the room was otherwise empty.

"What?" My father was puzzled, likely because I'd barged into his space without any explanation for my behavior.

I supposed it was still barging in even when the door had been open, but *this*? This was worth some rudeness.

"The people." I was very nearly fighting against the urge to laugh in both relief and excitement. "The people of your city are the key."

My father said, "I don't quite understand what you're getting at, Flower. Please begin from a place where this conversation will make sense. You seem to already be a decent way through it on your own."

"You've set it up perfectly, Father." I smiled, wondering how he couldn't understand with all I'd already said. "You and Anders. They love you here, don't they?"

When he still did not seem to understand, I pressed forward.

"I asked Jastin a question once about teaching physical training to people. He said Reapers are not allowed to share their knowledge with the citizens, that the sheer number of them is dangerous to the system."

My father blinked at me for quite some time, trying to catch himself up, I assumed. "You're saying you want the entire city trained?" His speaking was careful, and he looked at me as if he couldn't believe I'd come up with such an idea.

I hadn't come up with that at all.

"They would massacre each other with that knowledge."

"*No,*" I said significantly. "I'm saying you wouldn't *have* to train them. It's *love,* Father."

"What does love have to do with war?"

"*Everything.*" The smile stretched wider on my face, and I felt the only way to describe it was . . . *maniacal.* An intense urge to laugh bubbled up inside my chest, but I pushed it down far enough that it didn't come out. "Everything . . . or *nothing.*"

"*Oh.*" Anders drew the word out. "You are so very smart."

"You tell the people." I looked only at my father. "You tell them everything. Tell them about Ahren. Tell them about mine and Jastin's wedding." Very slowly I added, "And you tell them about the threats to our family."

"You're saying they would fight for us, if that were needed." My father's voice sounded thoughtful.

"They wouldn't have to," I told him in a strange mixture of exasperation and excitement. "You have hundreds upon hundreds of Reapers in this city, Father, but *thousands* more citizens. You make a public announcement and you tell them about the dangers we're facing, the dangers the entire *city* is facing, and they'll open their eyes." I paused. "How many spies do you think are currently here in Jarsil?" I fought against another laugh when I said, "Watch what happens if you make an announcement in front of the entire city. Those spies will be standing in a sea of our people who are finally looking around for them."

"It's possible," my father conceded. "But it is also possible they will escape and give word to their own cities."

"Our hand is already dealt, Father." I shrugged a bit, because it simply was what it was. "Everyone who has their eyes open has seen everything. We have nothing else to lose. But if we *choose* to . . . we could gain so much."

"I'm curious . . ." my father began, still using the thoughtful tone, "of what, *exactly,* you believe could be gained by this." It had not sounded demeaning, only curious.

"Your people know you take care of them," I said. "They love you for that, for giving them safety and comfort where they had none before. But if you included them . . . they would believe that you *trust* them. If you include them . . . they would feel like part of our family." I smiled. "That's what you told me about the kings when I was a child, wasn't it? That they loved all their people as though they were their own children. But more importantly . . . You would gain the happiness of your son for finally being acknowledged openly as yours."

"He'd never be able to go on another mission," my father stated.

"He's already lost his partner to me, Father," I said. "And I'm sure that, even if things had been different . . . knowing that you care for him as much as you do me would be more important to him than anything in the world. It should be worth it to you, even if it's only done for that reason."

My father analyzed my face for a very long time, which I remained silent during, before asking, "And you're *certain* about this? About putting yourself, Jastin, and your brother so at risk?"

"We're not at risk here," I said assuredly. "Not so long as the people we care about are safe." It was such a long chain, but if all links were strengthened, *reinforced* . . .

"How can you be so certain?"

Anders said, "I'm more curious where she learned her strategic way of thinking."

I brought my attention to Anders for the briefest moment to say, "By listening and watching." I looked back to my father. "I cannot tell you how many leaders I watched fall in New Bethel. More than a hundred over ten years, easily. They were all overtaken by hate, and greed, and other people who wanted power. Everything bad in this world. It was the evil that caused them to fall, always. Never good."

"And what of Hasting?" my father asked. "How has he not fallen if that's true? If bad falls and good stands, how is he still standing?"

"He must be an incredibly frightening man." I frowned. "But, Father, if we allow enough good to run, and we do things for the right reasons . . ." I shook my head. "He won't stand a chance."

My father sighed. "Are you wanting this done for the right reasons, Flower? It sounds as though it's all strategy to my ears." He just barely raised an eyebrow. "You can word it however you like, but I hear it there. Can you deny that?"

"Strategy or not," I said, "it does not change the fact that you would be doing good for your people. Do you need reasons for doing good things?" I paused and pursed my lips for a moment. "Good is good, Father."

He shook his head. "*Love.*"

Anders said, "It's so mad that it just might work."

"Father." I smiled. "Wouldn't my mother be happy if we were allowing people to have the things you were never allowed in your life? Even if everything goes wrong . . ." I shrugged. "It would be worth it, wouldn't it? To give people *happiness*?"

"How can you argue with that, Brother?" Anders asked.

"I'm not." My father sighed and shook his head again. "You're aware the likelihood this will fail on us is quite great, aren't you?"

"I won't deny that I am aware of it being a distinct possibility," I admitted. "But you said it yourself that we couldn't sit back idly, waiting for Hasting to grow stronger. It would make sense, wouldn't it, to fortify ourselves as much as we could and in any ways we can?"

"It would." My father agreed.

"I've been wracking my brain, attempting to figure out what his plan for attack would be," I said in frustration. "He's very smart, you all say. An abduction attempt would be risky, yes, but . . . when Chase left, you and I still had not begun fixing things between us. He won't know we have. I've thought, perhaps, that Hasting may believe I would come to him willingly. Perhaps he may send someone to me to sway me in that direction. Or attempt swaying.

"Still," I went on. "As everyone has said, now is the perfect time to make a strike at you. Would he take the risk that, if he spent his time focusing on that endeavor, it may not work out? So that brings me back to him abducting someone close to me. To use against me and lure me out, so I would come to him that way to be used against you.

"Then, I've thought about him waging a full-on battle against you, but he wouldn't do that, would he?" I shook my head. "Not here at least, one would think. Perhaps in your other city, to weaken you, but he would also weaken himself in the process. So . . . I believe an abduction of me specifically is one of the least likely options, with a direct battle just ahead of that in likelihood."

My father's eyes had been narrowed for quite some time before he spoke. "What is you're thinking he'll do? I can see on your face that you believe you've discovered it."

"Send enough of his Reapers here to do what he wants done," I replied. "I think he's going to send his Reapers here, not necessarily to take over the city because that would be ridiculous given your cities are on opposite ends of the land, but to kill you. It's so much easier, Father. The doorway to taking me easily has been closed to him. Why negotiate when he could simply kill you instead?

"*So*," I said and then took a deep breath. "You're going to make your announcement, Father. You're going to tell the people everything and inform them that, if they see *any* suspicious behavior, they're to find the nearest Reaper immediately. And at the same time, you're going to station more Reapers on top of the wall because some of the spies will flee. *Attempt* to. Not right then of course because it would draw too much attention, but within a matter of days, I would imagine. We will catch some of them with information from the people, and others as they attempt to leave. Some of them will still manage to slip through, I'm sure. . . ."

They surely would, but . . .

"Still," I went on. "You get the people looking, and when Hasting makes his move . . . he won't be able to touch us."

"And if you're wrong?" my father asked curiously.

My voice was firm when I said, "Then it is still so much better than sitting around doing nothing and waiting for it."

I wondered if my father's eyes were not narrowed or if that was simply the way they always were now. But of course that was ridiculous. "It's quite frightening, the way your mind works." His voice was not condescending but sad when he added, "You're just a girl."

"War is an awful thing, even when only between two people," I said thoughtfully. "But there's always some sort of logic in strategic decisions, which is the entire basis of war. Strategy. That's correct, isn't it?"

"Yes, Flower." My father chuckled as he shook his head. "That is correct." He took a deep breath and then released it. "You must've inherited your way of thinking from your mother."

"It's funny, Father," I said. "I thought I'd gotten that from you. You're the one who taught me how to think properly, after all. Weren't you?"

He smiled hugely at me, which made me quite happy.

It felt like an odd and yet pleasant sort of pressure inside my chest.

Then he sighed. "Well, I believe I must go inform my men to spread the word that I'll be giving a speech meant for the entire city tomorrow."

I smiled at his back as he left the room, but it dropped away when I heard footsteps behind me.

Anders was right at my back when he said, "Jastin, will you give us a moment?"

Jastin didn't respond verbally, but he did glance at me as he passed.

He had his hand on the door to close it when Anders said, "Leave it."

I suspected we were both watching Jastin's back until he rounded a corner. He didn't give a second glance back.

I turned to Anders, and he stared straight at my face until I asked, "What is it?"

"There was a point in time where your father had lost everything. We made our plans, and I watched him. He smiled, and he told a version of the truth that made people stand up and be willing to fall on their own blades for him. But truth isn't one-sided, is it?"

We were both silent, and I waited for him to make his point. It took a little while for him to speak again.

"I watched your father tell one side of the truth to everyone, and then he came to me with the other side. Both wanted to build up. One because it was what she'd wanted, what he'd wanted before life had stolen everything from him. And who could deny it was the right thing to do?" He paused. "The other side wanted to build it up and tear it down. Tear down the world and burn it to ash. He was more than capable. Then one day . . . he stopped coming to me with those thoughts he kept hidden from everyone else." He raised an eyebrow. "Can you guess why?"

I was sure Anders knew that things had changed with and for my father, but I didn't want to say it so I asked, "Can you tell me why?"

He smiled at me. "I'm going to give you several bits of advice and you can do whatever you wish with them. I suggest you listen very carefully and think very hard."

I was silent, waiting.

"You don't yet understand what comes with all this." He gestured around my father's office. "You'll come to, now that you'll allow it. The sooner you learn something, the better off you'll be. Its importance is unparalled."

He paused long enough that I asked, "And what is it?"

"When you live this life, there are so many parts to the truth, all of them only as true as what people believe. When you choose one truth, you must stick to it. If there is *any* doubt . . . they will tear you apart."

"So you're saying—"

"I'm saying if you choose this, you *choose* it." He interrupted me with more intensity than I'd ever heard from him. "You keep your mouth *shut* if opening it would contradict *anything*. You can't play this halfway with everyone watching."

"You're telling me to trust no one."

"Trust belongs out there." He pointed to the one window in the room. "Trust keeps you safe there. It gets you *killed* here. Either listen to me or don't with that. This is your choice and you'll deal with whatever consequences come from it."

He began to walk away at that, but he stopped and turned back around.

"Do yourself a favor," he said. "Don't mistake your father's kindness for weakness. He can afford to be kind here, in his position. But he is what he is. He's exceptional at hiding it, but it's there. If you ever find yourself doubting . . . ask yourself the questions."

"What questions?"

"All of them." Anders smiled. "You can start with *how is he still alive* and go from there."

He left me alone, and I found myself taking turns staring around my father's office then at the window.

Chapter Twenty-Six

TAKING CARE

I WAS ANTSY for the remainder of the day after speaking of keys and hearing about trust. I trained for a long while in an attempt to take my mind off everything, but it was not satisfactory in getting the job done. My thoughts were almost spastic, jumping or falling from one specific thing to the next. It seemed as though they were doing both, sometimes at once—jumping and falling. There were so many things.

My relationship with my father, my feelings and its potential. Marrying Jastin. Chase being the spy and all that pertained to it. The words Anders had said. The speech my father was to give. Value. Happiness. Responsibility. Trust. Truth. Windows. Cats. Change. Nature. Simplicity. Taking steps. Keys. My mother. So many things that made me wonder if *peace* even existed in the world at all.

I was only partially relieved from my anxiousness when lying in bed with Jastin that night. It was not full relief, but the closeness to him numbed me to it in some strange way. Quieted it.

"What if I'm wrong?" I whispered. "What if I'm wrong and the citizens turn on one another out of fear?"

What if it failed to that degree? It was possible. More than that. It was *likely*, if this was not done *perfectly*. It was still possible regardless.

He sighed. "It's possible. You inform people there's something lurking right out of their view, wanting to steal their way of living from them . . . Well, it's unpredictable, when all people react to things in different ways. There's really no telling what will happen, but I think it'll be all right."

"It would destroy everything my father's been building here if it goes badly." My voice was quiet. "I cannot believe he'd risk all that, simply on my word."

All he'd built and done for whatever reasons he had. Good was good, and risking *any* of it . . .

"You gave quite the argument for your case," Jastin said. "As you said, it's better than doing nothing."

"But what if it's not?" I whispered. What if what I'd done destroyed all my mother had hoped for? Died for. What if I was wrong and she'd died for . . . *nothing*?

"We'll just have to wait and see what happens, Star," he said apologetically.

He was right, of course. Things were already set into motion—because of me—and I could not stop them. The word had already been properly spread about the speech, I would imagine, and wondering *what if* would not change anything. Whatever was going to happen would happen. I just had to have faith that my plan was sound. I had to have faith in my father and all he'd built here for whatever reasons he had. My mother had believed in him and what he was capable of. I had to believe with her.

For her. If he'd done it . . .

This could work.

My mother and I could stand together on this.

It all made sense inside my head. I couldn't deny the rarity of that, and I just needed to believe in it.

I did not want to think any more on it. I'd spent enough of my day allowing it to occupy the majority of the space inside my head. It had done as much even while training. Tearing it all apart again would do me no good. The logic was sound, and attempting to predict results would be a waste of time when the path from here to there was already set. It would be what it would. I had to have faith. The logic was sound.

I breathed out in a huff and said, "I'm quite accustomed to touching your skin now."

Jastin laughed. "Are you?"

"Yes," I answered blankly.

His skin being close to me only caused issue at certain times that I couldn't quite grasp hold of. But I was fine with it.

"I'm curious what the next step is when taking things slowly."

"Whatever you want," he said. "It's what I'm here for."

That did not answer what had clearly been a question worded as a statement.

I laid there for quite some time, attempting to discover what the next logical thing would be, as Jastin wasn't helping. It would only make sense that, if I'd become accustomed to touching his skin, to touch it with more of my own until I was entirely comfortable with that as well. It seemed logical.

I sat up and removed my shirt, finding myself very thankful that females wore top undergarments where men did not. I doubted I would've been all right with this at all otherwise. I truly had no idea. I supposed it likely would've depended upon a number of things. I didn't throw my shirt across the room as Jastin always seemed to with his. I sat it behind myself, in case I needed it.

Needing it was likely.

Jastin had his eyes somewhat narrowed at me, but he asked me no questions. He lifted up his arm for me to settle in properly beside him.

I did.

I imagined that seeing a female in such a state was not an unusual thing for him. Of course, Chase had fooled me into thinking it was for *him*. Jastin had never tried to fool me in that way, though.

I did not allow myself to think on how many times Jastin had seen such things for very long because it sent some unpleasant feeling into my stomach. I was unsure what the proper word to explain it was, but it was similar to what I'd experienced the last time I'd thought of him with Cherise. It wasn't the same, though. Duller, but almost more unpleasant.

I laid there frowning for a while as I attempted to process and work through what I was feeling.

It didn't take me too long to realize I had no hope for getting anywhere with it.

Yet another thing. Perhaps time would bring some clarity with it. Until then, there was no point.

"This is different," I whispered. I was not whispering when I spoke again. "Why is it that this is so much different?" I did not think it should've been.

The arm of his that was beneath me, running along my back, did not help matters any. Still, I felt as though he was not even noticing my scars. It was strange. *All* of it was so very strange. It should not have been, because we always slept close to one another.

But there was *something* about him touching my skin. Was it *where* he was touching or *how* he was touching?

I didn't have a clue.

He asked, "Good different or bad different?"

"Well, I want to kiss you quite badly right now, so I'm suspecting it's mostly good," I replied.

He laughed quietly. "I don't think kissing is a very intelligent thing for us to do right this second."

I waited several seconds before asking, "How about now?"

He snorted. "Go to sleep, Star."

"I . . . I don't believe I can."

He kissed my forehead. "Try."

Though I didn't believe *sleep* was the purpose of this exercise, I grumbled, "All right."

He did not allow me to try to sleep. I didn't know if it was proof of my thoughts on the matter, if there was something wrong with me, or if it was even intentional at all on his part, but I mentally blamed it on him. I wouldn't have, had he not been doing what he was.

I imagined that his touching was meant to be comforting in some way, but it was so very far from it. I stared through the near darkness at his fingers running over my hipbone until I realized that, if his intent was comfort . . . he was not anywhere *near* achieving it. I closed my eyes tightly, hoping it would change the way I felt, but it did not.

I eventually told him, "I can't sleep with you touching me that way."

He stopped, but that told me nothing on the motivations behind it all or whether there even were any.

It only told me that he was respecting my obvious want for him to stop.

It told me absolutely nothing of use.

I took a deep breath and continued lying there, expecting for sleep to come to me. It did not because I still couldn't get his hands out of my head.

Nearly twenty minutes had passed, I was sure, before I asked, "Will you touch me that way again?"

He laughed quietly. "I thought you didn't want me to?"

"I was thinking it would make a difference if you stopped, but it didn't, and I would much rather you be doing it if I'm going to be thinking about it regardless." Perhaps then I might have a hope at figuring it out. I shook my head. "It's just so frustrating."

"What is?"

"Feeling like my entire body is going to explode everywhere," I said in exasperation. "I don't understand it. It makes absolutely no sense whatsoever. We're just lying here together."

He chuckled. "You're acting like you've never felt that before."

"I haven't."

There was a very brief moment of his body going entirely still before he moved into a position where he could look at my face. "You slept with Chase," he said once he was propped up by his arm. "You're telling me you've never felt that before?"

"Somewhat similar I suppose, but no," I answered. "Not like this."

"You're telling me that you've . . . never felt like your body was going to explode," he said slowly, like he was trying to work it out.

"I haven't," I said again. "Is that a . . . *normal* thing to feel?" It did not seem very healthy or good at all.

I could tell his eyes were wide as he laid there staring at me. He put a hand over his mouth to scratch at his lip, which made my stomach sink.

"Are you laughing at me?"

"No," he said quickly. And indeed, his tone of voice did not sound as though he were, but I didn't know why he was behaving the way he was. "I'm trying to figure out whether or not you're going to attempt to kill me when we finally . . ." He seemed unable to finish the thought for some reason.

I *believed* I knew what he was talking about, but I couldn't understand . . . "Why would I?"

"You're going to be surprised," he stated. "Either very pleasantly or very unpleasantly. Knowing you, I'm not sure which of the two it's going to be. If you were anyone else, I'd know the answer. Then again, if you were anyone else . . ."

"I don't understand," I told him apologetically.

"I'm trying to work this out." He put one of his hands over his face. "When you did that with him . . ." He paused and seemed to be thinking very hard about what he was trying to say. "You didn't feel a sense of . . . *completion*? Like . . . it was *finished*? That's what you're getting at, right?"

"I don't know what you mean," I said quietly. Then, I thought back on it and wanted to smack myself in the face. Agatha had told me I would feel things, but . . . "You're saying females can feel that way as well?" I didn't see how that was pos—

Jastin's mouth dropped open, and all he said was, "He is such a bastard."

My first reaction was to say I was sure whatever he was talking about hadn't been intentional, but . . . if Chandler had been telling the truth about Chase, that meant he knew all about this sort of thing. Did *everyone*?

I wondered if he'd thought it was hilarious. Jastin clearly seemed angry enough, so I was inclined to believe there had been some negative intent on Chase's part during. Whether that negative intent had been out of humor or something else . . .

I had no idea.

Tears threatened to well in my eyes, and I whispered, "I'm very embarrassed." It was worse than embarrassed, but I didn't know a word that would describe the feeling of it. The one I'd used was accurate enough, I supposed. It was the closest one I knew.

"Don't be," Jastin said. "You've clearly never had these things fully explained to you, and that's not your fault. So, I'm telling you right now that everything you're feeling is perfectly natural. It's what you're supposed to feel. It's okay. And whenever we take that step and you feel things you haven't felt yet . . . just know those things are okay too. I'm going to take care of you."

"What does taking care of me have to do with that?" That made no sense.

He smiled at me for what seemed to be quite a long time before saying, "You'll figure it out."

I did not have a clue in the world what he meant, but something about it made my stomach feel quite funny.

CHAPTER TWENTY-SEVEN

TERRIFIED

THERE WAS SOMETHING ABOUT WAKING UP next to Jastin while neither of us had the entirety of our clothing on that made me not want to get out of bed. It was . . . *warm*. Pleasant. Perhaps other, unknown things. I did enjoy something about the feeling of holding and being held onto at once.

I was contemplating never moving again when he said, "I know you're awake."

I shook my head.

"How are you responding if you're still asleep?"

I shrugged.

He laughed, patted my back several times, and said, "Time to get up. We have a lot of things to do today."

My response then was to latch onto him. I did not want to do anything else, and I was sick of always waking up and having to *do* things. That had been the story of my life. Wake up, do things, most of which I had no desire whatsoever do to, sleep, repeat. I didn't currently care about how I'd been doing my training daily, as *wants* seemed to easily change to *needs*. Some days they seemed to switch at random.

Stepping past certain points changed things.

"I'm giving you five seconds," he warned.

My response *then* was to throw one of my legs over him as well and latch on harder.

He sighed, stood, and began walking around the room as though I were not attached to him. I began sliding downward, and only at that point did he acknowledge me further.

He laughed loudly and tried to yank me off of him. "You're taking my pants with you!"

"Oh," I said as I willingly jumped down. "I'm sorry."

I was *not* sorry when I got a good look at what I'd done. His pants, as it were, were hanging extremely low on his hips. There was something quite breathtaking about the bones and muscles there, and I could not be sorry for what I'd done if this was the end result.

"What?" he asked with a grin.

"How is it that men have those sorts of muscles?" I asked curiously.

He chuckled. "Not all men do. Reapers are required to be in peak physical condition to do their jobs properly. I've lost about a third of my muscle mass since I met you."

"Why is that?" I asked. He did not look as though he had lost anything to my eyes, but then again, I'd not seen him with his shirt off until we'd been traveling for a number of weeks. It was possible, even if it didn't appear that way to me.

"Because you keep me from training consistently," he told me with another short laugh. "As much as I used to, at least. I try to fit in in when you're off doing other things, but . . . I'm around you almost all the time."

When thinking about his muscles being larger than they were now and how that would potentially look on him, I felt the need to say, "I very much like the way you look." I likely would've felt the need to say it regardless of whatever thoughts.

"The feeling's mutual," he said. It was only when his eyes went noticeably downward that I realized I was still lacking my shirt.

I blushed and made some sort of sound that was a mixture between an embarrassed giggle and some unknown thing. It sounded horrible and ridiculous, whatever it was. It made me feel quite foolish, but I blamed it on a lack of coherency due to having just woken.

I had to turn my back to him in order to retrieve my shirt, which made me think about what he would be seeing. When I nearly had it properly in place, I asked, "Why do you act as though my back isn't covered in scars?" I faced him again. "You've not looked at me any differently because of them. And when you look, or when you touch me, it's like you pretend they're not there at all."

"I know they're there," he said impassively. "Do you want me to treat you differently than I normally would because of them?"

"No." I shook my head. "I'm just curious. I'm sure Cherise likely has no scars at all on her. I'm simply wondering if you pretend they're not there because you find them off-putting."

"I don't find anything about you physically off-putting." His brow furrowed. "Least of all something that proves what you'll go through for what you believe in."

I smiled tightly at the floor. "It was just books."

"You and I both know it had hardly anything at all to do with the books by the end," he said. "You were proving a point."

I looked up, my gaze meeting his. "How could you know that?"

"Because your brother and I had a conversation immediately after Camden reported seeing you sneak inside the library." His voice was blank again. "We talked for a very long time about how he hadn't yet set things up to where he could show you preferential treatment. I was in the room the night you received your last beating."

My gaze shot to the floor, trying to process this.

He laughed a little, and it sounded quite uncomfortable. "Do you know why we talked for so long?"

When I said nothing, he answered the question for himself.

"We were hoping you'd be gone by the time we got there, that it could be shrugged off as misinformation. But you weren't."

I brought my eyes back to his.

"You were just sitting there, weren't you? It was like you were waiting for him. And when we walked into the room, you went and put the book back where you'd found it, walked over to your brother, and stared straight into his face. Do you remember what you said to him?"

"What are you waiting for, Sir," I answered quietly. I'd not asked that many times, as they rarely waited for anything, and I could remember being particularly pleased by the look on his face.

"So then we went down into that room," Jastin said. "You walked right into the middle of it and pulled the back of your shirt over your head, and you stood there waiting. You were expecting him to do it himself, weren't you? So when you realized it hadn't been him . . ." He trailed off and shook his head.

"Was it *you*?" I asked quickly.

"Of course not," he said. "It was some random Guard. Any Reaper would get killed by your father for that, and even though I didn't know you then . . . I wouldn't have beaten my best friend's sister any more than he would've done it himself." He paused. "I was standing next to Ahren the entire time. And then, when it was over, you came back in front of him and said . . . *Please sleep well, Sir*. You had the *tiniest* smirk on your face, like you were amused by the entire thing." He kept shaking his head. "I will *never* forget that moment. We stood there for the longest time before I said . . . *She thinks you're a coward*." He paused again. "It's what you thought, isn't it?"

I pursed my lips together into a hard line. It *had* been what I'd thought at the time, or close enough to pass.

I did not want to think about that, so I asked, "Why don't I remember you being there?"

"You didn't even see the Guard, did you?" he asked. "When I held the door open for you to his office a few days later you didn't look at me, but I could tell you were surprised someone had done that for you. You don't remember me standing there when you threw that fit to get his attention, the day he punched that Guard in the face. You looked right at me, but you didn't see me." He took a deep breath. "I was always there after I was. You just didn't look properly, not until you realized you could and allowed yourself to do it."

I had absolutely nothing to say to that because I could not think of anything.

"So . . . what point were you trying to prove, exactly?"

"The same one I proved to all of them except my brother." My voice was very quiet. "That they could do whatever they wanted to me, but they would all be dead long before I would." I cleared my throat. "I *did* enjoy the books." If it were so simple.

"I'm sure you did." A few seconds passed before he asked, "Are you angry I was there?"

"So was my brother." I took a deep breath and then released it. "Sometimes we're all required to do things we don't want to, simply because of the way situations play themselves out. I suppose one must play the part they must."

I felt my mind branching off in so many different directions due to the new information and thoughts on my past life. It was so strange to realize that my ten years of hell were now . . . *past*. Was I on my third life now? How many of them would I have?

Years of time, and memories, and experiences, all of them similar enough to be clumped together as one small part of an infinitely larger whole. . . .

"Chase told me . . ." I began, careful. "He told me that the leader who was in New Bethel when I first arrived . . ." I paused to take another deep breath. "He told me he cut off his hands and then, that after he met my father, my father killed him. He told me he'd called it . . ." I smiled tightly. "*A show of good faith.*"

I could not fully decipher the look on Jastin's face. A mixture of confusion and disgust, possibly? It took him a rather long time to respond. I was not quite sure what sort of response I'd been expecting, but I knew I did not receive it.

"I wasn't there, obviously," he began, "but I've never heard anything about your father going to New Bethel before he came to retrieve you. It's possible it's true yes, but . . . it's also possible Chase said that only to deceive you about your father, wanting you to think he'd been right under your nose and had left you there. Potentially sway you where he wanted you. I wouldn't know which of the two it is."

I nodded because I'd not really expected him to know.

"Those parties," I said. "The ones they threw in New Bethel when the Reapers would return home from successful missions. Jarsil doesn't do that, does it?"

"We don't celebrate death here," he said firmly. "Not anymore."

"Then why did my father laugh after our camp was ambushed while traveling?" I'd thought about that many times since, especially after arriving here. "Does he have issues with the leader of Maldir?"

"I'd imagine it had something to do with Stelin," he replied. "I don't believe your father wants to give him the impression that he's soft, in case he *is* still in contact with his father."

"You didn't answer the question."

His brow furrowed. "What does that matter?"

"Eliminating or opening up," I explained. "I find it relevant to the initial question asked, as it *is* one factor to include in his behavior that night being out of character."

I supposed he couldn't argue with that. My logic *was* sound.

It took him a moment, but he said, "As far as I know, what your father said that night on the leader you're asking about is accurate. They only have whatever issues with one another that they do, none of them personal. He's too smart. I hope to god none of those men meant anything to him though, or that if they did he doesn't find out who it was."

"Why is that?" I asked. "Do you believe he would retaliate?"

"I'm not sure." He shook his head. "But he's one of *very* few leaders people speculate *just might* be able to kill your father in a one-on-one. People bet on that sort of thing, get in fights over it."

My brow furrowed. "You're saying there are only a few people as skilled as my father at killing people."

"It's not simply about the act of killing, Aster. It's *everything*. Skill, intelligence, mental states." He almost laughed. "I suppose you wouldn't know."

My face was still in the same state it had been. "Know what?"

"What your father is."

"He's a Reaper. I *believe* this has been gone over."

"Sure." Jastin laughed then, nodding. "Sure. I mean, he *is*, but he's not. Most leaders get to where they do by a series of flukes. They're *just* good or smart enough to get ahead of the rest. But every once in a while, a child stands out in the schools. Flukes in the blood rather than any situations. They get sent out earlier in the hopes they'll be killed. They pose too much of a threat. If they *survive* and keep on the path?" He shrugged. "They're not really Reapers no matter what they're referred to as. It's the ones who keep their heads on with all the talk on *prodigies* that end up doing massive damage in some way or another. Or being capable of it."

"You're saying . . ." I tried to process this. "My father is a . . . *prodigy*?" Whatever that was. Was that what Anders had meant in saying *what he was*?

"Your father was *ten years old* when they first sent him out," he said, which felt like a blow to the gut. "There are only five prodigies in power. Your father, Hasting, the leader you're asking about, and two others. Hasting was sent out when he was eleven. One other at eleven. One at twelve. The only other sent out at ten still living and in power is the one you asked about."

"Are you worried he would or could kill my father?"

Jastin shook his head. "He *might* be able to manage it in a one-on-one, but I don't see that coming about. There's a massive age difference that would play into it in one way or another. He's larger than your father as well, so I've heard."

"My father is very large."

He nodded. "Anyway, it's nothing to be concerned over. He's too smart to come at your father like was said that night. It's never been personal. I just hope it stays that way. I've heard that him and his brother fighting together is a sight to behold." He smiled a little. "But *your father* fighting?" He sucked in a bit of air through his teeth. "I've heard that's the most terrifying thing in the entire world. I *do* wonder if a big part of that has something to do with how he is most often. But they say he was *much* different when he was younger. Not as bad as who you asked about. You won't hear a single good word on him."

"Is being intelligent not something?"

He laughed a little under his breath. "I like to think intelligence is only good when it is. Sure, whatever it is that's wrong with his head also keeps him away from your father and alternately this city as well. I'll give him that. It's how he uses it that's the problem. He's no better than the rest. I honestly don't know why your father hasn't killed him yet, but he hasn't sent anyone to Maldir in quite some time, and god knows it would take a small army to handle him." He seemed to think about it. "He hasn't sent anyone there in a while apart from Stelin."

"Why is that?"

He shrugged. "Who you're asking about caught all but two since he came into power, as far as I know. Not his men. *Him.* They say he can make anyone with nothing more than a glance no matter how good they are or how many other people are around. The two couldn't get near him. As far as I know, Stelin is the *only* person who's gotten close and not been made by him. How he dealt with the ones of ours he caught got progressively worse. I'd say that's part of why your father doesn't send anyone there. It might not be. We've had some caught and returned from other places in similar states and kept doing what we do. Only your father could tell you the real reason."

Interesting.

"But no, Aster." He shook his head. "It's not related. You could ask your father to be sure if he'd tell you, but *I'm* sure his behavior that night had everything to do with Stelin and his father. The leader you're asking about is and has been irrelevant since he stopped leaving his walls."

"Irrelevant how?" I hardly thought that an appropriate word, considering everything.

"Out here?" Jastin gestured around. "He's irrelevant outside his walls. That happens when they don't leave. He's irrelevant because he's no longer out in the world. He was out for a while when I was. What happens when there are active prodigies out is a complete avoidance of their cities. They can and will kill *anyone* they see outside walls. I know someone who rode two weeks out of their way *both ways* to avoid Maldir. A month, all in the hopes of not running into him while out."

Interesting.

I asked, "Are these *prodigies* truly that good? Are they, or is it preying on the fear people create with the scary stories they tell?"

Jastin rubbed at his face, seeming quite unhappy with this conversation. "Aster, the only other thing I'll say on it is that the *only* word heard on how he fights as far as I know came from people interrogated about him taking over Maldir. No other time or situation. Just the one instance. I've never heard of anyone managing to get away from a fight to potentially tell about it, only witnessing on his side. I've heard it takes *extensive* interrogating to get anyone who knows a word to say a word, and sometimes even that won't work. Because they're more afraid of him than any torture that's thrown at them, even from a place or situation they know there's no escape from. So yeah, I'd say so. But you can't imagine the sort of person. Your father is the only one I know of that isn't—"

He closed his eyes and held up a hand. "I'm not going to say anything else on it. I don't know if you're asking due to your father or Hasting. I don't want to confuse you about it. But a team of six avoiding a city to avoid one singular prodigy inside its walls?" He nodded. "It's completely feasible because, yes, they're that good."

Six had been the number supposedly sent by Hasting.

"Jastin," I said quietly, getting off all I'd just learned. I would think about it later, and he was clearly done. It *had* made me think about . . . "We can tell one another things, can't we?"

"Of course," he said without hesitation, seeming relieved at the deviation.

"Things that . . . perhaps someone else told us in confidence?"

He walked over to me quickly with a concerned look on his face and nearly whispered, "What's going on?"

"Stelin," I said warily. "I made a deal with him."

He shook his head. "What sort of deal?"

"While he and I were discussing my training the day when I told him I would allow him to work with Chandler . . ." I started and then stopped.

I lied and bent the truth quite often, but I'd not ever told another person something I'd been told in confidence. But there was something about it . . . something I needed an outside perspective on. My tone was a whisper when I said it.

"He told me he would work his ass off to help me reach my potential, and then . . . he wanted me to help him ensure his father ended up dead. He told me not to tell anyone."

Jastin's eyes went so wide. "You *agreed* to that?"

I nodded slowly.

He took a deep breath and looked away. "Have you thought he was—" He cut himself off and his eyes shot back to mine. "*That's* what you meant yesterday when you said he might send someone to you to lure you out willingly."

I nodded again. "Please don't tell anyone," I said quietly. "I need to be sure and, as of right now, I'm split down the middle." What I'd been told about *prodigies* gave me *much* to think on.

He stared at my face and it was quite a long time before he nodded. "Is that the first time you've ever told someone something a person told you not to tell?"

I nodded.

"Why did you tell me?"

"We're partners." The smile was tight on my face. "How can we properly watch one another's backs when we don't have all the information to know what we're looking for?"

"I'll keep an eye on him." He pulled me into a hug. "Discreetly."

I nodded.

"I've got your back, Star," he said quietly as he rubbed mine. "But please think on what I said and try to understand what it means."

I was only safe in any sense of the word with my father. That was what he was saying.

I said, "I understand."

"Good." It took him a moment to say, "Please don't tell your father you heard that word from me. He . . . doesn't like it."

I simply held onto his back tightly because I realized that I was more afraid than I'd ever been in all my life. It took me a moment to realize I wasn't afraid.

I was completely and utterly terrified.

CHAPTER TWENTY-EIGHT

EVERYTHING

AGATHA HELPED ME *prepare myself* for my father's speech. He required that I make myself more *presentable* than I normally was and, given what he was doing for or because of me, I figured it was the very least I could do for him. I thought it was ridiculous and an absolute waste of time, but he would know better than I would on these sorts of matters.

I made no complaints to him on the matter, though I did ensure he was aware of where I stood on it before going to do as required.

I had seen Agatha very briefly on a number of occasions since our arrival in Jarsil. I'd avoided her along with everyone else that first approximate month here, but I had run into her a few times. She seemed to be so happy here, which put a satisfied feeling in my chest. She was no longer a servant, but . . . given she had spent the entirety of her life busy, she was always doing something.

Father was still trying to find a proper place for her to fit, she said. He let her do whatever she wanted, so she was doing a lot of things she'd never thought she could. She helped some days with the crops, simply because she could, or assisted around the House. By the way things sounded, she did something new nearly every day. I had never seen her smile so much or so freely, but I did wonder if she was trying to find that place for her to fit more so than my father was.

Sometimes life was difficult to adapt to, even in the good ways. Perhaps even more so, when you weren't the slightest bit accustomed to positivity.

She seemed so happy.

She seemed like an entirely different person.

Things were still a bit strained between us, mostly on my part, though I was trying very hard to move forward. I'd not seen her since learning about Chase because I hadn't wanted to deal with the look on her face, nor had I wanted to speak of it at all. I still had not told her about Jastin and me, which was a great deal of the reason I asked for her assistance in getting prepared.

I wanted her to hear it from me and not my father as he was telling his entire city.

She deserved much more than that.

I felt badly that I had partially been tuning out her words as I prepared myself for her reactions. It wasn't that I didn't want to listen to her or was not interested in what she could possibly be saying.

I went through fake conversations inside my head and attempted to discover the best route to take when presenting her with the information.

In the end, I interrupted her in the middle of one of her sentences. And all I said was, "Jastin and I are getting married."

She stopped midway through some part of fixing my hair. She had a handful of it extended in the air when I looked in the mirror to analyze her face. I expected for her to ask me: *How did this happen?* Or: *What about Chase?* She did not ask me either of those things.

Very slowly she smiled at my reflection and asked, "Are you really?"

I nodded.

She did not share my brother's exuberant excitement, nor Jastin's sister's for that matter, but her smile was genuine when she said, "Congratulations, my flower."

"Thank you," I said with a tight smile.

She laughed when she saw it. "Well, aren't you happy?"

"Concerned," I admitted. "And . . . quite happy, yes." Amongst other things.

"Concerned why?"

"I feel as though I'm living in a dream half the time," I told her. "That, when I'm awake, the entire world is lies and strategy and worries. And then, when I'm alone with him, none of that seems so real. But life never seems real while you're dreaming, does it?" Close sometimes. Very close. "I'm so afraid that something will happen and I'll never be able to sleep properly again." I wiped at my eyes. "I don't want to wake up."

"Then let's hope you never have to." She spoke softly, but after a moment the smile on her face stiffened. "Your father told me about Chase."

I nodded, still not wanting to speak of it. I found no point to do as much.

"He's insisted I learn how to defend myself on the chance that they send a different set of Reapers here. But he told me that if I see Chase . . ." She paused and the smile on her face was the tightest I had ever seen from her. "He told me to run as fast as I could. Find the nearest grouping of Reapers if possible and keep running."

"That would be a good idea," I told her quietly. They would all know about her by now.

"It wouldn't make a difference, would it?"

I did not want to lie to her, so I remained silent on the matter. The only thing that made any sense at all to say was, "I'm sorry. For dragging you into this."

"My flower." She laughed. "You've not dragged me into anything. We could blame your father, his friend who gave you away, the woman who brought you to New Bethel, or the leader who assigned you to me." Her tone was very apologetic when she said, "It's simply the way it all worked out, love."

"I blame everyone," I admitted. I felt ashamed for saying as much, but it was true. I blamed everyone she'd listed and then some, every-one involved. I blamed myself. "Why is it that we all hurt people? Why is it that everything bad that happens only seems to affect the ones we love?"

"That's what love is, my flower," she said. "You make yourself vulnerable because . . . it's worth it."

Was it?

I STOOD ALONE WITH MY FATHER near a windowed door that led onto a balcony before he was set to give his speech. I stared out it with him, down at all the people who had gathered below. At least what could be seen of them.

"So many of them slept out there." His voice almost sounded sad. "I don't speak to them all often."

I said, "I suppose they wanted to be closest to you."

It was very strange, I thought, to sleep outdoors only to hear someone speak. Then again, I'd eavesdropped simply to hear someone speak when I could've waited a while and heard at least part of it later. Things often weren't accurate enough when you heard them after the fact, even from a source who'd been directly involved. I supposed it all depended on how badly you felt you needed to hear something directly from the initial source, the lengths you'd go to for just that.

Some things were more than worth sleeping outside for. I would've—

He shook his head slightly. "We've already found five spies. Three attempted to escape immediately after hearing word that I intended to make an announcement. Can you imagine how afraid they were to flee without listening to it?" He paused. "Two came to me of their own volition."

"What did they want?" I asked. "Bartering for their lives?"

"In a sense." A tight smile overtook his face. "They don't want to leave."

"How could you know they were being honest?"

"It's something we've been dealing with since we began implementing such drastic changes here," he said. "We've had a quite steady influx of Reapers from other cities who are unhappy. That's always the question. How do you trust them?"

"How can you trust anyone at all in this world?" I asked curiously.

"I don't know." He shook his head again. "I must admit it's more trusting the system as a whole than the individual pieces of it. I try to be objective with them, but all I can see is myself when I look into their faces. Your mother. I've been lucky thus far in the sense that when I lack the proper objectivity, someone else has it for me." He paused again before adding, "One of the Reapers who came to me has a family that he kept secret. He wants to bring them here."

"A non-Reaper family?" Why would any of them risk that?

"Yes," my father replied. "In an entirely different city than his own. He would always see them when he could, he said."

Quickly, I asked, "You didn't send him away to retrieve them, did you?"

"I am not so stupid, Flower." He sighed. "He agreed to let me send a team of my men to retrieve his family. He wrote his lady a letter to know she could trust them. He even let me read it before asking to. I saw nothing in there that didn't line up with what he said to me."

"And you would jeopardize a team of your Reapers for that?" For one family, one Reaper? Many for only one?

"It's what you said yesterday, is it not?" He was staring out the window rather than looking at me. "Happiness and love. Why not spare it, if we can? Apparently, some of us will choose to do so. I didn't order a single man in that team to go. They were in the room during and volunteered." He shook his head again for a while, then said, "He was smiling and crying the entire time he was writing that letter. I wish someone would've been willing to allow your mother and me our life together, with you and your brother as a family. Whole and intact as we should've been. A different world, without all this."

I took his hand in mine and smiled sadly at him when he looked at me.

"I know my mother is gone . . ." I began, "but you still have Ahren and me. And your brother. You're the one who's willing to allow it, Father. A different world. I'm sure my mother would be so proud of you for all you've done."

His eyes were welling with tears as he took and then released a deep breath. "I wish she could see you now. She would love your spirit." His eyes fell briefly on the necklace around my neck and he smiled tightly. "You're sure you want me to announce your engagement to them all?" He looked out of the window once more to add, "It's so many people."

"Abby told me we should celebrate and be happy, despite the bad things," I said. "That it was what leaders were supposed to do—to give hope to their people. I want them to think we're not afraid."

"But we *are* afraid, aren't we?" he asked. I assumed it was rhetorical. "You're saying you want to give hope to the people. What level of it are you talking about? Are you really telling me that you want to have them all at your wedding or are you simply saying to tell them of it?"

I chuckled. "I doubt hardly any of them would take the time to go, Father."

"Are you sure about that?" He grinned. "If I make the announcement, I can't go back on it, even if you change your mind later. It's all about consistency."

"What is?"

My father replied to that with, "Everything."

"What are we talking about?" Ahren asked as he came into the room with Jastin just behind him.

"She thinks hardly anyone in the city would show up if we allowed them to her wedding," my father said in a tone that bordered on amusement.

"You're so ridiculous sometimes." My brother pulled me into a hug.

"*Easy!*" I exclaimed. Whatever sort of contraption Agatha had put me in made breathing more than slightly uncomfortable and very nearly impossible.

"Is that even you under there?" Ahren asked as he frowned down at me.

"I already feel ridiculous enough, Ahren," I said in exasperation as I thought about the silly dress and my short hair pinned back uncomfortably to my head. "Don't make it any worse for me."

"Be quiet. You look beautiful," he said. "Doesn't she, Jas?"

I felt myself blushing when I looked over at Jastin and saw him smiling at me despite my foolish appearance.

"What do *you* think about the wedding?" my father asked.

When I glanced at him, he was staring at Jastin.

"He agrees with his sister," I answered for him.

"I never said I wanted so many people watching." Jastin chuckled. "Only that she may be right."

"Then we're in agreement on the matter." I nodded. "Wouldn't it be dangerous, though?"

"No more dangerous than the two of you walking about the city together," my father said nonchalantly. "We would have men everywhere."

"Why should something meant to be so happy be so stressful?" I asked, curious.

Ahren laughed. "You haven't even started *planning* it!"

"Planning what?" I asked. "You simply *do it*, don't you?"

My brother looked to my father. "And you're listening to her?"

Jastin said, "Planning weddings isn't the way your sister's mind works."

"I don't understand what you all keep talking about with planning," I said in exasperation.

All three of them seemed to ignore me, which was unfortunate. Perhaps I would discover what they were all going on about eventually.

"When was the last time there was a large wedding in any of the cities?" Jastin asked thoughtfully.

"If I've read the records correctly, it was one of the king's sons in Bethel," my father replied.

"Then strategically speaking it would be a smart move, wouldn't it?" Jastin asked. "I'm never going to be invisible again after we step outside. Might as well make that mean something."

"Are you *certain*?" I asked quietly.

"I don't care how many people are there," Jastin said. Then, he smiled at me. "As long as they leave when it's over."

My father nearly gaped at him. "Do you truly believe this is an appropriate time or place to be speaking of such things?"

Jastin shrugged. "She asked me a question."

I could not stop the small giggle that came out of my mouth, but I attempted to disguise it as a cough. I did not think I had fooled anyone.

"Are we going to do this?" I asked, attempting to bring focus back to what truly mattered, especially before my behavior was commented on.

My father sighed. "I suspect we should." He had his hand on a doorknob that would lead us out onto a balcony, and it lingered there. Under his breath he said, "I despise speaking in front of people."

So I was smiling in amusement when he opened the door, but only for a moment.

I'd expected silence.

You cannot hear anyone speaking unless you're silent, which was the purpose of what we were currently doing.

They were there to listen to speaking.

The people in the city were so very far from silent when the four of us stepped out into the bright sunlight. For an instant, I believed they were on the verge of rioting, as they were so *loud*. But then I looked at all that could be seen of their smiling faces and their hands waving and clapping.

"All the stars," I whispered under my breath when I realized. I saw the people looking at my father with tears of absolute joy on their faces, not at him returning from being away but for simply *being*, and it *finally* struck me.

Jarsil was once again a city that had a king. My father was *not* a Reaper at all . . . to them.

My father was so much more intelligent than I had ever given him credit for.

CHAPTER
TWENTY-NINE

STAR

I**T TOOK SUCH A VERY LONG TIME** for the people of Jarsil to quiet down and allow my father the chance to speak. Before they had, I took in as much as I could of the scene. It had taken me a moment to recover enough from the shock of what I'd stepped out to and thus realized to manage doing so.

The people were organized neatly into sections with Reapers patrolling up and down between all of them. There were Reapers atop the wall with bows in their hands and arrows in quivers attached to their backs, watching everyone and everything as entirely as could be done. I wondered how the people in the back would hear my father's words, but when he began speaking, that question was answered for me.

"I'd like to thank you all for coming to listen to my announcement."

Periodically, there were Reapers who were passing the message along to the people farther on in the sections. He must've had them memorize it.

"My daughter, Aster—" My father was cut off by a *preposterous* amount of loudness from the people. From where I was standing, I just barely caught the hint of a smile on his face through my wide eyes. When the people had become quiet again, he continued.

Clapping. Cheering. At my name. That was . . .

"She came to me yesterday and pleaded a case for the city. She told me that you all love me for taking care of you, protecting you. But she told me that I should *trust* you, along with all those other things." He paused. "I'll please ask that you keep my daughter's faith in you in mind while I'm trusting you with what follows."

And where things had been so loud before, you could've heard a feather hit the ground. It was so different, and it was also unnerving in a way I hadn't anticipated to have silence from thousands of people. They looked like ants, all stopped when they never halted. Ants, all stopped when they never did, staring up at one singular entity above them.

I took in a deep breath, hoping the things that followed would not destroy the entire city. What my mother had wanted.

"You all know that I was previously a Reaper for this city," my father said. "Back when things were not as they are now. I had a wife that I loved very much, and . . . the two of us had a son here."

There was a collective intake of breath from the people below us as my father stepped back and pulled my brother forward.

"This is my son, Ahren."

I hardly caught the look of bewilderment and shock on my brother's face. If he'd known about the speech . . . my father had not informed him of this part of it. What did he think he was doing up here? Standing guard? That seemed quite ridiculous, unless it was a normal occurrence. Even still.

Ahren turned his face away from the crowd and looked back at me. His expression was confused and there were tears in his eyes. Jastin squeezed my hand tightly where it was at my side, but he soon released it.

"As you can imagine," my father went on, "our son was taken from us, as Reaper children were back then." I knew he was crying too or at least on the verge of it when he said, "It destroyed the both of us and we decided to leave, knowing we would likely be killed. The thought of being so close and never being able to see him was too much to bear. Of course Reapers were sent for us, but we managed to elude them for quite some time. Until one day . . . a Reaper from Bethel had us cornered and we could not escape. His name was Hasting."

He'd brought them in? I hadn't realized . . .

I watched the people hurriedly look back and forth from one another and then up again to my father.

They knew of Hasting?

Was that because of the word Jastin had used to describe a select few or what he'd done as a leader?

"He offered to take us to the leader who was in control of Bethel at the time, saying that perhaps he would choose to spare our lives. We took the offer. It was several years there before my wife became pregnant with Aster. Hasting was already beginning his play at Bethel, and we could not allow another child to be taken and subjected to that life as it was, *especially* not under that man. So we ran."

My father turned to look at me, and while his head was turned, he wiped at his eyes. "My wife was killed shortly after our daughter was born. And I raised Aster for eight years in the wilderness, but . . . my wife and I had always spoken about wishing things were different than they were, that people would not be required to run in order to feel safe in their lives. So as my daughter was getting older, I began learning as much as I could about the events that were going in our world. And that is how I lost her. My daughter was taken to be a servant for the leader's House in New Bethel."

If the people had known that I was not here, they'd not known where I was and what I'd been doing there. That much was clear to me by their reactions. Some of them shouted, but I couldn't make out what they were saying and my father seemed to ignore it.

"I thought she was dead, so when my son gave me information that she was not . . . Well, you can see that she is here with me now."

I wanted to plug my ears then at the loudness of the people.

Cheering? Were they cheering again? Because of me, being here with my father?

Why?

My hands twitched at my sides. Truly, I preferred the silence, but I reminded myself I would have the quiet back soon. Once this was over, if the people did not riot or attempt a revolt.

"If we're being honest with you," my father went on slowly, "then I should tell you that my daughter is many things. She is kind, but she is also capable. While making our way here, she and Jastin— the Reaper standing next to her—were ambushed by two Reapers sent by Hasting to abduct her to be used as leverage against me. My daughter killed one of those men, but she also saved Jastin's life."

I fought against the urge to fidget, as my father had not informed me that he'd planned on telling his entire city I was a murderer. That would've been . . . nice to know.

"We've slowly been realizing things during her time here," my father said. "One of her companions, someone she trusted dearly, had intent to deliver her straight to Bethel. When I received information that Hasting was planning another abduction attempt for her in our city, that person was sent with a team of Reapers to intercept them because we did not know he was a spy. No one from that team has returned. We know now that they will not ever.

"It would probably be better if you were not aware of these things," my father said after a pause. "Everything I have ever done, or not done, has been for other people's well-being. Hardly anyone knows about my son because I could not risk Hasting discovering his existence in the world. But my daughter pleaded with me to ask for your help."

There was confusion, multiple outcries of, "What can we do?" and similar things.

My father continued on as though they were not speaking at all. "You may be asking yourselves why you should care. I am not asking you to care about my family, but I'm telling you that . . . if I am killed, I cannot promise the next person in my position will be concerned with your safety and well-being. You all remember the way things were before, and if I am killed, I cannot promise you anything. I cannot promise that Hasting himself won't come take over this city simply because he could."

And then there was panic along with the confusion. It was difficult to discern what was going on with so many people involved, but I could hear the panic in their collective tone.

"*Please remain calm*," my father shouted. Thank the *stars* for his carrying voice.

Everyone near the front seemed to get hold of themselves, momentarily at least, and it spread slowly down the masses. That made more sense when the quieting began and I could hear Reapers shouting for it, creating order at the beginnings of potential chaos. Keeping the ants stopped in the lines my father had made.

My father said, "I am not asking you to fight."

I heard several yells of people declaring they would. Those were clear enough.

My father shook his head. "All I'm asking is that you remain calm and open your eyes. There are spies in our city. It is what Reapers do. Now, most of them are simply here to report information back to their own leaders. Most of them have no intent to harm us, or any of you. I'm asking you to open your eyes. If you see *any* suspicious behavior, anything at all, find the nearest Reaper of ours and inform them of it.

"These spies will not be disguised as Reapers from our city. They will be disguised as citizens. Do *not* take matters into your own hands because they *will* attack if they're cornered, and they will *not* think twice about it. There is no telling how many people they could kill before they were apprehended, and it can be avoided if you do as I instructed. Find a Reaper and inform them immediately. Can you do that for me? For us?"

I bit my bottom lip to refrain from smiling at the reaction of the crowd. It was very nearly a wave that reached past where my eyes could see, of people who were willing to do absolutely anything my father asked them to. It took a rather long while for them to get quiet again, but I did not mind the noise so much right then. The Reapers must not have either.

My father said, "That's not all I have to share with you today."

And then there was silence again.

"My daughter informed me that someone close to her said leaders should give hope to their people, to show them there is still good to be found in the midst of bad."

That was not relayed. That meant . . .

He'd given me the chance to change my mind.

I almost reached out to grab his hand to stop him, but I forced myself to remain still.

He seemed to take a very deep breath before saying, "My daughter and Jastin are getting married, and they would like for anyone in the city who wants to attend to be there with them on that day. They want to show you that, even when people are coming to steal your life . . . it does not mean that you have to allow them to steal your happiness.

"I will fight for my daughter's happiness," my father said through the loudness of the people below us. "My son's. My future son's. Just as I will fight for the happiness of you all. We will stand together, and we will not hide any longer."

I did not try to stop myself from smiling then as I took in the cheering people. Jastin squeezed my hand to get my attention, and the two of us shared some secret little message. I thought we were both thinking the exact same thing.

My father is brilliant.

But then Jastin shook his head in what appeared to be disbelief and said one word. I could not hear him, but I knew what it had been.

Star.

I realized he did not think my father was brilliant.

He thought I was.

CHAPTER THIRTY

SHEEP

THE REMAINDER OF THE DAY after the speech was complete and utter madness. I could not take the dress and the squeezing, life-sucking contraption off. What was it Agatha had called it? A corses? Cor . . . Cor*something*.

Curses, more like. That's what it was to me anyhow and, in my opinion, it was the only word that made any sense whatsoever for it to be called. The curses was a torture device, and the longer I spent in it the worse it became.

My father had gone down to the courtyard immediately after his speech to speak personally with some of his people, whoever could or would get close enough through all the others to manage it. We were required to follow and do the same. So, until the sky went dark, the four of us were speaking with the citizens of Jarsil. I didn't know whether my father preferred the personal speaking opposed to what he'd done just before or if he despised both equally. If he disliked it at all . . . I couldn't tell.

Even his dislike of public speaking hadn't been at all obvious as he was doing as much. Not during. I suspected the personal speaking wasn't as bad for him. Or perhaps it wasn't the act of speaking at all but the thoughts leading up to it.

I hadn't needed to hear him say he despised it to be quite sure he did, but confirmation was always preferable. I wouldn't have known, had I not been in close proximity to him beforehand. It wasn't in any way obvious, save one thing.

Sometimes, one thing was enough.

Before going out to the courtyard, I'd asked Jastin and Ahren to give us a moment. I'd then very briefly spoken to my father about doing something to ensure what had been obvious to me wouldn't be obvious to others. It only seemed right after the discussion had earlier in the day about appearances.

He was chewing on a sweet but rather potent-smelling leaf when the two of us had caught back up with Jastin and my brother.

When responding to the inquiry of what I'd needed, I felt I was being truthful enough in saying, "I simply needed to speak to him on the correct thing to do out there."

That seemed to be good enough to suit them.

I waited a while to glance up at my father, finding him staring straight forward.

Though he was still chewing on that leaf, the corners of his mouth were just barely up. That went away when Ahren followed my gaze there.

Ahren then said, "I'll meet you all out there," and turned around.

I kept my gaze forward then, thinking on a number of things before ending up in the courtyard, surrounded by bodies all focused on me or the ones I'd been standing on a balcony with.

I tried to keep up with it and to do what I should despite the curses and how horrendous the entire experience was.

I kept reminding myself it would be over eventually.

It would be over.

All days passed.

People embraced us all, and they paid no mind to the Reapers who were nearly having some sort of catastrophic cardiac event because of it. The people did not even notice them there, but I watched them. It calmed me, somewhat.

If one were not paying close attention, they might've believed the Reapers of Jarsil were entirely composed, but I could see it there. Every time anyone was touched, their eyes would widen the slightest bit, their jaws would clench, or their hands would twitch and be balled into fists or their arms crossed. And every time anyone simply stepped near my father, it seemed they struggled against the urge to break the offender's neck. It made me think on a number of things, mostly differences between dogs, wolves, and cats.

The people hugged my brother. They hugged Jastin and myself and congratulated us endlessly.

I did not like it even a little. None of us knew these specific people on a personal level, nor they us, so *why* they believed physical contact was in any way acceptable . . .

Well, I truly couldn't fathom.

They asked us when the wedding would be.

Soon was all I could tell them. I said that one word more times than I could count. Eventually, I asked Jastin to answer them with it so I did not have to say the word any longer. I worried I would start shouting it at them even though I was aware that them not knowing as much until they were told wasn't their fault. I just couldn't understand why . . .

They *all* looked at *me* when inquiring about the wedding. They all looked at me, though I was one half of it on my own. They did not look to the other half.

Did you really kill a Reaper? I was asked that so many times. I would nod uncomfortably, expecting people to be afraid or disgusted. They were not because . . . why should they be? When they glorified their Reapers, not really thinking about what they did, why be disgusted? When they looked at me standing in front of them . . . how could they be afraid?

I would watch little girls' eyes light up, and grown women as well. *Hope.* Me being capable of killing a Reaper with its back turned to me gave them *hope.* It was ludicrous. And if they had the vaguest clue what they were hoping . . .

They would stop.

There seemed to be an odd, almost disassociation with what killing actually *was*. A failure to grasp. A lack of caring to.

It was more than somewhat disturbing.

How did you save his life? I was asked that more often than the latter. At first, I was surprised by that, but then I realized people didn't want to speak of death. They would rather skirt over it, pick apart a situation and pull out the good rather than take it as it was as a whole, bad and all. It was easier.

277

I let Jastin respond to the inquiries about me *saving his life*. I did not like thinking about it, nor did I believe any of my actions that night had been *heroic* as they all seemed inclined to think. I'd been an absolute mess despite anything I'd done. I did not believe that was the correct and complete definition of the word.

The killing was much easier for me to think about than almost losing him. I did not want that to come across. I was quite sure a dress and smile would still be what they were seeing if it did, though. I would show what my father had required and nothing more or less. Not even the possibility for more or less.

"I'd been cut and had lost consciousness from lack of blood. She carried me on her shoulders back to our camp." That was Jastin's standard response to the question, but it varied in detail from time to time depending on the sort of person who was asking.

She couldn't have, some people said.

Did she really? came from others.

They would look to him for that, as though I weren't standing right there. As though I were . . . not invisible.

Insignificant. That was the word. Insignificant despite them being incapable of stopping themselves to watch me simply walk down a street as they'd done *every time* I had.

Jastin had been correct in what he'd told me before. People were *exactly* like sheep. They asked the same questions and had the same general responses despite any small variations. It was almost as though the entire flock of them shared a single head to think with. The longer it went on, the more I felt a shifting in my perspective, and I began to understand. The dress and the smile. I understood.

The entire day was stressful, and exhausting, and so *unbelievably* repetitive. One of the only things that truly made me feel better was my brother pulling me aside at some point. He hugged me more tightly than he ever had before. I did not complain about the curses that time no matter what it felt like.

"Thank you," he said. I was quite certain those two words given at the exact point they were was the most sincere Ahren had ever been with me. Quite certain.

Look at the two of them together, came from several happy people around us. They didn't care about Hasting or threats in general. They cared about my brother and me hugging. That was what they wanted to see, for some reason.

Of course.

I squeezed Ahren's hand when he stepped back, but he said, "Sonofabitch," under his breath and the moment was over before having its deserved time in the world.

He had already begun to walk away because he'd noticed something, and I pushed my unhappiness from my mind.

I was concerned about a Reaper from another city, but then I discovered the cause for his frustration.

I was the smallest bit frustrated, but I was mostly unhappy at the thought of it.

Jastin was speaking with someone relatively close by. He was still within eyesight but a good distance away. And my father had just intercepted Cherise. I followed behind my brother to Jastin, thinking about words and promises. Words that created promises without the word being required to be said.

"Cherise is going to get herself killed," my brother said under his breath when the person speaking with Jastin stepped away.

Jastin looked at him in confusion and then glanced over his shoulder. He shook his head and sighed.

"What is she thinking, trying to start something in front of everyone?" Ahren was staring off at her.

Probably more than you realize, I could've said. But my father was leaving her, approaching the three of us, and she stayed where she was.

My father's gaze fell on me. "She wants to speak with you."

"With *Aster*?" my brother asked in disbelief.

I glanced back to where she was standing in the same spot, appearing uncomfortable.

"Yes, with Aster," my father said. "Alone."

When walking away, I heard my father muttering something or other about *distinctions* under his breath.

I had hoped to never see her again, but that was likely ridiculous of me regardless of how many citizens filled up the city to potentially put distance between. And even though I did not want to speak with her, let alone look in a direction she might possibly be, I found myself walking toward her anyhow. She was still technically a citizen of Jarsil, and she was still the mother of Jastin's child. I had never told her she could not speak to *me* after all, and I *was* remarkably curious.

I was unhappy that I found myself appreciating her impeccable black hair this time, but perhaps it was because the haughtiness was not on her face now as it had been before. She appeared quite drained and deflated, actually. The look of it was better suited for her face.

"They said you carried him on your shoulders for nearly half an hour." She spoke quietly to the ground. "That he was bleeding out and would've died if you hadn't. Is that true?"

"It is," I answered blankly. I had no idea of the time that night, but that was the amount of it that kept being said.

She nodded her head and looked up at me with tears in her eyes. "Congratulations," she said. "I wish happiness for the two of you."

"Thank you," I told her in the same blank way.

She forced a smile at me and walked away, and I watched her go until I could no longer see her. When she disappeared into the crowd, I went back where I belonged.

"What did she want?" my brother asked when I stepped back over to them.

My father was standing nearby, speaking with a citizen.

I said, "To congratulate us."

"*Cherise*?" Ahren asked it as if we had a slight mix-up in who we were speaking about.

I nodded and looked at Jastin, analyzing his face.

Ahren said, "That's not like her."

"Then good for her," Jastin said sincerely.

I did not say, *good for her that she's a manipulative liar*, as I was tempted to. It would've been quite nice if the sentiment had been genuine.

I somehow felt my father's eyes on me through the countless others. When I glanced over, I found him smiling at me. Was he proud that I'd handled the situation well?

My forehead was scrunched as I analyzed his face and attempted to discover the reason and emotion behind the simple action. He was not proud of me for my handling of the situation, but there *was* pride there.

I smiled back at him in a small way and then turned away.

When the strange interaction with my father was over, I pulled uncomfortably at my clothing, which made my brother frown and tell me to, "Act like a lady."

Firm, I told him, "If you knew that acting like a lady meant being strangled to death by a curses then you would *not* be telling me to act like one."

Ahren laughed. "A *what?*"

"Agatha put you in a corset?" Jastin asked as he laughed right along with my brother.

"You're laughing," I said unhappily, "but did you know that my breathing capacity is almost nonexistent with this thing on?" I tugged at it a little more and grumbled. "What is the point of it anyway?"

My brother said, "To make you *look* like a lady."

"All the stars," I said in exasperation. "Everyone knows I'm female. Why would wearing this contraption make any sort of difference? Are people so ignorant that they need to see such a thing to make a distinction on one's sex? That's the most preposterous thing I've heard in all my life."

I muttered under my breath afterward as I hid behind the two of them and tugged at it again to no avail. The only word I even registered myself saying was *curses.*

"I can help you take it off," Jastin stated.

"*Would* you?" I asked, excitement building in me.

He grinned mischievously at me, which was the only thing that led me to catching on to his meaning.

I giggled, just a little.

My brother said, "I'm leaving now."

"We're getting married!" Jastin shouted at his retreating back.

Several people nearby cheered toward us, as they had only caught Jastin's statement and not his reason for stating it.

I hid my face with my hand and snorted. "They have no idea why you said that."

He sighed contentedly and asked, "Isn't it great?"

THE HIGHLIGHT OF THE DAY for me was seeing two familiar faces—Francis, the Reaper who was stationed at the school and brought the Reaper children in to see their parents, and a little boy with black hair and nearly yellow eyes.

"We brought all the children to hear his speech," Francis said. "It was a direct order from your father, so . . . I figured I could get away with this."

Jastin and I both knelt in front of Aston. I attempted to do so in a ladylike fashion so that I would not destroy the ridiculous dress and potentially make both Agatha and my father angry. Not destroy the dress and not have the curses destroy my insides.

He did not hug us and he was not crying, but he was smiling and periodically checking over his shoulders at the onlookers. To Jastin, he said, "You're getting married."

"Yeah, we are." Jastin's smile was almost wary.

I said, "Unless you don't want us to."

I did not miss the look that Jastin shot me.

"You're going to be my mother," Aston said to me with his little smile. "Just like you said."

I was brought back to my conversation with Stelin that seemed like it took place such a long time ago.

I'm one of very few Reapers who have ever known their mother, even for a short time. After losing mine . . . Well, I think everyone should have a mother.

"Yes," I said quietly. "Yes, I am."

"Can . . ." Aston started and then stopped to look over his shoulders once more. "Can I be there?"

I laughed. "Of course you can." I said he could, so he could. I was sure I could make it happen if that was what he wanted. In all my attention being paid to Aston, I'd missed whatever had caused my brother to come over to us.

Ahren was taking turns staring from Aston's face to Jastin's. "This . . . this is your son?"

Jastin smiled tightly. "Yeah, it is."

"Who are you?" Aston asked my brother that as if he owned the entire place and all the people in it. I supposed he hadn't been close enough to see the speech and get a look at my brother.

"My god, he looks just like you," Ahren said in disbelief, disregarding the question he'd been asked.

"This is Ahren," Jastin said to Aston. "He's Aster's brother, and he was my partner for a long time."

"What happened?" Aston asked.

Ahren laughed uncomfortably. "My *sister* happened."

Aston seemed to think on that for a great while. I doubted he could possibly understand it.

"If you're going to be my mother . . ." Aston whispered to me.

"That's going to be your uncle," I told him with a smile.

I did not miss the ridiculously huge smile Aston had on his face when he turned back to my brother.

Ahren stood there blinking at him for quite some time before releasing a loud breath I hadn't seen him take. He must've been holding it. He forced a smile and wiped at his eyes before walking away. He did not go far. He walked over to where Francis was standing with his back turned to us.

I barely heard Ahren say, "I need to see my daughter." He paused. "Arlene. I need to see her."

"Well," Francis said happily. "Come with me, then." He turned toward us. "Come along, Aston."

Aston gave us quite an unhappy look, but Jastin said, "We'll see you again soon. I promise." Then he smiled again.

I did not miss the grin Francis shot my way as he left with my brother on one side of him and Aston on the other.

Jastin stood and helped me up from the ground. It was difficult to manage, but I did not complain about the curses again. In fact, I complained about nothing else for the remainder of the day. At least not until I went back indoors.

CHAPTER THIRTY-ONE

HEART

IN THE END, JASTIN DID NOT ASSIST ME in removing the curses from my body.

I believed the day would've been more tolerable, even if only just, had I been capable of breathing without inflicting pain on myself. I wished he would've helped me out of it as he'd offered, when he'd offered. I doubted anyone would've noticed a difference after the fact, but they surely would've noticed us slipping away. Even people leaving for a moment to relieve themselves had resulted in a ridiculous amount of questioning as to whereabouts. I was *very glad* for all the situations in my life that had taught me to at least *appear* patient.

What horrendous things to be in any way glad for no matter the reason. That had given me a great deal to think on, as if there hadn't already been so much else.

Agatha was the one to help me out of the curses, after an entire day spent.

"This is the most *evil* contraption I've ever seen in all my life!" I exclaimed as she was fiddling around with the back of it.

She laughed. "I'm sure it's not so bad, my flower."

"Let me trap *you* inside here," I threatened. "We'll see if you can say as much afterward."

She did nothing more to respond to my threat than chuckle quietly at me. If the curses weren't so evil, I might've worried my exclamation would've in part been done to in some way attempt to make up for all the shouting I'd wanted and been unable to do in the courtyard. It *was* evil, though. It was evil, and I did *not* appreciate all the laughing being done at my expense over it. I supposed that was an easy thing for people to do when they didn't understand something.

Every tiny bit of movement on Agatha's part put a little more air back into my lungs. I'd thought before, after my father came back into my life, about being unable to take a full breath. Couldn't and wouldn't were two entirely different things. I could see as much now.

It felt like forever, but . . . when she was done, I wanted to shout *sweet relief!*

I did not shout it because simply thinking the words was enough to suffice. I suspected it would've resulted in more laughing. I looked down and discovered I had these absolutely *horrendous* red marks running along the entirety of my torso.

"Perhaps it *is* quite bad," Agatha said with a slightly contorted face as she took in the sight of me while I was putting my normal clothing back on.

"Did you believe I was being dramatic?" Being *dramatic* when it felt like my insides were being destroyed and I couldn't breathe properly for an entire day while everyone laughed about it.

The grin I caught on her face was almost bashful. So yes, that was what she'd thought.

"When have I ever been?" I sighed quietly and shook my head because it was not important. "May I ask you a question?"

"Of course, my flower," she said. "You know you can ask me anything."

"How . . ." I started and then stopped. "How do be a good mother?"

"Are you pregnant?"

"Why does *everyone* keep asking me that?" I said in frustration. I took a deep breath to calm myself, realizing her question had been understandable when following mine. It had been understandable that time. "No. I am not pregnant."

"Why do you ask, then?" she asked. "Are you planning on having children?"

"It's not just that," I said slowly. "I'm sure we will at some point, so long as things don't get worse than they already are, but . . . Jastin already has a child, as I'm sure you know."

She sighed. "So what you're really asking me is how to be a good mother to a child that isn't truly yours."

"No." I shook my head, but then I thought harder on it. "Well, partially. You're the only mother I've ever known, Aggie. I didn't grow up with one to know what they're supposed to do when you're small. I don't think I would be very good at it, even with my own child were I to have one."

She said nothing.

I took in a deep breath and let it out as a huff of air. "We can't take Aston right now. Jastin said it would mess with his head, given his age and the training that's already been put in there. I can understand that and agree with it. I worry that, when and if we have children together and Aston is old enough to be with us . . . I worry that he would resent them. Hate them, even. I don't want him to think we'd love him any less."

Aggie stepped over to me and took my hands in hers. She was smiling when she quietly said, "You'll make a wonderful mother, Aster."

"I don't think so." Tears of frustration welled in my eyes. "I feel as though I'm far too stupid when it comes to life and the way the world works."

"Knowledge comes with time and experience," she said. "And you've *never* been stupid."

I did not want to tell her she was wrong about the latter of her statements, so I said nothing. I was saved from being required to speak at all when there was a knock at the door.

Jastin peeked his head in. "Ready to go?"

"What if I was still getting her out of that corset?" Agatha demanded as she dropped my hands.

At least he'd knocked then despite not waiting for a welcome in. That was something.

Jastin grinned hugely at me before looking at Agatha. "But you weren't."

Agatha seemed quite flustered—as she was grumbling something under her breath about Reapers—when I smiled at her and said, "Goodnight, Aggie."

She sighed again. "Goodnight, my flower."

Jastin was still smiling when I took his hand in mine and closed the door behind us.

"We can do this now, can't we?" I asked as we were walking down the hallway.

"Do what?" he asked. "Hold hands?"

"Anything we want." At least in that regard. I shook my head and we rounded a corner. "I could kiss you in this hallway and it wouldn't even matter, would it?" Everyone knew.

"I suppose." He chuckled. "Do you *want* to kiss me in this hall-way?"

"I want to kiss you everywhere."

He snorted.

I felt inclined to ask, "What did I say?"

"Nothing." The realization of how he'd taken my statement dawned on me, but before I could complain about it he asked, "So what's got you feeling this way?"

"I'm unsure," I admitted. "Perhaps I feel free because the curses isn't choking the life out of me any longer."

He laughed. "Aster, you know what it's really called."

"Oh, yes," I said assuredly, "but it is most certainly a curses to me. If you'd ever worn one, you would understand."

He would understand and would not be laughing at me over the most inappropriately named object in the world. Opportunity missed there, I thought.

IT WAS NOT LONG AFTER THAT when Jastin and I were lying in bed, lacking the same amount of clothing we'd been lacking the night before.

He analyzed the long red lines still running down my abdomen. "My *god* that thing did a number on you, didn't it?"

"Curses." Proof.

I attempted to ignore his fingers touching said red lines. And then his face was where his hand had been.

I heard myself loudly ask, "What are you doing?"

But I knew what he was doing. He was kissing my abdomen.

But *why?*

"Making it better," he replied.

I did not see how kissing it equated to making it better, not in any way.

My voice sounded far too high-pitched when I informed him, "It's perfectly fine, thank you."

But when he stopped kissing it and smiled up at me to say, "Okay," I realized how it actually *did* equate to that.

I'd forgotten all about the stupid curses. In fact, I found myself quite glad I'd been tortured for nearly an entire day, if that was what I got in exchange for my trouble. Not glad, but somewhat.

"I just lied." I heard myself say the words although my head had not given my mouth permission to speak. "It really feels quite terrible."

He laughed. "Does it?"

"No," I admitted unhappily. "Not in comparison at least, though it *is* quite uncomfortable. I'm sorry for lying, but I'm not entirely sure which thing I was actually lying to you about. You can . . . um . . . resume what you were doing."

"*Can* I?"

I did not know what to say and I felt it would be horribly rude of me to nod, so I simply laid there with my face burning.

"So . . . what you're really saying is I have your permission to kiss you everywhere?"

My mouth dropped open, I knew. It took an extremely large amount of focus to force it to close again. I cleared my throat and my voice was very quiet when I said, "Only if you'd want to."

"Oh, I *want* to," he said assuredly, "but I'm perfectly content with this for now."

Close your stupid mouth! my head screamed at itself. My mouth did not want to cooperate as I laid there staring at him while he smiled, biting a corner of his bottom lip. I realized then that my eyes had closed and not my mouth. Why wouldn't my stupid body listen to my head?

I opened my eyes, cleared my throat once more, then said, "Carry on."

He looked away and put a hand over his mouth in a futile attempt at concealing his amusement from me. After coughing once and shaking his head, he looked at me again. "If you insist."

I did insist. And he did carry on.

While he was doing so, I closed my eyes—consciously that time—and attempted to force my head into logical thought. It was difficult.

I thought of him smirking at me while traveling and telling me that I clearly could not keep up with him. Just because I was so less knowledgeable about things did not mean I didn't want to . . . *do* them or *become* knowledgeable about them. So, I resolved myself to getting accustomed to this.

It was strange. . . . Most definitely strange. I could not understand why being kissed on the abdomen would make the muscles in my shoulders feel funny, nor why it sent cold chills down the entirety of my back. How could it affect different places?

Everything you're feeling is natural, I told myself. *It's all right. It's perfectly normal, whatever it is. There is absolutely nothing wrong with you.*

Little by little, I realized it really *was* all right. It was strange, yes, but it did not feel bad. My eyes shot open when his kisses ventured slightly lower, near one of my hips.

How did *that* even feel different? Why was it that all the same things felt slightly different from one another—or drastically, depending on? It made absolutely no sense whatsoever. It all should've felt the same.

Only when opening my eyes did I realize he'd moved at some point and now had the majority of his body between my legs. How in the world had that happened? My . . . all the things that could happen without your knowledge while your eyes were closed.

I did not care, really. All I knew was that I wanted to kiss him, so I tugged on his arm.

I could tell, that first instant when he looked up at me, he thought he'd crossed some sort of line. He hadn't. And he realized as much when I kept tugging at his arm. Rather than bringing his face close to mine, which was what I wanted, he moved entirely.

My head was not working properly, so it took me several extremely long seconds to discover that he'd somehow managed to pull me onto his lap.

I could remember that first bit of traveling where I'd nearly been sitting on his lap—the opposite way—on that horse for days. I could remember telling him I was uncomfortable when I only partially had been.

I had only really been uncomfortable because it was strange and new. I hadn't known him and I'd been so aware of everything.

This was strange as well, but I was so far from uncomfortable.

One of his arms wrapped around my back and his other hand cupped my face. He nudged my nose with his and then he kissed me.

I did not want to, but I found myself thinking back on that time of being intimate with Chase. I remembered, at the time, feeling as though I were trapped inside a cage made by his arms and the rest of his body. I thought that was the way it was supposed to feel—a woman being trapped by a man. That was all it was, all it could be.

It was ridiculous, but it almost seemed as if Jastin knew as much and was trying to show me it was not supposed to be that way. Or perhaps that, even if it was, it did not have to be. I could move, if I wanted to move. I could breathe, if I wanted to breathe. And I could trap him, if I wanted to trap him.

I pushed him down onto his back, and I trapped him inside a cage made of my arms and legs. Not because I wanted him contained but because I wanted him close. I could not get close enough to him.

I didn't know why I started kissing his neck and not his mouth. It was not a logical thing to do. But was kissing of any sort logical, really?

I discovered in that moment that I did not like the way my head functioned, with logic and thought. Why did I always have to be that person? Why couldn't I ever simply . . . *act*? Why couldn't I ever be free of her, just for a little while?

I could not explain why I bit his neck any more than I could explain why he squeezed my waist tightly and made some sort of noise in response that sounded like a pleasant chiming to my ears.

"Time to stop," he said breathlessly.

I also could not quite explain the feeling of staring down at his face. I *did* know that I was very confused about his reaction.

I ignored my own heavy breathing when I whispered, "Did you like that?"

Why should a person like being bitten? Why had I bitten him? All the stars, this made no sense at all.

The only response I received from my question was another of those smiles where he bit his bottom lip. I supposed a person liking to be bitten on the neck was not any stranger than a person liking the sort of smile he was giving me.

I *did* like it.

And I would not complain about discovering something which could force that sort of sound from him.

I'd liked that as well.

I was just leaning down to kiss him again when he repeated, "Time to stop."

I did kiss him, but only briefly before asking, "Are you sure?"

His mouth said, "Yes," but his face did not seem to agree with the word he'd given me.

"Can we get married tomorrow?" I whispered against his mouth. I wondered how many times I would ask him that question.

He closed his eyes and squeezed one of my hips with his hand. "I'll tell your father we have to do it soon."

"He'll ask you why about the urgency." I laughed. "What are you going to tell him? That you want to be intimate with me but refuse to until after, so *please hurry up and arrange it*? I'm sure that would go over quite well."

I was still laughing when he wrapped his arms around me.

"I'm going to tell him the truth." Then, he rolled us both over onto our sides and smiled at me. It was a sweet smile. "That we just want to start our life together."

"We already *have* a life together," I told him in amusement.

"Yeah we do." He took a deep breath and tucked my hair behind my ear. "We have this foundation of trust and understanding. That's not going to change, but when we take that step . . . you realize what it will mean, don't you? We'll be tying ourselves together for the rest of our lives, and we'll both *know* that nothing can tear us apart." He took in a deep breath and laughed quietly. "So. You're not going to torture me until that happens, now that you've discovered you can. Because some things deserve to be special, and some people deserve special things. Please let me give that to you."

I nodded my head even though I didn't have a clue what he was talking about exactly. It sounded very nice. I wondered . . .

Could this be the way things could be?

Could that be?

He smiled and wiped a tear from my face. Then he leaned over and kissed my forehead before saying, "Go to sleep, Star."

He pulled me close to him, and I whispered, "I love you," against his chest.

He breathed out what I thought was contentedly. "I love you, too."

I fell asleep listening to his heartbeat. It seemed to be the only real thing in the world that was not bad in some way.

I did not let myself wonder why it always seemed that way.

Perhaps happiness was like training. If you tried hard enough . . .

CHAPTER THIRTY-TWO

FAITH

THE FOLLOWING MONTH was beyond stressful. And busy. It was so very busy, and there was so much to it.

As he said he would, Jastin had a talk with my father about when our wedding would take place. He insisted intimacy had not come up. I asked him to relay the conversation verbatim to be sure. It did not have to come up directly to be obvious.

My father had brought in a woman that next day—her name was Patricia—and she seemed to be in charge of planning mine and Jastin's wedding, whatever that meant. She asked me questions that I thought were entirely irrelevant to absolutely everything, and a lot of them I did not have any answers to at all. After half an hour or so of sitting alone with her on that first day, my father had come in to check on us. I'd contemplated leaving the room no less than fifty times, I was sure, before he arrived.

"Please excuse me," Patricia had told me with a very tight smile.

She'd stepped out with my father, and I heard her shouting at him through the door. I suspected that me hearing had been her intention. I could've been wrong. Perhaps she'd simply been unable to help herself or believed a closed door meant no one could hear what you were saying.

I heard her clearly.

"That girl is *impossible*! How am I supposed to do *anything* when she tells me *nothing*?"

"Flower," my father had popped his head in to say. "Would you prefer Jastin helped you answer these questions?"

I'd nodded in response and that was how Jastin ended up sitting with Patricia and me for approximately an hour every single day, talking about flowers, and food, and . . . Well, a whole lot of nonsense if I was being totally honest.

What did *colors* have to do with anything? Colors I preferred to and for what?

I could not understand, and it felt like such a waste.

Patricia tested my patience *immensely*. I suspected that had Jastin not been there, I might've eventually snapped. Even with him there . . . It was difficult. I told myself many times that it was sort of like training, as she tested me in ways that I was *not* accustomed to. I told myself *many times*.

To and for *what*?

I trained for several hours every day with actual training. I was distracted during that time, as I was always watching in an attempt to find cracks in stories. There were no holes so far as I'd found, so I looked for cracks instead. I looked, but I found none. That didn't mean the cracks were not there, only perhaps that I was not looking correctly or from the proper perspective. But I kept searching for them.

Jastin was there for my training, and while I was doing my movements, he did his own. At some point, he stopped assisting so actively with my combatives, mostly giving Stelin clear instruction, doing his own business, and coming to check periodically. Jastin would continue training after I was done, which was much faster than what it had been before. That wasn't due to massive improvement or a lack of need; it was because I had other things to do.

I would spend time with my father.

I spent quite a *lot* of time with my father. Some days Ahren was with us; some days he was not. Sometimes he would be with us for a while then one or the other would leave to do other things only for my father and I to meet back up later on our own.

Sometimes my father and I spoke of personal things when we were alone, but that was a rare occurrence. I did not deem it necessary to dwell on the past when moving forward, and he did not seem quick to bring it up. He'd never spoken to me of my mother when I was a child, after all, apart from the one thing.

He spoke of her now on occasion, tiny bits of information. I did not know whether he did it to prove what he was willing to do to make amends or if enough time had passed that he could finally manage it without causing himself too much pain. He even smiled sometimes when he mentioned her, but I would catch him staring off afterward, sometimes to the point where I would have to get his attention. I realized . . .

There were some things that could never fully be moved on from.

As much as I wanted to know about her or simply hear him speak the smallest thing of her . . . I did not bring her up. When he did, I didn't press him with questions, no matter how tempted I was. I let him say what he wanted to say, only that and nothing more, and I listened and watched.

It was somewhat rare, but it happened.

Most days, he and I pored over maps and discussed strategies. I'd been shown a map that had *all* the cities on it. There were more than thirty of them spread across the land. It was the one we turned to most often for one reason or another.

There were so many maps. Maps of landscapes and terrain. Maps of those cities. Maps of small towns between them. There were so many more of those, mostly empty, some utterly destroyed. Razed. Turned to rubble.

So many maps.

Endless stacks that flattened the world while somehow making it clearer.

Anders enjoyed being in the room while we discussed strategies. Some days, he seemed amused with or by me, but most of the time they both seemed to be impressed. We discussed ways to better Jarsil and Farin, my father's other city. They enjoyed my ideas, I thought.

I had a lot of ideas.

Ideas about the Reaper children. Ideas about finding what the citizens were best-suited to do and allowing them to do it. We discussed schools and infirmaries. We discussed morale, both for the citizens and Reapers. Some of our views differed slightly, and some more than.

I heard, "Aster, even if that *is* a perfect idea . . . it's *too* perfect," quite often. My father's logic on that made no sense to me.

I discussed trying to form alliances with nearby cities, but only when he and I were entirely alone. My father thought it was absolutely ludicrous. It seemed a good idea, both from a strategic standpoint and also given we could exchange goods between the cities— food and supplies. Assistance. *So many* possibilities.

"But have you *tried*?" I would ask.

"No, I've not tried to walk into Maldir just to get myself killed." My father laughed. "Bren would've killed me for such a thing before. Now I'm sure he would do much worse than that. He could certainly manage it in his own city. It was never personal, but you're aware that all things can change in an instant. I can assure you that, despite whatever it never was, he would've most assuredly tried to kill me had he caught me out. You've no idea the sort of people you're speaking about dealing with."

"Have you ever met him?" I had asked flatly.

"No, but you have not either," he'd responded. "If you'd met any of these Reapers or knew more than what you do about them, you would *not* waste your time with this idea." He paused to look at me significantly. "Do you want to know what happened to one of the few last men I sent to Maldir?"

"I'd imagine he was caught and killed, with the way you're looking at me right now." Likely in some grotesque way that he thought would stop the idea.

"No, he wasn't killed." My father shook his head, his brow furrowed. "I meant the last one caught who's still living. Would you like to meet him? He can give you a decent idea of who you're asking about, but it will take him a while to respond to anything you might ask. I could give you a clearer picture in the same way had the others returned to me alive not killed themselves after the fact due to the lasting damage he inflicted." He raised an eyebrow. "Would you like to meet the one who didn't? Keeping in mind that it got much nastier from there, of course. Still, this one can give you a rather clear picture. The beginnings of."

I didn't say anything.

My father stared at me for a decently long while before saying, "Keep in mind it's not necessarily about the actions. It's about the person who's behind them. Let's get you your first clear glimpse of that, shall we?"

I said, "If you believe glimpses of people are enough to suffice."

"Oh no, Flower." He shook his head. "We're not speaking on any normal sort of person with this. We're not even speaking on human monsters, though closer to. There's something worse, something I couldn't allow myself to speak to you on when you were a child. I'll ensure you learn now. You *must* learn the difference."

As time passed in my father's office with him, I began hearing a great many stories about the leaders of other cities.

I did not like hearing them.

For one thing, I did not believe that stories gave the proper measure of a person, no matter the sort, what was told, or how reliable the source. All sources were tainted with some bias or another, which brought inaccuracies no matter how truthful. Stories were not facts no matter any factual information included. For another thing . . . they were not typically nice stories to hear by any stretch of the word. Sometimes, rarely . . .

Sometimes *nice*, in its vagueness and openness, *could* be stretched far enough to cover unpleasant things. In some way. It depended upon a number of things.

"More people have to want good in their lives, Father," I told him one day with a sigh. "It's human nature, isn't it?"

"Human nature possibly," he had said. "Not Reaper. Not out there."

He was set on that, and there were so many other matters.

When discussing the Reaper children, I offered the idea that they could go home to their families at night.

They're safer in the schools, he would tell me. Also . . . *What about the children whose parents don't want them, Reaper or citizen? It would create discord in the system, an unfairness that would cause them to resent one another. If there is resentment, they cannot work together properly. That's how we function here now, and it's best. We cannot risk that being damaged.*

I offered up the idea that citizens who could not bear children themselves may be interested in taking Reaper children in as their own. Or perhaps just some of them might want to in general despite being able to have their own. That would solve the problem of discord, I thought. A family was a family. Aston did not seem to care that I wasn't his birthmother, so long as I'd be his mother.

Initially my father had laughed and informed me that no normal person would want a Reaper child. I had argued the case that, if a person could not have a child of their own . . . why wouldn't they? When he'd changed the way citizens viewed the Reapers of Jarsil . . .

Why wouldn't they?

He'd changed their perspective, if not his own. He sometimes needed to be informed of as much.

It had taken quite a while, but I could almost watch the idea sinking into his head. Still, they were safer at the schools where they were guarded. Even I could not deny that.

"What about allowing visiting hours every day while they're younger?" I'd asked. "Or once a week, even? Or, a family day even, where all the Reapers and citizens who want the Reapers as their own could be around one another? It would create a good deal of companionship, I think. Camaraderie, morale. And then, when they're older and more equipped to protect themselves . . . why couldn't they leave at night? Why shouldn't they be allowed families? It won't erase their training. If anything, I believe it would create improvements. Something to fight harder and keep themselves alive for. Speaking about keeping numbers up and all. That *just might* help, and in a good way."

He'd stared at me for quite some time before shaking his head. "Aster, I may not like the system, but it works."

"But how can we *fix it* if we don't make changes?" I'd asked.

"For now, I'm more concerned about keeping us all alive to ensure we'll be *able* to make changes," he'd told me apologetically.

"What would people think, I wonder . . ." Anders had started and then paused to laugh. "What would people think if they knew that your daughter is the one running the city now?"

"I'm not," I'd said in disbelief. "I'm only trying to help."

I'd stood at that and had almost made it to the door when I barely heard my father say, "She thought you meant you didn't appreciate her input."

Anders had run over to say, "That's not what I meant. I love your ideas, Aster. They're quite beautiful."

I had smiled tightly and left.

I preferred being alone when having discussions with my father. The more time passed, the more frequently that occurred. I realized he felt the same way when he began ensuring that happened.

We hardly ever spoke a direct word about Hasting or of Chase. Not unless there was something to say. There rarely was after a certain point that had been passed rather early in. There were so many other things, things something could or would potentially be done about.

Some days I listened to the people when they would come in to claim their issues. If I could, I would assist them personally. I helped a team of Reapers repair an old woman's roof one day. She had no family, and it had actually been a Reaper who'd noticed the issue and brought it to me. The next day I'd given my father the idea about making teams of citizens who would do such specific tasks regardless of occupation. It was one of the things he'd listened to me over and was beginning to put into effect.

I had also gone to both the Reaper schools and the normal schools, to speak to the instructors and children about any issues they might've been having. The children were not of much assistance when asking for their input, as they mostly just smiled at me. Most people had no ideas about how to better things. I would tell them to think on it and get back to me. Sometimes they would.

Ahren would accompany me sometimes. It was on one such day when I met my niece. She did not speak much to me, nor did she smile as freely as the other Reaper children seemed to where I was concerned, but she would speak quietly to my brother and he would relay messages between us. She was very strange, but . . . so was I. In comparison to the sheep.

I was beginning to worry that there was something quite wrong with our blood.

I did wonder sometimes on the definition of *wrongness*.

I'd been concerned about visiting the Reaper school and the proper way to deal with Aston there. I worried that openly showing him preferential treatment would upset the other children, but . . . there was no point in hiding that he was the child of the man I would soon marry. So, some days when I went, he would walk next to Jastin as he trailed along behind me. None of the instructors attempted to put a stop to it despite it being a short interruption to his training. Showing up at all created enough of a disruption for most everyone.

Life was long enough for a few disruptions here and there, I thought.

It had been later in the month when Aston had walked beside me and held my hand as I spoke to the other children. But it had been only a few short weeks in when the other children began speaking to and smiling at Jastin as well. Those were his favorite days, I knew, though he never told me as much.

There was a building where children who had no parents stayed, just normal citizens who had lost their families in some way or another. I went there several times and spoke to them after hearing about the place and the reasons for its existence, how they ended up there. There were so many children. I would listen to them and I would think that, in some way, my words and attention made them feel a little better, even if only for a short time.

I had asked my father to send them new blankets and pillows because the others were not in a proper state. When asking the lady who was in charge of that building—her name was Marlen—why she'd not gone to the House and informed my father about the issues, she said, "Hardly anyone cares, Milady."

She had cried the next time I saw her, because of the blankets and pillows. I understood the feeling.

I did a great deal of thinking on depth and capacity as days passed.

I went once to the infirmary, or I attempted to at least. They would not allow me in because they didn't want me to become ill. I could not even step one foot inside the building. I'd hardly even gotten close to the entrance. Reapers had ushered me away, in the opposite direction, the instant the ones following realized where I was headed. It was one of the only times they'd ever put their hands on me, but it happened occasionally due to the reasons it was required.

My brother went with me somewhat often when I made my trips into the city. Good for morale, for people to see the two of us together, going out and doing positive things as a family. Given Ahren could no longer go on missions, he did things in the city on his own quite often. That usually happened later in the day than what I did.

I could remember speaking to the Reaper before I'd left New Bethel. He'd told me about the Guard and about how so many of them were happy because they'd been treated better since my brother's arrival than they ever had before.

My brother was like my father. He would speak to people and

they would listen. They would smile at him and look at him like he was capable.

They would look at me like I was a kind little girl. I told myself it did not matter, that I was still doing good.

It *did* matter to me. And for the first time . . . I was jealous of a person. My brother. But I did not hate him for people's prejudice against women. It was not his fault. I'd ignored the people shouting at me to come down from the roof as I'd been helping them repair it, as did the Reapers I was with that day. I tried not to let it faze me.

"Just ignore them," they'd told me quietly while up on that roof.

I had tried. Very hard.

But it was as I was assisting in repairing a hole in someone's house that I finally lost my composure and had an outburst on a citizen. It was something I had told myself I would never do. They were always watching.

A man had been having words with a Reaper standing guard relatively close behind me. I'd been listening to him rattle off for over ten minutes to the Reaper, who wasn't paying him the slightest bit of attention.

"Why is she doing that? She's a lady. Surely there's someone else who can do it? My *god* women should not do such things, least of all *her*."

Minutes, and minutes that had stretched and told me along with his tone . . .

He wasn't going to stop.

I stood and walked over to him, and he became quiet immediately.

"My mother was a Reaper, Sir," I told him, my voice even. "She killed people for a living. How ashamed do you think my dead mother would be if her daughter was not capable of fixing a hole in a house?"

"But *why* are you doing it, Milady?" he'd asked in confusion, clearly not understanding. My mother had killed men capable of and expected to do what I was doing. "Isn't there someone else? Don't you have other things to be doing?"

"Like staring at flowers or embroidering curtains?" Both my eyebrows rose. "I am doing it because I *can*. Don't *you* have other things to be doing instead of harassing a person who is trying to help someone else? There are much better uses for one's time, but if you insist on being a hindrance, I'll insist you do it elsewhere. If you go against my insistence, you're going to have a *very* bad day."

I couldn't embroider anything even if I tried.

I started walking back to where I'd been to resume my purpose in being where I was when I heard the Reaper say, "I suggest you move along. I've heard she has quite the temper."

"I've heard she's the kindest woman in the entire city." The man's tone was thoughtful, confused in a different way than he had been, and oddly and disturbingly *lost* when he added, "Sure doesn't strike me that way."

"Perhaps that's because she's spent the majority of her life with people telling her she's inferior to them," the Reaper said. "Why would she be kind to you when you've been insulting her for the last ten minutes?" He paused. "You can either do as she asked or I'll remove you."

It was when I was done with my task that the same Reaper came over to me.

"He wanted me to apologize for him," he said. "I wouldn't allow him to do it himself."

"He would apologize for his words only because of what was said to him in response to them, not because he doesn't believe them," I stated. Then I sighed and shook my head. "Why would a woman be more likely to fall off a roof than a man?"

"You weren't on a roof," the Reaper said with a smile. "But the easy answer is that people are stupid."

I heard myself laughing a little. "You think so?"

"Oh yes," he said assuredly. "All Reapers know that women are just as capable as men, or most of them." He looked over his shoulders and took a step closer to me. His voice was nearly a whisper when he spoke again. "I shouldn't tell you this because we're instructed not to speak of your father's private life, but . . . I've heard him speaking of you. He said you have one of the most brilliant minds he's ever seen, that he's proud to have brought such a person into the world. So . . . what does everyone else matter?"

"It matters because I believe I finally understand why there's so much bad in our world," I told him sadly. "What do ideas matter when they fall on deaf ears? What do acts matter when they're witnessed by people who can't see? How can we make changes when no one is willing to change?"

"And now I understand what he meant." The Reaper stared off and shook his head for a moment before looking back down at me. "Keep faith in yourself and your ideals, Milady. I have faith that you can make the changes."

"You don't know me to have faith in me," I said, puzzled.

"I don't need to know you any better than I do to have that faith, Milady." Then he smiled tightly and walked away.

CHAPTER THIRTY-THREE

EXCITED

T WAS LATER THAT NIGHT on the same day the Reaper had spoken to me on faith when I found myself in bed with Jastin, crying. "Is there something wrong with my mind?"

"What?" he asked, concerned. "Of course there isn't."

"But why don't other people think like I do?" I asked. "They're all sheep, Jastin. They all think the same. Why is my head so different? Why do I have to think about ideas and strategies?" Why didn't anyone *ever* really understand? "And my *god*, I didn't fall off the roof!"

"I've never heard you say that."

I huffed out a breath because the fact that I'd said *my god* rather than *all the stars* did not matter. Out of *all the things* . . .

He rubbed my arms comfortingly. "Your brother told me he's jealous about your father, more or less. That when he's in the office with you, your father hangs on every word you say, looks at you like you're the most capable person in the world."

"But *everyone* looks at him that way," I said in frustration. "Because he's a man and he's kind to them like my father." It didn't matter to them that there was so much they couldn't see. He just had to open his mouth and smile as he did. Say some things.

"Yes, but I'm sure Ahren wishes he had that head you're complaining about." He cleared his throat slightly. "Someone wanted me to warn you about Stelin."

"What about him?"

"Have you noticed more Reapers following you when you go out into the city?"

"No." I answered slowly after I'd thought about it. "No more than usual, at least." It was an insane amount as it always had been.

"Reapers talk, just like normal people," Jastin started more slowly than I had. "They overhear things your father says, and Anders. Pretending you don't doesn't mean you don't. They hear us sometimes when we're talking. They know how hard you're pushing for the city, to make changes."

"What would it matter?" My brow furrowed and I had no idea how any part of what he was saying had anything at all to do with Stelin.

"It *matters* . . ." he paused to take a deep breath, "because you're putting a *very* large target on your back, like it wasn't already large enough."

Quickly, I asked, "With the Reapers in the city?"

"No." He shook his head. "With Reapers from other cities, and with Hasting. If they find out you're the one coming up with these things, that you're having a say . . . it makes things very dangerous for you. Even more dangerous than they already were."

"So more of them are following me without being told to do so?" I asked, trying to gather what he was getting at and disregarding the connection to Stelin now that I knew.

Jastin nodded.

"I don't understand." I'd thought they were all instructed to.

"Did your father tell you what happened to the kings?"

"He told me that Reapers from one city were sent to kill the other king and that they wiped out the entire bloodline of the king from their own city," I said. "What does that have to do with anything?"

"The kings' ideals destroyed everything they'd spent the majority of their lives building." Jastin was being so deliberate with his words. "Killing them was Bethel's Reapers' contingency plan, hoping it would take back the evil the kings had created, but it didn't. And nothing since, not *anything* has. Not until your father. I was informed that the Reapers in Jarsil have begun creating their own contingency plan now."

"Which is?"

"*You*." He forced a smile at me, but he could not keep it in place for very long. "If your father falls . . . their first priority is to keep you alive, to keep the changes happening." He shook his head. "Every word you've said to any of them, every word they've overheard you saying to the people in the city, everything they've heard about you . . . It was only natural."

I could not explain what I was feeling as I sat up quickly in bed, shaking my head furiously. "Anders, my brother," I said through my teeth. "That would make more sense. The people would prefer them. I couldn't *run a city*!"

"Aster, you're calling shots," Jastin said. "The citizens might not know it, but the *Reapers* do. If Hasting finds that out . . . he might not come to kill your father. He might come to kill *you*. So, for *god's sake*, don't let Stelin realize."

I nodded my head slowly.

"You need to give me your back."

"But we always sleep cuddled up together now," I said unhappily.

"Not anymore," he said. "You're going to give me your back because you're the only one of us that's really in danger. You always were. This is getting so large I can't keep pretending you're not who and what you are. I promised I would protect you first and love you second." He was almost crying, I thought. "*Please*."

I turned my back to him.

He held onto me more tightly than he ever had before. His grip did not slacken once in the night. I couldn't move to get more comfortable than what I was. I couldn't fall asleep. I was just so utterly . . .

Trapped.

THE NEXT MORNING, Jastin told me that he had to speak to my father about something, and he hurried himself before I was even prepared to leave the space. He wouldn't tell me what it was about, insisting it wasn't anything for me to worry on, but it left me with an empty sort of feeling. One that I knew I could do nothing for.

So, I simply did what I must. Prepared myself and went to make my way.

I felt a small jolt of joy in seeing that it was Stanley there, to walk with me to my room, but I kept it down. Though, because he'd spoken recently . . .

I said, "Good morning, Stanley."

He smiled a little in his typically small way. "Good morning." A few seconds passed, which were spent with him glancing down at me twice. "How did you sleep?"

My face scrunched minutely. "Poorly, I'll admit."

"It can be difficult adjusting to different weight in the bed, even after a long while."

"It's not that. I just . . ." I shook my head. "I just have such bad dreams."

"Even with him there?"

I nodded, also in a small way.

He said nothing.

It took me a while to get the courage to glance up at him, worried that—if I did—I would find him as uncaring as I believed he likely should be on the matter. But I did glance.

When I did, he looked down at me and said, "I like to think bad dreams are our spirits telling us something isn't right."

I stared up at him as we walked, contemplating. I could've asked one thing. Instead, I asked, "What would you think isn't right?"

"That's for you to discover, dear."

I thought on that for a moment before nodding, accepting it. I opened my mouth to say something then thought against. But then . . . "Perhaps w—"

He stopped walking.

So I stopped, looking up at him.

He waited.

I said nothing.

"Perhaps we what?"

I cleared my throat of nerves. "Perhaps we can sometime have a discussion on what you see *spirit* as."

The corners of his lips tugged up before he said, "I would love to."

I gnawed on my bottom lip for a moment, nodding. The smile I was attempting to conceal began fading, though.

"What is it?"

"I've spoken to my father. About my dreams." I admitted, "Not that I *wanted* to, necessarily, but there were two nights I didn't sleep at all, I believe."

"And?"

"His belief differs from yours. On why they occur."

A few seconds passed before his eyes just barely narrowed and he leaned the slightest bit down to almost whisper, "No one man knows all. Not even your father."

After a few seconds, I had to nod. "That's true."

He smiled a little again.

I WAS FULL OF UNWANTED KNOWLEDGE during my training that morning, but I made sure not to show as much to Chandler or Stelin. I behaved as I normally behaved, and I did what I normally did. Pretending of different sorts got much easier with practice.

It was two weeks before Jastin and I were to get married by that point. The weather was changing quickly and getting *much* cooler during the day, bordering on cold opposed to cool at night. I preferred it.

I despised the hour spent with Patricia every day, but I found myself intrigued when Jastin and I walked into the room and saw that she was not alone. He smiled when I looked at him.

"You'll enjoy this," he said quietly.

Patricia was doing as she often was—looking at papers. Over and over. The same papers. In my opinion, she was pretending to be more occupied than she actually was.

She didn't look up from them to say, "Now we come to the discussion of music."

Bemused, I asked, "Music?"

She did look up from those papers to ask, "Haven't you heard music before?"

"No," I said as I slowly shook my head. "Like singing songs, you mean? I don't know any songs."

Normally when I answered one of her questions, she became frustrated with me.

This time, she simply appeared to be confused. "You've never heard music?"

"No," I repeated more firmly. I'd *just said*. I always had to repeat myself *so many times. . . .*

She shook her head in a lost sort of way. "Please sit down and tell me what you think."

I did not. "What are those contraptions?" I pointed at the strange things the people were either standing next to or holding in their hands.

"Musical instruments," Patricia said without her usual haughty tone.

"I don't understand," I said to her. I brought my attention to Jastin, concerned, because some of those things looked like weapons to my eyes.

"Please begin," Patricia said to the people.

There was an extended moment of confusion over the noise. I blinked hard and shook my head.

How were those contraptions making those noises? How were the people doing that with them?

"Oh my," fell out beneath my breath. There were tears in my eyes when I smiled at Jastin.

He was smiling hugely back at me.

It was the most beautiful thing in the entire world! Like bells, and whistles, and chimes all put together in some way that was even better than the original sounds. I had never seen the purpose of concerning yourself with beautiful things, not until that very moment. I closed my eyes and focused on the sound of it, but all too soon, it was over.

"Oh my!" I essentially ran over to the people. "How in the world could you make those sounds?"

"Did you enjoy it, Milady?" one of the ladies asked almost warily.

"I loved it!" I exclaimed. "It was the most beautiful thing in all the world! What talented people you are to be able to do such amazing things!"

"You should know . . ." Patricia said as she came up behind me. "I've not seen her excited once since I met her. We've been planning her wedding and there's not been a bit of it."

"She doesn't get excited." Jastin laughed as he took hold of my hand.

"Did you hear those sounds?" I gaped up at him. "Have you ever heard such a thing in all your life?"

"Yes." Jastin was still laughing.

"Oh my." I put my free hand over my heart. "I've gone and made a fool of myself, haven't I? I apologize."

"Would you like to hear more, Milady?" a man asked.

"Oh, yes please," I said. I *very much* wanted to.

Patricia whispered, "Let's go and sit down so you don't make them nervous."

I laughed. "How in the world would I make them nervous?"

"Everyone wants your approval, Aster," she said in a startlingly believable way. "If I'd known this would make you so happy, I would've brought them in a month ago."

I was smiling in confusion when I sat down. And then I smiled in pure bliss when the sounds began again.

I did not know how long we sat there, but I was certain the hour had passed at some point. I did not care in the slightest. For once.

"Which did you prefer?" Patricia asked me.

"All of them," I told her happily. "I loved them all."

She smiled. "Then we'll have all of them."

"Oh, I wish we were doing it tomorrow so I could hear it again." I breathed out contentedly.

"We're very glad you're pleased, Milady," one of the people said.

"I'm so very far past that," I told them with a small chuckle. "Don't you think if people had that sort of sound in their lives, the world would be so much brighter a place?"

"It's why we do what we do, Milady," another said.

Was it such a strange thing to do something sort of useless, just to make the world better? I did not believe so in that moment. Perhaps I needed to reevaluate some things.

Perhaps building goodness inside could be something like building someone a home to live in. In that sense . . .

Not useless at all.

"Please call me Aster," I insisted. "I despise titles. I was forced to call men *Sir* for the majority of my life, and I wouldn't wish anyone to feel that way on account of me."

"Please enjoy the rest of your day, Aster," the same person said.

"Oh, I'll be hearing those sounds inside my head all day, so I'm sure it will be infinitely more enjoyable than the last," I told them. "Please enjoy yours as well. And thank you."

"Our pleasure," he said.

Once they'd all left the room, I said, "Oh, that was simply exceptional."

I was *sad* to see them go, I realized.

"I'm glad you enjoyed it," Patricia said with another smile. "Now . . . time to learn how to dance."

"Dance?"

I thought I had asked the question because I'd thought it inside my head, but I was standing there feeling my face contorting in confusion.

In reality, it had been Jastin who'd asked it in that disbelieving tone.

I TRIED AS BEST I COULD TO UNDERSTAND the purpose of dancing despite a decent bit of time spent internally debating time. I knew our hour was up, but I believed the *musicians* had remained longer than intended due to my enjoyment. Things always needed doing and sometimes that required extra time spent on one thing regardless of all the other things needing doing. I was unsure how this could *possibly* be more important than all else I needed to get to today. Still, I'd spent time doing something I'd wanted—essentially being useless as I sat doing nothing while others did something—and it had drastically cut into the next thing, which would then cut into the next thing and utterly destroy most a day.

So I spent that decent bit of time while first attempting to dance multitasking by having an internal debate about time and how one spent it, then all the repercussions that could occur from even small things. Or what seemed to be small things at one point and turned out to be very large things later. Not putting enough thought in. So on.

Once I'd gone through all that, *then* I tried as best I could to understand the purpose of dancing.

Patricia told me, "You do it to the music."

That made me like the thought of it a little more, but still . . . I would rather just listen than move. And I would much rather punch something than step on Jastin's feet as I *kept* doing.

He did not seem very enthused either.

He had this funny sort of look on his face that seemed to be a mixture of terror and unhappiness. I smiled every time I saw it, and when he saw me looking at him, he would smile back at me. As soon as he looked away, the cranky expression returned to his face. It made the entire experience more enjoyable for me by far. I laughed a great deal as it went on, and Patricia seemed to be quite happy for once as well.

I did not do *much* else that day because I had no time to. In the evening, I spoke with my father to tell him about the music. He'd laughed at me, but not seemingly at my expense or due to a lack of understanding.

"I've never really seen her excited," Jastin said from behind me. "Happy and somewhat excited, sure, but not to the point where every sentence begins with *oh*."

"Oh, be quiet," I told him.

I wondered for an instant why that made him laugh, but then realized I had said *oh* again.

Oh.

"I wish I could've seen it." My father chuckled. "But I suppose I'll see how happy she is in a fortnight."

"What a wonderful day that's going to be," I said somewhat dreamily.

"I know you're usually spending time around this time, but I think I should get her to bed." Jastin laughed again. "I believe she's worn herself out today. I don't know that her body can handle it."

My father frowned but said, "Go on, then. I'll see you tomorrow."

"Goodnight, Father!" I told him as I was walking toward the door.

He shook his head at me, but he was smiling when he said, "Goodnight, Flower."

I was at the door when he said something else.

"Don't let anything ruin what little remains of your day. And make sure you get a decent amount of sleep. Another long day tomorrow."

I'd halted in the doorway, but I looked back at him to nod.

Jastin and I had barely made it down the hallway before he laughed and asked, "What was that about?"

"Precisely what it sounded like." I shrugged. "He wants me to have a good day and sleep well."

"Right." He nodded, still laughing. "I suppose you didn't hear the tone."

I had. "So, what do you believe he was saying?"

"I suppose what he did say was what he said, but he's likely unhappy about you not getting your time together."

We'd gotten time earlier, during the morning rather than what was typical.

It had been necessary.

When lying in bed with Jastin shortly thereafter, he said, "I wish I'd known that music would make you so happy."

"Why?" I asked. I was curious, but then a strange sort of hopeful excitement bubbled up inside my chest. "Can you play an instrument that way?"

"No." He chuckled. "Playing instruments isn't exactly high on Reaper priority lists."

"Then why?"

"You mentioned singing songs earlier," he said. "Do you enjoy that?"

"I don't know." I shrugged. "I've only ever heard a person singing once—Francine, the main cook at the House in New Bethel. She had an *awful* voice. I left the room as quickly as possible. But my father used to hum sometimes while he was doing things, and I enjoyed that. I would always be *so* still when I caught him doing it because, if I moved and he heard me, he would stop." I chuckled a little under my breath at the memory and the realization that he'd been training me.

"I know some songs."

"*Do* you?" I asked excitedly. Then I shook my head. "How is it that you know songs when Abby doesn't?"

"Because I've been on more missions than she has," he replied. "I've been a lot of places to hear things. She doesn't go to any places here where she might hear one, and she doesn't associate with any citizens to hear from them."

"Would you sing me one?"

"How about this . . .?" He smiled one of his mischievous smiles at me. "How about, the night we get married, I'll sing to you."

"I have to wait?" I whispered. Why did *everything* require waiting?

He nodded. "But if you like it . . ." he started slowly. "Then I'll sing to you every night."

"Would you truly do that?"

"I'd do anything for you," was his response. He kissed me quickly and then smiled. "Now give me your back."

I did.

He latched onto it.

"Will you—"

"Will I what?" he asked.

"You know how you were touching me the one time? Would you . . ."

"Do that?"

I nodded. "Possibly . . . until I fall asleep? On my back, if that feels nice?"

"Star, it takes you *forever* to fall asleep." He paused. "And didn't doing that keep you awake?"

"That's why I said possibly on my back." I wouldn't think it would be so distracting if I could feel it at all. "I'll not have any trouble falling asleep tonight, I don't believe."

"You have trouble with it every night."

"As you said earlier about bodies being able to handle things." I wasn't sure I'd slept at all the night before, but I'd made it longer today than I thought I would.

Jastin removed his arm from over me. "Can you feel that?"

I shook my head.

"That?"

I nodded, smiling. It didn't feel like what he'd done the other time, more like pressure than sensation. I supposed scar tissue had its benefits.

I fell asleep thinking I could not ever possibly be any happier than I was in that moment, with the music inside my head, taking my focus and drowning out all the other things that would've kept me awake regardless of what bodies could or couldn't handle.

CHAPTER THIRTY-FOUR

FITTING

AFTER TRAINING THE DAY FOLLOWING the one where I'd heard music for the first time, Jastin and I found Patricia standing outside the designated door with Agatha and Abby. They all seemed quite excited over something, though I hadn't the vaguest clue what could be causing them to grin in such a way or why they were even there.

Patricia gestured at Jastin. "He's not to be with you today."

I frowned. "But why not?" Jastin was always with me for this. I had no idea how I was supposed to—

"Dress fitting," Abby said with a ridiculously large grin.

I did not understand, but Jastin began attempting to release my hand. I squeezed onto his tightly.

"It's fine." He laughed then kissed me on the forehead. "Try to have fun."

My frown deepened, but I released his hand.

"We'll be doing the same with you tomorrow," Patricia said to his back just after he'd turned.

He turned again, walking backwards down the hall to see us while still making his way. "Tell me you're not putting me in a dress."

Everyone apart from me laughed at his statement, for whatever reasons they had.

He shook his head. "I'll see you tomorrow, then."

"Make sure you bring her brother with you," Patricia said, again waiting until he'd put his back to us.

He didn't look back that time, but he nodded as he was walking away. He disappeared around a corner shortly thereafter.

I felt quite abandoned regardless of having other people near. Agatha and Abby didn't and likely couldn't answer questions. Jastin answered the questions. Perhaps we'd gotten past them and there wouldn't be so many today. It seemed we had a set *activity*, so that was possible.

I looked to Patricia. "Why does my brother have to be there?"

Her mouth dropped open. "Aster, have you been listening *at all* this past month?"

I smiled—a little too hugely—at her. I'd not been listening, really. Mostly while I'd been inside that room with her, I'd tuned out discussion of colors and food—along with countless other random things—and had been thinking about more important things to discuss with my father. Jastin had answered her questions, so she'd received what she needed. She'd never had to get it from me, though it had certainly taken her a while to realize as much, and I still wasn't *entirely* sure she'd completely grasped. I felt quite bad for not realizing until yesterday that perhaps this was more important, as was Patricia, than I'd given proper credit. It depended upon perspective.

I still didn't want to be left alone with her.

"Your brother will stand with Jastin," Patricia said slowly, "and Jastin's sister will stand with you."

"Will you repeat the purpose of that to me?"

"To have someone close to you standing with you in support and encouragement."

"She doesn't want me to," Abby said. I was almost positive that she was blushing, and not in a good way.

"Oh, of *course* I do, Abby," I said. "Who better to stand with me while I'm marrying your brother than you?" I took in a deep, contented breath. "That's quite a beautiful concept, isn't it? Yes, I believe it is." Shame I'd missed it when it had clearly been stated before.

"You said it was the music?" Agatha whispered to Patricia.

I disregarded that and looked at Abby's now-smiling face. "Who has the baby while you're here?"

She laughed a little. "Your father."

"Well, little James is in good hands, then," I said with a smile. "And I'm sure my father is having a wonderful time." Along with being relieved for an excuse to take some sort of break.

Any sort of break. Even if it was just an excuse to stand from his desk every so often to pick up a child.

Abby looked away from me and tilted her head at Patricia as if something were wrong with me. I disregarded that as well, thinking on the message my father had given me the night before.

"Will you be wearing a dress as well, Abby?" I asked. "I bet you'll look beautiful."

"Music?" Abby asked, still focused on Patricia.

Patricia shrugged. "Perhaps it's finally struck her that weddings are supposed to be happy events."

"What a wonderful day that's going to be," I heard myself say again.

I was still smiling contentedly—thinking about music and trying to figure out why one particular sound of it kept sticking out inside my head despite not being louder—when Abby asked Agatha, "Does she act like this ever? When she's alone, maybe?"

"I can't say I've ever seen such a dreamy look on her face." Agatha said. "She's always off in her head. Never seems so nice a place as what you're looking at."

"It feels good to be free of myself for a moment," I said thoughtfully. Then I shook my head. "Let's get to it, then." I had other things to do today.

"NOT THE CURSES." I backed away with my hands in the air. I was unhappy now that I always bathed after training. At least it would've given me longer to avoid that horrible contraption, if I had the excuse to waste my time. I should've waited. If I'd known what we were doing today, I could've altered my schedule. I was unsure whether I would've, but I *could have.* "Please don't make me."

"It's just for a moment, my flower," Agatha said where she stood several feet away with a curses dangling between us.

"You're going to ruin my wonderful day by having me stuck inside that thing," I said unhappily.

Patricia said, "You'll be so happy you won't even realize it's there."

"Oh, I'll *know* it's there," I said firmly. She'd clearly never been stuck inside one to know it couldn't be forgotten about no matter the day. Either that or she thought me so ignorant that some amount of *happiness* could make me *somehow* overlook the fact that I was being tortured. I wouldn't have been surprised. "*Please* don't make me."

"Don't you want to look beautiful for him?"

Abby laughed. "She doesn't even concern herself with matching her clothes to look beautiful for my brother. She doesn't speak that language, so I'll try a different approach."

I took several deep breaths and did what my father had told me to when I found myself feeling the way I currently did or wanting to do what I currently did. I took deep breaths, and I counted inside my head.

One.

Two.

Three.

Four.

"Aster." Abby looked to me, finally speaking to me directly and not again speaking about me like I wasn't there. "You know how, when you go out into the city and you're not helping people do things, when you're just speaking to them, your father requires you look a certain way? He requires Ahren be exceptionally presentable, just like you. You know how he makes you wear those dresses?"

I nodded my head in response. He required the dresses but not the curses being beneath them. He agreed it was both unnecessary and ridiculous. He'd also apologized for me ever having ended up in one.

"This is *just* like that," she said. "Only different."

"How?" My voice was quiet.

"Because the entire city is going to be watching you," Abby said slowly. "And . . . the reason the man can't see your dress until the day of is because it's supposed to be a surprise for him. Wouldn't you want to make yourself as beautiful as you can, to see the look on my brother's face?"

"But he always looks at me like I'm beautiful," I said. At least when he was looking for that sort of reason.

She smiled sweetly at me—I assumed it was accidental—and then quickly put her *focused face* back on. "Then don't you want to do it anyway, to see if I'm right or if you are? I'm telling you he'll look at you differently. Wouldn't you like to see that, if I'm right?"

I thought on that for a brief moment, but realized I was already nodding.

"Good girl," Abby said. "Time for the corset."

"*Curses*," I said under my breath.

And that was how I ended up standing there in my undergarments, the curses included, while two older ladies I'd met once before were gone to a corner of the room to *retrieve my dress*. I glanced over at Abby, who was in the same state myself, and smiled in amusement as she tugged and pulled at her own horrible contraption. Then I glanced over at Patricia who was distinctly staring away from me. I could see the expression on her face, though.

"It's the scars, isn't it?" I asked her apologetically.

Patricia looked over at me then, saying nothing. I supposed she didn't *need* to whether she was able to or not.

"The scars on my back. You look . . ." I paused, trying to figure it out. "*Sad*." Yes, that was the proper word for the expression, I believed. "Why?"

Agatha seemed slightly uncomfortable. "I warned them about it, to prepare them."

"Abby was already aware of them, I'm sure," I said. "All Reapers know I have scars on my back because they come up past my collar, and they notice everything. Isn't that right, Abby?" I didn't give her time to answer because I did not need her to. "But still, you were fidgeting to keep yourself from looking at me that way. Reapers don't fidget that much unless it's purposeful."

Was that guilt on Abby's face when she looked away from me? Being caught?

"What did you do?" Patricia asked quietly. "If you don't mind me asking."

I grinned a little. I couldn't help myself. "I looked at books in a library."

"Aster, if there's anything I've learned about you in our time together, it's that you're very intelligent," Patricia said. "Why would you do that if you knew you would get punished for it in such a way?"

"Because who were they to tell me I couldn't?" I asked, curious. I shook my head. "It's so funny, isn't it? I *waited* for one of them to be different when I was little. I waited for just one of them to understand, to look at me differently. They never did." I heard myself laughing quietly. "Do you know what most of them said when they saw my back before they'd beat me? Before they would add to it?"

Everyone in the room was silent because I had never even told Agatha, so I felt inclined to continue.

"'You must be a *horrible* servant,' they would say." I had to put my hand over my mouth because I felt ridiculous for laughing in such a way. "I was actually quite good at being a servant. I always did what was required of me, and I always did as I was told. Apart from the one thing, of course. So, when I got older, it was always amusing to me."

Patricia's lips released from the tight line they were in for her to ask, "How is anything about that amusing?"

"There are two types of men who come into power," I explained. "One type of man, like my father, wishes to do good things and actually does them. Those men are so very rare. So rare in fact that I'd not ever seen one in more than a hundred. And then there are the men who are so *blinded* and *ignorant* that, no matter their intentions, they can only do bad.

"It is *amusing* . . ." I spoke slowly so they might understand, "because it's their lack of vision, their stupidity, their *arrogance* that gets them killed in the end. It's funny because they could never, *ever* realize that anyone could *possibly* be more intelligent than they were. The very least of all some little girl who sits in a library and willingly walks into a room to be beaten for it. They never even realized what they were doing past the obvious. They couldn't *see* past the obvious." No one could.

"That Reaper I killed on our journey here," I said as I nodded my head. "He didn't *look* at me. Not *once*. They don't look at us, do they, Aggie?" I turned to her and found that her eyes were quite wide. "Stupid, arrogant men, thinking women aren't capable of *anything*. That's what allows women Reapers to kill them easily, isn't it, Abby?"

I laughed a little and looked at the floor, hearing no response.

"I understand what Jastin meant when we first began speaking," I said quietly with a smile. "Perhaps it *is* better for everyone to look at me like I'm a silly little girl who stares at flowers and looks at the pictures in books. What's wanted rather than what is."

I took a deep breath and brought my attention to all of them. Even the two older women had since come somewhat over and stared at me with their wide eyes.

"But you see . . ." I said deliberately. "I've always understood that. I just wanted to be proven wrong. But I see it every day here—those same looks from everyone. It is what it is, and it's better this way. I've always known." Their flowers and beautiful pictures weren't meant for me. My gaze fell on Patricia. "Don't be sad for me. Those scars on my back?" I nodded. "I did that to myself, and if you believe *I* am the *slightest* bit sad over it . . . you are mistaken."

I stared at Patricia only for long enough to discern that my explanation had done as intended and did not need to be elaborated on any further, which was good.

Then I turned to Abby and forced a sad smile at her. "Do you know why I fell in love with your brother?"

She shook her head.

"Because he's the only person who's ever cared to look at me, just a small increment past what's *easy* or *nice*. And that's something like what he told my father about me. Something like it. *So*," I said, some strange sort of discomfort rising up inside my chest. Jastin was real. "Please let's get me in that dress so I can look beautiful for him, to show him how much that means to me." I shook my head quickly. "My god, that makes absolutely no sense at all." I couldn't help laughing, shaking my head slower then. "And you all are looking at me as if *I'm* mad." But I knew. . . .

That was all I'd said that had made sense to them.

And yet they still didn't know or understand.

I tore it apart until it did make *some* sort of sense, but still . . . It was not logical to me. Perhaps . . .

Perhaps it was better that way.

CHAPTER THIRTY-FIVE

THE TIME

SPENT A VERY LONG TIME standing there while one of the older women poked and prodded at the heavy fabric hanging over me. I expected to be stuck with at least one of the pins she was using to make her adjustments, but she somehow managed not to do it. I suspected she was being particularly careful, given my *outburst*. I was sure they all thought my explanation on scars had been something like that—an outburst. She was likely concerned about my mental state and thought that accidentally sticking me with a pin would result in some extreme sort of unpleasantness. Considering scars had been the subject, if that was the reasoning behind her behavior . . .

Well, it would've perhaps been one of the most ridiculous things. Obviously I wasn't concerned with being stuck with a pin.

Not that I wanted it to occur.

Everyone in the room was likely concerned about my mental state, if the looks I'd received and their behavior were any indication. They were all behaving strangely, as though they were afraid I would do some unknown yet indescribably horrendous thing. Or perhaps they were all put off or disgusted. It was one or the other—either altering behavior due to feelings or expecting something horrendous from me. It very easily could've been both.

They could not understand. That much was clear, but I didn't know why. I'd explained, and I didn't believe it was difficult. There were many and *much* more difficult things in the world. I thought on it for a little while, feeling they should all understand, before it hit me.

We were all at the mercy of our circumstances.

Abby had been in Jarsil her entire life no matter how many— few—times she'd been out of it. She wouldn't have been old enough before my father's arrival to have been sent on missions, but she would've been old enough to remember the differences. Her adult life would've been what my father made it. It *was* what my father had made it.

Agatha had been a servant her entire life, owned first by a very influential man in New Bethel. At fourteen, he'd traded her to the leader, and she'd been at the Valdour House ever since. She'd not spoken much to me of her life before that time, but she'd made it quite clear it had been traumatic in some way or another. Traumatic to the extent that never stepping a foot outside seemed a worthy exchange. Not even a worthy exchange but a *good* one.

Everyone had a line, a certain point where *good enough* was reached. Life could go in so many directions. It could begin at the lowest point and have nowhere to go but up. It could start at the tip of a mountain and have no choice but to fall when the wind blew too strongly.

Those circumstances moved our lines. Every break that gave power to a step moved something along with us.

How could anyone understand anything when we were all looking at the same things from varying distances?

We could not ever. We could only choose to either accept the things we didn't understand, or not.

I was not content to simply accept things the way they were, nor was I content to wander around pretending to be satisfied with my own ignorance. I realized . . .

So many were not pretending anything with that.

When I reached that point of new awareness, I shifted my focus. While I was standing there, waiting for the pinning to be over, I thought about my brother.

I wondered . . . if you took away his training and our positions had been reversed . . . what would've happened to him?

He would've been too old to have been sent into Reaper training, but . . . I did not believe he would've ended up as a servant. What would've happened to him?

His back would not be covered in scars. He wouldn't have needed to do what I had, as he was not me and wouldn't have been no matter the circumstances. Would he have? Perhaps he would've had to do the same and I simply couldn't see it from where I was standing. I wondered if he would've had it in him to endure that. I wondered if he would've even found the purpose. Any purpose. I did not think he would be capable of enduring it, but I had been very wrong about my brother's character many times before.

Hope and faith only went as far as they did.

The other old woman—who was working on Abby—was done long before the one who was working on me. I suspected it had a great deal to do with the amount of fabric involved, but I didn't know. Then again, when they weren't concerned about someone's mental state . . .

Abby stepped over to me when she could, and though the dress was pinned and did not look how it would in a few weeks . . . "You look beautiful."

"Do you think so?" Her face scrunched more than a bit. "I've never . . . *worn* anything like this. I've never even *seen* anything like this."

"Yes, I suspect you'll take a great deal of attention from me," I stated. "I would hug you for that, but . . . I apparently can't move."

She liked hugs, I was quite sure.

She laughed. "Nobody will be looking at me, Aster."

It was true that people near me *occasionally* drew attention, but usually . . . No. If I were not myself but was still myself, that would've been different, just as it used to be. Still, there was one person I could count on looking at her rather than me.

I offered her a tight smile. "Chandler will."

"*What*?" she exclaimed.

I shrugged and was finally stuck with a pin in my leg. I felt air rushing in on the side of it at once.

"No blood," the old woman said in relief where she'd lifted up the dress.

Once the other woman had properly assisted Abby in removing her soon-to-be dress, she assisted the one working on me.

I hoped it would speed up the process.

"Do the two of you do this often?" I asked curiously some time later.

It took them quite a while to realize I'd been speaking to them.

One looked up at me, blinked, and said, "No, Milady."

"Aster," I insisted.

She nodded stiffly. "Well, your father doesn't have a wife." She seemed to think on her words for a moment. "At least not one living. Before he came along, we were required to make dresses for the wives of whatever leader was in power at the time, if they had one. Or for women they tried to impress. I'll admit we didn't do what we could." She shook her head at something I had no idea on. "It was quite a long time ago that we had a king in Jarsil, but it was a distant grandmother of ours who worked for the queen, doing this very thing. It's been passed down all these years to us."

"That's quite a beautiful thing," I said. I liked the thought of that—of families being together and all that could come along with it. "Do you have children you've passed the knowledge down to as well?"

"No," the other said. "My sister and I never had children. Couldn't bear the thought of bringing children into our world, and then when your father came along . . . it was too late for us."

Later, I would think—not for the first time—on the fact that people seemed to believe my father had simply appeared out of thin air when he'd been born here. It was not relevant to the conversation. At least not this one.

"So the knowledge of your skill will be lost with you," I said thoughtfully. "Have you thought of taking on an apprentice?"

They both stopped what they were doing and stared up at me.

"An apprentice, Milady?" one of them asked.

"Aster," I insisted again. "And yes, someone to pass the knowledge down to. I don't believe any sort of knowledge should ever be lost." No one would ever be able to dig themselves out of all this.

"There are a great many people who make clothing," one of them said, her voice sounding a bit . . . *biting*. It seemed she was frustrated, though I could not understand why. "We're finished. You can have a look at yourself."

I was assisted off the step they'd had me standing on, and I walked over to a mirror. My eyes went wide as I took in the image of myself.

"There may be a great many people who make clothing . . ." I began slowly, "but I'm quite certain they would not be capable of doing *anything* like this."

"Do you like it?" one of them asked. She almost seemed wary. Why did everyone always seem so wary when speaking to me?

"All the *stars*, this is remarkable," I said in disbelief.

There was so much fabric, but so many details into it. How in the world they had managed all this in a month . . . I didn't have a clue. They must've been working constantly on it. And here I'd been thinking nothing at all went into such an occasion.

I was taken aback at the wideset collar in the front. "All the *stars*, where did this come from?" I asked as I stared down at my chest. I knew it was there, but I'd never seen it look quite like it did.

Agatha laughed. "That's your curses' doing, my flower."

"Is *that* the purpose of it?" I asked incredulously.

"Partially." One of the old women chuckled. "And partially here." She put a hand on either side of my waist. "The two of you are so muscular that it doesn't make too much of a difference there."

"Muscular," I said in confusion. I shook my head and took a good look at my waist. "No, I can see the difference." I twisted and turned as much as I could manage, taking in as much of it as I could. I did not look like myself at all, just in shape. It was absolutely mad.

"Perhaps this will make people look at you differently," one of the women said in a thoughtful tone.

"I don't understand," I said apologetically.

"She's saying that perhaps people will look at you like a woman and not a child," her sister answered for her.

Interesting.

I looked to Abby. "Do you believe Jastin will like it?"

Her eyes lingered for an instant on my chest before meeting mine. Her face was scrunched up in what I believed was amusement when she said, "Yeah, I'd say he will."

It was a beautiful dress, and it was far more to look at than my chest.

Though the change to it *was* startling.

Patricia drew my attention by asking, "Are you pleased with it?"

"More than." My father certainly would be. Apart from possibly one aspect. I did believe it was a great deal *much*, and in one aspect *not enough*, but . . . My father certainly would be happy, I felt certain.

She smiled then pursed her lips together to try to conceal it from me. "Well, let's get you out of there. Now, I won't be seeing you tomorrow, but in two days we'll have another go at the dancing. Don't bother trying to hide your relief over missing a day. I know it's there."

I *did* feel relief for a moment, but then Abby's disbelieving voice rang out, pulling me from it.

"You've got my brother *dancing*?" She shook her head. "My god, he must love you."

"He's quite exceptional at it," Patricia said, "but it's clear he doesn't enjoy it. Has he never done it before?"

"I'm sure he hasn't," Abby said. "But all Reapers are pretty exceptional when it comes to proper movements. You can ask Aster all about it the day after she's married."

"Ask me what?" I asked. "About the dancing?" I'd already danced with him and could be asked about that now, but I felt I had nothing of value to add to what had already been said. . . .

Patricia put a hand on my arm and quietly said, "I don't believe she was talking about dancing, dear."

I looked down at her hand until she moved it.

Then . . .

Oh.

My face began feeling as though it were melting away. "I'm very uncomfortable."

Abby seemed quite pleased with herself. She should not have been.

"Let's get you out of there," Patricia said again.

I nodded stiffly and hoped she thought I was speaking about uncomfortable in the dress instead of what I was really speaking about.

She looked at Abby and said, "I'll expect you and her brother in here for your own dancing lessons in two days as well."

Abby blinked and asked, "What?"

Patricia didn't look at her to say, "You heard me."

I wondered . . . "Do you believe many people would enjoy dancing?"

"I suspect they would." Patricia nodded. "Why do you ask?"

"Is that something that's available to people—the knowledge of it—if they would be interested in doing it?"

Patricia shook her head in clear confusion, but also what I thought was response.

That caused me to say, "Perhaps we should change that."

"Why?" Patricia asked slowly.

"Well, to be honest, I spent a good deal of time yesterday thinking it was quite pointless," I said, contemplative. "I would rather just hear the music than move to it, but . . . I did enjoy myself. I laughed quite a lot, which I feel as though I don't do nearly often enough. Perhaps other people would have someone they would enjoy doing it with." I stared out the nearest window and felt the corners of my mouth tugging up. "Can't you picture the entire city dancing, and laughing, and smiling?"

"At your wedding?" Patricia asked.

My face was burning again when I very quietly responded with, "All the time."

CHAPTER THIRTY-SIX

HOPE

THAT NIGHT, I DREAMT OF DANCING. I dreamt about the little girl who'd lost her cat, peeking through a crack in a door and seeing her parents dancing and laughing with one another. She watched them, very much like the way I'd made myself so incredibly still to hear my father humming to himself at the same age. I dreamt about her smiling at their happiness rather than my own confusion as a child over my father's sadness.

Happiness, of the purest sort . . . *existed*.

I dreamt about the old man I'd spoken to on the street dancing slowly with his wife who'd been so concerned over me. They danced, not so people would see them but because they were alone. *Happy.* Safe enough to *be* happy. So simple. Two people loving another so much, so *completely* that any and all circumstances . . . They couldn't touch it. So simple.

People with blurry faces spun in and out of my vision. But I could always see the smiles. It was . . . *wonderful*. It was like breathing.

I woke up feeling quite ridiculous for it. Very sleepily I said, "Jastin."

"Hmm?" was the response I received.

I felt even more ridiculous because I'd gotten his attention to say, "I believe I very much enjoy dancing." Perspective. Everything.

"Do you?" He laughed groggily.

I nodded in response to his question.

"You're sort of bad at it, you know."

"Isn't it great?" I asked with a yawn.

He laughed quietly again. "Were you dreaming about it?"

I nodded. "I dreamt everyone in the city was as happy as I felt while dancing with you." That everything was much simpler than it was, or that it could be. That *safe* existed. That simple words were not so complicated.

Happy.

He kissed me on the back of my neck and jumped out of bed. I watched him walk around to where he'd thrown his shirt near my side of the bed, bend over, pick it up, and begin putting it back on. I watched the muscles in his back moving. They'd changed in appearance slightly over the past month or so, as had his arms. It seemed he was gaining back some of the muscle mass he'd lost on my account, finding the time for himself.

I was smiling where I lay on my side, curled up beneath my blankets as I watched him.

"What is it?" he asked with a grin when he turned to me. His face was scrunched up in amusement. Or what I believed was amusement.

"I was just thinking that I might finally understand what love is," I said thoughtfully. I'd been wondering what it was exactly. What it truly meant.

He chuckled. "Dancing?"

I shook my head and felt my face burning when I said, "Realizing I would be so unbelievably happy, just to watch you put your shirt on every morning."

He tilted his head and simply blinked at me for an extended moment, and then he came and knelt by the bed. "I don't know what's gotten into you," he said, "but I like it."

"You did. Have you forgotten?"

He smiled at me and leaned over to kiss my forehead. "I'll let you get ready." He stood and walked over to the door, but he paused there and looked back at me.

And for just an instant, it truly did feel as though the two of us were the only two people in the entire world where we smiled at one another from across the room.

But I knew that we were not.

I just needed to wake up.

"YOU'RE SO DISTRACTED TODAY, ASTER," Chandler said as he got in my face. "What is going *on* with you?"

Jastin still did not want me doing combative training with them while he wasn't there regardless of whether he was directly involved or not, so once he'd gone to do what Patricia required of him, I'd done more movements with Chandler and Stelin.

"She's turning into a girl." Stelin chuckled. "That's what's going on with her."

I fought against the urge to shake my head. "I've always been female, you idiot."

"Yes, you've always been *female*," Stelin said, "but you're turning into a *girl*."

I did shake my head at him then. "That makes absolutely no sense whatsoever."

"I wish you could see that dreamy little smile you have on your face all day now." Stelin chuckled again. Then he shook his head and added, "I thought you were better than that."

"Better than trying to let myself be happy?" I snapped.

"Better than being mindless," he stated blankly.

I recoiled as though he'd slapped me in the face.

"She's not *mindless*." Chandler's voice was firm. "She's getting married and she's excited. I'm sure she'll return to normal once it's over."

I shook my head where I stood there staring at the floor. Then I looked up at Chandler to ask, "Should a person always aspire to remain in the same place?"

He did nothing more than look at me.

"Never moving forward, never changing?" I went on. "What a sad existence that would be." I continued shaking my head. "What does it matter if I do my movements with a smile on my face? I'm still doing them; I'm still learning. So what does it matter?"

They had nothing to say to that, it seemed.

"We're all friends, aren't we?" I asked.

Chandler nodded, but Stelin asked, "*Are* we?"

"I should think so," I told him thoughtfully, "because I would wish to see the both of you smile all the time. Why don't the two of you think a little on that?"

"Are you done?" Stelin asked with a grin.

"Yes, I believe I *am* done for the day."

His grin went slightly wider.

Rather than punch him in the face—like I wanted to—I said, "I've been here for what? Four hours already? I have *a lot* of things that need doing."

Stelin nodded his head, as though he'd worked something out. "So you want to be a Reaper for four hours a day and a princess the rest of the time."

"I am *not* a princess," I said firmly. "And please tell me when I have *ever* said I wanted to be a Reaper. I can assure you . . . those words have *never* come out of my mouth."

"Why don't you clear this up for me, *please*," Stelin said. "What are you, Aster?"

I stepped close to him and stared up at his face. Through my teeth, I said, "You tell me when I have ever treated any of you like *what's* instead of *who's*." I shook my head at him and walked away.

I'd just been trying yet again to figure out which instrument made the sound that kept sticking out to me and, as per usual, had gotten caught up in the memory of it.

That was all.

RATHER THAN GOING TO DO any of the things I likely should've been doing, I went and sat down on the grass in the garden. A bit of open space surrounded by stone. I stared off into the distance at my living quarters and could just barely make out a spot of color from the flower the little girl had given me. Many other spots of color had begun fading throughout the city, but that one was still lingering. Clinging to brightness when all else started to fade. I thought it should've been gone by now, but it just . . .

Kept on.

The beautiful sight of it meant something different to me than what it did most or any others who would see it.

They could have their way.

I could have mine.

I closed my eyes and ignored the Reapers on the wall and in the garden. On top of the House. Watching me. Always watching.

There is good in the world, I told myself. *It's there somewhere. It's just difficult to see sometimes. Difficult to find. It exists. It does. It must. It's out there somewhere.*

I repeated that over and over inside my head until I heard a footstep behind me. I looked over my shoulder and forced a smile at Stanley as he came and sat down at my right. I was always glad to see him, whether he spoke to me or not. Whether he came close or not. Most often not.

Stewart stood off in the distance, pretending as if he were not paying attention to me—what I was doing, where I was, and who was near me. He often did just that here. They both did, in their ways. It was comforting. Something about the ways they did it or just them in general was always a comfort.

I did miss Stewart's conversations with me about nothing, his easy laughter and smiles that had disappeared after leaving a very small portion of New Bethel. More often as days passed, I found myself missing them more and wondering . . .

What had I done?

I fought against the urge to pull up a blade of grass and rip it apart. I rested my hands on my legs and stared straight ahead. "You're not from Jarsil, are you, Stanley?"

"How did you know?" he asked curiously.

"Because the one day you went with us to the Reaper school, you weren't looking around for your daughter," I replied, still not looking at him. "You would've been, if she were here. Where are you from?"

"I suspect you wouldn't like the answer to that question if you don't already know it."

When I finally brought my gaze to his face, I found him frowning. Not in his usual way, which I also found to be of some comfort. The new frown was different, and I didn't like it at all.

"Bethel," I said and then took a deep breath.

He nodded his head slowly. He didn't have the accent, but neither did Stelin. It had taken me a while to realize that Stelin *did* have the accent, but he'd buried it inside himself. It had taken thinking back many times on starting back up with combatives.

Let's play, sweetheart.

It had come out then, though not anything the likes of the Reaper on the way here. That had given me a great deal to think on, where people were concerned.

I did wonder what Stanley's real voice would sound like, were it not being hidden. I wondered what it might try to say about him.

For a multitude of reasons, I couldn't help frowning as well. "Did you know my parents there?"

"No," he replied. "Reapers aren't very friendly as a whole with one another there. Not anywhere apart from here, really. I knew *of* them, of course. We're always informed when Reapers join a city and when they go rogue. But I know you're aware of what your father was, so I'm sure you can partially understand me saying his reputation certainly preceded him. It was a rather large deal."

"Did Hasting kill my mother?" I asked the ground. I hadn't wanted to be callous by asking my father.

When Stanley said nothing, I looked back at him. Only then did he nod his head. I somehow managed to keep my reaction completely contained. It was like a knife in the gut, but I kept my face even. I could do nothing for the tears prickling in my eyes.

The sadness in his voice was palpable when he said, "I can still remember him bringing her body back to the city. Clear as day."

"Why?"

"I'll never answer that question for you," he said stiffly. "You wouldn't want to know even if you think you do or think you *need* to. You *shouldn't* know. Not that. But you have the right to know he did just that. I'm one of *very* few people in your life who both can and will confirm that for you."

There were so many things I could say to his words, but there was nothing I would.

"It was *very* shortly after that when he took over Bethel," Stanley explained. "He and his followers gave us all the chance to stay or be killed. I'd already had my daughter by that point so I stayed instead of running, hoping I would be able to protect her one day. Take her and her mother away when I wasn't so afraid."

That meant Stanley's daughter was older than I was. He must've looked so much younger than he actually was.

"How old are you?" I asked, curious.

"Thirty-seven," he said with a stiff smile. Apparently he was *precisely* as old as he appeared. "You're wondering how I could've already had a child by that point, aren't you?" He didn't give me the chance to answer. "She was an accident with a girl I'd grown up with. I was seventeen when she was born, as was her mother."

I thought on what I'd just learned, and I felt there was only one question to be asked for now. Only one I would or could. "So . . . why did you leave?"

"I'm sure Stelin believes only a few people know what happened to his best friend," Stanley said, the stiffness returning to his voice. "He would be correct about that but wrong about the precise number." He paused, clenching his jaw for an instant. "I left Bethel because Hasting murdered my daughter."

"June was your *daughter*?" I whispered as my face contorted in disbelief. Stelin's best friend had been Stanley's daughter? Was *that* what he was saying?

He nodded his head slowly. "Stelin doesn't know. No one ever concerns themselves with the parents. I'd never been able to speak to her, but her mother and I watched her from a distance as she was growing. I'll admit we were both concerned the first time we saw them together. He was a few years older, and of course we knew whose son he was. Then we happened to see something that changed our minds." He smiled a little at whatever he was remembering, and it only got sadder the longer it spent on his face. Then it fell away completely. "We thought she'd be safer, growing up close to him with him watching her back. We should've known better."

"But where is her mother?" I asked, confused. She must not have been here, because I'd never seen Stanley with a woman. But . . . I supposed I didn't see everything.

"She stayed," he said with a forced smile. "We'd heard whispers about your father making a play at Jarsil by that point and both of us thought, perhaps, he may understand. In the end, she was too afraid to leave. She worried Hasting would kill us one minute after setting out and that if he didn't . . . your father most certainly would. His time there added to the fear of it. His life there was *not* pleasant. Throwing a new Reaper in was always dangerous, but someone with that sort of reputation?" His face scrunched the slightest bit. "It's very much like wolves. The inconsequential ones are what they are. Do you know anything about the behavior of wolves?"

I nodded. "I read a book about it in New Bethel." I likely wouldn't have, if not for the similarities to human behavior that I'd caught onto early in.

"So you understand the pecking order?"

I nodded again.

"You can think of your father like an alpha. The big dog. So people hear that he ran off from here and they make the mistake of thinking it was weakness that sent him running. When throwing a big dog into a pack where he's presumed weak?" He sort of shrugged. "The masses try to get their bites in, thinking they can. Trying to pull them down because people can't help doing that when they think they can manage it. But people like your father?"

He shook his head. "You can't get people like that on their back unless they let you or you have enough to overpower them." His brow furrowed. "He did what he must, which I'm sure you can understand, and Mara?" He sighed. "She didn't understand that your father and Hasting were *always* two different people. She was set that one or the other would kill us if we took a single step in that direction. There was no option, in her mind.

"Mara and I weren't together in the sense you likely believe we were," he continued. "We were just very close friends. It hurt me to leave without her, but I still did it. I miss her very much, but it would've been far worse to stay under Hasting. I could've never lived with myself if I had. It had been hard enough, but I *couldn't* after what he'd done. Everyone is entitled to make their own decisions in life and deal with the consequences of them. Or they *should* be entitled to it.

"My consequence for doing what was best for me is living a life without her. Not a day goes by where she doesn't cross my mind, where I don't wonder how she is or if she's still alive. What I could've done to convince her to go. It took me five years to stop lying to myself." He shook his head. "She didn't make the decision. I abandoned her to it. I'll always have to live with that."

I blinked back tears. "Why are you telling me all this?" I almost whispered.

Stanley had never been one to divulge much of anything to me. A few lessons here and there, but nothing personal about himself. Him speaking to me on my parents was one thing, but . . .

"Because we live in a world of secrets and lies," he said. "I'm telling you because you give me the hope that . . . one day? The world we're living in may change. Just like your father has given me that same hope since I stepped in front of him and rather than killing me, he said . . . '*I am so sorry. This is my fault.*'" He paused. "There will come a time when your father is gone. Perhaps soon, perhaps not for another twenty years or more. But his ideals will never die. Not if you're alive to carry them on and move them forward."

"But my brother and Anders, Stanley," I said in exasperation. I was frustrated to be having this same argument again. "They would be so much better equipped, and they're both easily as kind as I am." In different ways, perhaps.

"No, they are *not*," Stanley said firmly. "You see the problem with Reapers, Aster, is that you never *truly* know who they are. Not unless they open themselves up to you. Even your father." He spent a few seconds shaking his head before continuing on. "It's trained into us relentlessly. Every person is an enemy. Every person is a threat. So, no matter what your father or any of them would do . . . it can only reach so far. Our minds are limited, sculpted and honed into what they want us to be. You don't carry our same limitations."

He stared at me for a moment before saying, "No matter the shared blood that runs in all your veins, they are *not* better equipped, Aster. The two of them did not get whatever fluke that blood carries in it. Your father got it. I've heard your mother was quite brilliant as well, so you got *something* from them. The difference, Aster?" He raised an eyebrow. "Your head isn't filled with all that your father's is. They put walls inside there that he can't or won't break. But he taught you to think, did he not? And are you not trying your hardest to break them down?"

He continued staring at me for a rather long while. I did not want to hear any more about people wanting me to be in control of the city or anything about any part of this.

"How many people know?" I asked instead of saying anything else I could have. "About your daughter."

"Only your father and now you. Stewart as well, of course. I'd be ashamed to admit to most anyone that the jackass knows almost everything about me and my life."

I couldn't help smiling at that.

The corners of Stanley's mouth barely tugged up for an instant, but they hurriedly went back down. "I'm telling you because I believe you have the right to make your own distinctions about my allegiances. I'm not talking about on a personal level. It's the same right I believed your father had when I came here." He smiled a little, differently then. "I don't believe we can ever truly have peace in our world, but you give me the hope that one day . . . I may very well be proven wrong."

Stanley stood and almost started to walk away, but he stopped himself, staring down at me. "Don't give up on those walls. All things can be overcome. You just have to figure it out. Understand?"

Slowly, I nodded. I wasn't going to say, but . . . "My father's walls are very much like these mountains surrounding us."

To that, Stanley said, "We all have our own mountains, and they can *all* be brought down. Don't give up. Not even when you stand alone at the bottom of a mountain and feel tiny when staring to the top." He shook his head. "You're not."

I couldn't blink back the tears then, so I just looked away.

CHAPTER
THIRTY-SEVEN

BAD

I DID NOT DREAM OF DANCING AGAIN that night as I'd hoped to.

I dreamt I stood on the balcony where my father had given his speech. I wore a curses beneath a beautiful red dress. The two old women had made it for me to wear while I gave my own speech to the people. I stood in front of the entire city, and before I could open my mouth to speak to them, they all began laughing at me. They pointed and they held their stomachs because their amusement was so great.

Silly little girl in a dress.

My Reapers—and they *were* my Reapers—frowned up at me from where they stood below, surrounded by sheep.

"Give the order," one of them said from beside me. I didn't know who he was.

"I won't give that order," I told him.

"Then we will do it for you." His voice was void of anything. "It is the only way." He shouted something from the balcony, and one by one, the Reapers below began killing everyone in the city—*my people*. The Reaper near me grabbed hold of the banister and dropped down onto the ground to join the others. The fall did not harm him.

I stood there silently, and I watched because I could not do anything else.

I was so angry at them, wasn't I?

I was angry because they looked at me, but they never really saw me. They looked and never saw anything.

They kept laughing, those people. Archers from the wall shot them down. Reapers on the ground slit their throats. Broke their necks. Stabbed them and they would fall. They were powerless against the Reapers, but they did not even attempt to put up a fight. They were far too preoccupied. Only when they were dead did they stop laughing.

The longer it went on, the more the world seemed to match my beautiful dress. The longer it went on, the more the world seemed to come to the silence I usually preferred. Didn't. Did. I stood in that silence, watching it happen and wondering if I could've stopped it.

If I should have.

If I cared to.

Why I wasn't saying anything.

I did nothing but watch.

When it was finished, my Reapers stood over the dead bodies of my people and smiled up at me as though they thought I would be pleased with them.

No. That was the wrong smile.

Silly little girl in a dress . . . all alone with us now.

My brother and Anders stepped out onto the balcony and all the Reapers dropped to their knees at the sight of them. They didn't seem to care about the poolings of blood they were knelt in.

"What a good job you've done," Anders told them as though he were speaking to a child. The strange voice people spoke to infants with.

"My father," I whispered. "Where is my father?" No. That was not the correct question because there was someone else, wasn't there? I was so confused. Who would keep me safe and who to keep safe? Two paths and only one choice. I shook my head. "Where is Jastin?"

"Don't worry, baby sister," Ahren told me with a smile. "They're well taken care of." That smile widened. "Trust me."

Urgently, I opened the door to go back inside, but I stopped in my tracks. There was a pile of bodies in the room. Agatha, Abby,

Stanley, Stewart, Chandler, Stelin, the Reaper who told me he had faith in me, the little girl and her cat, the old man. My father.

But it was Jastin standing there with a hand and a knife held in front of his neck that had stopped me from moving forward.

"I wanted you to see this one," a familiar voice said. "I've been waiting."

Jastin blinked a tear from his eye right before Chase slit his throat. I watched him bleeding out on the floor, and I did not care that Chase was there or that he was going to kill me too.

I ran over to Jastin, and I screamed as my hands turned red. I could not tell where his blood ended and my dress began.

No.

I heard laughing when I was sure that Jastin was dead. Still, I shook him and screamed at him to stand up and move. I had to take him to someone who could fix him. Couldn't someone fix him? Someone *had* to fix him.

It was too late. This could not be fixed. Some things could not be moved on from. Recovered from. Fixed. Changed.

When Jastin did not move and I stopped moving him, I looked up at Chase and realized that I had never wanted to kill anyone so badly in all my life. *Wanted.* Wanted him to bleed.

He laughed. "My god, if you could only see yourself there. All the blood and tears, like you didn't know this would happen. Do you *feel* it? *Can* you? Have you heard it? *Hard and cold as ice. She can't feel a thing.* Are they wrong or are you putting on a show? Playing pretend?" He smiled so widely. "It's just me here." He held my knife in his hand, dangling it between us. "Did you leave this for me to use or take it off because you had to? Because he gave it to you? Are you heartless or stupid, *Star?*"

It felt as though everything inside me had died on the floor. I stood up slowly and stared into Chase's face. "Do it, then." My voice sounded dead in my ears. Normal.

"With pleasure." He took a step closer.

I did not flinch when he smiled again and reached a bloody hand out to touch my face. I was not afraid of him.

"They say you can't feel anything." He sort of pouted at me. "Let's prove them wrong, shall we?" He put his mouth right next to mine to whisper, "I'm going to make it hurt. If you can't feel it, I'll find it."

"You're a monster," I told him firmly.

"I'm going to enjoy showing you what the words you use actually mean. I'm going to enjoy making you *finally* understand what we are." He grabbed my face, his brow furrowing. "We can always get inside if we're good enough, no matter how high or fortified the walls. Did you think you were safe in here?" He tapped on my chest a few times with my knife. "Did you really? You're not. There's always someone good enough. Someone better. You poor thing, thinking you're safe behind the walls you built for yourself. How many times?"

I said nothing.

"How many times do you need to be told before you *listen*? You've no idea the sort of people, Flower. I have to enlighten you. It's for your own good." He stared at me, a new smile stretching. "I'm going to find where it's hiding. Ask me what."

"What?"

He whispered, "That fluke in your blood. That place inside you where you hide everything that hurts. I'm going to find it, and I'm going to *break it*." He laughed. "And then?" He nodded. "I'm going to break *you*." He shook his head then, squeezing my face tighter. "You've *no idea* what you got involved in, you *stupid* girl. I *must* show you. Just remember, it's for your own good."

The last thing that happened was his smiling mouth pressing against mine before I was flailing around in the darkness.

I was being shaken, I knew, but it was Jastin's voice that caused me to stop flailing.

"*Star*," was all he said.

Over and over, he said it.

He was not dead.

He was alive.

It had only been a dream. Just a horrible, *horrible* dream.

It had felt real, but it was not real. Just a dream, and he was alive.

So I kissed him. I kissed him like I had never kissed anyone in all my life.

It did not last for long because I was crying hysterically and he was concerned.

"What were you dreaming about?"

I could see Jastin's face scrunched up in confusion and I looked at it so hard, taking in every bit of it that I could see in the darkness.

His tone was softer when he repeated, "What were you dreaming about?"

I told him and I cried. I cried so much and so hard that it physically hurt.

He did not laugh at me, no matter how ridiculous it was to have gotten so upset over something that wasn't even real. What he *did* do was pull me out of bed, take one of my hands in his, and begin leading me in dizzying circles around the room.

Dancing.

We were dancing. My head knew as much, but my body could not understand it. When Jastin realized I couldn't do it properly right now, if I ever actually could, he picked me up and held me close to him as he spun us both around in those circles.

I held onto him, and I breathed him in. He was here with me. He was not dead. He was alive. Everything was all right.

It had just been another bad dream.

Just another bad dream.

I WOKE FEELING VERY CONFUSED. I did not remember falling back asleep, but I was most assuredly in my bed with Jastin behind me. The new-morning light was barely filtering in through the curtains in the same way it did every morning. Everything was normal enough that I was almost positive I'd dreamt of dancing instead of the other thing. At least until Jastin sleepily asked, "Do you feel better now?"

"I'm sorry." Tears of embarrassment began welling in my eyes.

"Nothing to apologize for." He yawned widely. "Not unless you want to apologize for dreaming I'm incapable of killing Chase. Which would be a ridiculous thing to apologize for, given that you can't help what you dream about."

"Do you think you could?" I asked quietly.

"Not positive of course, but pretty sure." He yawned again. "He likes to play and I don't. I guarantee you if he came with intent to kill me, he would play. So that would give me the perfect opportunity to take care of it." He paused before asking, "Will you make me a promise?"

"What is it?"

"If we ever see Chase again, I want you to run."

"*What*?" I demanded. Had I ever run from anything in my life? I did not believe I had.

No. I had.

Feelings. I had run from feelings.

"You heard me," he said firmly.

I rolled over to frown at him.

"I'd have a better chance at killing him if you weren't there."

"How is that?" Anger started welling inside my chest, and when it reached a certain point . . . it began spreading.

"Because, just like in your dream, he would want to kill me where you could see, and if he was going to kill you, he'd want to do it where I could see," he said. "Take one of us out of the equation and it would remove a good deal of the *fun* from it for him."

Calm down, I told myself.

One.

Two.

Three.

Four.

Five.

Six.

I asked, "How do you know that?"

"I've had quite a few talks with Chandler."

"About Chase?"

He said, "About the things Chandler saw when he followed Chase on his missions."

Numbers disappeared.

"Why didn't you *tell* me any of it?" I demanded. Wouldn't it be better to know?

He pursed his lips for a moment. "I didn't want you to have dreams like what you had last night. I didn't want any of it in your head."

Numbers.

Rather than point out that what should and should not be in my head wasn't his right to decide, I asked, "How did he never catch Chandler when he was following him?"

"I asked him the exact same question," Jastin said. "He told me it was a rare occurrence for him to go once Chase was older, that when he was first being sent on his missions, he'd gone to ensure he came back alive. It's not an unusual thing. A lot of older siblings do that without telling anyone when they're able to get away with it. But he said that when Chase got older, he rarely ever went. Once or twice a year when Chase seemed particularly distracted over something or other."

"But if Chase is the way Chandler says he is . . ." I began slowly. "I don't believe he wouldn't have known he was there."

"Chandler said he was almost positive Chase knew he was there. But I asked him for more definitive proof of whose side he was on a while back. This is probably going to make you angry, but . . ." He almost seemed to be bracing himself. "He was the one Agatha spoke to. He was the one who found a Reaper to give word to your father."

"Are you *serious*?" I asked in disbelief. After eavesdropping on the meeting, I'd always assumed he'd simply overheard the question I asked Agatha that night.

He nodded. "I spoke to Agatha about it as well. She confirmed it."

"Why didn't you tell me immediately after?" The anger returned, more intense than the first time. There were no numbers.

He sighed and forced a smile at me. "You've been so happy lately. I just wanted you to enjoy that feeling for as long as you could."

"If you *ever* know something I need to know . . ." I told him firmly and then stopped. *Breathe.* I took in a deep breath. The only acceptable thing I could say was, "Don't do that again."

"Heard." The word sounded quite guilty. He stared at me for a moment then shook his head. "This is the first time you've been angry with me in quite a while."

"I'm not angry with you." I was angry at the situation. "I'm disappointed."

"You've never been disappointed in me."

I forced a sad smile at him. That was only as accurate as what it was. "I suppose there's a first time for everything."

There was a first time for everything, and then there was the first time something was out in the open. They weren't always necessarily the same.

CHAPTER THIRTY-EIGHT

FIXING

I'D GOTTEN MYSELF PREPARED for training and left my quarters as fast as I was able after having learned that Jastin had withheld a great deal of relevant things from me. Not only relevant but quite personal as well. I knew I should've attempted to learn more of what he had or might have, but I just . . . couldn't. I didn't believe I'd be able to maintain an acceptable amount of composure.

That was if he'd even say another word of it. He clearly didn't want me to know.

I supposed I should've expected nothing more.

It was not even an hour after the unpleasant talk with Jastin that Stelin and I were running around the perimeter of the room together and he asked, "Trouble in paradise?"

"No."

I glanced at Jastin out of the corner of my eye, and it was almost like he knew because he stopped in the middle of what he was doing to look back at me. I stuck my nose a bit in the air, brought my gaze forward, and kept running.

"Hey." Stelin tugged on my arm, just enough to indicate that he had something to say and wanted to stop.

I stopped moving, but I glared hard at him.

"I need to apologize."

"What for?" I asked in exasperation.

"Are you going to make me say it?"

When I did nothing more than blink at him, he breathed out a huff of air and looked away.

"I'm sorry for being an ass yesterday. I'm . . . jealous."

"*Jealous?*" I asked with an uncomfortable laugh. I was getting *so* sick of the word. "Of *what?*"

"Of you," he said. "Jealous of how happy you are with what you're doing. And jealous of the way everyone looks at you here. You know . . . when I was still in Bethel, everyone was afraid of me because of who my father was, apart from June of course. Everyone loves you because of yours. No . . ." He looked away again and shook his head. "They just love you. And they would anyway, regardless of your father. Wouldn't they? It's like . . ."

He did not continue on for a moment, and I didn't know what to say to him.

He brought his gaze back to mine. "It's like no one can help it. Like you just have this *way* about you that everyone is powerless to. It makes me angry sometimes."

My brow furrowed, partly because that was ridiculous due to a number of people *not* liking me *very* intensely, which had been something my father and I occasionally—sometimes regularly—faced. Partly because I didn't understand . . . "Why would that make you angry?"

"Because no matter *what* I do . . ." He paused to laugh humorlessly. "I'm still Hasting's son. No one can get past that."

"No one can get past that I'm a woman, either," I told him, my voice quiet. "So . . . it seems we all have reasons to be angry or whichever word you feel would be best to use. It's all a matter of whether or not you allow the anger over other people's stupidity to ruin you."

"This is *exactly* what I'm talking about." He threw up both his hands. "Where do you come up with these things in your head?"

"In . . . *my head?*" I raised an eyebrow. "You're smiling."

And he was. I'd seen a great deal of smiles from Stelin, but hardly any of them had ever been genuinely amused without some sort of restraint or coldness. He pursed his lips, and there it went.

"Perhaps . . . perhaps if you attempted to adjust your attitude, people would be more inclined to look at you differently."

"But you see, Aster, I've *tried* that." He almost sounded sad. "I tried that with you, but you still look at me for where and who I came from instead of who I am. There was this bit of time where I thought *maybe*, but no. You can say whatever you want about what's and who's, but we both know. Don't we? So do you think we're *friends* when you don't even *care* to get past it? I've given an extensive amount of time to account for your way of being, and you just don't care to. I must not use that word as loosely as you."

I needed to make a decision right then about how much to trust Stelin, because what he'd just said made it necessary. Or perhaps not even how much to trust him but how much faith to have in him. I did not truly believe he was bad, but neither did I believe a person loving their own father would *make* someone bad, no matter who or what their father was. No matter what they'd done. I would put faith in him and hope my risk would be rewarded in the end.

I asked him, "Can you blame me?"

He blinked at me in confusion. "What?"

"Can you blame me for having concerns that the deal you made with me was only to lead me to your father?" I asked. "I'm just a silly little girl in a dress, aren't I? How could I help you with what you asked of me? Even if I *wanted to . . . How*?"

"You've thought—" He looked away and nodded. "No, I can't blame you for thinking that. But I asked you because I'm too afraid to do it alone, and I'm too afraid that . . . if I was looking into his face?" He shook his head. "I wouldn't be able to do it regardless of anything." He took a deep breath. "Our deal is off."

"What?" My brow furrowed. "You're not going to help me?"

"No, I'm going to keep helping you." He nodded. "But I'm also telling you that if my father comes . . . I'm going to run. I'm not going to protect you and I'm not going to protect him. I'm going to *run*. The least I can do is help you learn how to protect yourself, if my blood comes for yours."

"I was your contingency plan," I whispered in understanding.

He nodded.

I could not explain why I heard myself asking, "How long did you know that Chase was the spy? No . . . *How* did you know?"

"I started having suspicions before we arrived here." His voice took on the even, businesslike tone Reapers so often used. "Those suspicions grew over time, but I didn't know for *sure* until after he'd gone. And I knew because, when I watched . . . I could see that he wasn't in love with you like he claimed to be. It took me some time, but I could see it. I wasn't sure, but I was sure enough."

"You *knew* I was pregnant," I whispered. I'd had my own suspicions over that for a while. "You knew I was pregnant with his child. Didn't you?"

I watched tears beginning to well in his eyes. He sniffed in through his nose and shook his head as though he were attempting to shake the unwanted feeling from himself. "Are you going to tell your father?"

"I'm going to tell you what I've wanted to tell you for months now." I waited until he was looking at my eyes to say, "*Thank you*. It was an extremely painful experience, far more emotionally than physically, but . . ." I nodded. "Thank you."

And that was how I knew Stelin was not working with his father. He had intentionally saved me from having a child with his father's spy. He had saved me from being more vulnerable than I already was to his father. I did not think I could ever repay him for what he'd done, no matter how horrible a thing it had been. In a sense . . .

He had saved my life. Perhaps he had also saved my father's life, and Jastin's, and my brother's. Perhaps Chandler's. Perhaps he had saved the entire city. And no one would ever know.

But *I* knew. I could see it in his eyes that he was telling the truth. He'd known I was pregnant. He'd known whose child was. He'd thought about it. Didn't want to but felt he must. Perhaps he'd realized the potential far-reaching repercussions at the time or perhaps he hadn't. I was quite sure I knew the motivation behind.

He'd been saving *me*. From his father. No ulterior motive because he'd not told his *good deed* until I'd asked, for it to potentially alter anything. He'd been saving me from his father in whatever way he could for absolutely no reason but because he felt he must or should. For once, something simply was what it was and was simply simple. Such a rare thing.

Stelin said nothing to me thanking him. There was nothing *to* say because there was no hidden motive and he was not proud of it. In a world of sheep . . .

Stelin was a different thing.

I felt inclined to say, "I feel I should also thank you for the vine blankets."

"I don't know what you're talking about." He said that, but he *almost* smiled.

"Sure you don't." I nodded. "I do still have them on my bed. I like them very much."

Both his eyebrows rose. "I hope you know I was being an ass with that."

I couldn't help smiling. "I know."

He seemed unable to help himself from doing the same then. Just a little. He then nodded as a gesture. "Let's get back to it."

We did.

I knew what Stelin had done. And I would not ever forget it.

I DIDN'T THINK ABOUT SPIES AND ALLEGIANCES for the remainder of my time spent training, though I likely should have. I thought about Jastin instead. I thought about his lack of telling me important information and his reasons for doing so.

I was quite accustomed to being kept in the dark, as it happened a great deal when you associated with Reapers. After spending more time with my father, he was excluded from that. He both was and was not a Reaper. The more time passed, the more he told.

But Jastin *was* a Reaper, no matter what any piece of paper said. He may not have told me in a satisfactory time frame, but he *had* told me—sooner than essentially anyone else would have, at that. And he'd been more open with me than anyone had been in all my life.

Essentially anyone.

I thought about him dancing me around the room in the middle of the night, regardless of the fact that he didn't like it, simply because I was upset over a dream.

Should I fault him for a shortcoming when he never faulted me for my own? Weren't people entitled to small slipups now and then?

Nothing catastrophic had occurred from it. Nothing changed.

Did I always have to be so harsh? Did I always have to be that person who used logic and thought only with their head and not their heart? Was I nothing more than a Reaper without the training?

What would I turn into after years of their training, if I didn't properly straighten out my head? What sort of walls might that create? What sort of mountains?

I thought about dancing and, though it made no sense at all, I realized . . . I preferred it.

"I'm finished for the day," I told Chandler and Stelin immediately upon my realization.

"What?" Chandler asked. "We've only been working for two hours."

"Would you like to learn how to dance?" I asked them quickly.

"*What*?" they both exclaimed. The expressions on their faces was quite a wonderful thing for me to see.

"*Dance*," I said. "Abby will be there with my brother. I'm sure you can have a go. Or . . . whatnot. And Stelin, you can take turns dancing with me if you'd like. I'm quite bad at it. Worse than at combatives, if you can believe. I'm sure you'd both find it amusing." I grinned. "Or *perhaps* if you don't want to go, Chandler, Stelin could swap out Abby with my brother."

"I'll go," Chandler said immediately, as I'd known he would.

I smiled and then turned to Stelin. "It'll be fun. When was the last time you had any fun?"

"Yeah, I'll go." His face contorted into something that was nearly absolute horror, and he seemed quite shocked to hear the words that had quietly escaped from his mouth.

"Wonderful." I nodded. "Now go ready yourselves and meet me back here in . . ." I thought hard, "one hour."

Stelin asked, "How does one *ready* themselves to dance, exactly?"

"Well, I suspect Chandler would like to go bathe beforehand." I shrugged. "You might ought to as well."

Chandler pursed his lips for a moment, I assumed to hide the grin on his face from me. "What are you going to do?"

I looked down to scratch at an itch on my leg that didn't truly exist. "I'm going to go kiss Jastin is what I'm going to do." Not for an hour, but for a bit of it.

"See you in an hour," Stelin said as they both made a hasty departure.

"What's this about kissing?" Jastin asked from behind me.

I stepped up close to him and poked him in the chest. "Don't do that again, with the not telling."

He smiled one of his lip-biting smiles at me and nodded.

"Now that that's settled . . ." I stood up on my tiptoes and kissed him.

He wrapped his arms around me and pulled his face away after a short moment. "Well, now you've kissed me in your training area. Is there anywhere else you'd like to—"

"Oh, be quiet." I interrupted him and then kissed him again.

CHAPTER THIRTY-NINE

BOTH

JASTIN AND I WERE ONLY KISSING inside the training area for a short while before I told him I had something to do and went on my way. I usually spent most of the time with my father in the evenings, but he and I both would stop in with one another throughout the day, so it wasn't unusual for me to drop by his office. I did bathe first, so I only had a few short minutes of helping him with what he was doing before someone stepped inside and informed me of the time.

I looked to my father and said, "See you this evening, Father."

He looked up from his work, smiling. "Looking forward to it, Flower." He waved a hand. "Go on. Remember what I said."

I smiled as well, nodding. I then went back to my training area as intended. I was in very high spirits when Jastin, Chandler, Stelin, and I came upon the designated room. Abby and my brother were already inside it with Patricia.

"What's this?" Patricia asked when we stepped inside.

I grinned. "I've convinced these two to learn how to dance."

I did not miss Abby trying to hide her smile from Chandler. When she couldn't manage it, she looked at something near one of the walls instead of at him.

"Have you really?" Patricia asked in disbelief.

I nodded.

"If you'll give me just a moment, I'll go retrieve my daughter."

I hadn't known she had a daughter, and I momentarily felt quite horrible for not having asked her if she had children simply for the sake of *polite conversation*, but I said, "That's not necessary."

"Oh, I believe it is." Patricia nodded, both eyes widening. "I have a difficult enough time keeping two of you in line at once. My daughter's quite an exceptional dancer. She'll be a great deal of help for me."

"All right, then." That was logical. "We'll just wait here."

Patricia was gone for nearly half an hour. The very first thing Chandler did was step over to Abby and ask her where James was. She blushed and told him that James was again with my father. I must've just missed her bringing him in.

The two of them spoke in hushed tones with one another and my brother had quickly walked over to Jastin and me, making some sort of gesture that was clearly about the two of them with a questioning expression on his face.

I just smiled at him. I managed it.

It had not been long at all before I'd noticed the two of them together, and the three of us together, leaving Stelin all alone and uncomfortable. It didn't matter so much that I wasn't involved or even listening to any conversations had near to me, partially because listening to Jastin and my brother interact was something like knives scratching at plates to me. I'd been thinking on things after a short bit of time pondering utilization.

I stood on my tiptoes to kiss Jastin on the cheek and then went over to Stelin. "Would you like to dance with me?"

He seemed quite confused. "She's not in here to instruct me how."

I grinned again. "Well, as I said . . . I'm quite bad at it, but I'm sure we can manage. As with a great many things, I know how it works *in theory*. It's the execution that's the problem."

And that was how I'd ended up holding one of Stelin's hands, while he had hold of my waist with his other, and stepping on his feet periodically for nearly twenty-five of those thirty minutes.

He and I both laughed a great deal despite the strangeness of it, with the touching in the way it was being done and whatnot. I was glad to see him enjoy himself.

He stopped both moving and laughing at once when Patricia entered the room again with her daughter in tow. His eyes widened only a little before he looked away.

"Aster." The expression on Patricia's face was almost a frown but almost a smile at the same time. It was peculiar. "Have you been trying to teach him while I've been gone?"

"Yes, and I've probably only made things indefinably worse for him," I admitted as I dropped his hand. He seemed to have forgotten I was still holding it. "If your daughter is as exceptional as you say she is . . . it would probably be a good idea for her to make up for the damage I've likely done." I smiled at the girl who was very nearly hiding behind her mother and said, "Hello."

Her face turned very red. "Hello, Milady."

"Call me Aster, please," I insisted. "What's your name?"

"Michaela," she answered. "But you can call me Kay, if you'd like."

Kay *was* quite stunning, enough for Stelin's reaction toward her to be understandable. She had dark hair and warm brown eyes that nearly matched in color his generally cold ones, or made up for them. I wondered if her mother's eyes had been so warm when she was younger. She was built very small, even smaller than what I was at least in height, and appeared as though she could break at any moment. And yet she didn't at all look like a child. She seemed very kind and quiet, but I could almost see a tiny bit of fire behind her eyes. I wondered if she knew it was there, or perhaps I was only seeing things.

"Well, Kay," I said with a breath. "I believe I've put a horrible knowledge of dancing inside Stelin's head. Perhaps you can fix that for him."

She smiled at me. "I will try my hardest." And then she turned that beautiful smile on Stelin. "Hello, Sir."

He just stood there, the poor thing.

I patted him on the arm, which made him look at me with his wide eyes. I gestured with my hand for him to do *something* because I did not want him to make a fool of himself.

He shook his head and looked at Kay. I could've sworn I heard him swallow before he said, "Hello, Miss." I'd thought he would handle females better, but perhaps there was *something* about this particular one. Could that happen with just one look at someone?

It seemed quite ridiculous no matter what stories I'd heard on things. No matter what all I knew.

"Please call me Kay."

He nodded, and I took in a contented breath.

"Shall we proceed, then?" I asked happily.

Patricia nodded, and I went over to Jastin. He was shaking his head at me for quite a long time as we went about things.

"What?" I whispered after having stepped on his right foot on four separate instances.

"Do you want everyone to be happy?" He whispered his question curiously while Patricia was saying something to Abby.

I almost laughed. "Yes, I do."

I glanced at Stelin periodically during our time in that room. It took him a while, but eventually . . . he began smiling. By the end of our time, he was smiling even when Kay was taking turns with both Chandler and my brother. He was even smiling when she was trying not to be flustered because my brother was *my brother*. My father's son, more like.

It happened.

Girls got *very* silly over him.

Jastin didn't look away from me and scowl about the dancing that day. He looked at me and smiled the entire time. I stepped on his feet *a bit* less than I had before. I believed we all had a great deal of *fun*. It was odd, and interesting, and enjoyable.

As we were walking toward the door at the end of our time, I heard Kay ask, "Will you be coming back tomorrow, Stelin?"

I looked over at him, unable to help my mouth tugging upward.

He glanced from her, to me, then back. "I believe I will."

She didn't even try to hide the ridiculously large smile on her face. "I shall see you tomorrow, then."

I barely heard him tell her, "I'm looking forward to it."

I was smiling the rest of the day, or a great deal of it.

I was smiling inside my father's office while holding little James just after the dancing. It did not scare me as much as it initially had, perhaps because I'd become somewhat accustomed to it, or perhaps because he'd grown since I'd first seen him, which made it a little less scary. Or perhaps for another reason.

I was smiling when Abby came alone only a few short minutes after I'd arrived to retrieve him then went on her way.

I was smiling when I insisted my father and Anders go with us the next day, and that Agatha go as well.

I didn't have bad dreams that night, and I was smiling most the next morning while training.

"It's all right, you know," I told Stelin quietly when Chandler had gone off to speak with Jastin.

I heard the two of them laughing about something in the opposite corner of the room. They enjoyed doing their training together, for some reason. It made no sense to me, as they both disliked one another quite a lot so far as I could tell.

It was not my business.

I only hoped that Jastin's arms would not grow to be as large as Chandler's.

It was not my business, but the closeness irked me somewhat.

"What's all right?" Stelin asked as we were doing our own movements together.

"Letting yourself feel." I kept telling myself it was, and I thought he needed to hear it as well.

"I don't know what you're talking about," he said nonchalantly.

"That Kay . . ." I began. "She's quite breathtaking, isn't she? Moves so gracefully like the wind too, which is quite unusual for someone who isn't a Reaper. Very kind as well, it seems. There's *something* pleasant about her manner of being."

It took some time for him to speak, and his voice was quiet when he did. "I don't think I'll go back with you today."

"Oh, you most certainly will." I stopped moving to stare at him. "You just might enjoy the realization that you have a heart. I already know it's in there, but I should very much like to see the look on your face when it finally dawns on *you*. And if you hurt that girl for nothing more than your own selfish reasons, then you and I will simply have to fight." I paused for an instant. "But you're not going to do that."

Only then did he stop doing his own movements and look at me. "How do you know that?"

"Because you *want* to be and have good," I told him assuredly. "You're simply afraid of moving away from that place where you've settled yourself in the middle of all things."

"Aster," he said, his voice unyielding. "I don't want any more people to get killed because they care about me."

"We're not in Bethel," I whispered. "Your father has no power here. But . . . if you *like her*? The *instant* you're concerned for her safety, you let me know."

He did not ask me what I would do, or what I *could* do.

Instead he asked me, "Why would you care?"

"I care about everyone here," I informed him. "Most of all anyone who could make one of my friends smile when they so rarely do. And yes, Stelin." I nodded. "I *do* think we're friends. Maybe looser than what would make you use the word, but that does *not* mean there's a lack of care in moving past. It's not you. It's this place and all that comes with it. I like you, when you don't try to make me not. Even sometimes then. But I just . . ." I cleared my throat. "I've not had good experiences in getting close with people, and I honestly had no idea *you* cared to. But yes. I would very much like to see you smile, as I said. As much as possible."

"Isn't it exhausting?" His face scrunched a bit. "Concerning yourself with absolutely everyone? Always thinking about other people and doing things for them?"

"Yes," I admitted, "but it's so worth it to see the smiles on their faces. Perhaps you should try it sometime so that you may understand what I mean."

"How?" he asked, curious.

"As you well know, I spend several hours a day doing—" I stopped myself. "Being . . . what did you call it? A *princess*?" I huffed out a breath at having to say the word. "I know you're concerned about the way people look at you here. I believe I know the perfect place to show you that you're wrong and are simply in need of a shift in perspective. Will you go with me there?"

Very slowly, he nodded his head.

I'd started to carry on, but . . .

"It's different."

I raised an eyebrow at him.

"It's the same thing," he said. "But it's different."

"I have *no idea* what you're talking about."

His face reddened. "I'm trying to be sensitive of your issues with speaking directly."

My brow furrowed.

"One of your male friends being interested in a female. It's the same situation as Chandler and Abby, or close enough. But your reaction is different. The words are the same. *I want you to be happy,* but now you actually look happy. It's not the training, right?"

I did not know how he knew about me having told Chandler that I wanted him to be happy, pertaining to that, but . . . "In what sense?"

He sighed. "You know what sense, Aster. I'm giving you an option that isn't relevant. Because you and I both know it's not the same. You *do* know that now, don't you? You're genuinely happy at the thought of me being happy, and you know in your head that you want him to be happy, but you're just not. You've gotten that figured out properly, haven't you? Because your father's been working with you to understand. Right? And you understand that it's not different because of the females. It's different because you don't feel the same about us."

I meant to only glance at Chandler across the room, but I watched him with Jastin.

Not long at all passed before Jastin moved to do something with movements, and Chandler shot me with a look behind his back. Looked like . . .

Do you see what I have to tolerate?

My mouth tugged up.

His sort of followed.

He then shook his head and followed Jastin off.

I was still watching them when I said to Stelin, "My father and I have had a great many conversations on value. Currency. Occupations. Commodities. Resources. People. If you saturate with one thing, its value decreases. What is a smile worth?"

Stelin said nothing.

I looked up at him.

Then, he said, "I would say that's subjective."

"If there's one thing I've learned, it's that nothing is subjective. There is always a set and controlled factor. If something seems subjective, the control is simply out of view."

"And yet feelings don't listen to *controls.* Has your father convinced you that there's logic in feelings, or have you done that yourself to get through the days?"

I said nothing to that.

What I did do was ask, "How did you know? That I'd told him about wanting him to be happy."

Stelin said very deliberately and with a tiny smile, "Believe it or not . . . we *do* speak when you're not in the room. Sometimes." The smile dropped away and his eyebrows rose. "He told me. After you'd left the room."

Careful, I asked, "For what reason?"

In the same deliberate way, he said, "Because people don't always understand you. And sometimes, figuring *anything* out is a group effort."

My lips pursed. But then tears began welling. I turned my back to the other side of the room and looked Stelin in the eye. I mouthed . . .

Does he know?

Did he know and was just trying to be kind in not letting me know he did?

Stelin's eyebrows rose again, and he said in the most believable way I had perhaps ever heard anything, "*No.*"

I nodded, taking in a breath of relief.

DANCING WAS MORE ENJOYABLE with my father, Anders, and Agatha in the room than it ever had been before. Patricia and Agatha took turns dancing with either of them.

My father, Reaper or not, was *horrible* at it. He was possibly even worse than I was.

I believed his blood had doomed me from ever being remarkably good at it in the way that Kay was, but I didn't care because it was so unbelievably amusing, as was him getting frustrated with Patricia. I was quite sure no one else apart from possibly Anders knew the frustration had occurred.

My father sounded only curious when he asked, "Is it the counting or the movement, Patricia?"

She replied to him with, "Both, Sir."

He sounded only calm when he stated, "It's one or the other."

"I promise it's both."

He took in a deep breath and released it before saying, "Counting is *cold*. Movement is fluid, which would be *warm*. They do not go together. If you're counting steps, would this not be done for the show of it? If you're focused on the feel of the movement, would it not be done for the individuals? The difference between external and internal." He paused for the briefest moment. "How am I to focus on the feel while *counting*? It's one or the other."

Patricia shook her head. "That makes sense of some things."

Kay was smiling so widely when she said, "That's the beauty of it, Sir. It can be anything. Cold or warm. I suppose you could likely compare it to your training. You repeat something until it becomes natural. You count until the numbers are music in your head. It is what you *make it*. It can be both. It can be *everything*."

My father, along with everyone else, stared at Kay until he nodded. Then we got back to it after the disruption. Having a proper explanation, my father was no longer frustrated.

My brother was exceptional at dancing after only what time he'd had, so I had to assume my mother would've been as well and he'd inherited her dancing blood. I'd certainly gotten some parts of my father's blood.

I did wonder what parts of her I might've gotten beyond appearances.

I danced with my father for a while and the two of us laughed as we stepped on one another's feet. I'd made a joke under my breath about us counting together. No one else would've understood it. He made a few jokes under his breath as well, when Patricia would be speaking to cover them. It was better that way. I enjoyed myself immensely, and I believed he did as well.

When we were all done, I was in the process of walking over to Stelin when I heard Kay ask, "Would you like to stay for longer?"

"I can't." He seemed quite sorry to say as much. "I promised Aster I would go with her to . . ." He looked over at me.

I'd just made it over to them and said, "The orphanage."

His eyes went wide, which I pretended not to notice.

Kay's brow furrowed. "Why?"

"Those children have no one in this world, apart from the few people who take care of them," I said. "Not enough to give them the proper attention by any means. They have such brilliant little minds and children seem able to see through everything, but it takes so very little to make them happy. Simply allowing them to speak to you, the *knowledge* that someone in this world cares about them in some way . . . that's all it takes. They don't care what anyone says. They make their own distinctions about everything and everyone." I paused. "It's quite an amazing thing to see."

They had a certain way of looking at and seeing things.

Kay quickly asked, "May I go with you?"

"Of course you may." I laughed beneath my breath. "No one should need permission to do good for other people."

"Do you go there often?"

I nodded. "As much as I can. It's one thing of many."

"How do you find the time to do all these things?" Kay's nose scrunched a bit in an adorable sort of way.

Jastin came up behind me and laughed before saying, "She hardly ever sleeps."

"I sleep." I shook my head. "But there are some things worth losing sleep over."

The orphanage was one of many things that had caused me to lose a *great* deal of it.

Chapter Forty

TRUTH

E TOOK A RATHER LARGE PARTY to the orphanage, which was quite strange. I was not accustomed to so many having intent to go inside. Most Reapers who followed would remain out with only enough inside to do whatever they felt they must. I suspected nearly all of them would've remained out, if not absolutely all, had they not felt obligated or whatever nonsense to do otherwise. So the large party with intent was strange. I felt good about it and ignored the small voice in the back of my head, telling me I was ridiculous for this pertaining to Stelin. I was confident and it was not ridiculous. The logic was sound.

Anders joined us, as did my brother. Patricia even came as well.

My father remained behind, claiming he had work to do. I suspected that was only a partial truth, as there was *always* work to do, but I didn't call him out on it and I didn't believe anyone else had noticed. My father was very good with children, so I suspected no one could or would put together his feelings on the orphanage. He was a busy man and that was a good enough excuse for most things, but there was an obvious reason as to how the blankets and pillows had gotten into the state they were before replacement. It wasn't for lack of caring, as he'd been *very* upset over not knowing what they needed. The orphanage?

Well, it wasn't a place most wanted to step a single foot inside of for whatever reasons they had. It was typically easy to discover those reasons if they existed, so long as one knew what they were looking at. Or for.

I had my own reasons, but none of them would stop me from going.

They weren't good enough.

Jastin was bombarded with children the instant we opened the door because he'd promised he would read them a story the next time we came.

Stelin was overwhelmed by it all, I could tell, so I squeezed his hand in encouragement. I then kept it, hoping that might in some way help.

"Who are these people?" the children asked excitedly.

They never concealed their excitement. They had no need to. I enjoyed being around them because of it, but that was not the only reason.

I began pointing to each of them with my free hand. "Well, this is Anders." This was not the first time my brother had come with us here, so I didn't need to introduce him. "Patricia here has been planning *all* the details of mine and Jastin's wedding. This is her daughter, Kay. She dances beautifully, by the way. And this here is my very good friend Stelin." I wiggled his hand a bit with mine rather than pointing. I then released it.

And then *they* were all bombarded. Anders was surrounded by little boys saying they had *seen him with the king*. He smiled because he thought it was amusing more so than any other reason he could've possibly had, I was sure. They called my father *The King* here, and I did not contradict them. It seemed to make them quite happy. I did like that they thought so highly of him.

Patricia was surrounded by little girls who *demanded* to know about my wedding. Something or other about colors.

My brother and Jastin were both dragged away by a flood of happy children.

Kay had knelt down and was explaining what dancing was to quite a few them. The little boys scrunched up their faces in what appeared to be disgust, but several of the girls asked her if she would show them how.

Kay's face lit up, and I heard her say, "I would *love* to."

A little girl tugged at the bottom of Stelin's shirt as she looked up at him. She waited until he brought his gaze down to her face to speak. It took him a moment. I believed he'd been hoping she would go away if he didn't.

She didn't. She wouldn't have.

"You're Princess Aster's friend, Sir?"

I blushed furiously at the word being used so casually to him, especially with certain remarks he'd made. After having contradicted the children several times as to what I was and was not and seeing the sad looks on their faces . . . I'd decided to stop. Someone would explain it to them when they were older and could understand, and I didn't want to be the person who squashed their happiness into nothing when they had so very little of it. I refused to be that person. If believing I was something I wasn't made them happy, if *anything* could . . .

Stelin looked over at me and blinked several times before shaking his head minutely and bringing his attention back to the little girl. "Yes, I am."

"I saw her holding your hand, Sir, so she must like you very much," she said. "May I hold your hand?"

I could see it on his face—the urge to ask her why she wanted to, or perhaps the urge to tell her there was no use in hand-holding. He did not say anything, but he held his hand out for her and watched the smile on her face as she took it. It wasn't long before another little girl—that one even younger—came and tugged on the other side of his shirt. He offered her his other hand without her having to ask for it. It was precisely what she wanted.

I was smiling as I walked over to where Jastin was sitting on a bed, surrounded by children on the ones nearby. They were watching him intently as he was reading through a book of stories about the king. They were true stories and not ones that had been passed down where there was so much room for exaggeration. These had been written down by some unknown person. At least . . . I assumed they were true, for the most part, but I supposed I couldn't know.

When he had finished one, a little girl asked, "But what did the queen do? We never hear stories about the queen."

Jastin closed the book and smiled at her. "They say she used to paint these extraordinary pictures and that she'd put them in her favorite places throughout the city."

"Paintings like that one?" A boy pointed to a painting hanging near the door. It was of trees and little spots of color that I presumed were flowers.

Jastin smiled wider. "Paintings exactly like that one."

"Did the *queen* paint that?" a little girl asked in excitement.

"I'd say she did," Jastin said. He couldn't know that, but it didn't hurt anything to say what he had. Sometimes it was best.

"But why would she like coming here?" a boy asked. "No one likes coming here."

I told him. "*We* like coming here."

That boy looked to me. "But why?"

"To see all of you, of course," I said. "The days I get to see all of you are some of the most cherished I've ever had in my life."

My attention was torn away from the boy because I felt eyes on me. I looked over my shoulder and found Stelin standing on the opposite side of the room—with the little girls still attached to his hands—staring at me. He smiled a little and shook his head again.

The moment was interrupted by a boy asking, "Are you *married*?" to Anders and Patricia, who were dancing together in order to show some of the children how it was supposed to be done.

"What? *No*," one of them said.

"Of course not," came from the other at the exact same time.

They were then pestered with a string of questions about whether they were married to other people and why they were not married, either to one another or to anyone else. It was very awkward, given Anders did not say anything else and Patricia had to explain that her husband had died several years previously.

Perhaps that was the reason for her unhappiness.

Again, I found myself feeling guilty for how little I knew of her, but by the expression on her face . . . it was a subject she'd rather not speak of. Children unfortunately could not make such distinctions. Adults often seemed to find great difficulty in that as well. The larger problem was how far children could drag things out. What wasn't a problem with the problem was that children did not do as much for the same reasons as adults.

"Will you dance with me, Sir?" the more vocal of the two girls with Stelin asked, which drew my attention back to them. The other wiggled his hand, and I took it to mean she wanted to dance with him as well.

He shot me a look that clearly said he didn't know what to do.

I nodded minutely and heard him very awkwardly tell the two of them that they could take turns.

"Do you dance with *her*?" a boy asked Jastin as he nodded his scrunched-up face toward me.

Jastin said, "Oh yes, I do."

"*Why*?" he asked, disgust clear in his tone.

"Because it makes her happy," Jastin replied. "She enjoys it very much. I don't care much for it, but she likes it enough for both of us, and she can't do it alone."

The little boy seemed to think quite hard on the response he'd received before looking at me. "Would you like to dance with *me*?"

I tried as hard as I could not to laugh. "Of course I would. But I should warn you, I'm quite bad at it."

"I didn't think you'd be bad at anything," a little girl said quietly at my left.

"I'm bad at a great many things." I could not help myself from laughing then. "Most of all things that require following other people's instruction." I'd been left to my own means, mostly, in New Bethel. I looked at the little boy and extended my hand to him. "I believe you owe me a dance."

He scowled at my outstretched hand.

"You'll have to hold it if you wish to dance with me."

He must've wanted to quite badly, because he took it. Whether that was because Jastin did it and he wanted to be like him or because he thought it would make me happy, I had no idea.

It was not long before most of the children were dancing with one another and we were all laughing. They took turns with the adults in the room, and I had a line of them near me. I assumed the little boys didn't want me to think that any of them were any braver than the others, though some of them had no issues at all. It was quite amusing.

The people who ran the orphanage came in, wondering what could have the children laughing as they were. They watched them, standing there in confusion and disbelief for a moment, and then they smiled.

Very slowly, people began trickling inside from the streets. They rarely heard laughter from this building, I was sure, and definitely not so loud if they ever did.

They were greeted by smiling children who did not understand that it was curiosity and not caring that had drawn the newcomers inside their space. Children did not care about whys. They only cared about what was happening directly to them at any given time. So they would ask the adults who entered to dance with them. The adults would look at me, I knew, and then tell the children they did not know how. And the children would always say something along the lines of . . .

"Don't worry. I'll show you how."

Some of them would take their hands, and some would not. Most of them did. I didn't know whether they did it because they genuinely wanted to or if, like searching for the little girl's lost cat, they felt as though they were required to. Obligated, for some reason, because of me.

More Reapers had come inside due to the influx of people near me. They'd come inside to keep an eye on me, to make sure I was not attacked. By that point, I'd found myself in a somewhat exhausted sort of dreamy-like daze and was standing against one of the walls, smiling as I watched them all. Most of the Reapers had no choice but to dance with the persistent children, but a few of them stood near the wall with me, watching the scene with me and watching me.

"Who's going to keep your princess safe?" I heard one of them standing near me ask a child who had come up to him.

She'd hugged his legs at that and run away to rejoin everyone else.

Stelin walked over to me eventually, and he didn't care about the Reapers standing near or the same two little girls *still* attached to either of his hands. He almost desperately asked, "Why did you bring me here?"

I did not look at him to say, "You know why."

"They're children." And I knew what he was really saying to me despite not hearing it in his tone. What did children's opinions of him matter?

"They're the future," I said as I stared off at the room of people rather than his face. "In any number of years, they're going to be the ones standing outside, looking at a man and *hoping* upon *all* hope that the man will take care of them."

I was sure he understood what I meant where it pertained to him. In any number of years, the children would be adults who had formed their own opinions of him. He could have a say in what those opinions were. He could have as much a say in his future as he was willing to speak up for.

He stared at me as I looked at the people, and he very quietly asked, "How are you so good?"

I laughed a little and shook my head. "Every person has two people living inside them. Someone good, and someone bad. It's all a matter of which of those people they allow to control their body and mind." I shook my head again. "It's nothing more or less than that." I laughed humorlessly once more and finally looked at his face to say, "People tell stories about men. Happy stories about the good ones and scary stories about the bad. Bad women are forgotten entirely while the only things left of good women are disregarded paintings hanging on walls."

He blinked at me, and I forced a smile at him.

The little girl who was quieter than the other kept hold of his hand, but she tugged on my dress with her free one. "You're crying, Princess. Are you sad?"

I knelt in front of her and smiled at her to say, "I'm very happy."

She looked quite confused so I was about to clarify in a way she might possibly understand when Jastin cut in from where he'd stepped over a few seconds previously.

Jastin knelt beside me. "She had a dream about the *entire city* being happy enough to smile and dance."

Stelin wiggled their hands a little and said, "It looks like Princess Aster's dream is starting, doesn't it?" He turned quickly and began leading the girls away, but not quickly enough for me to miss a tear falling from his own eye.

CHAPTER FORTY-ONE

ENOUGH

EXPECTED PEACE IN MY DREAMS that night. I expected to see visions of the children's smiling faces. I expected a dream of the people in the city caring about one another, moving just a little out of their way to make things *better*.

Instead, I dreamt about my hand holding a brush and dipping it into colors that I would spread across a canvas in front of me. It felt like hours passed in my dream, seemingly endless hours of painting I could never really do because my hands refused to work in such a way. Hours that passed in bursts of instants.

"Are you done?" I heard behind me as I stared at the product of all my hard work.

"I believe I am," I said. "I've no idea what else to do."

"Where are you taking this one?" the same person asked.

"The orphanage." I smiled sadly at the painting that truly hung on the wall in the orphanage. "A window to a world they will never see."

"They see it every moment they spend with you." Whoever it was still spoke at my back.

I stared at the painting I'd spent hours of my life making for the children, and I had a nearly uncontrollable urge to destroy it. I didn't. I just stared.

The person came up behind me, wrapping their arms around.

I didn't move. I didn't want to. I couldn't. A tear fell from my eye when I said, "I only wish I could do more."

"You don't have to do this alone."

"Don't I?"

"Don't you know?"

I said nothing for a long moment, continuing to stare at the painting. "It's so small." I could've sworn . . .

"Then make it bigger."

"It's the size it is. I can't with this."

"Then start over," he said slowly, "and make it bigger."

"What about this one?"

"Is it good enough?"

I shook my head. "They never are."

His arms moved away, going at my back with the rest of him. When they were in front of me again, they didn't wrap around. I watched a knife cut the canvas before it disappeared behind me.

He said, "If it's not good enough for you, it's not good enough for me either. Get it right or don't bother. It's too important. Do it right or not at all."

I still stared at the now-damaged painting, feeling . . . *better*. I felt better. It hadn't been right.

I asked, "Who are you?"

His arms went back around me. "Don't you know?"

I looked down with intent to look at his arms where they were, but . . . "Am I bleeding or are you?" There was a pooling of red on the floor, and I didn't know . . .

"Are you afraid of a bit of blood? If you are . . . What are you thinking?"

"Can I see you?"

He whispered, "You don't want to do that, do you?" He released me, pointing at the canvas. "Fix this."

I turned immediately, but . . . there was no one there. The room was empty apart from myself and a pile of canvases. I looked down, finding the pooling of blood gone.

I stepped over to the blank canvases. I did not know how long I spent searching for the largest. I took it back to where the damaged one was, tossing the latter into a pile of destroyed work. I could've sworn it hadn't been there before.

When I put the new where the old had been, I stared at it.

I could've sworn the other had begun the same size.

I took the brush back in my hand, and I just cried.

It wasn't going to work.

I couldn't do it.

"The same picture is the same picture."

I jumped at the voice, turning myself and still finding the room empty.

"If I scare you, that's your fault." Hands from behind moved me until I was again looking at the blank canvas. "Fix this."

I looked down, finding more blood on the floor. "Who—"

"*Fix it.*"

"I can't."

"*Fix it.*"

"I *can't*. Why can't y—"

A hand moved again from behind me, toward the canvas. It pressed against then ran down, from the top to the bottom. Red smeared down. Dripped. "I can't."

I stared at the red.

"Am I a monster?"

I reached a hand out to the canvas and touched from top to bottom, watching red smearing in a line next to the other.

I stood there, looking at the two streaks next to one another, feeling . . .

It was beautiful.

I had to ask . . . "Where are you?"

I felt a tapping on the back of my head.

I turned around.

The room was empty. The blood was gone.

I did not wake up flailing, but tears were falling from my eyes as they had been in the dream.

Jastin's breathing was slow and steady behind me, so I'd not woken him. I was glad for that.

Very carefully, I managed to get out from beneath his arm. *Very* carefully.

I crawled out of bed and spent a moment staring down at his face. He used to not sleep so peacefully, I remembered.

I smiled, though it felt strained on my face. I put my shirt back on then left the room.

I sat down on the grass close to where I'd planted the flower the little girl had given me, and I cried. I cried and wished so badly that I did not need to feel as though everyone's happiness and well-being was my concern. I wished I did not need to feel that *everything* had turned into my concern.

I also wished that, if I were required to feel that way, I would at least be a person who *could* do more. I wished I could be a person who was capable of achieving what they aspired to. I wished I could be a person other people believed in.

It should've been pleasant to dream of accomplishing something I was incapable of, no matter how minuscule it seemed in comparison or how it hadn't been good enough. Was it minuscule that my own hands could not do as they should? *My own hands. . . .*

How could anyone have *any* sort of faith in me? How was I supposed to do *any* of this?

I heard a footstep and reached for the knife attached to the strap on my arm on instinct. It took me a moment to realize through the darkness, but it had been intentionally placed and . . . "You were at the orphanage earlier."

"I was," the Reaper said as he walked closer. He still stayed a good distance away, and I put my hands in my lap. "I assume you want to be alone, considering you didn't wake Jas up, but . . . I just wanted to make sure you were all right."

"I'm fine," I said tightly. "Jastin . . . do you know him?"

"For most my life," the Reaper said. "Or . . . I did, I suppose. Well enough."

"What do you mean?"

"He's an entirely different person than he used to be, so in a way . . . I don't know him at all," he said. "They say you have that sort of effect on people."

"Why do people always say that?" My voice was quiet as I shook my head.

"I suppose because it must be true."

"People can only be changed by another person if they allow themselves to be," I told him. It was something I'd told Amber a very long time ago. "Anyone who changes after being near me must want to make the changes. It's not my doing. It's their *own*." I did not want to get lost again in the frustration of perspective. "What's your name?"

"Shawn."

I nodded and quietly admitted, "Today is my birthday, Shawn."

He smiled in the darkness, seen easily enough in the moonlight. "Is it?"

I nodded again.

"What do you intend on doing?"

"The same thing I do every day," I told him. It was just another day.

"Were you crying because it's your birthday?" he asked. "Strange reason to be crying, one would think."

"No." I laughed a little, humorlessly. "Bad dreams."

"Do you have bad dreams often?"

"Yes." I shook my head a bit. "Don't you ever wish the world were a better place? That the people in our past hadn't messed it up so badly and left us all here to either pick up the pieces or do nothing more than kick those pieces around in the dirt?"

His brow furrowed. "Is that what you dream about?"

"No," I said, "but in a roundabout way, I suppose that was what tonight's dream was about." Part of it, at least.

He smiled a little. "I wish that every day."

"Perhaps one day I'll wake up and take in a breath of relief that those bad things are gone." I sighed. "That *bad* is nothing more than a distant memory, haunting me in my sleep."

"I never took you for a dreamer," he said. "Not from the things I've heard about you."

"Everyone has dreams," I told him with a quiet laugh.

"That's not what I meant."

I knew it hadn't been.

He'd misunderstood me.

"Then the simple answer is that I allowed myself to be changed." I forced a tight smile onto my face. "I spent far too much of my life telling myself there was no good at all left in our world. I can see little bits of it now, tiny little slivers of hope."

"And yet you're not happy."

"I don't want to see *slivers*." My voice was so . . . *desperate*. "I fear the things I want are unattainable."

He grinned, but it was not taunting, only amused. "You want to see people dancing in the streets?"

"I want people to be *safe*," I said. "Safe and happy enough that, yes, they could dance in the streets if they wished to do so. Safe and *free*. Free to live their lives as they see fit, without worry of being punished for making the right decisions for themselves." I stopped short when I realized that was basically what my mother had said in her letter to me.

Quietly, Shawn said, "People have that here."

"Here isn't good enough," I told him. "What about everyone else? What about those innocent people in Bethel and the rest of the world who are living their lives subjected to tyranny and oppression? For no reason apart from that *no one* will *stand up*. What about *everyone else*?"

The door to my living quarters swung open, crashing into the wall.

Jastin was staring at Shawn, who quickly said, "It's just me, Jas."

I could almost see the relief pass over Shawn's face when Jastin removed his hand from the hilt of a knife on his arm. It wasn't necessarily the sort of relief one would expect.

"My god, you scared me to death," Jastin said as he picked me up from the ground.

"I'm fine." I forced out a chuckle. "I just needed some air."

"You know we've all got her back," Shawn told him.

"It's not good enough," Jastin said. "How easily could you have been someone else?"

"I'd be dead if I were any closer to her." Shawn chuckled then pointed up at the wall where nearly ten Reapers stood with arrows notched in bows, all of them aimed directly at him. Then he pointed up on top of the House where there were nearly ten more Reapers doing the exact same thing.

"Why in the *world* would you risk talking to me right now?" I demanded. "My god, it's dark out. They wouldn't know who you were!"

"You were crying," Shawn answered nonchalantly.

"I do that quite a lot," I told him. "It's nothing to risk losing your life over. Believe me."

"Well, I'm going back to my post." Shawn said it almost as if I hadn't spoken then looked at Jastin. "I'll see you in a little over a week."

Quickly, I asked, "What's going on in a little over a week?"

"Well, we're getting married for one thing," Jastin replied.

"That clearly wasn't what he was talking about," I stated.

"My god, she's a handful, isn't she?" Shawn asked.

Jastin said, "Sometimes."

But I said, "It was nice to meet you, Shawn."

It was clearly a dismissal, which he must've realized because he actually walked away as he said he would.

"A little over a week?" I asked Jastin expectantly once Shawn was a suitable enough distance away.

He grinned. "I'll tell you that if you tell me why you've suddenly put so much trust in Stelin."

I frowned as I thought about it.

Jastin would be angry, I was sure, but . . .

"Deal." I nodded. "On the condition you don't do anything, or *say* anything to *anyone*, regardless of how angry you get over it. And you have to go first."

Very warily, he said, "Deal." Then he sighed and seemed to brace himself for something. "Your brother has insisted he get me drunk the night before."

"*What*?" I demanded.

He shrugged. "He insisted. I was thinking Abby could stay with you that night and—"

"I am *not* happy," I told him.

"I've never been allowed to drink." He almost seemed embarrassed. "Neither has your brother. So . . . kind of just thought it would be a good idea to try it once."

Interesting.

"And you believe the night before our wedding would be the perfect time to try it?" I was attempting very hard to work out the thought process behind this. It made absolutely no sense to me whatsoever. "That's preposterous. You do realize that, don't you?"

He nodded and the expression on his face seemed quite guilty.

"My god," I said in frustration. "I've seen drunken people, at that stupid party in New Bethel my brother made me go to. All men want to do is grab women when they drink. So . . . how do I know you're not going to get drunk and go off touching random women?"

"Are you *serious*?" Jastin laughed. "We're not going out into the city, Aster. It would be too dangerous. We're not that stupid."

I said, "I'm not so sure I agree with that particular statement."

He pursed his lips and said nothing.

"I'm warning you right now that if you show up still drunk, or if you're too hungover to properly appreciate the day . . . I shall never forgive you for it. And I *will* talk to people beforehand, and if I find out there were *any* women with you . . . I simply won't marry you at all."

His mouth dropped open.

"Don't look at me that way," I warned him. "How would you like it if Abby and I went off and got drunk and you had to worry about what I was doing and whether or not I would even show up there, either due to drunkenness or being killed over my own stupidity? Let *alone* the fact that you're willingly not going to be with me that night." I shook my head. "I am not happy with you at all right now."

He sighed loudly. "What about Stelin?"

I stared into his eyes and said, "He elbowed me in the stomach on purpose that day."

I watched Jastin's eyes widen and his nostrils flare. "*Please* tell me how that equates to trust. *Please.*" His jaw clenched.

"Because he saved my life," I answered evenly. "How easy would it have been for his father to have gotten his hands on me when I'd been pregnant with a child from his spy? You should thank him for it. I already have."

"I think you're wrong about him."

"I think I'm not." I grinned. "I suppose we shall see who's right."

He shook his head—not in response to anything—and sighed again. "Do you want to try to get some more sleep?"

"No," I told him firmly with that same grin. "I'm quite angry with you right now. I'd like to go train. I have a great many things to do today."

"You might be angry with me," Jastin said slowly, "but I know you're aware you should've told me what you just did when you first found out about it. And once you're done being angry with me, you're going to realize you just did the *exact* same thing to me that you were disappointed in me for doing to you a few days ago."

"You're saying you're disappointed in me?" A horrible feeling attempted to slip through my anger. It was not entirely successful.

"Is that what I said?"

I held my nose in the air as I stepped past him to head back into my living quarters so I could prepare myself for training.

At my back, he said, "This behavior isn't my favorite thing."

I stopped to tell him, "I can assure you that the *behavior* would be more to your liking than me letting loose of all I'm stopping myself from saying to you right now. I suppose you don't have to thank me. But for your information, it's not the *exact same thing*. What occurred with me is only your business if I make it so. Your situation *was* my business. I do hope that clarification offers you some clarity and allows you to get this sorted inside your head. You don't need to take out the guilt of your bad decisions on me. *I'm* not the one making them. But I suppose if that's what makes you feel better, that's what makes you feel better."

"Are you done?"

"Unless you stop me again."

Chapter Forty-Two

Between Siblings

’D ALREADY BEEN INSIDE my training area for *quite* some time before Stelin arrived. Once he stepped over to me, I whispered, "I need you to do me a favor."

"What's that?"

"My brother somehow seems to think getting Jastin drunk the night before our wedding is a *spectacular* plan." I attempted to rein in my frustration. I'd been attempting that since it had first appeared and had thus far been unsuccessful. "I want you to go that night and ensure no females are there. And if they are, I want you to give me your word that you'll tell me before I marry him."

He stopped moving, looked at my face, and laughed. "Are you serious?"

I blinked hard at him and very firmly said, "Quite. Can I trust you to do that?"

He shook his head and laughed a bit more, though I didn't know what was so funny about it. "Yeah." He nodded. "You can trust me with that, as long as they'll let me go."

"Oh, they'll *let* you go," I said assuredly.

"How do you know that?"

"Because I say so." I shrugged. "You can be my little Reaper spy. Just for the night, of course."

Stelin laughed, louder than what he'd previously done. "My *god*, that sounded dirty."

"Did it?" I asked curiously.

He nearly fell over as the realization dawned on my face. It took a moment.

"I suppose it sort of did in a way. Possibly if you have an overactive imagination." That would surely be the only way.

His laughter eventually died down, but it took a while. When it did, a frown began appearing on his face and he became visibly uncomfortable. "After you left the orphanage yesterday . . ." he began slowly. "When I was walking her home, Kay asked me if I was in love with you."

"All the *stars*!" I exclaimed. "Why in the *world* would she ask you that?"

"That's what I asked her," he said. "Not with your little star thing of course, but . . ." He paused to shake his head. "She told me it would be understandable if I were, that you were . . . *extraordinary*."

"Well, that was a very kind thing for her to say," I said distractedly. Then I got myself back on the proper thought path. "I hope you told her the truth."

"I contemplated telling her I was." His laugh was uncomfortable then. "But then I thought about all the things you said, and . . . I told her the truth."

"Well." I took a breath and patted him on the arm. "I'm very proud of you. Now, I must be going. I have things to do."

"I just got here." I thought he almost sounded sad. "Surely he did as well." He gestured to Chandler across the room.

"Yes, but I've been here for hours already," I informed him. "I have something I want to do, and I'm waiting to see my brother."

"Can I go with you?" Stelin asked. "I'm pretty sure I'd enjoy bearing witness to that particular conversation. I'll catch up on the training later for that."

I shrugged, which I could tell he'd not truly been expecting. "I don't care. I'm quite sure you'd enjoy it as well, though I doubt you'll enjoy the rest of what I'll be doing while I'm waiting."

Wariness creeping in was clear on his face. "What is it?"

All I did was smile in response.

THAT WAS HOW STELIN ENDED UP nosing through a good number of the rooms in the House with me. I'd given my father instruction to send Patricia to me as soon as she arrived opposed to me being sent for, and though she did not feel right assisting us, she *did* assist once I explained myself to her. She did make quite a few remarks on all the things that needed done.

I told her, "There are always things that need doing. One must prioritize. Jastin's not here for those other things. You're more than welcome to find him, but I'll be doing what I am today."

After, I tuned out anything else she said on the matter. I'd given her a reasonable alternative option.

I'd also given my father instruction to send Ahren to me as soon as he was awake and moving around. My brother enjoyed being up most the night and sleeping away a good portion of the day, the moron. So it was nearly midday by the time he found me.

"What in the world are the three of you doing?" Ahren asked when he stepped into the room.

"Oh, there you are," I said, relieved. *Finally.*

"Father said you were quite adamant about seeing me." Ahren glanced around the room. "But . . . I just so happened to run into Jastin on the way."

"Meaning he sought you out to warn you," I stated.

He narrowed his eyes at me but did not confirm or deny as much. I didn't need him to.

"Well, come on properly inside and explain to me the reasoning behind your idea. Try as I might, I could not find one *bit* of logic in it."

Very slowly, Ahren closed the door and stepped over to me. "Just for a bit of fun."

"The night before our wedding." I nodded my head. Then I shook it and said, "No. Still not making any sense."

"Why are you looking at me that way?" Mostly he appeared bemused, but there was the slightest tinge of wariness in his voice. Not wary in the way Stelin had been before accompanying me. Stelin's had been much lighter a thing. Good senses.

"Because I'm contemplating whether or not . . . if I punched you in the face, it would be healed in a little over a week," I replied. "I'm not entirely certain it would." It would, if not for one, singular thing.

Ahren nodded his head slowly. "You want to punch me in the face for wanting to have fun with my best friend the night before he marries my sister and is gone to the world forever." He'd missed it.

"Unless you swear to me there will be no women there . . ." I nodded. "Yes."

And he grinned. "Maybe just a few of them."

He was such an asshole. An asshole and an idiot.

I feigned throwing a punch with my weaker arm, knowing he would grab hold of it on instinct. So I was almost smiling when I landed a punch on the left side of his face with my dominant one. But I was not smiling at all when I pushed him down. Not even close. I couldn't.

"It was a *joke*!" He shouted once his rear was done skidding across the floor.

I stomped over to him and said, "I remember that party you forced me to go to, Ahren. Don't you remember? Don't you remember that man touching me inappropriately and Chase breaking his wrist? I suppose you wouldn't remember the things I heard men saying that night because you were too busy watching me from a distance and ensuring I did as you'd instructed. So . . . please forgive me if I don't find men's drunkenness with women as *amusing* as you do."

"Shit." Ahren said that under his breath as he stood. "I'm sorry, Aster. There won't be any women there, I promise."

"Oh, I know there won't be," I told him assuredly.

His brow furrowed. "Then why did you hit me?"

"To make you understand," I said. "If there *are* any there, and believe you me, I *will* find out if there are . . ." I paused to laugh. "I did that to show you I can now. Every other time I've done it, you've allowed me to. If you break this promise to me, I'll do more than hit you."

"*Aster*!" Patricia exclaimed from relatively close by.

I smiled at Ahren and said, "Thank you for ruining my birthday, big brother."

"It's your—" He closed his eyes. "*That's* what . . . Sonofa*bitch*. Father's going to kill me."

"No, he won't." I shrugged. "So long as you don't break your promise to me, he'll never find out about this conversation. I'm sure you can come up with some sort of excuse for the bruise that will appear on your face. I would've hit you harder, but I didn't want to break anything. But I'm promising you," I went on slowly so he would comprehend, "if *anything* happens to Jastin because of your ridiculous idea . . . I'm holding you personally responsible. I'm sure you're smart enough to know what I mean when I say that to you."

He gaped. "Are you threatening to *kill* me?"

"Promising," I said evenly. "If he gets killed because of you . . . that's *exactly* what I would do. Just because you're the big *high prince* of the city doesn't give you the right to put other people's lives at risk for your own amusement. You know he has a target on his back, just like you and me and absolutely *everyone* else we care about. You should really take a moment to think very hard on that, big brother."

"Are we going there?" Both his eyebrows rose. "Are we going to pull out the *prince* and *princess* cards? Believe me, Aster, you and I have enough issues as it is without dragging that into the mix."

"You know . . . I've been trying to figure out why in the world you could *ever* have any issue with me." I chuckled. "Are you angry that I have a head, Ahren? Angry that I care? Angry that I've worked things out with our father? Is that what it is?"

"I'm not angry with you for anything," he said firmly. "I'm frustrated because I can't figure out why you care about these people. They're nothing to you. And my god, where have you been all your life to have some sort of feeling for them?" He closed his eyes and put his hand over his face the instant the words had left his mouth.

"Where was I while you were here in your city?" I could not force a smile onto my face no matter how badly I wanted to when I very slowly said, "I was locked away inside a House and beaten for ten years for looking at books in a library. That's where I was, big brother. That's where I was while you were in our city. Didn't you know?" I shook my head. "If you're jealous of me for that . . . you are the biggest imbecile I've ever seen in all my life."

"Of course I'm not jealous about that!" he shouted. "Not any more than you could be jealous of the fact that I spent the majority of my life without our father, stuck in that Reaper school and then having to murder innocent people. But my god, don't you see the way they look at you here? They look at you like you're some sort of *god* that fell out of the sky to help them!"

"And they look at *you* like you're someone who would be capable of protecting them!" I shouted back. "They may look at me how you say, but they don't even think I'm capable enough of not falling off a damned roof! Please tell me which of us has the right to be jealous of the other, Ahren. *Please.*"

I blinked tears out of my eyes when he said nothing in response, thinking hard—with what information I had on the word—about him believing they looked at me that way. And yet it in a sense was only as relevant as it was.

"If I were a man, you would likely have proper cause to be jealous of me," I told him. Then I shook my head and looked around the room in confusion.

"They left." His voice had turned blank.

I laughed a little under my breath at the floor. "And this is the part where it's pointed out that you *would* be much better equipped to keep them all safe," I said quietly. "I can't even notice when two people leave the room."

"I wasn't going to say that."

"You don't have to." I began walking to the door.

He followed me.

"Please just leave me alone."

"Aster." He tugged on my arm.

I jerked it away from him and rounded on him. "I have to go speak to our father."

"What about?"

"All the stars," I said through my teeth in frustration. "I've already told you I wasn't going to say anything to him about our conversation. I need to speak with him about what I've been doing all morning."

"I figured you'd changed your mind," he barely said.

"What's an argument between siblings?" I asked with a tight shrug. "I don't go back on my word. Not unless I must. You should've realized that about me by now. Perhaps one day you'll see me clearly, big brother. I only hope I'm alive long enough to see it happen."

CHAPTER FORTY-THREE

SAYING A WORD

AHREN FOLLOWED ME to our father's office. I assumed he did it because he wanted to ensure I didn't mention our altercation the instant his back had turned despite saying multiple instances that I wouldn't. My father didn't say a word about my birthday upon our arrival, nor did he behave differently toward me at all. I'd not expected him to, as he hadn't when I'd seen him earlier either. It had been such a long time since he'd been required to remember it, and it was all right.

"My *god* what happened to your face?" he asked Ahren once we were inside the room with the door closed behind us.

"Aster punched me," he said, which made my eyes go wide.

My father's attention fell on me. "Why would you do that?"

Technically I could not say anything because I'd given Ahren my word, so I stood there in silence for a moment, staring at my father until Ahren spoke.

"She was angry with me, for good reason."

"And what reason was that?" my father asked him.

My mouth dropped open when he said, "Because I wanted to get Jastin drunk the night before their wedding. She believed I was being insensitive to her and certain experiences she's been subjected to, which I can see now that I was. And she believed I was being irresponsible and playing with his life, which . . . I can also see now that I was."

"Ahren." Though my father's face was nearly blank, apart from a slight pursing of his lips, his unhappiness had been apparent in what little he'd said.

I almost wanted to smack myself in the face when I blurted out, "I threatened to kill him." But . . .

"*Aster!*" my father exclaimed.

And for just an instant while he was looking at me in the way that he was, I felt like a child again.

A child who'd done something wrong that they should've known better than to have done.

Then the moment was over and I found myself happy it was. I'd done some thinking . . .

My father sighed and closed his eyes. "Anders decided to get me drunk one night after your mother and I told him she was pregnant with you." His face scrunched a little at Ahren, not in amusement but something that appeared similar to pity. "Be very glad in this instance that you're dealing with your sister and not your mother."

Curious, I asked, "What did she do?"

"Came in while we were drunk and beat the daylight out of us both," my father said with a quiet chuckle. "She had the most satisfied look on her face the next day when she asked . . . *'Do you see how easily you could've been killed?'*" He cleared his throat. "It's natural to want to do things you've never done before, but it's also natural to deal with the wrath of a woman when a woman believes those things are ignorant and irresponsible despite other people doing them." He laughed a little. "Anders' nose never quite healed properly."

So *that* was why his nose was slightly crooked. . . .

"What's the moral of this story?" Ahren asked.

"That both of you are right in your own ways." My father shrugged. "Everyone is entitled to make their own decisions, but they also have to deal with what follows, whether good, or bad. Now," he turned to me, "what did you need to speak with me about?"

"Clothes," I replied, which made both of their faces scrunch up in confusion at me.

"*Clothes?*" My father asked it like he was attempting to ensure he'd heard me properly.

I nodded.

386

"What about them?"

"Well, there are so many nice sets of clothing hanging in wardrobes and stuffed into drawers here," I said slowly. "I was thinking you could give them away."

"For your wedding?" my father asked.

"Why *is it* that *any time* I talk about nice things for people, everyone always assumes it has something to do with my wedding?" I asked the question mostly to myself.

Ahren asked, "What use would they be otherwise?"

"What use are they at all being stuffed in places and never worn or looked at?" I asked. "Perhaps a woman would like to dress up nicely for her husband one day. Apparently that's something women want—to look beautiful for men." I shrugged then went on. "Or perhaps a couple would want to have a nice dinner together on some occasions. Anniversaries maybe? Or perhaps a man would want to impress a lady? Or perhaps a little girl would want to play dress-up. I saw a leader's daughter do so once. Regardless, there's a great deal of children's clothing here." I shrugged again. "Take your pick."

Ahren then asked, "And if they wanted to wear them to your wedding?"

"Then they're more than welcome to." I threw up a hand. "I don't care how people dress, I can assure you. I'm assuming some people do because one of the first things Abby ever said to me was that my clothes didn't match themselves." I still didn't understand how they couldn't *or* how clothes matching themselves *apparently* altered the way one looked.

"Then why?" he pressed.

"Because shouldn't everyone be able to have nice things?" I asked evenly. "And as I said, they're not doing any good here. I'm sure it would make *someone* happy."

"Out of all the things in the world you could concern yourself with . . ." my brother said deliberately, "and you choose *clothing*?"

"Granted it's not anywhere near as important as keeping us safe, but given I don't have a clue in the world how to do that . . ." Little more than that, but . . . I took a deep breath. "It was an errant thought that took hold in my head. At least I'm concerning myself with other people and not my own amusement."

Ahren threw up a hand, much differently and higher than I had. "Can we not get past the arguing today, Aster?"

"You insulted me by belittling my ideas," I told him. "Don't expect me not to retaliate when you make a personal attack on me."

"Well, how about this one?" Ahren asked. "How about you tell both of us why you suddenly trust Stelin."

My father looked to me. "*Do* you?"

"I *do*." My voice was firm. "And my reasons for as much are personal between he and myself. I'll not tell them to either of you. Not even privately." Ensuring my father knew to not press it later.

"You realize you allowed him to witness a personal argument between us, don't you?" Ahren asked. "That would be perfect for him to tell his father—the things we were arguing about. Don't you think? And you willingly brought him with you, knowing it would happen."

I raised an eyebrow. "Which of the two ushered the other from the room in the middle of it?"

Ahren blinked at me.

"Did Patricia pull Stelin toward the door, or was it the other way around?" I pressed. "I know you saw it because they were both at my back."

Ahren said nothing, so I knew what the answer was. I hadn't needed to see this particular scenario to know how it had played out.

"Don't you believe that, if he were working for or with his father, he would've stayed inside the room?" I asked. "Or that he would've been *somewhere* in the hallway when we left? Eavesdropping? He wasn't, was he? He was long gone. Was he not?"

"Yes, and he could've done all he did simply because he knew you'd come to that point," Ahren stated.

"Oh, I'm well aware." I nodded. "But you see . . . he's already done enough to prove himself to me, which he knows. He doesn't need to do anything more than he already has." Not for me.

"But you *do* realize he could be working for his father?" Ahren asked. "Don't you?"

"I won't deny it could be a possibility," I answered impassively. "But you could say . . . You could say I have faith in him as a person, more than I trust him. I can see a desire to do good in him. I'm quite certain I have a proper feel for him as a person."

Ahren grinned. "Do you?"

"More than I do you, big brother," I told him.

He recoiled as though I'd slapped him, which had not been my intention. I'd only been telling him the truth. I thought it necessary to explain.

"He's more consistent than you are. And . . ." I paused. "If he wanted me to believe he was solely good, he would not show me the bad side of himself willingly, which he does. It's a struggle for him, and it's understandable. But you can see the confusion when a person shows you good and tells you they love you and then always seems to act in the exact opposite way."

Ahren gaped. "Aster, do you realize what you do to *me*?"

"You tell me when I've ever hit you or said hurtful things to you at *any* time when it has not been in direct retaliation to something you've done or said to me," I urged. "Please."

Our father hadn't even pretended to not be listening to every word of our conversation. I watched Ahren's gaze shoot to him and then back to me. And I could clearly see now that he blamed our current conversation on me.

I shrugged. "I wouldn't have said a word."

"But you did."

"Only because *you* did, Ahren," I told him firmly. I could've said a great deal more, but I did not.

He shook his head at me and left the room. My father and I both watched him go.

I wondered if *normal* parents would attempt to force their children into working out their issues with one another. I wondered if a normal parent would've called after my brother and urged him to come back and resolve issues. Attempt to. But my father was a Reaper, in a sense, and Reapers understood that only the strong survived. He was who he was, and he understood. This.

I would not let anyone weaken me, least of all my own brother. He'd been trying very hard to do just that in several different ways.

"What do you think of my idea?" I asked my father once I'd gotten my mind back on the proper path.

"I think it's a wonderful idea." An almost sad smile appeared on his face. "I heard all about your evening at the orphanage. The positive before the negative that we dealt with after."

I didn't want to speak about the negative that had occurred after. "Did Anders tell you?"

"Well, yes," he said with a quiet laugh. "But we've had a great deal of people wondering if they could learn how to dance. Patricia had already told me what you said before, about how we should make the knowledge of it readily available. It's sort of amazing." He shook his head. "They want to do any and everything you do."

"That's quite silly," I said. "Why can't people want to do things simply because they want to do them?"

"Oh, Aster." My father pulled me into a hug. "If more people were like you . . . the world would be such a brighter place."

I did not smile about his statement or the kiss that he placed on top of my head. I believed that if more people were like me, they would never, ever be happy. I'd learned that parents had the tendency to be biased where their children were concerned.

"Now, you go on and be organizing that clothing in the way you want it done," he said when he released me.

"Would you like to do it with me?" I tried to hide the hopefulness in my voice, but this would be the eleventh birthday I'd spent without him if he did not.

"I have other things to do today." But he smiled to add, "I know you're capable of getting it done."

I nodded and forced a smile at him before leaving the room. At least I got to see him on this one. At least I knew he was still alive. At least I knew so much more than what I had before. That was something. I supposed it was good enough.

Why didn't it feel that way?

CHAPTER
FORTY-FOUR

STOP

I SPENT NEARLY THE ENTIRE DAY removing clothes from their respective places and organizing it all into stacks by general sizes, types, so on. *Types* was sort of an issue for me, and it required questioning. There was an absolutely ludicrous amount of clothing hidden away, easily enough to give an outfit to every person in the city. It was absurd to me—having something useful simply lying around, never being touched. Just because I thought it was quite useless in the way other people seemed to think of it, that didn't mean everyone else would agree. It could still serve a purpose no matter my opinion. At the very least, it was something to put over yourself, and that was good.

I'd asked several Reapers following me around for their assistance, direct opposed to typical, more than clarification on types. Some of them asked me what I was doing and why I was doing it. Some of them simply did what I asked them to without any question or word at all. They might've thought it was silly of me, whether before any response or after, but none of them said or acted as though they did.

It embarrassed me, in a sense, but it also made me quite happy.

Quite a lot of them would not assist me. They said they could not do their jobs properly if preoccupied with something else. They changed out periodically—the ones who'd been watching to helping and the ones who'd been helping to watching. Even if they *did* think it was ridiculous, they still seemed to want to be part of it. It made me feel a bit better about the way my time was being spent. Perhaps they understood. Perhaps they didn't care either way. The thought that they might understand well enough nearly sent me to tears. Nearly. Just the partial relief.

I spoke with a few of them, simply trying to get to know them a little better as people. I knew it was selfish, but I partially did it because I wanted company on my birthday despite reminding myself however many times that it was just a day. I'd been reminding myself of that for years, but it always felt wrong. Them speaking to me did not mean they cared, or would.

Amber and Agatha both helped me for a short while, but not even an hour passed before they'd gone. I tried not to be sad about it.

My brother was brought up on a few occasions by a couple different Reapers. I supposed me initiating speaking would make some of them do the same. One of them asked if I seemed so down because of the arguments I'd gotten into with him. It appeared I was followed more closely than I ever really paid attention to. Or perhaps I was simply getting accustomed to it. Complacent.

"I wish we could just get along," I told that one of Ahren and me.

"You should see me with my own brother." He'd laughed, but I did not think it was funny. And if things were worse between them, I had no idea how he could think it was either.

Shawn had come up to me sometime in the early evening to say, "I happened to overhear Jas and your brother speaking on my way here."

"Oh?" I asked.

It was easier to see how Shawn carried himself in the light. He had an interesting way about him, though I couldn't quite place why.

"Yes, Ahren was quite put out Jas hadn't informed him of how much better you'd gotten at your combatives." Shawn laughed. "He said he should've been informed, considering how often you seem to hit him." He smiled. "I saw that nasty bruise starting on his face. I'm assuming you did it?"

I pursed my lips to stop myself from grinning because I should not have been pleased with myself. But I'd hit a Reaper in the face. I couldn't not be pleased—that I'd accomplished it, if not on whom I had managed and it having to be done at all.

"And I'm assuming you did it because of his idea?"

"Stupid idea," I grumbled under my breath. I didn't have to attempt to stop smiling then; it happened naturally.

Shawn laughed again. "Don't be surprised if your brother is walking a bit funny the next time you see him."

"Why is that?" I asked, puzzled.

"Because I also happened to overhear what it was, *precisely*, your brother said in order for you to have hit him." He was trying not to grin. "Jas got a good hit in there, too. I suspect your brother will be pissing blood for a while."

I blinked at him until he clarified.

"Right in the kidney."

I still did not know what a kidney was, only that Jastin nearly had his own cut while we'd been traveling. I supposed I also knew now that, if you got hit there, it made you piss blood. It did not seem like a very pleasant part of the body.

I pursed my lips again for a moment. "He hit him over that?" I didn't want to have asked that, but I couldn't stop myself.

"Yeah, told him to stop being—" Shawn cut himself off and stared off for a few seconds. "Told him to stop being stupid."

I chuckled. "Not in those words."

He shook his head in response.

I took a deep breath before asking, "Why did you tell me that?"

"Figured you'd like to know." He shrugged. "Make your day a little brighter, especially considering what it is."

I looked away and proceeded about my business, but it wasn't long before he spoke again.

"Why are you doing this, anyway?"

"To hopefully make other people's days a little brighter," I replied.

"My god, you're something else."

I stopped and looked at him again. "I don't know what you mean."

"I mean Jas is very lucky." He shook his head. "I can see now how you managed to do what you did to him." He narrowed his eyes and asked, "How old did you turn today?"

"Nineteen."

"Still a little baby." He grinned. "So much space left in your head for knowledge you don't have yet. I suspect the two of you will have a great deal of fun taking up that space."

It didn't take as long as it normally did for me to catch onto what he was saying. My mouth had dropped open, I knew. It took me a moment, but I cleared my throat and said my standard response for the subject. "I'm very uncomfortable."

Shawn was fiddling around with some of the clothing, but I didn't miss the smile on his face when he said, "I'm sure he'll enjoy breaking you of that." Then he seemed to realize what he'd said, and he looked over at me with wide eyes. "Don't tell him I said that. Or your father. *Especially* not your father. It just slipped out. It's easy to forget who you are when actually speaking. My god, I'm sorry."

I didn't tell him that I would not so, for nearly an hour, he stole nervous glances at me as I proceeded about my business. He didn't speak to me again. But when Jastin came in, Shawn stood against one of the walls, rigid as a board as he attempted to pretend that he was not intending to eavesdrop on our conversation. I didn't mind if he did, as I knew he was doing as much. Knowing things made all sorts of differences, or could.

Jastin said, "I've been looking for you."

"Are you still *disappointed in me*?" I asked as I kept doing what I'd been doing for nearly the entire day.

He grabbed hold of my hand to get my attention. His face was slightly scrunched when he stated, "I never said I was disappointed in you."

"Basically," I informed him.

He shook his head.

"Well then you said what you did in the hopes I would be disappointed in myself."

"Well, if you're done feeling that way, come with me."

"And if I'm not?" I asked. I hadn't been.

"Come with me anyway." He smiled and wiggled my hand a little.

I turned back to the clothing. "I'm busy."

"Star," he said firmly.

I frowned at him.

"For just a little while . . . stop being so busy." He smiled sweetly and repeated himself. "Come with me."

I pursed my lips and allowed him to lead me from the room,

leaving in the middle of what I'd been doing. I didn't like doing that. It happened sometimes now, but I *really* disliked it.

I expected him to take me back to my living quarters, but he stopped outside a door I'd never been through in the House. His smile was almost wary before he opened it.

Wariness, it seemed, was the mood of the day.

I had an extended moment of confusion as I looked at the rather large crowd of people inside, but then none of it really seemed to matter because Aston came running over to us.

"*Happy birthday!*" he exclaimed as I knelt down to hug him.

"How did you know it was my birthday?" I asked him in disbelief.

"Your father came to see me a week ago to tell me." He was almost wiggling in his excitement. "We made something for you."

"Did you really?" I asked, baffled.

He held out a hand that he'd had concealed behind his back, and inside it rested a twisted piece of metal.

"What is it?"

"A bracelet," he said excitedly. "Garin helped me cut it off the fence near our school."

"Did he really?" I asked with an uncharacteristically loud laugh.

"*Yes!*" Aston exclaimed. "He said *never touch this fence again*. Do you like it?"

"I *love* it." I took it from him and slid it over my left hand. It was a *bit* large, but I didn't care in the slightest. "I shall wear it always and you'll know that I'm thinking of you." Then I picked him up and propped him against one of my hips. "But never touch that fence again."

He'd not ever allowed either of us carry him, but he didn't protest against it. He just nodded in response to what I'd said. I grabbed Jastin's hand with the one that was not holding onto his son.

"What is all this?" I asked as we walked over to everyone else.

"You didn't think I'd forgotten your birthday, had you?" my father asked as he pulled me into a hug. I did not miss one of Aston's little arms wrapping around him too.

Quietly, I said, "I did, actually."

"Of course I hadn't." He laughed. "Why do you think I didn't help you today when you asked me to? Patricia, Jastin, and I were getting this whole thing properly organized."

I looked around the room—it must've been some sort of banquet hall—and took in everyone's smiling faces. Patricia, Anders, Agatha, Chandler sitting next to Abby who was holding onto James, Amber, Stanley and Stewart, Stelin sitting close to Kay, and my brother sitting with Arlene on his lap. His smile was apologetic rather than happy like everyone else's.

I was overwhelmed with so many feelings that it brought tears to my eyes when I whispered, "Thank you."

I ensured I walked behind my brother as I made my way to my own seat. I mussed up his hair as I went, the way he did mine sometimes when he was happy with me. Or the way he'd done before things had changed, when we'd been some sort of friends rather than siblings. I did not do it because I was no longer angry with him, only because I did not *want* to be angry with him.

I did not want things to be the way they were with him, but . . .

I sat down when I reached my seat.

CHAPTER FORTY-FIVE

EVERY DAY

"YOU'RE GOING TO SPOIL HIM, letting him hang on you that way rather than having him sit in his own chair." Anders gestured to Aston, who was still latched onto me. He did not give the same message to my brother, still sitting with Arlene in his lap.

I supposed it was acceptable to spoil girls and not boys. I did not believe that was right. Perhaps it had something to do with age, but I didn't believe that was right either. My father had let me sit on his lap as a child, so I supposed that was a normal thing. I saw nothing wrong with it.

"You deserve a bit of spoiling, don't you?" I asked Aston. I honestly didn't see how this had anything at all to do with spoiling, though.

He smiled bashfully at me, but I didn't believe he understood what the word actually meant.

Anders chuckled. "Are you going to let him eat off your plate as well?"

"No," I said haughtily. That wouldn't have been even slightly all right. "Whenever he feels like eating, he can get down and sit in his own chair. It's his decision whether or not he wants his food to be cold."

If he wanted cold food, he could have cold food. If he would rather be on my lap than have warm food, it was what he would rather. I was just glad he could make the choice. I would've eaten every meal freezing cold to have had my father all the years I didn't. Gladly.

To have ever been near to my mother.

"He's going to be a handful, that one," Anders said with a grin.

"Oh, that's ridiculous." I looked at Aston to ask, "You're not going to be any trouble at all, are you?"

He shook his head and climbed down to get in his own chair on the other side of Jastin to eat.

I brought my gaze to Anders. "You see?"

My father laughed. "Francis told me he's already asked two different little girls to marry him."

I glanced a little way down the table to look at Aston, who was now grinning over his plate of food. I took that as confirmation.

What I said was, "He's only five." But in my head, I was thinking . . . *Perhaps he may be some trouble*. I would've thought he'd done it simply because his father and I were getting married, but that *grin* . . .

Jastin seemed to think it was funny. I almost thought he wanted to clap his son on the back and tell him he was a good boy. He did not do that, so I said nothing about his amusement on the matter. I did not think it was even *slightly* amusing.

"Five or not." My father shook his head. "If that's a preview of things to come . . . you're in for a world of sleepless nights. And who do you imagine those particular little girls are going to come to with their broken hearts?"

Me. I'd already had more than one little girl crying to me over that sort of thing. I'd been horrified, but my father had told me I handled it quite well, in his opinion. He did suggest a few adjustments for the next time, which had already occurred. Several more after.

I felt as though I were endlessly being taunted at the table, but I'd exhausted myself today with all the arguing and upset, so I managed to keep my mouth shut. I would worry about that sort of thing with Aston when it became a more pressing issue. There was a *very* long time to go before we reached the point of *potentially sleepless nights*. There was no point thinking about it now.

No point.

I remained quiet for most of the time while we were eating, and I listened to everyone else as they discussed things.

Mine and Jastin's wedding was talked about, as was the dancing at the orphanage and the clothing I'd been sorting throughout the day.

It was after we were done eating that my father stepped away and returned with a glass in his hands. He set it down on the table in front of Jastin.

"What is that?" I gestured to the clear liquid. "Why would you bring him water when he already has some?"

Jastin's nose scrunched up when he sniffed the air near it. "That's not water."

"I simply figured it would be best to see now whether you had a taste for it or not." My father shrugged as he walked away and replaced himself in his own seat.

Aston had since finished eating and was again latched onto me. He was facing his father in my lap.

"What is that?" Aston whispered in my ear.

Jastin blinked at me, then at his son. He pushed the glass away from himself and leaned back in his chair.

"Go on," I urged.

Jastin shook his head. "I'm all right."

I nodded my head toward the glass and more firmly repeated, "Go on." If he wanted to do this, then he could at least do it in front of me and his son.

He reached for the glass and held it near his mouth. His nose scrunched again.

I watched him take in a mouthful of it and I was expecting to want to punch him in the face.

I was not expecting to want to laugh.

He spit it back into the glass and sat there with his tongue hanging out of his mouth. "Sonofa*bitch* that's *disgusting!*" He almost shouted. "My *god.*" He made several disgusted noises, and I was almost entirely certain one of them was nearly a gag. "Why would *anyone* like drinking that shit?"

I'd thrown both my hands over Aston's ears at the start of it. "*Language.*" We'd *talked* about that.

"I'm sorry," he said as he shook his head. "But my *god.*"

There were several snorts around the table as people tried very hard not to laugh at him. Or perhaps they were laughing at me for covering a Reaper's ears due to language, child or not. I uncovered them.

Abby didn't attempt to hide her snorting like most everyone else did.

"You have a go at it!" Jastin shouted at her. "I promise you'll do the exact same thing."

She laughed. "I'm not drinking your spit."

He was still making a noise that sounded very much like some extended form of *ugh*. "I'm sure it destroyed any of my spit left in that glass," he said. "Ahren, you can do what you want, but I'm good. My *god*, I think it's eating away at my tongue."

"It's still there." I laughed as I was speaking.

"That's good," he said in what was clearly relief. "I need that."

"What for?" Aston asked curiously.

There were several laughs disguised as coughs from around the table. Given Jastin had explained a great deal of . . . *things* to me, I simply turned my face toward the wall and closed my eyes tightly.

"To . . . *speak*," Jastin told him. It had sounded more like a question than a statement when leaving his mouth.

Aston looked to me. "Why is that funny?"

I couldn't answer him. I simply could not do it.

Ahren laughed. "You'll find out all about speaking when you're older, Nephew."

"I don't understand," Aston said quietly.

Clearly uncomfortable, Jastin said, "Probably best to just . . . put it out of your head for now."

It seemed the one time *I* was not extremely uncomfortable about something of that nature being discussed, someone else was. I looked over at my father, who had his fingers plugging his ears. His face was red, his jaw clenched, and he seemed quite on the verge of getting out of his chair to do some unknown thing I likely would not approve of.

I glanced around the room and took in everyone's smiling faces, apart from my father's face, which was not even *close* to smiling. Reapers with their children sitting with them around the table. This was the way things should've been—not just on special days but every day. Because every day was special.

Why couldn't anyone else see as much?

Why was everyone else so content with good enough?

Why?

When it was nothing more than what they accepted to get through the days . . .

Why?

JASTIN, AHREN, AND STELIN volunteered to return the two children to the Reaper school. Along with an escort, of course. Aston was asleep in Jastin's arms by the time that occurred. I took a mental painting of the image when Jastin reached the door and turned to smile at me, committing it to memory and vowing to never forget it or the way it made me feel.

"You knew he would hate it," I said to my father once everyone else had gone and it was just the two of us alone in the room. Standing to let most everyone think we were going our separate ways as they did. Stanley had made a gesture at us before leaving. I knew what it meant.

Privacy.

It meant he would ensure it.

"Oh yes," my father said. "I made sure to get the strongest I could find. If it had been any weaker, he very well may have enjoyed it. I'd say I properly put him off to it. That's one less thing for you to concern yourself over."

I nudged him with my arm. "Thank you. And . . ." I took a deep breath. "Thank you for this. And thank you for spending a bit of time with Aston. It means a lot to me."

He shook his head a little, and he was not smiling. "Every year on this day for the ten before now, I've gotten drunk out of my mind. I'm sure you can imagine the extent I was guarded during, that enough figured it out, and all the nonsense after." I'd never seen my father so visibly uncomfortable. He wouldn't even look at me. "I thought you were dead and . . . it was better for me than being miserable and thinking I'd never get to spend another day with you again. But here we are . . . making new memories together. I never thought it would happen."

"Sometimes I miss being a child," I admitted. "I miss not knowing about all the things in our world, where the only bad was contained in your stories. Everything was so simple then. You were there and you loved me and protected me. Nothing else mattered." I laughed humorlessly under my breath. "But you always knew about the bad, and you tried to protect me from it. It's not fair, is it? For you to have had that knowledge when I didn't? For you to have been sad the whole time I was happy?"

"Here's to the future," my father said with a sad smile. "And the hope that we can live out the rest of our days happy, despite that knowledge."

"And the hope that we can allow others the same," I added for him.

"My daughter," he said on a breath as he cupped my face in his hand. "You will do such good in this world. I only hope I'm here to see it happen."

I could see then, in that moment, why my brother was jealous of me. It truly was the way our father looked at me. But it did not mean that I didn't want for him to look at me that way. It did not mean that I didn't want one of the only people who seemed to have faith in me and my capabilities to stop having it. He was my father, and I felt I finally knew who he was. The *what* didn't matter past that. *What* was only ever words. *Who* was what mattered.

"You'll always be here, Father."

He shook his head slowly.

I nodded my own and quietly said, "Yes, you will."

I had not understood that as a child, but . . . I understood it now.

CHAPTER FORTY-SIX

HAPPY BIRTHDAY

"**A**RE YOU STILL ANGRY WITH ME?" Jastin asked when we were lying in bed together that night, before I'd have to roll over and give him my back. I liked as much time before that as possible.

"No," I replied. "I was angry about the situation and the thoughtless decisions, not at you. I wasn't happy about your attitude, but I understand and it wasn't as important. I didn't want to worry about you being killed. Now I don't need to worry about it."

"I'm still going to spend that night with him," he said. "Do the same thing we were intending to do, minus the alcohol."

"Which is?" What else had that ridiculous plan entailed?

"I don't know." He shrugged. "Reminisce about life, I suppose. Spend some time being glad those days are over and new days are coming."

"Ahren said he wanted to do that," I said quietly. "Something about spending time before his best friend married his sister and was gone to the rest of the world." Whatever that meant.

"Yes, I'm assuming he's sad about it in his way." He exhaled a rather loud breath. "But I'm so far from sad about it."

I smiled a little to myself and, after a brief pause, he went on.

"Stelin invited himself, said you'd insisted he go."

"I did," I admitted. "And he told you why?"

"Oh yes, he told us exactly why." Jastin chuckled. "Your brother said it wasn't necessary, given I wouldn't be drinking, but . . . he still insisted. He said he'd told you he would inform you whether or not any females were there and that you'd said nothing to him about your intentions for him changing if I didn't drink. He said he'd made a promise to you and didn't care whether either of us liked that or not."

Stelin and I were moving from deals to promises together. Interesting.

"So that's why he went with the two of you," I said in understanding. "I was wondering about that."

It hadn't made much sense for him to accompany them, as he seemed rather indifferent to them both. I did know that him seeming one way did not mean it was an accurate reflection of the insides and that his feelings leaned hard one way. He seemed rather indifferent toward nearly everyone, as that was simply how he was, but I *had* caught him laughing with Stewart twice. That wasn't difficult to manage, if Stewart wanted it to happen. He could speak civilly with Chandler. Apparently, he could speak—presumably civilly—about me with whoever was in the *group effort*, which I believed was in fact just Chandler, Stanley, and Stewart. That was it that I'd seen. Also, despite how well Stelin had done with the children at the orphanage, I hadn't thought he would put himself near another large grouping of them by choice.

I'd thought him accompanying them might've had something to do with what I'd asked of him, when going through possible options inside my head. Now I had that confirmed.

"Yes, I'm pretty sure he said it to further dissuade your brother from going against what you wanted," Jastin said. "He likely figured Ahren might try to have females there now, just to make you angry. It would be ignorant but not anything I'd put past him. We both know he can be petty sometimes."

He could indeed.

Jastin pursed his lips tightly for a moment and the amusement dropped away from his face. "Your brother said you have your hands in everyone's pockets. The two of them nearly got into a fight over it. Very well might have if they'd been alone. I suppose it's true that Stelin does feel some sort of positive attachment to you to damn near come to blows with your brother on your account. But I still hold on my opinion of him. I think he's an asshole. I don't want to get into another thing about the *definition of the word psychopath.*"

I knew he was, or *could be* the thing Jastin had decided to call him this time, and I knew that Jastin and essentially everyone else thought as much. I also knew they thought as much in a different way than I did. But I shook my head because . . . "I don't know what that means. The *hands in pockets* bit."

"Meaning you have too much of a say in what other people do," he explained, which was only as much of an explanation as it was. "I know your brother well enough to know he only said it because he's frustrated. He was heckled by quite a few people today for the arguments between the two of you, and then again after for the one I got into with him. People say things they shouldn't sometimes. I've never seen him treated that way. It's getting to him."

"Why shouldn't he say it if he believes it's true?" I asked curiously.

Plainly, Jastin said, "Because it's not true."

"It *is* true," I informed him.

He raised an eyebrow at me.

"I had a dozen or so Reapers sorting through clothing with me today."

Apparently he hadn't put that together.

"*Reapers* sorting through clothing," I reiterated. "Just because I asked them if they might want to. No other reason."

"They would've been watching you anyway." He shrugged. "Might as well be doing something with you. It's no different than your father asking them to patch up people's houses."

"It *is* different," I said assuredly. "It's different because I'm nothing to them. Why should they listen to me or do what I say? I'm not a Reaper. I'm not their leader. Contingency plan or not . . . I'm nothing to anyone outside my immediate vicinity. Or I shouldn't be, at least. My brother sees that."

Jastin narrowed his eyes. "What did he say to you?"

"Nothing." My voice was quiet.

"Aster," he said unhappily.

"It was *nothing.*" I took a deep breath and shook my head. "It's just so frustrating. I understand that my brother would be better equipped at keeping everyone safe. I really do understand that. I mean . . . I saw the way he took care of New Bethel in the short time he was there, but he's so damn inconsistent. And as I said to him earlier, he seems to be more concerned with his own amusement than other people's safety."

Jastin said nothing to that.

In a whisper I admitted, "I can't stand the way he looks at me sometimes. He was so much nicer to me in New Bethel. We got on so well while we were there together."

"You got along there because you weren't any sort of threat to him," Jastin said, blankness taking over. "That's the only way a Reaper can get along with anyone. Usually not even then."

"He feels I'm stealing everything from him, doesn't he?" I asked quietly. "Our father, our city, our people, our Reapers. . . . Why can't he be content to share and work together? I don't understand."

"Just give him some time. I think he'll get everything straightened out in his head eventually."

"Yes, either that or come to hate me enough that he—" I stopped speaking and shook my head.

"That he what?"

"I don't want to speak about it anymore right now."

"Are you worried he'd try to kill you?" Jastin whispered in disbelief. "Or start working with Hasting?"

"I'm sick of always watching over my shoulders," I told him, frustration swirling around inside me. "I should be able to trust my own blood, shouldn't I? I don't know how people live this way all the time."

"You'll have to get used to it," he said apologetically. "That's the rest of our life."

"My god," I said on a breath. "Can you imagine what it would be like having children and worrying about keeping them safe?"

He just laid there and blinked at me.

"It's different with Aston right now because you have faith the Reapers guarding the school will do it for you," I said. "Can you imagine having a child in a crib in here and worrying someone's going to slip in through the window? I don't think I would ever be able to sleep."

He kissed my neck. "I'm sure we could find ways to keep ourselves occupied while not sleeping."

"Stop trying to distract me!" I laughed as I pushed at him. "It's not a joke."

He sighed and propped his face up onto his elbow. "You're right," he agreed. "But . . . won't you be happy we'll be able to have that worry and share it together? Can't you just picture little versions of us running around here?"

"That's a frightening mental image."

"No, it's not." He smiled. "They'll grow up seeing how wonderful you are, and they'll see how much we love them. They can be the future, carrying on what your father started here. It's going to be amazing."

I wanted to say . . . *We can hope it will be.* Instead, I smiled and said, "They would have your eyes."

He grinned at that. "How do you know?"

"Because even James has those eyes," I said. "You and your sister. Whichever of your parents gave those to the two of you . . . Well, it must be something that insists on being carried down."

"I saw the page of your mother that Ahren has," Jastin said. "Maybe they'll have blue eyes like she did. Or green like you and your father."

"I suppose we'll have to wait and see," I told him with an almost bashful smile. "How many children do you want to have?"

He laughed. "Fifteen."

Firm, I told him, "That's *never* going to happen."

"I was just joking," he said. "I don't know. Enough." He shrugged.

"What do you mean *enough*?" I asked in confusion.

"I don't know," he said again, shaking his head. "I suppose until either of us looks at the other and says *enough*."

I heard myself giggling over that for quite a while. I didn't believe he would come close to getting as many as he wanted with me if that was the way he wanted to do it.

"You know," I said after I had managed to quiet myself. "When we first met . . . I would've never taken you for the parenting type. But seeing you with Aston and how good you are with the children at the schools and orphanage . . ."

He grinned again. "It makes you want to have babies with me, doesn't it?"

"Kind of, yes, in a way," I admitted. I could feel my face scrunching in confusion.

I'd never really thought I would *want* to have children. I would have them, after thinking about it, but I'd never thought I would really want to. Did seeing the man you were with being good with children unleash some sort of instinct that made you want to have them? I didn't know. It still wasn't even that I *wanted* to have them, but I felt a bit better about it now.

"Still," I said after a moment, "I think we should wait a while. At least until Hasting is taken care of. Or that we should try very hard not to have them until then." I didn't know how that was possible, save one thing, but we needed to try very hard.

"I agree," he said. "When do you think that will happen? Hasting."

"He's going to wait," I said thoughtfully. "I know what everyone believes about opportunities, but he's going to wait until after we're married and have settled in properly. I know he's heard about it in one way or another. And then he's going to leave Bethel with some of his Reapers to come here. But he'll wait until he believes complacency has settled in. I give it six months to a year, give or take."

"Why do you think that?" I didn't want to glance at his face, but I could hear the curiosity in his tone. "I thought *now* was the perfect time?"

"Several reasons," I replied. "As you said before, I believe he's going to come to kill me as well. He'll likely attempt to wipe out my entire family in one fell swoop now. Giving it some time would ensure we had our guards down, but . . . it's not just that. I'm sure he's heard about the things going on here. He'll want to let the people have hope so he can take it away from them. The more hope they have . . . the worse it will be for them if we're all gone. *Perfect* can change with how you're looking. The situations have changed. His perfect plan will have changed with them. Everything has changed. That's what I think."

"How do you know?"

"Because it's what I would do," I admitted quietly. "If I were evil."

I was starting to believe he was, that I could not hold him to any set of standards I'd held anyone else to. It had changed the way I looked at the situation. Everyone was on different levels. One did not necessarily have to get on the level of another to know where they were. They simply had to *see it* and *understand it*.

Jastin asked, "You think he'll risk getting himself killed by coming here?"

"You would think it illogical, wouldn't you?" I shook my head. "It's *only* illogical in the sense of self-preservation. Stanley said he could still remember when Hasting brought my mother's body back to Bethel."

I ignored the way Jastin's body stiffened in response to my statement, and I took it to mean he hadn't known where Stanley came from. Or perhaps that he hadn't known that I knew who'd killed my mother.

"He'd gone himself to kill both my parents," I went on. "That gives me reason to believe Hasting truly doesn't trust anyone to do what he wants done, that if it's something important to him . . . he'll do it himself if there's no other option." I shook my head again, thinking also on Stelin's wording when speaking of it. "Reapers don't trust anyone, do they? Not if they consider them a threat. An intelligent person in power would consider *everyone* a threat, even if they might not be. That's precisely what he is, at the core of things. So it would be logical, wouldn't it, that he would want to be the one to finish what he'd started?" The ultimate lesson. I paused and tugged uncomfortably at my blanket before adding, "The complete extermination of my blood."

He asked, "Do you believe you could kill him?"

"No," I replied evenly. "If my mother who'd trained her entire life couldn't do it . . . I'm not foolish enough to believe I ever could. Some things in life can come down to flukes. This will not. Whatever he does will be controlled enough that no space for flukes exists. We both know what he is, and we both know I could never manage killing someone like that myself. But someone can, and someone will. I suppose now it's all a matter of who will be the one to do it when the time comes and how many of my people he'll manage to kill before someone takes him down. I only hope I'm there to see it happen."

I spent a moment thinking about seeing bodies and how necessary it was. It took me quite a while to realize Jastin was lying there staring at me.

"What?" I asked.

He shook his head at me slowly. "I wish I could get inside your head for a little while. Just to see what it's really like in there."

"You're always in my head."

"No, I'm not. You and I both know you know that wasn't what I meant. I might understand you, but I've never been in your head. Every time I've thought I might be, I realize I'm not as close as I thought I was. Head and heart aren't the same."

"You wouldn't like it in there." My face burned. "It's quite awful, if I'm being honest." I cleared my throat. "Now . . . it's still my birthday. At least for a little while longer."

"You know . . . I tried and tried to think of something to get for you." He shook his head. "I couldn't think of anything you might want."

I fiddled for a moment with the bit of metal on my wrist and said, "I have everything I could possibly want for now and the hope other things will come in time."

He finally grinned at me. "Then why were you hinting you wanted something?"

"I don't know what you're talking about."

He narrowed his eyes at me, which made me sigh in an overly dramatic sort of way.

When had I started being dramatic?

Perhaps when life had turned into a show.

"All right," I said. "I was just thinking about the . . . *speaking*."

He rolled over onto his back and laughed up at the ceiling. "My god, that was awkward." He put one of his hands over his face.

When he realized I was not laughing about the situation right along with him, he looked over at me in confusion.

"What about it?" Then he blinked and his eyes widened slightly. "You're not wanting me to . . . You're not, are you?"

I shrugged. "It's my birthday."

He laughed. "And you want *that* as a birthday gift?"

"Well, I've been thinking about it," I admitted.

"*Have* you?" He was not openly laughing anymore but smiling hugely with a great deal of amusement on his face.

"A little." I was almost whispering. "It sounds quite . . . *interesting*. And I still can't fully understand the purpose of it, which I believe is what makes me think about it occasionally."

He nodded his head a bit. "And you were thinking if I did that and you discovered the purpose of it, you would stop thinking about it."

"Well . . . yes." The difference in understanding something in theory and being able to execute it.

"Won't work," he told me with a grin. "I've already told you, the purpose of it is to—"

"Yes, you've already told me what the purpose of it is." I interrupted him because I did not want to hear it again. "But I simply cannot figure out what you would get from it."

He smiled and bit down on the corner of his bottom lip.

I looked away and cleared my throat. "You said Abby will be staying over with me the night before we get married?"

"Yes, why?"

"No reason." I realized that I had a great deal of questions I was certain Abby could answer for me because I believed I finally understood what Jastin had meant before when he'd talked about taking care of me. At least partially understood.

"My little liar." His voice was affectionate as he pulled me close to him. "Whatever it is you want to talk to my sister about . . . I think I'd rather not know."

He was not going to do what I'd hinted at, I knew, but that was all right. We'd said we were going to wait, hadn't we? I could wait for that as well, despite it not being part of the initial insistence, even though I wanted to understand it.

When my back was properly to him, I whispered, "Do you think you can break me of how uncomfortable I am concerning that sort of thing?"

"Star." He laughed. "Given what you just asked me . . . I'd say we're already well on our way to getting there."

I smiled a little to myself. Fixing broken parts of me was the best birthday present he could've given me. Was it possible there wasn't anything wrong with me, really? That perhaps I simply required making a few tweaks here and there on myself to get to the point where I could be happy and function like a somewhat normal person?

It really seemed like something was wrong with me.

I was quite certain there was.

He kissed me on the back of my head and whispered, "Happy birthday, Star."

I stayed awake for some unknown stretch of time, staring through the darkness at what I could see of a painting hanging on the wall.

CHAPTER FORTY-SEVEN

MINE

THE DAYS DID NOT PASS QUICKLY, as I'd expected them to. I kept myself busy, and though part of me wished the days before mine and Jastin's wedding would disappear into oblivion, I found myself appreciating the fact that they were not. Every moment began standing out vividly to me. Colors somehow appeared brighter, time more relevant, and smiles more meaningful. Information sharpened, blurred, and then sharpened again. Everything seemed to be clicking into place. I assumed it was only me feeling that way, but I wished everyone was. Perhaps it was best.

Nearly every time I had a spare moment indoors, I caught myself staring out windows. Every time I was out in the city, I would at some point of it or another catch myself glancing over my shoulder in the direction of the House.

Patricia followed me around almost constantly when she could, rattling off details about things. I tried to listen to her sometimes, but I felt as though I'd spent so much time not paying attention to any of it that I couldn't possibly have any idea what she was speaking to me about now. That made attempting to listen an improper use of time.

It was an even more improper use than trying to remedy the confusion I still felt over the individual sounds instruments made. I kept replaying the music inside my head, attempting to pick it apart to discover the source of what was undoubtedly the most pleasant frustration I'd ever experienced in my life. It was very much like an itch that couldn't be scratched inside my head—not knowing what made the sound I kept hearing through all the others. And yet it was so different from every other reason I ever felt the same way. With everything else, when the feeling occurred, it kept itching incessantly. With that sound?

Every time I replayed the memory in an attempt to discover what I didn't know, I became lost in it.

I believed that to be a better use of my time than attempting to listen to Patricia. It was just as unproductive, only it was *much* more enjoyable for me.

I tried to remind myself it was all important, whether I was grasping or not, but I still didn't care about colors. I had no issue admitting to myself that I found the new vividness interesting and something worth thinking about to question. I didn't truly care much about or for them past that, certainly not as much as she still expected me to. Nowhere near. She'd *still* not given me proper explanation or response on it.

A few days were spent distributing clothing. I didn't know how my father managed to keep the people in his city organized and under control even with the enforcement of his Reapers, but . . . he did. I only assisted with that for a short while on the day after my birthday. My presence was not helpful in the slightest, which meant I was hindering rather than assisting with my own idea. That gave me a great deal to think on.

"I cannot accept this, Milady," people would tell me.

I'd urged them to take it, which they did, but they didn't seem happy. The people being happy was a great deal of the purpose of it.

After leaving the space to move on to the next part of my day, I'd watched from a doorway for a short time, keeping my body mostly concealed and peeking around the corner. They could take what was offered to them happily so long I was not there to see them do it, or so long as I was past the limits of their vision.

I thought it very strange. It was . . . illogical. My father and I spoke on it and related matters. By the end of that particular discussion, I found it more upsetting than anything. It took me several hours afterward to discover the appropriate word to replace *upsetting* with in that instance.

Disappointing.

My father and I then discussed that word thoroughly, in the context I was feeling it. It was easily one of the worst conversations I'd ever had in my life, and yet it was also perhaps the best at the same time. Funny, how that could work. But life moved on, no matter the words.

I experienced a great deal of confusion over a great many things, many that I spoke to my father on where he would then attempt to assist me in working through them. His methods of doing as much weren't always what I would consider helpful, sometimes more confusing than anything, and yet he was still as patient as ever.

More often as the days passed, I began finding bits of clarity or deeper understanding, sometimes in the most mundane of things. Or seemingly mundane. No matter what clarity I found myself discovering, it did nothing but cause me to feel I knew even less.

Things that seemed unchangeable I realized were in fact not. Perceptions altered through perspective, and when being asked to open my eyes in ways I'd previously been unable or unaware to . . .

I discovered that all things not only could change but inevitably would. Did. Must.

"All things move," I realized and said to my father one day.

"And what's got you thinking of movement and seeming so disturbed, Flower?"

"I needed Stanley earlier. I knew he'd be eating, so I went to the general dining assembly. And there was a moment, Father—a moment where I slipped inside to get to the corner where he goes with Stewart, and I went unnoticed. My guards at the time I suppose seemed like nothing more than anyone else in the space, in the sense of people moving with purpose. It was a moment, Father, an odd sort of one, and I can't—" I didn't know how to say that there was so much *can't* pertaining to it.

My father sat in silence for nearly a minute as I tried to work through things. When I couldn't and he realized as much, he said, "There was presumably a moment where you existed within the movement until one thing noticed you, which caused the others to, which caused all the world to stop. And you presumably are struggling with what you always have—being the different thing amidst the rest. Only now it's a realization, again presumably, that all things move but you now stop all things from moving."

Tears that I'd been struggling against welled and fell faster than I could've stopped, but I stopped them before they made much of a way. "I keep thinking of butterflies. Caterpillars and growth. They're constantly growing until turning into some beautiful thing, but . . ."

"But?"

"What then?" I shrugged stiffly. "When all things have moved and grown in the way they will . . . What then?"

His brow furrowed. "What are you truly wondering?"

"About the growth between people," I admitted. "If our relationship is the movement of growth and we've gone from a caterpillar to a butterfly stretching its wings and flying . . ." I shook my head, not knowing . . . "What then?"

He said, his brow still furrowed, "Flying, Flower."

I shook my head, that time at him because he wasn't understanding. "What *then*?"

"You're truly wondering about what you would consider in this context *the inevitable end*. Correct?"

I nodded.

"Do you believe all ends are the same? And do you believe that butterflies fly with the thought of the end inside their heads?"

I said to that, "Father, if you believe you can know what thoughts a butterfly has, I need to reevaluate my opinions on you."

He chuckled a bit at that, but he said, "Think on what I meant."

So I did think on it. I thought on it a great deal as I went about life and began seeing such movement to it.

Almost as if to punish me for putting so much thought into it, something occurred that showed me both the wonderous moment of flying and the beginning of what would be the inevitable end. It was one of the most beautiful and painful things of my entire life, but it told me . . .

While I'd done no daydreaming, I'd done some dreaming.

No matter how necessary sleep was to getting through the days . . .

With some things, it was best to be so acutely aware of the impossibility of them that there was no chance to ever—not even while sleeping—mistake reality.

Stelin had not been present to witness it. He'd left the room then returned to it once I'd been left alone inside. I didn't believe he'd eavesdropped.

He had no need to.

Anders had said before about trust belonging where it did and things never contradicting anything.

Sometimes, there were certain people who knew certain truths whether you told them directly or not. That nearly always to me was a horrendous experience, full of fear and worry.

Inexplicably, Stelin knowing the one he knew was one of the most relieving things I'd ever felt, though I was unsure why and what the differences were.

And it was strange how, after one of the most painful moments of my life, Stelin sort of swooped in, figuratively scooped me up, and carried me away from it.

As he and I walked and spoke that day on a great many subjects, I discovered that perhaps not all things that flew were as fragile and fleeting as butterflies.

ABBY AND I had another dress fitting together, and I passed the time during in a productive way, by thinking over a counterargument to my father's last argument, where mountains were concerned. He was so set on what he was, but I just had to push harder. *Smarter.* Find the crack that would tear it down, or make one. I had to be smarter.

By the end of the dress fitting, I'd been back to believing it impossible. Upon stepping out of the room, I'd found Stanley waiting in the hall, and he just smiled at me in the small way he sometimes did. I felt as though . . .

In a sense, I felt as though some force of the world had put Stanley there to smile at me in the way he did to remind me of what he'd said before about believing in me with it. It was illogical, but it was of both comfort and assurance that I could not give up. I would think of something.

I would.

Abby had seemed startlingly excited during the dress fitting about staying over with me the night before I would marry her brother. I thought that was very strange as well, and I could not really understand it.

Jastin seemed to be as happy as I did. Possibly more so. But happiness was a funny thing. *Happy* was such a complicated word.

He would find me sometimes during the day and pull me away from whatever I was doing. He would kiss me and then smile. Sometimes he would give the explanation for his actions as, "I just wanted to see you." Then he would leave and return an hour or so later.

I thought it was silly, but I did like it. Sometimes more than others, depending on what I was doing.

I also liked the time spent with my father, where no one entered the room without legitimate reason. I very much liked that, even when it was frustrating. I got far more frustrated with myself than my father while inside his office whenever I felt the word. If I couldn't come up with satisfactory points, arguments, and solutions . . . That was *my* fault. Not his.

I kept trying.

I paid great attention to the Reapers around me. They did not attempt to conceal themselves from me or anyone else now, not even a little. Whenever I would find myself smiling after one of Jastin's visits during the day, I'd almost always catch one of them grinning and shaking their head as if they thought the *both* of us were silly.

Then, I would purse my lips and proceed to go about my business so they would not think I was an ignorant little girl. But still, sometimes when I was not thinking directly about their presence, I would find myself smiling again. I simply could not help myself.

Sometimes.

Perhaps . . .

Being happy sometimes was a very good thing.

It was better than never.

The day before our wedding, I attempted to leave the House and go out into the city. Patricia had been following me for nearly twenty minutes, speaking about things, and had been completely unfazed by my pace when moving. I'd attempted to faze her with my pace, but her legs were a great deal longer than mine and she'd been focused. I was just in front of the door to exit when she shouted at me.

"You *cannot* go out there!"

My brow furrowed. "But why not?"

"We're already setting things up, Aster," she said in exasperation.

"And I'm . . . not permitted to see it?" I asked slowly. I had no idea how or why.

"No, I want you to be surprised."

"But what if I don't want to be surprised?"

A Reaper standing near me coughed and looked away.

She began tugging me away from the door. "You'll thank me tomorrow, as hard as I'm sure that is for you to believe."

When she properly had me far enough away to suit her, she walked away in a tizzy and began nearly screaming at the people filing in and out of the House with assortments of unknown things in their hands. I paid no mind to what any of those things were as I watched her go and for what felt like the thousandth time wondered why she was the way she was, but I noticed a great deal of color from the corners of my eyes.

"What use is having bodyguards if they allow people to tug at me like a puppet?" I asked the dozen or so Reapers who seemed to be my constant companions now once I gave up yet again on human behavior. They were interchangeable. Every few days I would see the same ones, but never really at the same times.

"You would've been angry if we'd removed the woman from your arm," one of them said with a grin. "Wouldn't you have?"

I stuck my nose in the air a bit—looking up at him—and responded with, "It's likely." I glanced around myself and realized that I now had absolutely nothing whatsoever to do. Nothing useful, due to a number of things. It was something I was not accustomed to. "My *god*, will this day never end?"

"Anxious for tomorrow?" another asked.

"Anxious for today and tomorrow to both be over," I answered then blinked. "That sounded quite bad, didn't it?"

"Understandable to be anxious for your wedding night," one of them said.

"Yes, I am quite anxious about that," I admitted dazedly. "He won't hardly kiss me for longer than five seconds right now, as though the entire world might end if he does. It's driving me mad." Again, I blinked. "I'm being highly inappropriate. I apologize."

"Nothing to apologize for." The same one shrugged. "And don't worry. No one will be near enough to your quarters for you to concern yourself over."

"But . . . isn't that risky?" I asked in confusion.

"Still within sight, of course," he said, "but hopefully out of hearing distance."

I shook my head. "That doesn't make any sense."

I felt my face burning when several of them snorted at me.

"I suspect you'll find out tomorrow night precisely how much sense that makes," another stated.

I did not tell them that I was very uncomfortable. I scrunched my face up and said, "I suppose that's a possibility. Is . . ." I stopped and took a deep breath.

"Is what?" one asked.

I smiled. "Never mind." I would ask Abby later.

"We'll be especially on top of things tonight, given that your soon-to-be nephew will be in your quarters with the two of you," one of the oldest told me.

"Thank you," I said quietly. "Is anyone going to be watching Jastin while he's away with my brother, to ensure nothing happens to him?"

"Already taken care of." He nodded. "He's followed even when he's not with you. And some intending to be with he and your brother tonight are doing so simply to watch after him. Jastin knows as much, but your brother doesn't."

I'd not known any of that either.

I wondered now how much more I could've been learning all this time if I'd simply opened my mouth rather than attempting to ignore their presence.

Curious, I asked, "Do any of you follow my brother?"

"He won't allow it," someone said. "Pride of a certain sort gets people killed. I hope your brother realizes that before something happens to him. It's a wonder he's still alive, but you didn't hear that from me."

I fought against the urge to nod. "Do you think . . ." I started and then stopped, warring with myself to voice a necessary request. Necessity always won out. "Do you think someone could watch over him, not just tonight but all the time?"

"He'll notice," the same one said. "And if he's informed you sent someone to tail him, I'm sure you're aware what he'll believe your reasoning is." He narrowed his eyes. "But you already know, don't you?"

I stared up at him and evenly said, "I don't know what you're talking about, and I don't care what he thinks." I shook my head. "I want him alive. I want him alive long enough to realize he's being a complete imbecile. And then I want him alive after that hits him so he can actually live up to his potential." Quietly I added, "One day, he'll realize everything."

"Do you really believe that?" one asked me.

I chewed on my lip for a moment, uncomfortable. "Jastin does." My voice was still quiet. "That's good enough for me with this." I frowned up at all of them and whispered. "Do you all *truly* believe I would be better equipped to run things than he would? You realize he could keep everyone safe better than I ever could, don't you? I mean . . . you'd *have* to realize that."

"This is the only thing I believe you don't understand," one of them said thoughtfully. "A leader doesn't technically need to keep everyone safe with their own hands. It's *decisions* they need to make. Keeping everyone safe?" He shrugged. "That's what we're here for. All we need is someone to point us in a direction and tell us to go."

"And why would you *listen* to me?" I asked in disbelief. "I'm not a Reaper. I've not had any training in understanding tactics, or anything of that nature. I'm just a girl. Why would you listen if I pointed you in some direction? It would be illogical for you to believe a silly girl would know proper directions to save her own life, let alone the lives of other people."

"Because you wouldn't tell us to go unless you were certain you were pointing us the correct way."

"How do you *know*?" I demanded.

"Let me ask you this," the same one said. "If you were in control of Jarsil, would you send Reapers as spies into other cities?"

"I would," I admitted without hesitation.

He grinned. "For what reason?"

"To see if the leaders could be swayed to join our cause," I replied. "And to attempt to discover how many Reapers in whatever city were unhappy with their circumstances, and if their leaders were not willing, how many of them would choose to rebel against them for the greater good." I'd done a great deal of thinking about that sort of matter over the past months.

"Not to listen for whispers of threats?" His voice was curious enough it nearly verged on taunting, but . . . it was not.

"Well, yes, that as well of course," I said evenly. "But mostly for the reasons I said."

"And you would ally yourself with other cities?" one asked.

"Cities you had no control over?"

"Only if they agreed to certain things," I replied. "Standards of living both for their Reapers and citizens. It's not about control in the way you're thinking of it. It's a different sort. Similar, but on a wider scale." I paused for a moment. "Can you picture it? An alliance for a free world, a *better* world?"

"How could you ensure the standards wouldn't fall when you were not directly in control of them?" another asked.

I laughed a little beneath my breath and looked at the floor. "One city entirely united would be a frightening thing," I said quietly. "But several of them united together? All of them standing together and fighting for the same things?" I shook my head. "The standards would not fall."

"Out of fear."

"Fear is necessary in life," I said. "And it's something leaders should gladly bear the brunt of for their people. No one should be in power if they're not afraid. If they're not afraid, it means they have no care. Why should a person be responsible for people they have no care for?"

"Are you afraid, Milady?" one asked.

"Every second of every night and day," I admitted. "Even my dreams are terrifying things, because . . ." My brow furrowed. "No one else can see them." I smiled stiffly at them and began to walk away. I listened to the nearly silent footsteps of my Reapers trailing along on all sides of me.

My Reapers. And they *were* mine, at least in a sense. If Ahren was not followed, our father did not want him followed. If I could *get* him followed despite that . . .

They were mine. At least for now.

I wondered when that had happened, exactly. It gave me a great deal to think on.

CHAPTER FORTY-EIGHT

SISTERS

"**G**OODNIGHT," I told my designated Reapers as I stepped inside my living quarters that evening.

Some of them simply smiled, and some of them returned the sentiment before walking away. One did nothing more than nod. I was perfectly all right with that. They would change shifts, I knew. It wouldn't happen all at once, but periodically others would come to relieve them through the night. It happened every few hours, even during the day. One would come and one would go, but never more than one at once and never at precisely the same time of day. Constantly.

I'd always thought the Reapers following closest had been ordered to, but I wondered now if I'd been wrong. Jastin said more were following of their own volition. Had they switched out at some point? Were they all doing it of their own volition now?

If they had, if the ones on order had changed to those who volunteered . . . my father must've known. He was allowing it. Of course he was. I did wonder . . .

Who was organizing their movements?

Someone *had* to be.

I watched the Reapers' backs as they walked away, going to their respective posts, feeling Abby's presence beside me.

James was already asleep inside, or lying quietly in the crib that had been set up for him here.

I smiled when I saw Jastin running up.

The smile on his face was ridiculously large. "Didn't want to be gone for the night without seeing you first."

"Are you sure you won't come back later?" I asked sadly. I couldn't stand the thought of him not being here at night. No matter how I felt about Abby, she wasn't an equal replacement for me.

"And get shot by archers on the wall?" He laughed. "No, I won't be coming back at all tonight. You and I won't see one another again until we're getting married."

"We're getting married." My voice was quiet as I attempted to wrap my mind around his statement.

Won't see one another again until we're getting married.

Madness.

"Yes, we are." He sounded so happy, but wariness slipped in when he spoke next. "You're not going to stay in there and decide not to show up tomorrow, are you?"

"Of course not," I told him with a quiet laugh. "You're not . . . going to not show up, are you?"

"My god, I love you," he said before kissing me.

I laughed a little.

He smiled at me. "I'll see you tomorrow."

He kissed me again.

"Time to go." I heard Abby's exasperated voice behind me. "You're ruining my first and likely last stay-over. Let me spend some alone time with my new sister. You'll have her all to yourself soon. Well, yourself and the rest of the city." He kissed me quickly again which caused her to make a frustrated sound and say, "Good*bye*, Jastin."

"Love you," I whispered.

"Love you," he said back.

I watched him go.

Abby said, "You two are so damn disgusting."

I cleared my throat, closed my eyes for two seconds, opened them, and then closed the door.

"I was wondering how all those men around you all the time didn't drive my brother insane." She nodded. "I've got it now."

"What do you mean?" I asked curiously. "I mean, it's often frustrating, but they're there for protection. I don't see how or why it could drive him insane."

I disliked it much more than he did. Generally.

"*That* is what I mean," she said. "You don't even see them, do you?"

"The Reapers?" I asked, baffled. "Of course I see them. As you said, they're around me all the time."

"Their *faces*," she said. "You don't see them, do you? It's like they're nothing more than bodies taking up space, bodies that can talk to you if you want them to. You don't see them as anything more than that. You don't look at faces unless you know the person it belongs to. At but not really."

"I've always been that way," I told her uncomfortably. "When you spend such a long time trying to stay invisible . . . you learn faces look back when you look at them. Reflex. So you train yourself around it and look past." I cleared my throat again. "So what is the purpose of . . . What did you call it? Stay-overs?" I shook my head. "Why are you so excited about staying here with me?"

"I can remember thinking the exact same thing," she said with a tight smile. "I would see the girls walking home with their friends from school. Not the Reapers, but the normal girls. They would smile and giggle, and I could *not* understand what they were doing, how they could be *so* blind to what was going on around them."

I asked, "What changed it for you?"

"When Reapers are old enough to be sent on their missions, they're allowed to leave the school," she said. "We always do when we're younger—sneak out just because we can and see which of us gets caught. But when we're older, we can leave. There are different schools for different ages, and we get more leeway every time we move to a new one. But there are always rules and curfews. Only . . . when you hit the last school, they don't enforce the hours."

I had no idea how she thought I didn't know all that now. I hadn't gone, but I'd been involved with things here long enough now to know all that. I didn't bother pointing it out, letting her get to her point and not mine.

"*So*," she went on. "Once I reached that last school, I decided to follow a couple of girls. It was three of them, not sisters, and they all went to one of the girl's houses. They were a little older than I was at the time." She grinned a little. "I sat outside their window and listened to them talking for nearly the entire night."

"That's the purpose of it?" My brow furrowed. "Talking?" I couldn't imagine . . .

She nodded her head in what seemed to be excitement. "My god, I learned half the things I know about boys from listening that night." She laughed. "I almost threw up, which is so funny now." She sighed contentedly before saying, "It was great."

Slowly, I asked, "That you almost vomited?"

"You know how some animals live in herds?" Her voice took on a thoughtful tone.

I nodded in response to her question.

"People are like that. That's how we learn things—by other people telling us, or experiencing things for ourselves and telling other people. It's human nature to help the others survive with knowledge. We're basically animals that stand up." She shrugged.

I believed that to be far more accurate than she likely did, but at least we were in agreement. That was a *rare* occurrence.

How she put it was far better than how it typically sounded.

"Now," she said brightly. "You're going to get over your uncomfortableness with things and we're going to be girls and talk. For tonight, I'm not a Reaper and you're not a princess. We're just friends."

"I'm *not* a princess." I obviously needed to remind her of the fact. Repeatedly. How she couldn't get that through her head was beyond me.

She pointed a finger at me. "Don't ruin it for me."

I nodded, though I didn't know how saying what I had might do as much. I likely would do as much unintentionally if telling her the truth would ruin it for her. I supposed intentional or not could be argued there. Either way, it seemed she and I had the same idea for tonight, only she was ridiculously excited about it and I was not. It was strange to realize that something useless was precisely what I needed, at least in one regard.

There were so many regards. I just had to work on them.

MY FATHER STOPPED BY before it was entirely dark, which was somewhat unusual. He only came to see me here when he had something to speak of past our usual hours. He got ideas at odd hours sometimes.

I supposed we both did, though his were odder than mine, in my opinion. He would disagree with me on that.

Regardless, my lack of sound sleep often gave him opportunity to drop by at odd hours. I often slept better afterward, depending on a few things.

"I just wanted to check in on you." He stepped inside with his hands concealed behind his back. "I had to do it before it was dark enough that my men would shoot me dead outside your door. I didn't feel like wasting the time up on the wall to inform them. By the way . . . best to stay inside. They're on high alert tonight."

"Yes, Father, I was planning on walking outside and getting shot with an arrow," I told him. "Don't you believe it sounds like the best thing to do right now?"

He didn't get frustrated with me because he knew how I meant it. He smiled a little, and I smiled a little because he'd known as much.

He looked at Abby. "What are you shaking your head about over there?"

She was indeed shaking her head when she said, "It's so hard to tell when she's joking. She always sounds the same."

My father said to that, "Perhaps she and I should have a more thorough discussion on sound being the sound or the movement behind and through it."

I said, "Father, you surely didn't come here to argue with me."

He laughed.

Abby asked, "Would that cause an argument?"

His eyes widened. "You've no idea. Should you have any doubt in your mind on capability of sound, hearing her shout at me would surely offer you clarity."

She again shook her head to say, "Sir, I can't keep up with you when you're talking like her."

He laughed again at that and moved on. "I've brought some things for the two of you. Jastin said you were excited about having a proper stay-over. I must admit I didn't have a clue what the word meant in the way you think of it, so I did some digging." He pulled a basket full of unknown objects from behind his back. "I *believe* I've put together the appropriate things for such an occasion."

Abby was giggling as she ran over to him, entirely changed by such simple means. "*Pajamas*!" she exclaimed as she held up a bit of fabric.

I asked, "Sleeping clothes?" Were they cause for excitement?

"Those girls called them pajamas," she said dreamily. "Oh, and snacks. *Oh my god*." Her eyes went unnaturally wide. "Is that chocolate?"

My father grinned. "It is."

I asked, "What's that?"

"Only the best thing in the entire *world*," Abby said. "Or so I've heard. How did you get it?"

"Don't worry about it," my father said dismissively. I knew how he'd gotten it, roundabout. She should've as well. "Just enjoy your time, have fun, and ensure the two of you don't stay up the entire night. Best for her to not fall asleep while she's getting married."

"I'm getting married," I said quietly. And then I realized . . . "You're going to be my sister."

"I've never had a sister," Abby said with a ridiculously large grin.

I knew she hadn't. Perhaps that was what *normal* girls did—told other girls useless information. Perhaps that was how they could stay up talking for an entire night.

I laughed. "Neither have I."

Perhaps useless information could be fun. And perhaps some non-useless information could slip its way into our . . . *talking*. Though I sincerely doubted any of it could be useful in any sense past personal. That was something either way.

CHAPTER FORTY-NINE

OVER

THAT WAS HOW ABBY AND I ended up in those . . . *pajamas*, which were nothing more than sleeping-dress sorts of things, sprawled out on my bed and giggling over the contents of the basket. I liked them much better than normal dresses, if only due to all the aspects of comfort. I would still return to my usual sleeping attire at the first opportunity.

They'd not been the only thing in the basket brought to us by my father.

"I don't like it." I extended my piece of chocolate toward her. We'd split it in half.

"Are you *serious*?" she demanded.

"Too bitter." I held my tongue out of my mouth for a moment, wishing the taste would leave it. It was one of the most disgusting things I'd ever had in my mouth, apart from Fandir root and poison. "Honey is *much* better than that." Just about *anything* was much better. Just about.

She reached into the basket and extended a wrapped-up object to me. "Trade you."

I grabbed for it greedily, unwrapped it, and then felt as though I were inside a bubble of pure bliss. The feeling struck me before I even put it into my mouth.

"See?" I asked as I sucked on a bit of the honeycomb. "Why can't people just share?"

"Oh, what's this about?" she asked excitedly.

"Just my brother."

Her response was, "Your brother is *gorgeous*, by the way. Just thought I would let you know. I sometimes feel the need to shout it at you."

I frowned at her, and she shrugged.

It took me a moment to somewhat recover from the knowledge that she thought my brother was *gorgeous*. I didn't know how I'd missed it. Perhaps because I'd only seen her near Ahren with Chandler there as well. She seemed *quite* unable to look at anyone else when he was no matter what she thought they were.

Once I had recovered, I asked, "Do you and Jastin have jealousy issues?"

My father and I had spoken about Ahren's jealousy issues several times, how it and they had affected his life in other ways before me. How they had worsened because of me, and in what ways they differed.

"I suppose," she said thoughtfully. "I was always jealous of how well he did his job. Jealous that he was partnered with your brother. Jealous that he was a boy." She shrugged again.

"You see." I held up a hand. "That's my issue. Why should women wish they were men so people would look at them differently? Why can't we all just look at one another as equals?"

"Oh, we *are* equals," she said. "They're stronger and we're smarter. It evens out. It's not their fault they're dumb."

I snorted.

A rather thoughtful expression took over her face before she continued. "Or maybe we're dumb because we're the ones stuck carrying their babies. Who knows?"

"Do you like being a mother?" I asked her.

"It doesn't matter what I like," she said quickly. "I'll still have to give him up and go back to work."

I was much more hesitant when asking my next question. "Do you like being a Reaper?"

"Yes and no." She shrugged. "I enjoy knowing I can do more than most men can, but sometimes . . . Sometimes I just want to be a lady."

"A *lady*?" I asked in confusion.

She scrunched her face up at me. "*Yes*, a *lady*."

I'd never considered Abby to be particularly lady-like, at times very much the opposite, but I supposed what one wanted to be didn't necessarily have to correlate with what they were. I supposed it made sense, even on that level.

I asked, "If you could do anything in the world . . . what would it be?"

I was not entirely pleased to see her as uncomfortable as she often made me, only partially.

"It doesn't matter," she answered again.

"But if you *could*?" I pressed.

"You'll think I'm stupid." She looked away from me, bringing her gaze to the nearest wall.

"Try me," I urged.

She smiled bashfully. "You know those old women who made our dresses?"

I nodded.

"I'd like to do that."

"Make clothing?" I asked.

"Make clothing that looked like that," she answered. "It would take so much skill to make something so exceptional."

That was very, very true.

I asked, "Would you rather do that than be a Reaper?"

"Yeah." She was clearly uncomfortable, or perhaps . . . *sad*. "Yeah, I would. I'd get to keep my son that way, too. Get to be with who I wanted to be with. Not have to kill anyone or watch over my back. Just make beautiful things and be happy." She shook her head. "No point thinking about it."

"Are you in love with Chandler?" I had to ask.

"No," she said quickly. "I can't be." She took a deep breath and then let it out as a sigh. "And even if I was, even if the two of us were together . . . we'd still have to give up any children we had together and make children with our assignments. It's only a matter of time before he gets assigned a woman if he chooses to stay here. There's no point to it."

"That's *preposterous*!" I exclaimed. "You'd still have to have children with other people if you were married to someone?"

I did not tell her that Chandler would *not* be getting assigned to anyone. My father and I had already discussed it. He'd been more than happy to oblige on that.

She nodded uncomfortably. "We're not all as lucky as you when it comes to that sort of thing." Her tone was not snotty. It was almost apologetic.

"My god, that would be one of the first things I changed," I said under my breath. I couldn't *believe* my father hadn't told me about outside-marriage reproduction, but there were so many other things.

"What?" she asked as she tilted her head. Then she smiled hugely. "Are you already planning out your reign?"

"No," I said. "Only saying, if I were in that position . . . I would change that. Anyway." I had to know, though . . . "Why are you thinking he's getting assigned someone? You know he's not from here."

"I know. But I've heard it spoken about."

Carefully, I asked, "By whom?"

"Just some females." She waved a hand dismissively. "Talking about the good blood."

"Saying he's handsome, you mean?"

She nodded. "I'd ask if you think so, but you've likely never looked at him." She laughed at that. "And if you're attracted to my brother . . . likely not. But yeah."

I took in a deep breath then told her, "I would expect you to know that listening to random people who have no idea what they're speaking of isn't the best thing to do."

"Yeah, but it's only a matter of time."

One.

Two.

I took in another deep breath. I released it slowly. I then asked, "You're not in love with him?"

"No." She shook her head. "I like him, yeah. And my god would I *want* to make babies with him."

My brow furrowed, because I knew how much it upset her about having to give up James when it was time. "Why?"

"Have you seen his arms?" Her eyes went wide. "I just want to lick them."

"That's disgusting." It was disgusting and just . . . *no.* Along with . . .

It said a great deal.

"Agree to disagree." She shrugged. "No, really . . . I do like him a lot. He's really good with James now. I think the couple years make a massive difference from what I'm used to, and . . ." She took a deep breath. "I like the way he looks at me. Do you know what I mean?"

Arm-licking aside, that much I could understand. I nodded. I said nothing about how it was more than *a couple*.

"People say you've brainwashed my brother." She shook her head. "They give him shit about it sometimes, which is ridiculous. All Reapers are brainwashed from birth. It's like you erased it from him and told him it was okay to be who he is underneath all that. I wish someone would look at me like I'd fixed them that way." She sighed and shook her head again. "I think everyone's jealous. Of the two of you."

"Why?" I asked curiously.

"How could a person not be?" Her eyes widened again. "The two of you are just so . . . *happy*."

Perception was all down to perspective.

"Why would people be jealous of someone's happiness?" I asked, bemused. "It has no effect on their life whatsoever."

"Because they don't have it."

Interesting.

"Your brother is . . ." I started and then stopped. "He's the only thing in my life that seems to make any sense, the only real thing I have in this mad world. My days are what they are, then I come here and have a moment with him. Perhaps it's understandable for people to be jealous of that, but . . . they can't be jealous of anything else. Not of the worry that someone's going to stab him in the back the first time I turn my head, or worse. The fear of losing it? I don't know." I smiled tightly at her. "I'm so afraid of losing it."

She saved me by saying, "Let's not talk about that. We're supposed to be having fun."

"The man you had James with," I said, which made her scrunch up her face. "How do you feel about him?"

"My assignment, Richard . . ." She took a deep breath. "He's all right. Good-looking like all assignments are and . . ." She shook her head. "He's nice, I guess." With her stiffness . . .

I whispered, "Your assignment isn't James' father, is he?"

Her eyes went wide again—wider than they had before. "Don't tell anyone. *Please*."

"I don't make it a habit to share things people tell me in confidence." I wouldn't have to tell anyone. I *would* have to alter a few things. "Who is it?"

A few long seconds passed before an uncomfortable smile took over her face and she said, "My best friend, Shane. We, um . . . we're friends. James was an accident. I'd planned on waiting until I turned twenty to get my assignment, but I had a year to go and woke up throwing my guts up one morning. So, I ran down to the assignment office and met Richard."

"And no one knew?" I asked in disbelief.

"Well, him of course," she said. "They all thought James was just a bit premature."

I laughed a little, which transformed her smile from uncomfortable to genuine.

"He's going to be *so* angry I told you. Probably best if I don't inform him of it."

"That's ridiculous." Better me knowing to get it down and potentially prevent accidental inbreeding later. Better me knowing than my father. I narrowed my eyes. "May I ask you something?"

She nodded.

"Shane . . . are you in love with *him*?"

"*No.*" She drew the word out, which somehow made it both more and less believable. But then she said. "He's just . . . He's just my friend."

"Then why?" I asked curiously. "Why do . . . *that* with him?"

She said, "Because I could."

"Is . . ." I could ask her the question I'd intended to ask her now that there was a proper opening for it, the question I'd stopped myself from asking a group of people earlier. "Is it enjoyable?"

"Well, you see . . ." she started slowly. "After hearing those girls talking, I was curious. So I figured, who better to try what they were giggling about with than him? Was it enjoyable the first time?" She paused to shake her head dramatically. "I couldn't figure out why they'd been talking the way they had about it, so I figured we'd try it again. Maybe we didn't do it right or something. Second time still wasn't so great, but eventually . . . yeah. Clearly, given we were doing that for three years before I got pregnant."

"How in the world did you manage not to for so long?" I asked in disbelief.

I'd gotten pregnant by doing it *once*.

She laughed. "I'm sure my brother can tell you that much." Then she looked away and scrunched her face. "Eww."

"Yes, I've been saying *eww* every time you've brought the subject up." I laughed. "Are you finally getting it?"

"Well, mostly I just said things to make you uncomfortable," she admitted, which was something I was already aware of. "Totally different when you're actually talking back to me about it."

"Well, you see . . ." I said. "I spent a very, very long time being afraid of that, hearing it was bad, and my one and only experience with it was . . . Well, it was nothing special, apart from that I'd done it by my own choice to."

"You've done it before?"

"Not with your brother." Under my breath I added, "My god, this is strange. I would imagine those girls were not with any of their friends' brothers to make their talking so awkward."

"Don't feel too bad," she said. "I've slept with your brother once. Okay, not once, but a few times. Well . . . maybe more than a few times. That's partially why I've wanted to shout about it." She must've seen the look on my face because she shrugged and asked, "What?" Then her eye twitched and she loudly said, "*Don't* tell my brother that. Not *ever*. That would go *really* badly. Brothers are exhausting."

"All right, I'm going to get this conversation on a different path." I took a deep breath. "Or at least back to where I was going with it, which isn't entirely different, but not . . . not anything to do with either of our brothers." I paused. "That spy? Chase? Chandler's brother? I did with him once. I think he intentionally ensured it was . . . not like it could be. Does that make sense?"

"Okay we're in more comfortable territory now." She took what seemed to be a breath of relief. "I'm not entirely sure I know what you mean, but . . . Chase? He's really bad, isn't he? Chandler's told me he is." Were conversations about such matters really so easy to change direction so quickly?

"It would seem that way, yes," I answered quietly.

"And did he know your issues with that sort of thing?"

I nodded because Chase knew and had known very well about my issues with it.

"How did you feel afterward?"

"Kind of strange," I admitted. "Fine, I suppose. A little stunned. Well, a *lot* stunned if I'm being wholly honest with you." I'd had time to get past that, but immediately after had been mad.

"Listen," she said apologetically. "I've heard men talking about women. We listen and hear things we shouldn't, things people shouldn't even say. They always talk about women seducing men, but . . . men can do the same thing. And there's a certain kind of man that lives for hurting people. They think it's funny. So . . . I'm going to assume he acted a certain way to get you to be comfortable enough doing it and did just enough to not put you off towards it, but not really enough that you'd care to do it again. I'm only assuming that by the way you're talking about it, but . . . usually when men do that, they *want* women to want to do it again, at least until the men have had enough of them and move on to the next. It must not have been what he wanted from you."

"That . . . sounds about right," I whispered to my blanket. And was further proof that different types of intelligence mattered.

She very much was not stupid in some ways that I was.

"They say women are heartless." She shook her head. "We're not. We give too much of ourselves to people who don't deserve it, and then . . . we don't have as much left to give. He must not have hurt you too badly for you to be able to feel the way you do about my brother."

"It wasn't a matter of hurt, really," I said. "I was embarrassed after the fact, for falling for it and for him."

"It's nothing to be embarrassed about."

It actually *was*.

"He always treated me like a girl," I said. "Like I needed to think for days over one subject, and like I wasn't capable of things. I couldn't see it then, but I do now. And I remember, the morning after I did that with him, I went to my brother's office because he'd thrown a fit and I wanted to work things out with him." I laughed a little. "Your brother, he said . . . 'It's funny how love twists and distorts little girls' minds.'"

"That sounds like him at the time." She frowned. "But how is that funny?"

"Because when we went in my brother's office and I asked Jastin why he'd flirted with me before if he thought I was a little girl, he said . . . 'It's what your father and brother would think, isn't it? Clearly you're not.'" I paused to laugh again. "My god, it had taken me over eighteen years to figure out I'd at some point turned into a woman, but . . . nobody had ever looked at me like I was before. Do you know what I mean?" I shrugged. "I'd slept with Chase, but he hadn't looked at me that way. It took me quite a while to understand the way Jastin looked at me that day."

She sighed. "Great feeling, isn't it?"

"It is," I admitted. "But I'm afraid that, after tomorrow . . . he'll stop looking at me that way."

Her face scrunched again. "Are you really?"

"I don't have a clue in the world what I'm doing." I shook my head. "Don't know what's normal to feel and what's not, or anything."

"I'm going to regret asking this." She closed her eyes. "Are there some times where you just want to . . . rip his clothes off?"

"Yes," I admitted as my face started burning.

"Totally normal thing to feel." She shrugged. "There's nothing wrong with your body. Your head is the only thing holding you back, and you can work with that. But Aster . . . you're an adult. You're getting married to my brother tomorrow. The two of you love each other. Even if you don't have a clue in the world what you're doing, he's not going to look at you any differently, and the two of you will get that stuff worked out over time." She smiled what seemed to be apologetically at me before adding, "There isn't *anything* wrong with physically showing a person what they mean to you."

"*That's* what it's supposed to be?" I whispered.

She smiled a little and quietly said, "Yeah. That's what it's supposed to be." Then she chuckled under her breath. "Good thing for people like me it's a whole hell of a lot of fun as well."

"Is it?" I asked curiously.

She grinned. "Oh yes." Her nose scrunched a little. "Give it some time."

CHAPTER FIFTY

HEARD

ABBY AND I DID NOT STAY UP the entire night talking, but we came much closer to that than we likely should have. I'd never really enjoyed talking very much, at least not for extended periods of time or about nonsense. But I enjoyed it with her, in some ways. In some ways, I enjoyed it a great deal. Was that what it was like, having a sister? Or simply being a *girl*, as Stelin had said? I did not know, but I liked it. It made me feel strange, sort of, a bit . . . *lighter* somehow.

Perhaps speaking of nonsense unburdened you from some of it, in which case it would not be useless. It would not be useless and could perhaps be remarkably beneficial, no matter how difficult that was to believe.

I wondered now just *how many* enjoyable experiences I held myself back from for one reason or another. There was no way to know. I didn't have the time to put thought into it. Perhaps at a later date.

Doubtful, with so much else.

I knew the mechanics of doing . . . *things*. I'd done them after all, and Agatha had explained it to me, but I had no idea about the feelings.

After talking with Abby, I realized there really *wasn't* anything wrong with me, like I'd thought all this time. Or at least, if there was, the same thing was wrong with her as well. Or at least there was nothing wrong with my body if not the rest of me.

It was illogical to think she and I were the only two females who felt that way, so . . . I had to assume we all did. Hearing it from another female was entirely different than hearing it from Jastin. He clearly was not built the same way to know for certain. But Abby and I were built the same, at least in the most basic of ways. Not really any other ways at all, apart from the one. We were *very* different people otherwise. That seemed to be the way it went and was.

Although I'd not wanted for her to, she told me about how her . . . *liaisons* with my brother had come about.

He'd seemed sad and she was bored.

I'd not known that people didn't need any more reason than what they had to do such things willingly. Apparently . . .

Well, apparently sometimes they didn't.

Also apparently you could sometimes find people physically attractive enough that nothing else need play into it. I'd heard as much before, but it still baffled me. That seemed to be the consensus no matter how mad and ridiculous I thought it was. I just couldn't imagine, and I *believed* it was best that I found it unfeasible. Not even the most handsome man I'd ever seen would I have considered doing as much with nothing else involved.

My father and I had conversed before on the matter of people's willingness to overlook things due to appearances, in how it pertained specifically to work. He did not find it unfeasible. He found it a great many other things I was inclined to agree with. All but the one. The one *baffled* me no matter how many times I'd heard it.

Abby talked about the Reaper schools and how they'd changed since my father had arrived here.

She talked about clothes and explained a little to me about matching past what I'd learned and figured out while organizing clothing the day I had. I still did not entirely understand the purpose, but I supposed there was *some* sense to be found in it after proper explanation. She also said some things about colors, in the sense of matching clothes, that made me do some thinking on them as a whole.

She talked about Chandler's arms and face a great deal. I did not know how she could transform statements about Chandler's body into things that made the muscles in my face twitch, but she somehow managed to. And I did not know why, at some point through the conversation, I began thinking they were slightly more humorous than disgusting. Perhaps it was not so different from fear in that exposure changed some aspect. Or perhaps it was realizing that she was concealing some amount of depth with shallowness. That . . .

I understood.

I giggled a few instances and was quite surprised to find myself making random points on matters here and there without any spurring on at all. We spoke about Jarsil and the people here. We spoke about the places she'd been and New Bethel. We woke James by laughing too loudly on two different occasions.

When we were both on the verge of falling asleep, I said, "We should do this again sometime. Perhaps invite Kay as well."

"Would you really want to?" she asked in disbelief.

"Yes, I like Kay well enough," I said. I liked her more for making Stelin smile than I liked her. "Do you not?"

"No, I meant do this again," she clarified. "She *is* a bit *much* in the sense of sweetness. We'll compare this to chocolate and honey, but if you like her . . ." She sighed. "But no. I was asking if you would really want to do this again."

"Oh, yes," I said quickly. "I always feel I don't laugh nearly enough. I'm certain I laughed more tonight than I did in all ten of the years I spent in New Bethel. I've never had a female friend, let alone one near my own age." I supposed Agatha could be considered a friend, in a way. It depended upon how one looked at it.

She grinned. "I thought we were sisters now?"

"Sisters tomorrow, but still friends as well," I said with an extremely large yawn.

"That sounds nice." She caught my yawn. It was so mad to me, that happening. "Time to give me your back."

I frowned at her.

She smiled and shrugged. "Sisters and friends or not . . . I'm still a Reaper, and I still have orders. It's different to have orders I actually enjoy."

"That's ridiculous," I said in exasperation. "There are so many Reapers outside. We'll be fine."

"Don't get complacent," she said quietly. "You'll get yourself and my brother killed if you do."

I nodded and rolled over. Her logic was sound and I could not argue with it any longer.

It felt quite strange when she latched onto me, given she was much smaller than what I was accustomed to having my back. It was not as strange as it likely should've been. I'd slept close to Agatha for ten years until my brother had given me my own bed.

"I've thought about putting traps in the windows," I said. "To worry a little less."

"Traps?" she asked in confusion.

"Yes, sort of like how people trap animals sometimes when they're hunting them," I said. They could still eat without actually *hunting*. "Only a trap meant to incapacitate a person rather than . . . *trap* them. I suppose it would be called the same word regardless of what's intended to be trapped or incapacitated. I apologize if that sounds insensitive or *inhumane*."

A few seconds passed. "How do you know about that sort of thing?"

"By reading a book about it in New Bethel," I replied with another yawn. "Took me nearly a quarter of a year to get through because of the damned writing in it. The drawings were quite helpful, though."

"Do you think you could do that?"

"No, but I'm sure someone could," I replied. That seemed to be the answer of all answers. *Someone could.* "We should probably figure it out before they do. I'll talk to my father about it after the wedding. Well, not directly after of course, but perhaps the next day."

"Do you have all sorts of ideas like that in your head?"

"Oh yes," I said. "More of them now than I used to, but I started thinking about that particular one while I was still in New Bethel."

"Why?" she asked. "To hurt people there?"

"Of course not," I said. "It was just an errant thought after watching Chandler climb up the side of a wall and slip in through a window. I didn't want to let myself think about how many people he'd killed that way, but . . . well . . . You think about it. So, it was kind of just an idea about how to prevent that from happening. What a surprise that would be to any Reapers from other cities who tried to slip into our buildings undetected."

441

It took her quite a while to say, "You're kind of scary sometimes. Did you know that?"

"Why?" I laughed. "I'm sure someone's already thought of it. And if they haven't, then they should have. The problem is that . . . if there were spies, they would likely know about the traps anyhow. It would depend on the sort of mission they were sent on, I suppose. Perhaps intelligence levels."

"Now I know what Jastin meant about you hardly sleeping," she said. "Is your mind always going this way?"

"Yes," I admitted. *Worse.* "It's quite exhausting."

"I can imagine." She chuckled. "Try to get some sleep. You're getting married."

"Do you think very many people will show up?"

"Oh yes." She sounded quite sure.

"That's unfortunate," I said under my breath. "I don't like being looked at."

"You're going to have to get used to it," she said apologetically. "That's your life now."

"That's unfortunate," I repeated in a whisper.

She laughed a little and kissed me on the back of my head. "Goodnight, new sister."

"Goodnight," I told her with a smile that she couldn't see. I hoped she'd heard it in my voice.

"Get up!"

Patricia was shouting and I was being shaken.

"Oh, hello," Patricia said exasperatedly when I peeked one of my eyes open at her. "I've only been in here yelling at you for the past ten minutes."

I suspected Abby and I had stayed up for far longer than I'd even realized because the light was not in the same place as it usually was on my curtains the next morning. It was normally barely there at all, given I was always awake just as the sun was coming up in the sky or before it, but it was bright today instead.

"Sorry," I said groggily as I sat up in bed. I would've slept through a Reaper attack just then, I was sure.

Abby left immediately to grab James so she could feed him. She'd been shaking me.

"We're already running behind schedule," Patricia said. I wondered if she was talking to herself instead of me.

I asked, "Ten minutes behind schedule because of me?"

"No, about an hour because of everyone," she said in frustration.

"Surely it's not—"

"Oh, I can assure you it's *quite* a big deal," she said firmly. "It's going to take *hours* to get you ready."

My eyes went wide. "*Hours?*"

"My god, Aster, do you *ever* listen to me?"

"Sometimes." It was better than . . . *Not often.*

I heard Abby snort in the other room.

"Well, you say things, and occasionally I don't know what you're talking about. . . ." After seeing the look on Patricia's face, I said, "I'll just be quiet now."

"Out of bed," she ordered.

I did as she instructed and attempted to find some clothing.

"No." She extended fabric to me. "Just throw this on over what you're wearing now. We have to go." She raised the volume of her voice. "Abby, I'll expect you as soon as you're done feeding James. Garin said he wants to watch him, so you can just take James to him."

"Heard," Abby said loudly from the other room as I was throwing some sort of covering over myself.

Patricia looked to me, confused. "What does that mean?"

"That she heard what you were saying," I answered blankly. How could anyone not *possibly* understand that?

Patricia shook her head and began ushering me from my bedroom.

"Don't ruin her day for her by being grouchy," Abby warned Patricia.

"It's the schedules." Patricia shook her head again. "People waiting and moving, talking and asking questions, and—" She threw up both her hands. "My god, Aster. How do you have so many things in your head at once and not lose your mind? God knows that's all you did during our time together is sit there and work things out in your head. It's obvious."

I shrugged uncomfortably. "Everything will be fine, Patricia." I ensured my voice was calm. "There's no reason to worry so much. I'm not so concerned with the details. I'm concerned about marrying Jastin. That's all that matters to me today." It was the plan for the day.

She took a deep breath and smiled a little. "Come along, dear," she said in her kinder voice as she tugged on my arm.

Though I was happy for her to use that voice, I was not happy she'd called me that.

"See you soon, Abby," I said. I hoped she knew I meant that I would like for her to hurry and not leave me alone with people fussing over me for too long.

Abby laughed. "Heard."

"Heard what?" Patricia asked as we began walking at a very fast pace through the garden toward the House—*too fast* for just waking with no threat in sight.

"Um." It was all that came out for a moment while I processed the fact that there *was* something threatening in sight. "That I would see her soon?"

CHAPTER
FIFTY-ONE

PREPARATIONS

OH, AND THEY DID FUSS over me.

Agatha insisted I needed assistance *bathing*, for god's sake, as if I hadn't done it on my own nearly all my life and was *somehow* incapable of doing it properly today. Counting only worked as much as it did, when it did. I pushed at her hands more times than I could count on both my own. She pretended not to notice, and she asked me a plethora of questions that I attempted to answer as politely as I could possibly manage.

Not losing my temper was maddeningly difficult. I did a *great deal* of counting.

When I was done bathing, and shaving, and doing all the necessary cleanliness things—and had stopped bleeding from the shaving—they began rolling my short hair up into some strange little contraptions.

I asked, "What is the purpose of those things?"

Abby had since joined us and somehow thought my question was funny.

"Curling your hair," Patricia replied.

"That doesn't explain the purpose," I stated.

"My, she's exhausting." Patricia shook her head. "Has she always been this way or has her father made it worse?"

"Ever since the day she was thrown onto my floor." Agatha laughed. "So I suspect she always has been, yes. I'd imagine her father has worsened it though, for her to give voice to things that drive her mad. She wouldn't always, but I'm sure you know how that eye of hers gets to twitching." She laughed again. "I also suspect her father will teach her how to stop that from happening. God knows he had to learn it himself."

It had been discussed.

Count, or scratch that itch until it's open and bleeding to heal itself.

"Aster, for just *one day* can you allow yourself not to think about the purposes behind things?" Patricia asked me. "I know you get it from him, but *one day*?"

"But if you explain the purpose of curling my hair to me, I'll stop thinking over it," I told her slowly, hoping that would help her grasp. "Is my hair not acceptable straight?"

"Your hair is lovely," Patricia said, which made it all the more baffling. "Well, it would be much lovelier if it was not so short, but you'll be beautiful when we're done with you."

"Jastin thinks I'm physically beautiful the way I am." I personally did not care either way, but I hoped she realized what she was doing had nothing to do with either of us so far as I knew.

"I'm sure he does, dear." Patricia took a deep breath. "Have you thought of growing your hair out?"

One.

Two.

I said, "It was always long."

"Well, what in the world happened to all of it?" She held a bit of it in her hand, as if she could make it grow unnaturally fast by sheer force of will. Or possibly as though that might help her discover where it had gone.

"Cut it off with a knife, didn't you?" Agatha laughed again. "You should've seen it. Looked like her entire head was lopsided before Amber got hold of it."

Patricia stopped what she was doing and stared at me in the mirror.

I looked absolutely *ridiculous* with those things on my head, and I knew it would only get worse as they added more of them. I hoped they intended on removing them from my head before I was expected to leave the room.

Patricia's voice was disbelieving when she spoke. "Why in the *world* would you do that?"

"Because Jastin liked my hair," I admitted quietly, feeling my face burning.

Nearly everyone in the room snorted, apart from Patricia.

"Came out of the trees with a great handful of it and threw it right at him, didn't you?" Agatha laughed again. "Oh, you looked *so* pleased with yourself. All the *stars*, everyone had gone absolutely *mad* that day."

I cleared my throat. "That was the day when we kissed for the first time."

"Before or after you threw your hair at him?" Agatha asked.

I did not look into the mirror to see her grin, but I heard it in her voice.

"After," I answered quietly. "First time he told me he loved me as well." I laughed a little under my breath. "He also told me I would never hear him say it again, but he says it all the time now. Funny, isn't it?"

"What?" Patricia asked.

"How, in hindsight, sometimes good days will end up being bad," I said. "And days you think are horrible at the time turn out to be some of the best memories you have." I smiled a little to myself. "That was a very good day looking back at it now."

Patricia said, "Well, hopefully today will be another of those very good days for you."

"I would've preferred marrying him in front of no one." I laughed. "So . . . all those details and schedules you're worried about? It's going to be a good day either way."

THE DRESS WAS HEAVY, quite a bit heavier than I remembered it being. It was difficult to stand there as they were trapping me inside it by lacing up the back tightly with pretty, white ribbon. That pretty ribbon was a deathtrap, cutting off the circulation of my body to my body.

"My god, he's going to be so frustrated trying to get this thing off you." Abby laughed. "Let alone your curses underneath."

One of the old women laughed as well. "Oh, but that's the point of it, isn't it?"

"What's the point?" I asked in confusion.

"Watching his fingers fumble all over the place, trying to get you out of it," she answered.

Disbelieving, I asked, "Is *that* why there's so much of it?"

The only sort of response I received was more snorting. Why did everyone think *everything* was so amusing? It really wasn't.

"I still don't understand."

"Our grandmother told us something about the queen once," the same woman said. "Our mother would've never said a word about it because she was a prude, just like my sister."

"Oh, be quiet," the other woman said.

"What did she tell you about the queen?" I'd only ever heard one thing about her, which had to do with the paintings.

"That when she was young, she used to come and ask our very distant grandmother to make her special corsets to wear sometimes beneath her dresses." The old woman who had called her sister and mother prudes answered the question.

"For what reason?" I shook my head. "Why would anyone *want* to wear them?"

"Watching the king fumble around with it as your husband will be doing with you tonight." She laughed. "We were told she used to speak a great deal with that distant grandmother of ours. She made her dresses all the time and . . . Well, topics come up. Said she used to laugh about her husband sometimes."

"*Laugh* about him?" That made no sense to me whatsoever.

"Never talk about the queen, do they?" she asked. "We heard she was a kind woman, always caring about everyone, but my god . . . she had that man wrapped around her finger. Did anything for her that she wanted, all the time."

I spoke carefully. "So you're saying she was bad."

Both of the old women snorted then.

"Of course not," the one said. "I believe all women are capable of doing that to a man. They just have to find the right one. And I also believe all women enjoy it."

"I don't believe that," I told her.

"We'll see if you change your mind by the morning." She peeked around my shoulder to wink at me.

"Or maybe she won't," her sister said. "They say that boy can't go an hour without coming to see her."

"Because he loves me," I stated blankly. "That's what love is, isn't it? Wanting to be with the other person?"

"But you're not the one going to see him, are you?" the prudish one asked with a laugh. I was beginning to wonder if her sister was wrong about her. "Too many things to do and you make him come to you. *Power*."

"*Love*," I insisted.

"Oh, I wish I could see how amused you'll be, watching him try to get you out of this," came from the non-prudish one. "Fingers fumbling everywhere."

"He's a Reaper," I said. "I highly doubt he'll be anything but composed."

"Reaper or not, he's still a man." The non-prudish one laughed. "A man pacing in a room right now, at that. Doesn't sound as composed as you'd think to me."

"I highly doubt that."

"He's most certainly wearing a path into the floor." Patricia laughed. She hardly ever laughed. "Your father told me as much this morning. Said he didn't know if Jastin had slept at all."

"I'm sure he was simply worried about my well-being is all," I said beneath my breath.

One of the old women laughed, though *none of this* was or had been funny. "If that's what you want to tell yourself."

My stomach suddenly did not feel good, and it was not the curses. "What if he doesn't show up?" I asked quickly. "He didn't tell me he wouldn't." Perhaps that was the reason for his pacing.

"My god, Aster." Abby laughed. "He'll be there."

"But what if he *isn't*?" My voice was far too high-pitched to sound normal.

They all laughed at me, but I was not laughing with them. That seemed to be the way it was and went. Everyone laughed at everything, and no one put enough thought into anything.

CHAPTER FIFTY-TWO

BEFORE

IF I'D THOUGHT STANDING THERE while they trapped me inside the dress was a difficult thing to do, sitting and breathing inside it was worse by far. It was nearly impossible to do both those things at once. But I sat there, patient and silent as they made up my face and then took the curler contraptions out of my hair. It looked ridiculous, even without them. I really didn't like the way it looked.

They began pinning it up, which I was grateful for, but I was quite certain it defeated the purpose of curling it in the first place. Couldn't they have simply done their pinning without all that extra work? Speaking of time and being *behind schedule*. . . . It seemed an improper utilization to me, right along with people making things worse or more complicated than they had to be.

It was certainly something to think on.

I stopped paying any attention to them, as it made no difference in anything whatsoever and I had no say in it regardless. So I sat there, not looking at my reflection, contemplating the way I would feel if Jastin was not there.

I contemplated how it would be dealt with.

How to handle it.

What to potentially say.

450

My god, hours passed. Hours stuck inside that room getting fussed over on the outside and worrying on the inside. They were still working on me after Abby was done, which I did not think was entirely fair. So, she stood there next to me, looking absolutely beautiful with her face and hair and in her dress. At least, if she was that beautiful and Jastin did not show up . . . perhaps no one would see my reaction. That was a positive point to think over, at least.

"Stop biting your nails!" they told me several times.

"I'm *required* to bite my nails," I shot back at them eventually, after becoming tired of hearing it.

Patricia's face scrunched in the way it often did—as if she'd stepped past something with a foul smell. "Why in the *world* would you be *required* to bite your nails?"

"So I don't rip them off or cut my palms open while punching things," I replied. "I can't cut them as short as I need them." My hands weren't cooperative enough. I suspected if I tried, my fingers would end up bloody messes. It had been difficult enough for me to cut them longer without damaging myself. Hands were bad things to damage. They were also bad things to be uncooperative. Horrendous things.

"She never bit them before," Agatha said in an apologetic tone.

It was almost like saying that, without my long hair and nails, I was not a girl. But, *oh*, I had been one before at some point.

I was more of a *girl* now than I'd ever been by far. I was *required* to be.

That particular conversation was dropped after that.

They talked amongst themselves, but I hardly listened to a word they were saying. I felt better, with Abby being there grinning at me all the while. It somehow made it all slightly more bearable. Like she thought it was amusing and perhaps I should as well. I didn't, but it helped in whatever way it did. It also made me reconsider some things.

It felt like forever until I heard the two words I'd been waiting to hear.

"All done."

"What's the purpose of this thing?" I asked as I pointed toward a strange-looking, thin piece of fabric that was *somehow* attached to my hair.

"To cover your face," one of the old women answered.

"That is the most ridiculous thing I've ever heard," I said in exasperation. "What was the purpose of doing all this only to cover it up?" Then I shook my head and said something that rarely came out of my mouth. "It's irrelevant. I don't even care."

Stupid. What an *utter waste* of time. But it was what it was, and it would be over soon. I believed.

"I'll go retrieve your father," Agatha said and then walked away.

I finally looked at my hair again. Somehow, they'd managed to pin it up while keeping the curls intact. I did not know how they'd managed that any more than I knew how the fabric was stuck on there.

"That looks quite nice," I said of my hair. "Strange, but . . . interesting and . . ." I sighed. "Yes, quite nice." They'd hardly put any sort of extra coloring on my face, for which I was very glad. Only enough that it made my eyes appear a little wider and my mouth look slightly different.

"Well, come over here and look at the full effect." Patricia sounded excited as she tugged me out of my chair.

"Curses," I reminded her as she tugged on me.

I'd learned curses did not like large and sudden movements, and I got a clear reminder of it just then. I would've used that as a valid point to keep myself out of them had my father not agreed from the start.

Sometimes large and sudden movements were quite necessary.

We stopped in front of a large mirror, the same one I'd seen my dress in for the first time. That dress looked slightly different now, with all the bits of excess fabric hidden and tucked away without pins, and there was something else about it that I couldn't quite place.

I could remember such a long time ago looking briefly into a small mirror and realizing I did not look like myself before being forced to go to a party for a Reaper's successful death mission. For *Chase's* successful death mission. I'd looked away from the image of myself then, but I did not look away now. Being different was not so frightening to me any longer.

"I'll go prepare Jastin," Patricia said quietly.

I asked, "When will I see him?"

"Very, *very* soon." She smiled.

I nodded. I could deal with all this, so long as I could be with him again soon. Get past this madness because all things passed. Then Patricia was gone.

"Are you happy with the end result?" one of the women asked as I wiped at my eyes.

"Don't touch your face!" the other exclaimed.

I sighed and dropped my hand. "I look like . . ." I started and then stopped speaking because I could not locate the appropriate word inside my head. "Like . . ." I struggled with it.

"A princess?" one of them offered.

I almost closed my eyes as I was shaking my head, but then I noticed . . . "You changed the back of it, didn't you?" I blinked in astonishment as I turned sideways and looked at my partially exposed back and the scars that ran along it. They would be visible to everyone, Reaper or not. "It wasn't cut this way before."

One of them smiled almost warily at me. "We did."

"Why?" I asked on a breath.

"Because no matter what you said during that first fitting . . ." the other started. "You wish people could see you for who you truly are, the people of Jarsil most of all."

"They're going to feel badly for me," I said firmly. "Have that look on their faces like Patricia had that day. They'll think I'm some poor little thing, won't they?" I could clearly see the benefit of being seen as less than what you were, but *that*?

"Perhaps," she said as she nodded her head. "Perhaps some of them will. But perhaps some of them will look at you, neither like a little girl or like a woman. Perhaps some of them will see it in you."

My brow furrowed. "See what?"

"Capability." The other answered and then shrugged. "Strength."

"If you wear yourself proudly . . ." I heard my father's voice behind me. "Some of them will have no choice but to see it. If someone looks at you and doesn't? They're not worth it." I turned around to face him and his eyes were only on mine and not my scars in the mirror when he stepped closer and said, "You look beautiful."

Quietly, I said, "Thank you."

He looked quite dashing himself, but I did not feel like telling him as much. I was sure he knew and had likely been told a ridiculous amount of times already. People, Reapers included, fawned over him like mad when they got the chance. He had some issues with that rather often, especially with the opposite sex.

"Couldn't convince her to take that necklace and bracelet off," one of the women said.

"No, I suspect not." My father chuckled. "That was her mother's necklace and Jastin's son gave her that bracelet." He smiled at me to say, "When Jastin gives you the ring back, you'll never *have* to conceal it from anyone. I'm so very happy to tell you those words. It was something your mother always wished for."

"I'm very happy to hear it," I whispered.

"Stop making her cry!" one of the old women exclaimed. "If she does any more of it, we're going to have to fix her face."

My father pursed his lips and narrowed his eyes at her, partially over being shouted at and partially because of the *fix the face* bit. But then he sighed and looked back to me. "You remember what happens next, don't you? We've gone over it—the words and all that."

I nodded because we had gone over and *over* it all. "Am I really doing this?" I asked him, hardly believing it. "Is this actually happening right now? It doesn't feel like it is."

"Oh, it's happening." Abby laughed beside me which caused my father to turn his attention to her.

"My god, aren't you stunning?"

"Isn't she?" I laughed. "I'm very much hoping she'll draw attention away from me."

"That's funny," my father said with a quiet chuckle under his breath. He saw the confused look on my face and shook his head. "Another time." Then he put the fabric over my face and said, "Let's go do this." He paused when taking my hand. "Try very hard not to be overwhelmed."

Wary, I asked, "By what?"

"Everything," he replied.

I was already overwhelmed, and that did not give me very much hope for how the rest of my day would go.

Then he smiled a little. "All things shall pass. Tomorrow is a new day." He tapped beneath my chin a few times with the side of his pointer finger. "Remember."

I smiled a little as well, nodding.

CHAPTER FIFTY-THREE

ALONE

Y FATHER PAUSED before we reached the door we were required to exit through. Abby had to go before us, though I still did not quite understand the purpose in any of it. She stood there waiting for an order from my father, far enough away not to overhear anything said, but he still put his back to her.

"Do you truly love him?" he asked me, so quietly. He'd barely said the words.

"I do," I answered without hesitation.

"I'm going to ask you again. . . ." His eyebrows rose. "Are you *certain*?"

I nodded. "I do love him, Father." I took in a deep breath. "This is the right thing."

He nodded in what appeared to be acceptance, and he seemed prepared to move on. "My daughter." His voice was full of affection as he squeezed my hand. "If I had been told eleven years ago that you and I would be standing where we are today in the positions we're in . . . I would never have believed it. Not of myself. But *you*?" He paused for a moment to shake his head at me. "You were always destined for something greater. I feel as though I was put in this position by some outside force, only so you could end up here."

"That's ludicrous, Father," I whispered. He had to know it was.

"Is it?" he asked. "Anders and I should've died. Many times. But here we are." He paused to smile at me before continuing on. "Our people love you for what Anders and I have done for them. My men love you because they can't help themselves. They are much harder to sway than normal people, though you likely can't see it. And one day, my dear girl, you're going to do everything you dream about with all of them standing behind you. You're going to free the world of our evil."

"How can you say that?" I asked him on a breath.

"Because you won't stop," he said assuredly. "Not even after it's done. Nothing will ever be good enough for you, so you will continue to fight until long after there's nothing left to fight. So, when you step through these doors . . . don't look at the nonsense around you. Look at our people. Watch their faces. And when you reach Jastin, look at the man who will be standing beside you the entire time, long after I'm gone. The city will be yours one day. Our men will ensure it. So, you look at the person who knows beyond a shadow of a doubt almost as well as I do that you'll be amazing when that day comes."

I thought my father was being absolutely ridiculous, but I did not want to tell him as much.

I reached my hand up and wiped away a tear as it was rolling down his cheek. I had a strange urge to rub his chin, but he was clean-shaven all the time in Jarsil, unlike how he had been at our small home in the wilderness.

He smiled, stiffly. "I'm telling myself that you will always be my special little girl. This day does not change that, just as you looking as you do now hasn't."

Tears welled in my eyes. "Of course I'll always be yours, Father."

I glanced over at Abby and saw her wiping gingerly at her eyes. She smiled at me a little.

"Go on," my father said to her.

And she went.

There were not a dozen Reapers standing with my father and me in the corridor that would lead us outside. There were only six of them and they would follow behind me as my father and I made our long walk. Every Reaper in the city was working today, patrolling up and down the lines of organized people that were just through the doors we were standing in front of. Every single one, supposedly. I hoped it was unnecessary. I hoped there was maybe only one small grouping of citizens.

My father squeezed my hand again. "I love you, Flower."

A tear fell from my eye when I said something I'd not said in nearly eleven years. "I love *you*, Father."

He did not allow me to wipe the tears away from his own face again. He took my arm in his and opened the door with them on display for everyone to see.

It was not a small grouping.

I was overwhelmed.

Silence, absolute silence, from what had to be thousands of people who were all turned to look at me as I would pass by them. Thousands. We exited through a side door of the House and would walk the long way to reach the courtyard that was positioned in front of the House. It was the same walk the queen took when she married the king. Strategic moves that truly, in this moment, did not matter to me at all. I was getting married, and for just a moment, I did not care so much about logic and strategy.

And the flowers everywhere.

No, I was not to look at the nonsense, my father said. I was to look at the people.

I kept my face forward and my back straight as I walked, and I watched their faces before I would pass. And afterward, in my wake, I would hear breaths catching in throats. But they didn't even whisper. The only sounds I could hear were my own breathing over theirs, my footsteps, and their feet as they turned while I passed.

We walked forever, it seemed. I wanted to close my eyes, but . . . I also wanted to remember this moment and the absolute absurdity of it. The madness.

The only time my face was not directly forward was as we were passing under one part of the wall through the city. I looked up at the Reapers with their bows, patrolling above us like protective gods that had fallen from the sky and dangled there, just above everyone's eyes and reach.

That was their intention, their purpose from being transformed from normal people into the monsters everyone thought they were past the walls of our city. My father had saved the Reapers of his cities, but I wanted to save them all. Fix them. Remind them they were human and had the right to things all humans should have the right to. Children, families, love . . . the right to sleep at night without being haunted.

They should not have to be so haunted.

If the kings could see their creations now . . . they would be so ashamed of themselves for destroying people's humanity. *Their* people.

But they were not destroyed, not all of them, only lost. Lost and needing to be pointed in a direction and told to go.

I needed to fix it.

I was still thinking over that when Jastin came into my view.

He had cut his hair, I could tell. It wasn't shaven closely all over like most Reapers because he was not required to do so anymore, and he knew I liked the waves in his hair. Still, it was shorter than it had been and was nearly shaven on the bottom, but not quite. I liked it better now.

What a ridiculous thing to think about.

My brother looked quite impeccable where he stood beside him. The bruise I'd made on his face was entirely healed, and he was actually smiling what seemed to be genuinely at our father and me as we walked together. I was surprised. Abby stood farther off on Jastin's other side and was smiling at us as well. But it was Jastin's face that struck me.

It wasn't necessarily a smile there, but it was almost as though every one of his breaths showed on his face. The closer we came to him, the more I could see. I saw every emotion passing across his features—excitement, anxiety, happiness, worry, contentedness, relief.

He did not truly smile until my father placed my hand in his, and then . . . he did not stop smiling.

I was glad the thin fabric—a veil, they had called it—concealed my face enough so that he could not so clearly see the tears running down it if he could at all.

I looked backward at my father as he scooped up both Aston and Arlene and held them close to him under either arm. His grandchildren. Chandler standing nearby him caught my eye very briefly with James in his arms. He did not look terrified now of the small thing in his arms. I—

My father caught my attention and nodded forward.

I turned to the man who would marry Jastin and me.

I'd been introduced to the man and had seen him several times so that we could go over this moment. The words. The words in some strange language that neither Jastin nor I understood a single bit of. I doubted anyone at all understood the man as he began speaking.

Praying was what my father had called it, though it was not praying the likes of which I knew of the word.

He'd told me that, in the time of kings, people had believed in gods—some otherworldly beings that made the sun come up in the sky and the crops flourish or fail. It was another word I'd not ever heard in that sense, not as a believed real, literal thing. He'd told me that there were men and women who would instruct people how to live their lives in satisfactory ways and that they had their own special language to speak to those gods.

The Reapers had forbidden the practice of worshiping of any sort, and they had killed most everyone who refused to follow by their rules. But not everyone. Knowledge was something that could not ever be entirely repressed and forgotten, not so long as there were people who refused to forget. And some people refused to forget about their invisible gods.

It was risky, I believed, to have one of them here openly in front of everyone. I believed it would put the man in front of us in some sort of danger. The man did not care and . . . was I not hoping that people could be free to do what they thought was best for them?

I personally did not truly believe in any sort of god, nor did I believe that hardly anyone else here did either, but . . . I would not complain about someone who *did* believe in such things wishing good for Jastin and me to them.

When he spoke in that other language, he did so almost beneath his breath.

Eventually he began speaking our language, but I hardly listened to him. I stared at Jastin and waited for my cue to speak. He and I were only required to say six words apiece and we both said them at our respective times after the man had given off a rather lengthy list of things that we were supposed to do for one another. I did not need to be told what to do for him.

"Until I draw my last breath," we both said when we were required to.

I cried. And he cried, though I did not know if it was for the same reasons as I did.

I removed a ring from my right thumb and put it on the fourth finger of his right hand, and he removed my mother's ring from the top of his left pinky and put it on the fourth finger of my left one. Rings went on the non-dominant hand because the person you marry is supposed to make you stronger in the ways you're weak. I liked that idea, but he and I had discussed switching the appropriate hands to confuse people.

The man said something I didn't quite hear, and Jastin moved the fabric over my face.

There was no one in that moment. No one standing beside or behind us. Only his face and his hands cupping my cheeks, both his thumbs wiping tears away as they fell. Only his mouth when he kissed me.

Even when the thousands of people began cheering . . . there was no one else. The sounds drifted and floated away like the people who were making them while the two of us stayed firmly on the ground with one another.

We were alone when we got married, just like we'd wanted.

460

CHAPTER
FIFTY-FOUR

ONLY

I WAS SWEPT AWAY in a sea of those floating people. I kept one hand in Jastin's as we were pushed and pulled in directions we did not want to go. I feared I would get lost if we were separated and that we'd have no hope of finding one another again in all this. So, I kept one hand in his, holding onto him as though my very life depended on it, and he had Aston tucked away under his other arm.

His son smiled at us endlessly and, in a way, it felt as if the three of us were inside a bubble together, somehow closed off from that sea of people despite being in the middle of it. Despite being moved by it. How we didn't want to be. Where we didn't want to be. Powerless to stop it. Incapable.

Aston had his head resting contentedly against Jastin's neck, tucked under his chin, but he stared at me. I could not hear his voice over the cacophony when he said it, but I knew precisely what it was that he'd said.

My mother, his lips read. So simple.

Jastin must've heard him because he moved slightly and kissed the top of Aston's head. I was certain we all had tears in our eyes as we smiled at one another.

It was later, though not very much, when I felt tiny little fingers on the top of my back when it was turned to the two of them, tracing the lines there.

When I looked back at Aston and saw the expression on his face when he took a deep breath, I knew someone had seen in me what the old women hoped they would.

Strong, his little eyes said as they blinked at me.

If the only person who saw that in me was my husband's son . . . I was happy. It was far more than enough.

No one asked me about my scars. No one mentioned them at all when they spoke to me, but I could feel their eyes when Jastin would remove his hand from mine and rub there when a somewhat peaceful moment in the storm came. Their eyes were on us anyway, so I pretended not to notice.

People spoke to us endlessly. They asked us questions and we answered, responding to them on instinct. I did not truly know what I was saying to anyone, nor did I particularly care so long as I gave the correct responses. The only conversation that stood out clearly to me was when the two old ladies who had made my dress came over to us.

"We thought it would be no matter if our knowledge was lost," one of them said quietly. "I'm thinking now that we've been wrong."

"I am glad to hear it," I told her. "What changed your mind?"

The other said, "The realization that there may very well be a queen walking the streets of Jarsil again one day."

I pursed my lips together tightly for a moment and said nothing on that particular matter when I spoke. "Have you decided to take up an apprentice?"

"Two, if you'll permit it, Milady."

I sighed and did not insist again that they called me by my name. "I have an idea in mind about one, if you have no objection toward me having a say in the matter. And the other . . . Will you take a child from the orphanage?"

"What do you mean . . . *take a child from the orphanage*?" one asked in confusion.

"Those children have no homes, no families," I said. "You both said you couldn't bear the thought of bringing children into the world until it was too late for you to have done so. Kill several birds with one stone. Give a child a home, have a family for the remainder of the time you've been given, pass along your knowledge." I stared hard at their blinking faces. "I'll make arrangements and accompany you there in a few days' time, if you'd like."

"Are you certain your father wouldn't object, Milady?"

"Quite," I said. "You may go ask him yourselves or allow me to deal with it for you, which I will do once this day is over. If that's what you want, I'll ensure it happens."

"You are . . . a remarkable woman," the other told me. They took one another's hands and began to walk away.

"Thank you," I said quickly. "For spending so much of your time on this dress. It's beautiful."

"I'm hoping you'll be wanting our services again very soon," one said. I would have to learn their names at some point. "Nice thing, seeing that our heads weren't filled with entirely useless knowledge all our lives."

"I'm sure I will," I told them with a smile. "And I'm glad you're happy."

"Please enjoy your day," the other said. "Everyone will return to their homes at some point."

She waggled her fingers at me a little which made me disguise a laugh as a cough.

I looked at Jastin and he narrowed his eyes at me, but he said nothing.

After that, Aston insisted Jastin put him down though I did not know why. He took turns holding either of our hands, usually depending on who was being spoken to at any given time. The one who was not speaking directly to anyone had to hold his hand. I thought it was quite funny. He played with the bracelet he'd given me several times while he was holding mine. I would smile down at him and he would seem pleased.

I would catch him looking at the Reapers who were standing guard near us, entirely businesslike and impartial as they watched the people. Aston did not smile as much, the more time he spent watching them, but he smiled while he was not.

After *hours* of that, Jastin whispered, "I want to show you something."

I smiled at him as he led me away from the people and into the House. They followed after us, organized by the Reapers.

We went into the room directly adjacent to the main door of the House, which was space I'd never been inside of. It too was some sort of banquet hall, I discovered upon entry, though it was easily twenty times the size of the one we'd had my birthday get-together in. So many rooms and so much space that was so rarely put to any sort of use.

There were flowers everywhere. Flowers on tables and flowers in strange vase contraptions. Flowers near the musicians who were getting their instruments set up and in place. I hardly noticed any of that, and I did not wonder where they'd all come from because I was looking up.

There were paper stars hanging from the ceiling by some sort of string. Hundreds of them.

"The children made them," Jastin said. "Every child in the city made one for you."

I smiled through my tears and heard myself laugh quietly. "Was that your idea?"

He bit his bottom lip and narrowed his eyes at me. Then . . . he nodded.

"I love it."

He grinned. "I figured it would distract you from the flowers."

"That's not why you did it," I said with another quiet laugh.

Aston tugged on my hand, which made me look down at him.

He was clearly confused when asking, "Why are you so happy over paper stars?"

"Because your father calls me Star when he's happy with me," I answered and then wiped at my eyes. I unfortunately remembered too late that I was not supposed to touch my face.

"Why?" Aston asked curiously. "Your name is Aster."

Jastin spent a very short moment wiping his thumb near my eyes. I supposed I'd smudged something. Then he knelt in front of his son and pointed up at the ceiling.

"You know how you look outside at night and see all the stars in the sky?"

Aston nodded.

"You know how there always seems to be one that's bright enough to draw your attention away from all the others?"

Aston shook his head then.

"You'll see it one day," Jastin told him. "And when you do . . . you won't ever care about the other ones again. She's the only star in my sky and she lights everything up for me, like daylight in the darkness. That's why I call her that. You'll find your own star one day." Aston smiled, which made Jastin clarify with, "When you're much older."

CHAPTER FIFTY-FIVE

STEPPING ON

E ATE FOOD, THOUGH I ATE VERY LITTLE. The curses did not like food, and I didn't have much of an appetite due to the people staring at me anyhow. I did not care about their staring at all when there was music and I was dancing. I did not even care about the curses while I was dancing. I wouldn't let the curses not liking dancing ruin it for me.

I felt as though I danced with everyone.

I danced and laughed with all the people I knew and then so many that I didn't.

The Reapers in the room were not so happy about random people being near me, or Jastin, or my father, or my brother, or Abby, or nearly anyone, really.

I would dance with the Reapers as well and they would not be happy at first, but I would get them smiling by stepping on their feet and then apologizing for it endlessly. Sometimes I did it on purpose, sometimes I did not. Sometimes they would accuse me of doing so on purpose, and sometimes they would not.

Either way, I would get them smiling and then move or be passed on.

And I was indeed passed on. Like an object. An object to be used for a purpose.

466

Jastin and I never stayed out of one another's eyeshot, apart from a few times where he left for a short while. He was never gone for long, though I had no idea where he went. He would make funny faces at me while he was dancing with his own random people, and I would smile. I realized I'd spent so long smiling that my face felt quite strained. It was not entirely unpleasant, only strange.

Aston hogged a great deal of my attention for a rather long while. He would frown in my direction occasionally, depending on whomever I was dancing with at the time. If he did not like them, he would come and tug at my dress. When whomever it was that he did not particularly like had gone a suitable enough distance away from me, he would return to where he'd been standing nearby. He would continue watching and waiting until the next time he felt required to come and save me from the next person. It was not *too* long before Jastin noticed and came to scoop him up, putting a stop to the exercise.

That had been my favorite part of the day, as exhausting as it was in a sense. Trying to discover all the reasons why he'd done as much would take some thinking and reflection, I was sure.

Chandler danced with Abby for nearly the entire time. I would catch the two of them smiling at one another, and I believed she'd lied to me when she told me she was not in love with him. Perhaps she did not know what love was to be aware of it when she was in it.

Did anyone?

Chandler danced with me for a short time and would pinch me when I would laugh at him. It was funny to me, for some unknown reason, to see him dance. Or perhaps it was simply funny to dance *with* him. Or perhaps it was something else. I did at some point begin feeling odd and started to be on the verge of crying. We parted ways then.

When Stelin was not dancing with Kay, he would watch her and smile to himself. It took him a very long time to come dance with me.

"No females," was the first thing he said.

"I assumed as much. You would've told me earlier if there had been." I did not tell him how long I'd spent watching the doorknob while being prepared.

He smiled at me a little, but he could not keep it on his face for very long.

"No one trusts me," he said. "You should've seen your brother's face when I told him I would be with them that night. It's like he thought I was going to try to kill all of them." He shook his head and looked over the top of mine. "And they all watched me like they thought the exact same thing last night."

"All of them?" I asked curiously, which brought his eyes back to mine as we spun around together. "Did Jastin?"

He shook his head in response and his brow furrowed. "Why do you trust me when no one else does? I know it goes against your better judgment. You know the likelihood that you're wrong about me, and you know the consequences if you are."

"Wrong or not, people can change."

He nodded. "So you believe you're wrong."

"I didn't say that," I told him. "Sometimes . . . sometimes taking a leap of faith is worth the risk that you'll fall."

The two of us stopped spinning and stood there staring at one another.

"This isn't only your life that you're risking, Aster." His voice was both firm and quiet at once. "Your decisions on things like this affect *everyone* now. Do you realize that?"

"If I were taken out of the equation and it was only the people, I would admit that I would be *very* worried about you."

His face barely scrunched. "What does that mean?"

"You've been looking for a friend for a very long time," I said. "You wouldn't allow yourself to betray one after you found them. You may not care about many people or much, but you care about *me*. That's enough for me."

"How do you *know*?" His jaw clenched.

"Because I can picture precisely what would happen in a literal leap of faith," I said slowly. "I can picture myself jumping over a gap, missing the mark, and dangling off the side. I can picture you being the only person there to pull me up."

"And you think I would."

"I think you would stare into my face." My voice was so quiet. "You would stand there while I was slipping away and I would see the indecision on your face when I looked up at you. You would be torn, wouldn't you? I know you would. I know that as well as I know that you'd pull me up before I fell. Doubts and hesitations don't change the end result." I paused. "You wouldn't let me fall. You couldn't do that to me. Letting something happen on any terms but his doesn't *stop* it. I know you know that."

"You're guilting me," he said in disbelief.

"If that was what it took . . . then *yes*." I nodded. "I would do that to save you from yourself."

"Is that why you've been doing everything you have been?" he asked. "Is that why? So when you're dangling I'll be obligated to help you?"

Though I did not know what had upset or shaken him past fear . . .

I smiled a little at the floor and shook my head. "You understand the purpose of friends, don't you? Every day, you jump a little more and take the risk they won't be there when you need them to be. Every time you jump and they're there for you, it builds up a debt. So the two people build up some giant mountain of things they owe the other that can only be repaid by making the other person's mountain larger. It chips away and then grows again on both sides.

"You've already saved my life once, Stelin," I told him. "More than that. More than anyone could possibly know. I would do whatever it took to show you, to *prove* to you it was worth your while to have done so. No matter what anyone else believes, no matter what *you* believe of yourself . . . you have a friend in me. Only you can break the trust I have for you. And as I said, I know you won't do that. You wouldn't allow yourself to, even if a part of you wanted to—the part that still loves your father no matter how much you hate him. That's what matters. That's what's important to me. The two people inside you are irrelevant when both of them care for me. Both of mine care for you as well. And I understand, Stelin. You and I are choosing our mountain."

He shook his head, but he reached out and pulled me close to him.

And that was when we hugged for the first time.

"You shouldn't put so much trust in people," he whispered. "Hardly anyone deserves it."

"Yes, but some people are worth it," I said against his chest. "One day you'll realize that you are, even if it takes me beating it into your head for the next ten years."

"And would you do that?"

"I promise I would," I told him without hesitation. "That's what friends are supposed to do. Now, go on back to Kay and tell her that Abby and I would like to have a stay-over with her sometime in the future."

He took a step back with the most baffled expression on his face. "A what?"

"I'm sure she'll understand." I smiled. "I'm finding I very much enjoy having friends."

It was not such a very long time ago, despite how it felt, that I'd not even believed they truly existed.

IF IT HAD TAKEN STELIN A LONG TIME to come dance with me, it took my brother twice as long. So many people had already gone, but still nowhere near all of them.

"I've had a tail since yesterday," he said as soon as he had one hand in mine and the other on my waist.

"Yes." My voice was impassive.

He slowly nodded his head. "You've sent Reapers to follow me."

"Yes," I admitted.

"To tell you what I'm doing?"

"To keep you *alive*," I said firmly. "I don't care what you do on your own time, which, if you spoke to whomever it was, they would tell you as much." I pursed my lips for a moment. "You and I need to come to an understanding, big brother."

"Which is?"

"For you to understand that I'm not trying to steal anything from you," I said. "These people around us are not yours or mine. They're not even our father's. They're our *responsibility*. If we can all work with one another, things will be better for everyone. And we cannot work together until you get it through that thick skull of yours that I'm not trying to steal your life."

"Aster, those people might be ours . . ." He spoke deliberately. "But the Reapers? They belong to our father, and to you."

"Reapers are people too, Ahren," I told him quietly. He didn't understand.

"You wouldn't say that if you'd seen the things we've done."

"Perhaps that's why they're biased against me," I said. "Because I haven't seen as much and I'm not biased against them. Stop for a moment."

He did.

I gestured around. "Look at them. Look how proud they are to be doing what they are, to be protecting everyone. That's what Reapers were intended to be, not what they'd all turned into. They *are* people, just like *you* are a person."

"You don't understand our potential to do bad." He shook his head. "The knowledge in our heads, how *easy* it is. You don't understand."

"I have a better understanding than you believe I do," I told him. There was a very brief moment where I saw Chase smiling as he flipped a knife at the end of a hallway. Jastin paralyzing a man before interrogating him. Anders, making a joke while a man bled out on the floor only a few short feet away. "But I also understand a Reaper's potential to do *good*. Knowledge is only knowledge, and you can tell me it's easy to carry it out, but . . . even if it is at the time, it's not easy afterward. I know that as well as you do. And I also know that . . . people don't *want* to do those things. Not most of them, at least."

Ahren said, "You cannot *change* what we *are*."

"Our father did," I stated evenly. "Tell me he hasn't. Tell me he hasn't at least started the change."

"You believe you can." He sort of gaped. "Fix everything and everyone." His brow furrowed. "Some broken things cannot be repaired, baby sister. Sometimes the best option is to dispose of them."

"I *know* I can," I told him firmly. Then I took a deep breath and shook my head. "And if I can't . . . I'm still going to try. Please tell me it's not worth putting things aside and working together. It's worth not giving up hope in you all."

My brother looked at me and then looked at the Reapers standing near enough to be overhearing the entirety of our conversation.

Most of them pretended as though they were not listening, but I knew they were. They were inescapable.

"You lied to me," I said quietly, which made his eyes dart back to mine. "The day I told you Jastin and I were getting married. You lied when you told me you don't hate me. A part of you does."

It took him quite some time to say the word, "Yes."

I nodded my head and blinked a tear from my eye. "I would very much like to stop worrying that your hatred for me will be the thing that gets me killed."

"Are you saying that because they're listening?"

"I'm saying it because it's true," I told him. "And they're *always* listening. I'm telling you because I'm hoping if you know that, for now, I'm more concerned for myself because of you than I am Hasting . . . it might make you see."

"You're legitimately worried I would try to kill you," he said to the floor. When he looked up at me, he had tears in his own eyes. "That's a lot different than worrying I'm a spy."

"It's along the very same lines," I said. "But yes, infinitely worse. *Hate*?" I shook my head. "It's the most evil thing in our world, and it makes people *do* very evil things. I want that evil gone from you because you're so much better than that. I can see that you are, but I'm not certain whether you do or not."

He clenched his jaw and said nothing.

I very hesitantly reached out to take his hand.

"We must at least *try* to fix things," I nearly whispered. "Can't you see that we *must* try? If we don't . . . we'd only be perpetuating the evil cycle our world is stuck in. We must try to be better. And if you and I cannot even fix things amongst ourselves . . . what hope would *either* of us be to this city?"

He said nothing.

I shook my head and sighed. "We *must* try, big brother. If we don't . . . then I fear everything good in this world will be gone. And you and I? We would be responsible for it. We must do more." Desperately I asked, "Can't you see?"

He still said nothing in response, but he returned his other hand to my waist and began spinning me around in circles. I did not step on my brother's feet the same way I did everyone else's. I supposed some things depended on more variables than what was initially apparent.

One must clearly see all potential variables to cut down the likelihood of flukes.

CHAPTER
FIFTY-SIX

SEASONS

J ASTIN AND I WERE NOT SPINNING in circles but holding one another closely and hardly moving at all. Some people stood around and watched us as we moved, I knew, but some people were still dancing near us. I did not think they would ever leave, so I pretended as though they weren't there at all.

Stewart came up beside us and said, "You know you have to share the bride."

Jastin asked, "How many dances have you already had with her?"

Stewart laughed. "A few."

I had no idea who I'd danced with or how many times, as they'd mostly been blurry faces to me. I *did* know I'd danced with Stewart four times. I did also know that the stepping on his feet had been intentional. It had been quite enjoyable as a whole, but it had also been somewhat upsetting.

Jastin leaned over and rested the side of his face on the top of my head. "I have to share her all the time. I believe I'm done sharing my wife for now."

I smiled, my face against his chest. His wife. I was his *wife*. What a strange thing to be to a person.

My eyes were closed so I didn't know when Stewart left, only that it was some time later when my father came up and said, "He's out."

Jastin said, "I'll take him back to the school."

"No, no," my father said quickly. "I'll go with Ahren to take Arlene."

I finally opened my eyes and stared for a moment at Aston, fast asleep in my father's arms. I reached out and pushed a bit of dark hair away from his forehead.

He did not stir at all. I wondered what age Reapers were when they could wake from the slightest sound or touch. I hoped he had many, *many* more nights before that time came upon him.

I wished so badly that it never would.

It was after my father had gone that I asked, "Do you think we could slip away without anyone noticing?"

Jastin laughed. "You know we can't."

They were all watching.

"Yes, and I also know that I don't care," I said against his chest. I took a step back and looked up at him. "Do you intend on kissing me for longer than five seconds when we leave?"

A very slow grin spread over his face before he nodded.

I took his hand. "Let's go. I'm dying to get this damned dress off." Everyone had seen it. It had served its purpose.

I IGNORED THE STARES, and the grins, and the giggling girls as Jastin and I went. Girls as a whole giggled quite a lot more than I did, I'd noticed.

Quite a lot more.

I felt rather lightheaded as we walked together through the halls that would take us into the garden, and then, into my living quarters. I decided to account that to an entire day spent in the curses rather than some euphoric feeling of being married. It was more logical. Wasn't it?

Perhaps not; because when I directly thought the words *I'm married* inside my head, the strange feeling only intensified.

I did not hear the Reapers as they trailed along on all sides of us, but I saw them. I pretended not to. I pretended we'd stopped in the garden simply because we wanted to do so and not so they could do a sweep of my quarters to ensure no one was inside.

I did not allow myself to think about how risky they likely believed it had been—allowing so many people inside the House with such easy access to where I stayed.

The archers on the wall would've shot anyone down, I knew, and I did not want to think about any of that. I did not want to think about Reapers, and spies, and killing.

I was surprised by how . . . *bright* it seemed when we stepped inside and closed the door behind us, finally making us alone. There was too much brightness coming from my bedroom.

Was it Jastin's bedroom as well now, technically?

Was everything ours and not mine or his?

I almost asked him if he had any things that he would want to bring here, but I stopped myself and made a note inside my head to ask him at a time when it felt a more relevant thing to speak of. I was thinking about more pressing issues, currently.

Him leading me into the bedroom, for one. And two and three. Perhaps four as well.

I wondered what the purpose of all the candles in the room was. It was a fire hazard, most certainly. Did people want to see the sort of thing they did on their wedding night clearly?

He was grinning at the—likely confused—look on my face when he said, "It's supposed to be romantic."

"I'm not familiar with the word," I told him. "What does it mean?" If I knew what the word meant, I could understand the purpose of it. If I understood the purpose of it, I could stop myself from thinking about it unnecessarily.

He smiled, but he did not laugh at me. "It *means* . . ." He put a hand on either side of my waist. "That someone does something for another person because they believe they'll like it and that it would make them happy." He scrunched his nose a little before adding, "More or less."

"*Oh*," I said. "That sounds nice. Did you do this for me, then?" I decided against counting all the candles in the room because I was quite certain it would entirely defeat the purpose of them being there.

He narrowed his eyes. "Possibly."

I pursed my lips because he was silly and I didn't really know what else to do. Why not just say as much? It took me a moment to get around that.

"You're very romantic, aren't you?" I asked. "You're often doing nice things for me and saying nice things to me." I gestured around the room. "I very much like the way this looks in here, although I cannot exactly explain why."

"You're nervous," he said slowly. "You ramble that way when you get uncomfortable."

I spent too long a moment thinking over the word *romantic* and wondering if there was much more to it than I had understood in his explanation.

I said nice things to him quite often, but . . .

I thought about the differences between when the two of us said nice things to one another.

I'd always thought Jastin and I were quite similar, but I wondered now if I had been mistaken about that. When he spoke to me, he spoke with feelings. When I spoke to him, I spoke with facts even if feelings were involved.

I thought about the way it made me feel when he said certain things to me, explaining about stars and talking about the ways I had changed his life. There was a certain tone of his voice and a look on his face—something that made the words more than words, something that made the words everything they had the potential to be.

I realized I wanted to fill my entire world with those words said in that tone of his voice and that look on his face.

"You know we don't have to do anything if you don't want to," he said believably.

I was hardly listening to him as I stood there thinking.

"You know that, right?"

But shouldn't he be able to feel the way I felt when he spoke to me and looked at me in the ways he did? I didn't want to be exceptional with other people and yet rubbish at being in love with my husband. I wanted him to feel as special as he made me feel.

I only spoke words to him; I could see that now. Words and nothing more. Words about feelings I felt without showing him the feelings behind them. Emotionless words about love.

I was *exactly* like those blank-faced Reapers who followed around me, feeling things but never truly showing them to anyone.

I was worse. I was quite sure . . .

I was much worse.

My entire life could be purpose and logic, but . . . I did not want it to be that way with him. Couldn't I be free of myself with my *husband*?

I had a husband, and he was standing in front of me now. I had a husband.

I fought against the urge to clear my throat and was startled that I won. I never won against myself.

He looked very confused at the smile on my face. It felt a little strange where it sat.

A tear fell from my eye, and I didn't ignore it because it was not irrelevant, like I normally told myself they were. I paid the proper attention to it as it rolled down my cheek.

My voice was very quiet when I said, "I want to show you the way I feel about you."

"You show me every day," he said with an almost wary smile.

I shook my head shortly at him. "I love you." There was something different about my voice, though I could not understand what it was.

It struck me only long enough for me to pause slightly and realize it must have sounded different to him as well by the expression on his face.

"I love you so much it hurts," I said. "Like every second I'm not near you, my heart rips apart. I don't want you to leave when you do, and I don't want to leave when I do. I often don't want to be around anyone else, or even myself if you're not there. And I've tried not to smile while I think about you because I was worried everyone would think me so weak if they knew. And I didn't show you any more than I have because I couldn't."

I understood the difference in my voice when I felt the tears rolling down my face. I understood the difference because I had never known that it almost tickled when they fell. I nearly laughed when I realized I'd never really felt them before, in all that had fallen, but I could not laugh because of what it meant.

So cold, Jastin's voice said inside my head.

I was so cold, like endless snow in a never-ending winter. An ice princess stuck inside an ice prison she'd built for herself.

I smiled because I did not feel cold in that moment. I did not think about how strange it felt when thawing out like the snow in the spring as my own season was coming to an end. I did not worry that it was bad or that there was something wrong with me.

There was not anything wrong with me.

I quietly said, "I don't feel so cold right now."

I watched his face. He was not confused or wary like I'd believed. He was stunned.

I reached up and touched his face, and then . . . I kissed him.

I'd shared so many different sorts of kisses with him, but this one was so different from all the rest. Had I never realized the way it felt? Had I never really allowed myself to feel it properly?

I closed my eyes tightly when I pulled away and said, "*Please* get this dress off me."

He did not smile. He just nodded.

He walked around behind me and spent a very short moment touching the top of my back before attempting to begin the process of releasing me from my cage. I could hear his breathing and tell that it sounded almost . . . *frustrated*.

I peeked over my shoulder.

He pursed his lips briefly when his eyes met mine. "You should see the knot those women put on this thing."

I watched him shake his head as he tried, and failed, again.

"I told myself I wasn't going to act like an idiot," he stated to the back of my dress.

Something popped into my head, some tiny little snippet of the women's conversation earlier that I'd not been paying much attention to at all.

I heard the non-prudish one's laughter when she said . . . *Tell him to pull, dear.*

I hadn't known what she was talking about at the time and she would not tell me when I'd inquired about it. I supposed I understood perfectly now.

"They said for me to tell you to pull," I told him quietly.

I watched him pull on one part of the ribbon. It did nothing. He pulled on another and it did nothing as well. And then, on the next, the knot seemed to just . . . disappear.

He shook his head like he was either amused or impressed. I was not certain which one he was, nor did I particularly care.

I'd expected for him to remove the ribbon entirely, as it had not been on the dress at all before the women had put it on. He didn't. He simply tugged it loose from the top to the bottom. It took him several go's to get it loose enough at the bottom to remove.

I'd thought I would feel self-conscious when the dress fell to the floor, leaving me standing in my curses and the strange bottom undergarments they'd made me wear. I had told the women that they were impractical, as lace hardly covered enough of anything to be of use. Lace was for things like curtains, not for wearing.

You'll see how useful it is, they'd said.

When I turned around and stepped over the dress to look at him, I believed I understood.

"It's nothing you haven't seen before," I said in both confusion and amusement.

His eyes were wide as they went from the bottom of my body to the top, like undoing the dress in reverse with his eyes. They lingered for slightly longer than I expected near the top of the curses before settling in on mine.

"The lake while traveling, remember?" I reminded him. "You said that you'd looked."

He opened his mouth, but no sound came out of it.

I was very, *very* confused. The curses covered far more than he'd seen that day, far more than he'd seen most nights as we slept. Was there really something so different about how I was standing in front of him now?

His eyes kept moving from mine, downward, and then back again. It seemed as though he needed a little help.

I took his hands and put them on either side of my waist over the curses. "Would you like to take this off me?" I asked him encouragingly.

He still didn't speak. All he did was nod his head very slowly.

I could not help the smile that took over my face. I turned around and, as his fingers were fumbling around with the back of the curses . . . I did not stop smiling.

I listened to my heart pounding in my ears, and I listened to his breathing. And every bit of tightness from the curses that dissipated felt as though I were being released from a prison. When it came off in his hand and I turned around to see him drop it onto the floor . . . I finally felt free of myself.

Epilogue

Gifts

JASTIN AND I DID NOT GET MUCH SLEEP on our wedding night, nor did we leave my living quarters at all the next day. In such a very short time, I believed I'd discovered a more . . . *distinct* understanding about several things in life.

I understood, very well, what Jastin had meant about taking care of me. I had not tried to kill him for it, though I hadn't the vaguest clue what I might've done without *some* sort of warning. I understood what the Reapers had meant when they'd talked about being out of hearing distance. More importantly, I understood what Abby had meant about that sort of thing and what it was supposed to be.

Most importantly, I understood more about myself. I understood what had been holding me back and keeping me locked away in my ice prison.

Fear.

A fear I hadn't even realized ran so deep within me. The fear that I could not trust anyone. The fear that I could not trust myself.

I *could* trust myself, and I could trust him.

We spoke a great deal. My voice did not revert back to its normal speaking tone. My laughter sounded different in my ears. He must've enjoyed it because he kept doing things that brought on fits of it. It sounded *free*. I enjoyed the sound of it as well, and the feeling of it. It did scare me a great deal, though.

We laid in bed together that next night and did something I'd never done before.

He and I made up a perfect dream world together, where each of us offered details of what that perfect world would entail. A little house in the wilderness with children running around. No Reapers, no people, just the simple freedom of being alone and making our own choices together. Surviving and striving toward better things for ourselves and no one else. Not all hoped-for things aligned. That was life. It was all right because . . . It wasn't real.

We smiled as we were speaking about it until I began crying because we could never have it.

My father was the leader of Jarsil and his Reapers intended for me to carry on for him after he was gone. *He* intended it. The reality of the situation was that, because of my father and myself . . . I could not ever have that life I wanted. I would be here, in this city, always thinking of the people inside its walls.

There would always be people. No trees, no solitude. No dancing alone where no one but our children could see. No words spoken that would not be overheard by people who had no business hearing them. No secret smiles that were only witnessed by the two of us. No secrets at all. That was our life. My life. His, because of me.

Our conversation about our unattainable future was sort of like the dream I'd had of painting. It was a window to a world I would never, ever get to see. It didn't make me happy, because the trees and flowers were not real. What use was seeing them and dreaming about them when I could not touch them?

But still, I felt free in a way because of it, free that I could dream and cry with someone. I felt free because I did not have to do it alone. I felt free because I could allow myself to do it now. It hurt, but it didn't hurt like it could have. It hurt differently.

So, the morning after that conversation, I trained as I normally did. I spoke to my father about the things I had promised and intended to speak to him about. He and I came to an agreement on the matter after a rather long discussion. Once we'd negotiated and had all our stipulations in place, I had a Reaper escort me to the home of the two old women who'd made my wedding dress. Beatrice and Dorothy. I still did not know which was which, but Jastin had informed me of their names at least.

They seemed quite surprised to see me.

One of them laughed immediately upon my arrival. "I didn't think you'd leave your bedroom for a week."

Why people always thought a week for that, I had no clue. Past people being as people were.

I smiled tightly. "Things must always be done, and I gave you my word that I would take care of something for you."

"You've spoken to your father?" the other asked seriously.

"I have." I nodded. "Have you prepared yourselves for your new apprentice?"

"We have," she replied. "We childproofed our home as best we could. Put sharp things well out of reach. Still, we weren't sure you could do what you said."

"I always do what I say." I did not like hearing my old tone of voice in my ears, but . . . when speaking with everyone else . . . it was necessary. It was what they expected from me. I didn't know how I felt about it feeling more natural. Me. It was me. "Come along. I've already sent a Reaper ahead to tell the woman who runs the orphanage to prepare herself for a meeting."

"The Reapers," the non-prudish one started and then stopped. She glanced briefly at the one who'd followed me inside and furrowed her wrinkly brow at me. "They do as you say?"

I forced another tight smile at her because I did not want to ever hear myself say that everyone did as I said.

I reached for the doorknob, but she grabbed hold of my arm.

The Reaper who had followed me inside twitched slightly, but he did not move otherwise.

"The changes that have been made since your arrival . . ." the same one started. "Are they because of you or your father?"

"My father instates all changes made in Jarsil," I answered as something of a reflex.

"You know that's not what she asked you," the other said.

I stood there staring at her for a short time before evenly saying, "I'll accompany you to the orphanage, and I'll explain to Marlen our peculiar circumstances. I'll ask her if she knows of one child in particular who seems distinctly artistically inclined. Once she has a child in mind, I'll inform her to make the child's departure from the building as discreet as possible, and then I'll leave you to the rest."

"Why?" the same one asked. "Why would you leave?"

"Personal moments should remain personal." It was not technically a lie, but it was not the complete truth.

I wondered how the people of Jarsil would feel about me if they knew how often I did not tell the complete truth.

I DID EXACTLY WHAT I HAD SAID.

I went to the orphanage, and I spoke with Marlen. Eventually, she thought of a child, once I explained the purpose of it to her and gave her a letter from my father. It should not have stung that one needed direct permission from my father to listen to me, especially someone who'd seen me far more than they had him. I couldn't allow it to bother me.

I informed her to make the departure discreet, and then, I made my own departure. I did not stop by the children's large, shared rooms because I couldn't bear the thought of seeing all the ones who would be left behind.

Not today.

When I vacated the building, I did not go far. I stood out in the street and spoke with the people who approached me. They always came up to me, when the Reapers would allow them to. The Reapers only allowed them to when I permitted it.

They asked me why I'd taken the two women in there, and I told them a partial version of the truth.

"I asked that they take up an apprentice." I had not asked, only put the idea in their heads and said I believed they should do so. That could be considered asking.

The people would ask me why, and I would stretch it.

"So their services can still be of use long after they're gone." Sometimes I would add, "Beautiful dress, wasn't it?" But I could not force myself to smile, and I could not force the appropriate amount of lightness into my voice to make it properly believable.

They believed me anyhow. I knew why.

I stood, and I waited with my back to the building a short way off. And eventually, I felt a tug on the back of my dress. I turned around to find Beatrice and Dorothy standing there with a familiar-faced little girl. She was holding one of each their hands with either of hers. It was the same quiet little girl who'd held Stelin's hand for hours, the one who'd asked me why I was sad. I smiled down at her.

"Princess," she said with the hugest smile on her face. "These women are giving me a home." She seemed as though she could not believe it.

"*Are* they?" I asked.

"Yes," she said quietly. "They've told me they're going to teach me to make dresses for you."

"Is that something you would like to do?"

She nodded her head in clear excitement.

"Then I'm very happy for you. I'm quite certain I'll be seeing you again soon."

She looked up when one of the women wiggled her hand slightly and said, "Come along, Jadis."

She offered one last smile at me before following them away.

As soon as their backs were to me, my own smile fell away from my face.

I did not turn when the Reaper who'd been following the closest to me all day came up behind me.

"Why did you not remain inside if you were going to wait out here to see which child was taken?"

"Guilt," I answered as I stared at their retreating backs.

"Guilt?"

"Nothing will ever be enough," I said quietly. "No matter what I do, what *anyone* does . . . it will never, *ever* be enough."

"You've been lying to everyone," he accused after a short moment more than likely spent thinking over my answer. "Why?"

"Because I must."

I WAS INTENDING TO FIND ABBY to ask her a question, but I wanted to stop by my quarters beforehand to change my clothing. My father had informed me that he'd moved her and James into the House so they could be looked after more thoroughly. I could walk around the House in whatever clothing I saw fit, matching or not, and I did not want to be wearing a dress for any longer than necessary.

I found myself stopped halfway between the entrance to the garden and my living quarters, staring at a tiny bit of redness on the ground. It was just a tiny smudge, but it stood out quite vividly against the faded green of the grass.

"Where is my husband?" I asked quietly.

I looked up at the same Reaper following closest, who had no answer for me.

I firmly ordered, "Find my husband. *Now*."

And then I hurriedly went the rest of the way to my living quarters. Several Reapers had since noticed the change in me and attempted to push their way past.

I did not allow it. I stood there for a moment, staring at another bit of redness just in front of my door. And I held my hand up, motioning for them to stop.

They did.

Everything was precisely as I'd left it when I stepped inside. I looked around quickly, trying to find something to explain . . .

Paper, lying on a table and smudged with red. I kept my hand up as I walked over to it, and I recognized the writing even before I slowly removed the papers from the table.

Aster,

Here is the letter you asked me for. Two lines connected together doesn't say enough, but that would depend, wouldn't it?

I suppose you know everything now, don't you? I must admit that I underestimated you. I'm quite ashamed of myself for it. I watched you for such a long time, so I should've seen it there. I can't believe I didn't. You're probably thinking the exact same thing about me, aren't you? You're probably nearly as embarrassed as I am.

I would imagine my traitor of a brother told you some things about me that he likely shouldn't have. Do me a favor, please, and inform him I'll let it pass for now because it truly doesn't matter. I might change my mind eventually.

I'm ashamed that I feel torn right now. A part of me wants to apologize to you. Maybe, if I'd told you everything, you'd be with me right now instead. You probably think I wouldn't want that, don't you? I never lied to you directly, just as I promised, so everything I told you was true enough in its own way. I <u>did</u> see you that first day you arrived in New Bethel. I <u>did</u> follow you. I <u>was</u> beaten for it. Maybe if I'd told you that your father was not the only man I met while I was away . . . maybe it would've made a difference.

I wonder how much of a monster my brother has made me out to be. I wonder how much he's told you and how much he's spared you from for whatever reasons he has. We're all monsters, Aster. If anyone tells you any differently . . . they're lying. And if you believe them, it's your own fault.

I'm ashamed that I feel torn. I'm even contemplating lying about the things I've learned of you. He'd believe me if I did. I'm very good at lying. I haven't made up my mind yet.

Why shouldn't I want you dead, though? You're not anything to me now, are you? So why shouldn't I? Maybe I'd feel bad for contributing to the end of something so innocent.

I'll admit that I'm smiling to myself now. I've contributed to the end of so many innocent things. Why should you be any different? You shouldn't be.

I wanted to tell you congratulations. That was my intention for writing this. Also . . . you looked beautiful on your wedding day. I'm looking forward to seeing you again. I wonder if you'll see me the next time. I wonder how many of your Reapers will look past me. It's funny.

All of it is so funny. And I'm so angry at myself because I feel like a part of me is lying when I write that to you.

I _did_ love you, in a way. As much as I'm capable of, at least. I can't decide whether I want to take it away from you, like you took it away from me. A heart for a heart. I'm sure I'll make my mind up eventually.

Tell my brother I might be seeing him. Tell your father he'll be seeing him. And I promise I'll be seeing you. Whether or not you'll see me too remains to be seen.

There was a large smudge of redness near the bottom of the last page and a postscript written hastily. It was much more difficult for me to read.

You asked me once if I could do something, didn't you? I'm sorry I had to do it. They followed me here and tried to *take me in. I didn't break the deal I made to you, even though it should be voided. Count it that way now. They were a direct threat. Cut three more crosses into your arm because it's your fault for not informing them I could. I warned you that I could, didn't I? Don't you remember? Why didn't you tell them?*

Your wedding gift from me is on your bed.

My hands were shaking as I stepped over to my bedroom door and opened it with my Reapers following behind me. On my bed, as promised, were three dead Reapers—two men and one woman.

I heard cursing all around me, and I took in a deep, shaky breath.

One.

Two.

I released it.

I turned to the living, and to the closest one I said, "Inform my father Chase has been in the city and killed three of our men. And for *god's sake*, someone find my husband."

They all stood there blinking at me until I said what was necessary to get a proper grasp on the situation.

"That was an order. *Go.*"

They went.

DEAR READER,

I in a great many ways struggle with human nature, questioning why we do the things we do. It at times can be an almost debilitating hurt when facing facts. One fact?

People hurt people. Sometimes on purpose. Sometimes not.

But I believe we have choice in life, even when the choices of others leave us with seemingly none. *Will this break me? Will I learn and become better for/from it?*

I like to call it: Making fertilizer from the . . . manure. (I don't typically use that word, if I'm being honest.)

I will say it probably a million times in life that I wish everything could be nothing but sunshine and daisies, and yet one thing I know from my own life far more than any writing of books has taught me?

Had I not gone through my own hurts and difficulties, I wouldn't be me. My strengths wouldn't be my strengths. I wouldn't know what all I do (not even half). I wouldn't be me at all but a person with the same face.

Finding gratitude for the difficulties is a long and difficult road, but I (personally) have found a peace in trying my best to facilitate growth in what others could consider barren soil. I like to think it's one point to life—growing ourselves inside. But that's just my belief.

I hope so much that you'll continue Aster's journey with her, difficult parts and all. We all could use some friends and some care as we go about life, you know?

If you're struggling through your own hurts and difficulties? Know you're not alone. And keep that chin up, even when every single thing tries to force your head down. If you do it for long enough, it'll become part of you.

<3 C

If you enjoyed this book, I hope you'll consider leaving a review or telling a friend or family member.

Stories are much better when shared. Thank you for sharing in Aster's story with her (and me).

<3

WHERE YOU CAN FIND ME

WWW.CMILLERAUTHOR.COM

Email: contactcmillerauthor@gmail.com

Amazon: www.amazon.com/author/millerc

GoodReads: www.goodreads.com/CMillerAuthor

Facebook: www.facebook.com/CMillerAuthor

WordPress: www.cnmill.wordpress.com

Instagram: @dolly_llama

Twitter: @cn_mill

My website is where any and all information is and will be available. Any news, any updates, information about books and where to find them. If you're looking for any of that, it'll be there!

If you want to stay up to date on new releases, please consider subscribing to my newsletter. It's strictly for relevant information (NEW BOOKS!) and perhaps an occasional letter.

I am quite 'shy' and tend to shy away from social media as a whole. I do have accounts and would be happy to connect with you there, but if you're looking to get in contact with me, messaging me through my site or email would be the best way.

Questions, comments, or just wanting to say hi? I'd love to hear from you!

CONTINUE ASTER'S JOURNEY IN ...

TO FALL

DECISIONS AND CONVICTIONS HAVE REPERCUSSIONS.

Aster could never have anticipated being anything but invisible in life. With her new role, she finds herself in a position of visibility and significance, where action and inaction both have consequences that stretch farther than her own hands could reach.

Being determined to do what she must leads Aster down a path of both expected and not, where she learns that even the things we know with certainty are far larger than we could ever imagine them to be.

Made in United States
Troutdale, OR
03/02/2025

29425314R00289